THE
BLOW OUT

ALSO BY BILL ROGERS

BILL
ROGERS
THE
BLOW OUT

Published by Thomas & Mercer, Seattle

www.apub.com

Amazon, the Amazon logo, and Thomas & Mercer are trademarks of Amazon.com, Inc., or its affiliates.

ISBN-13: 9781503904972
ISBN-10: 1503904970

Cover design by @blacksheep-uk.com

Printed in the United States of America

blow out
1. extinguish by a current of air
2. an easy victory (in golf)

Chapter 1

FRIDAY, 13TH OCTOBER

The two electric buggies came to a stop. The middle-aged quartet decamped, selected their clubs, and trudged up the wooden sleeper steps onto the seventh tee.

'Three bogeys, two pars, and a double bogey on the last,' said Nathan, the tall thin one with sunken cheeks. 'You two are going to have to sort yourselves out. At this rate you'll be getting the drinks in all night.'

'It's Jack's driving!' Steve complained. 'Seventeen out of our thirty strokes came on the even holes.' The smile on the face of the British Bulldog tattooed on his right bicep widened as he scratched his bald head with a gloved hand.

'Well, I doubt you'll get any joy on this one,' said Ronnie, the ape-necked powerhouse to whom they all deferred. 'Gem of a hole. Deceptive little beggar. Hundred and seventy-seven yards, par three. You've got two options. Ignore the fairway. Play straight over the pond. That's going to leave you with two putts for a par.'

'Providing your first shot doesn't end up in the drink!' chortled Nathan.

'Or,' Ronnie growled, 'you can ignore the pond, take the coward's route, and play the fairway. Lucky for you we're playing a two-ball foursome. One of you can go for it. The other one can play safe.'

'That'll be you, Jack,' said Steve, stepping forward to address his ball. 'I'm going route one.'

The three of them watched as he took several practice swings with his seven iron before unleashing his shot. The ball rose above the trees behind the hole, appeared to hang for a moment in a sudden crosswind and plummeted into the ditch at the front of the green.

Steve's curse was drowned by the laughter of his fellow players.

'Bad luck that,' said Ronnie with a broad grin. 'Another two feet and you'd have been sitting proud. Should have used a six iron.'

'Sodding wind,' said Steve, bending to retrieve his plastic peg.

Nathan landed his shot on the fairway, leaving a chip onto the green. Jack followed suit.

Ronnie placed his ball on the tee, took several warm-up swings, addressed the ball, and waited for the breeze to drop. A woodpigeon broke cover from the woods off to their right, their late autumnal coats shimmering russet and gold in the morning sunshine, and flew directly across his line of sight.

'Bird's got a bleedin' death wish,' he muttered. He raised his iron, judged the downswing perfectly, and struck the ball on the sweet spot. As his follow-through reached its peak he cried out, dropped the club, and slapped the right side of his neck.

'What's the matter, Ron?' asked Jack, his eyes still on the path of the ball.

'Bloody wasp stung me!' he replied, rubbing his neck with vigour. 'Either that, or one of those damn horseflies.'

'Shame it wasn't a fraction of a second earlier,' Steve moaned. 'Looks like you're three feet from the pin, you lucky josser.'

'Luck doesn't come into it. I keep telling you. You gotta practise.'

'You saying they had a practice range in Belmarsh?' said Nathan.

Ronnie rammed the six iron into his golf bag and climbed onto the buggy.

'I've been making up for lost time,' he said. 'Played at least one round every day since I got out. If today's anything to go by I bet that's more than you've played all the time I've been inside.'

He was still rubbing his neck as the two buggies wound their way around the pond, and their voices faded on the wind.

Chapter 2

Day One – Monday, 16th October

Jo placed the last set of bubble-wrapped plates in the crate and closed the lid. She stood up, dusted the knees of her tracksuit, and looked around. The lounge had an air of desolation. The TV and sofa sat forlorn in a sea of packing cases. It was not that long since she'd stood here, feeling alone and abandoned. Now all that was changing.

It was only a fortnight since her civil partnership with Abbie had been dissolved. Abbie was already eight months pregnant by the donor she'd found for herself, and desperate for her share of the apartment. To Jo's surprise, a cash buyer had appeared and offered the asking price. The only problem was he needed her out by the end of the month, and there was every chance of completion within the next ten days. Fortunately, a perfect apartment had come onto the market on Salford Quays, close to work, and also to Agata who had a place on the opposite side of the Huron Basin. It was too early in their developing relationship to think about moving in together. Jo had the impression that Agata would have been happy to do so, but for her it was a case of once bitten.

She glanced at her watch. If she got a move on she could make the early-morning session at the gym. If anything was going to shake off her melancholy blues, an hour of Krav Maga would do it. She went through to the bedroom, picked up her kitbag and briefcase, and set off.

Grant, Jo's Krav Maga instructor, raised his eyebrows as she entered the room. The usual suspects were already there, pounding out push-ups, burpees and star jumps like there was no tomorrow. Two bankers from the financial district, two teachers, a female lecturer from UMIST, a fireman, and a door supervisor, aka bouncer.

'You're late,' he said. 'You'd better do your warm-up while this lot help me get the equipment out.'

Three minutes later, with the blood coursing through her veins and her body covered in a slick sheen of sweat, she joined the others facing their instructor, their backs against the wall.

'Right,' said Grant. 'Today we're revisiting limitation training. It's a while since you've done it, so remind me. What are we talking about here?'

'Fending off an attack in a confined space,' said one of the bankers.

'Such as?'

'In an alleyway.'

'On a staircase,' said the second banker.

'In an elevator?' suggested the fireman.

'Sitting down on a train or a tram or a bus,' said the lecturer.

Grant nodded appreciatively. 'And what is our mantra for limitation training?'

'Manage the distance to manage the damage!' they chorused.

'Exactly. Fortunately, we've got a couple of experts here to show us how it's done. Jo, let's start with you backed up against the wall. Alex, you're going to face her as the aggressor.'

He threw the bouncer a large black padded strike shield.

'Here, this'll help to protect your ugly mug.'

They laughed on cue. It was a well-worn joke. Alex was probably the most handsome bouncer in the North of England. At six feet five, weighing in at a muscular 190 pounds he was, like Jo, a five-bar-level Krav Maga graduate. He was also an instructor, as Jo could equally have been, had she so chosen.

'I'm not going to give you any instructions,' said Grant. 'I want you to demonstrate the three position scenarios one after another. When you're ready.'

Jo brought her fists up to her chest and waited. Alex pressed the strike shield against her with the full weight of his body behind it. She could smell garlic on his breath and see individual drops of sweat trickling down his forehead. He nodded to show that he was ready.

She bent her knees, then exploded upwards striking with the crown of her head against the shield where his chin – and a normal person's nose – would have been. As his head and shoulders jerked back she struck the centre of the shield with her left elbow and then the right. Then she pivoted away from the wall and drove her right knee into his thigh. As he bent forward she hooked her right arm around his neck and flung him into the wall.

Alex stepped back. This time Jo turned sideways on to the wall and waited for him to close on her. She struck first with her right fist into the abdomen, then her left elbow, a headbutt and a knee strike, before wheeling away, and ending as before with the arm hook.

The final scenario, with her back to Alex, looked deceptively easy. She drove her right elbow into his right side, then into his back as she spun free, and kicked his right knee, before grabbing his T-shirt at the shoulder and using that to fling him into the wall.

Jo placed her hands on her knees and gasped for air as the group applauded.

'Good,' said Grant. 'Bloody brilliant given the difference in height between the two of you. Jo used his clothing to drag him down and forward, because she couldn't reach his neck. You always have to be ready to improvise. Okay. Now I want the rest of you to try it. Then we do it again, this time in the stairwell.'

An hour later, showered and changed, Jo felt amazing, as she always did at the end of a session. Andy Swift, her National Crime Agency behavioural psychologist, had explained why that was. She already knew about the pain suppression and euphoric feeling that endorphins produced, but this was something about the fight-or-flight reaction releasing a protein called BDNF that protected your mind and body from stress, and left you feeling clear-headed and ready for anything. She didn't care how it worked, so long as it did.

She was just about to unlock the Audi when her phone rang. It was her boss, Harry Stone.

'Where are you, Jo?' he asked. He was abrupt and focused. Not at all like Harry.

'Outside the gym. I'll be in the office in fifteen minutes.'

'Don't bother,' he said. 'Get yourself over to Manchester Royal Infirmary, Jo. The Critical Care Unit. There's a suspicious death Greater Manchester Police want our help with.'

'Is Max going, too?'

'I've just asked Max to work on an operation looking into what looks like an organised honour killing crime syndicate. The rest of the team, too. I'm afraid you'll be on your own on this one. Although you'll be able to draw on NCA resources, obviously.'

The way he said it, it didn't sound obvious at all.

Harry homed in on her silence. 'Are you alright, Jo?' he asked.

'I'm fine,' she replied.

'Only given everything you've been through since you joined us . . . not to mention what happened before that . . .'

'I told you, I'm absolutely fine,' she insisted.

'Only nobody would blame you if you wanted to . . .'

'What is this, Boss?' she demanded. 'Have I ever let you down?'

'No, but . . .'

'Then can we please just move on?'

There was a long pause before he answered. 'Very well, if you're sure.'

'I'm sure. So, what more can you tell me about this suspicious death?'

'I'm sorry, Jo,' he said abruptly. 'Got to go. GMP will brief you. Good luck.'

That's ominous, she thought as she put her phone back in her bag. *Harry Stone doesn't believe in luck. And neither do I.*

Jo laid her head back against the rest and took a moment to reflect on their exchange. He hadn't needed to elaborate. Three investigations in less than three years during her secondment from GMP to the NCA, two of which had ended in her having to discharge a weapon and face an internal enquiry. The most recent of which had seen the perpetrator make her a target of his sickening fantasy. But, as always, Harry had been right. It was the backwash from her abduction in the Bluebell Hollow case that was threatening to resurface. *Think of it as dealing with grief*, the counsellor had told her. And she had. By acknowledging it for what it was. Then throwing herself back into her work. By taking up Krav Maga. By seeking new challenges with the National Crime Agency. And now, Abbie's departure had become a second grief. Prodding her defences. Testing her resilience.

She took a deep breath and exhaled slowly.

'Manage the distance to manage the damage!' she intoned.

Experience had taught her that it wasn't just the physical dimension of wellness where that applied. She inserted the key in the ignition and revved the engine. Felt the power beneath her foot. Took back control.

Chapter 3

'Assistant Chief Constable Gates rang,' Ged, the Incident Room Administrator, continued. 'She would like you to urgently attend Manchester Royal Infirmary to investigate the suspicious death of a—' She looked at the note in her hand. '—Ronnie O'Neill.'

DCI Gordon Holmes remembered him. A ruthless gang leader. Short, stocky, muscular, shaven-headed. A pocket battleship. He'd be in his fifties by now. 'I thought he was doing a stretch in Belmarsh?' he said.

'He came out on parole,' Detective Sergeant Carter said, 'a month ago. Looks like someone was waiting for him. You're welcome to this one. Whoever topped him has just stirred a bloody great hornets' nest.'

Gordon followed Ged across the room, pausing at Carly Whittle's desk.

'Detective Constable Whittle?' he said.

She looked up at him, pushed back her chair and leapt to her feet. 'Yes, Sir!'

For a moment he thought she was going to salute.

'Whatever it is you're doing will still be here when you get back,' he told her. 'I want you with me.'

'Yes, Sir!'

She grabbed her bag from the side of her desk and straightened up. Gordon found it strangely unnerving that they were standing eye to eye. Hers shone with excitement. As he turned to lead the way he was grateful that she was wearing low wedges and not high heels. With those blonde curls piled on her head she was already taller than him.

'Just one thing,' he said as he opened the door to the corridor. 'It's not Sir. It's Boss, or Detective Chief Inspector.'

'Yes, Boss!' She'd almost shouted it.

Gordon sighed and headed for the exit. 'Come on,' he said, 'the meter's running.'

———

'Ronnie O'Neill,' said Gordon. 'Tell DC Whittle what we know about him, Nick.'

They were speeding down Alan Turing Way, blue lights flashing. DC Carly Whittle in the passenger seat, DS Nick Carter in the rear.

Nick braced himself on the back of Carly's seat as he leaned forward. 'Long-standing boss of a South Manchester crime syndicate. Suspected of running a drugs empire, extortion, armed robbery, kidnapping, and grievous bodily harm. Far too clever though. Only ever convicted once, for the GBH. He all but killed a guy from Stockport trying to muscle in on the city centre clubs.'

Gordon glanced up at the rear-view mirror. 'That was in 2011, if memory serves. How come he's out already?'

'Released from Belmarsh last month on parole for good behaviour. Given non-association and place-restriction orders. He's rebranding himself as a reformed character and pillar of the community.'

'And pigs'll fly,' muttered Gordon.

'That's the general consensus,' said Nick. 'You know about Operation Cortez?'

Gordon nodded. 'Gang they christened The Albanians, working a dial-a-drug scheme in the city centre clubs. Twenty of them arrested back in February. They've just been sentenced?'

'A total of eighty years between them,' said Carly, who was beginning to feel left out. 'Most of them are awaiting deportation.'

'The word is,' said Nick, 'O'Neill's mob is looking to fill the vacuum left behind, with him pulling the strings at arm's length.'

'Sounds like a motive, Boss,' said Carly. 'There are bound to be rival gangs wanting a piece of the action?'

'Let's not get ahead of ourselves,' said Gordon as he turned on the sirens and swung onto Plymouth Grove. He glanced over his right shoulder as they sped past Longsight Police Station, where his FMIT career had begun. 'O'Neill will have made more enemies than you and I have had hot breakfasts.'

'Can I ask you a question, Boss?' said Carly.

'Take that as read.'

'Why are we using blues and twos? I mean, he is dead after all.'

Nick snorted his disapproval.

'No,' said Gordon. 'It's a fair question. When someone like Ronnie O'Neill snuffs it at his age, rumours are going to abound: it's payback from someone he crossed in the past, it's a rival gang hoping to muscle in on his business, or an internal takeover—'

'The King is dead. Long live the King,' Nick interposed.

'—or someone believes, rightly or wrongly, that he's informed on them as a way of getting an early parole.'

'Like The Albanians?' asked Carly.

Gordon nodded again. 'Exactly. But they're not the only ones. Titan have been really motoring over the past twelve months.'

'Titan?'

'The North West Regional Organised Crime Unit's overarching operation,' said Nick. 'I'd have thought you'd know that.'

Gordon sensed DC Whittle squirming with embarrassment beside him.

'We have to move fast to try and prevent revenge attacks, Carly,' he explained. 'Even when there are no suspicious circumstances. The last thing we need is a vigilante gang war breaking out.'

They lapsed into silence for the final stretch to the hospital, allowing their imaginations to run riot.

Chapter 4

'Looks like it's already kicking off,' Nick Carter observed. 'And isn't that SI Stuart's car over there?'

Gordon Holmes pulled into the only remaining designated bay between hastily parked police vans, a patrol car, and Joanne Stuart's Audi. Leaves skittered across the tarmac as Hurricane Ophelia began to make her presence felt.

The three of them climbed out of the car.

Jo alarmed her car and turned to face them.

'Jo,' said Gordon. 'What are you doing here?'

'Good to see you too, Detective Chief Inspector,' she replied. 'Congratulations on your promotion, Gordon. I thought you'd never do it.'

Gordon pulled a face. 'Don't tell anyone, but Marilyn gave me an ultimatum. Go for promotion and boost the pension or move into the spare room.' He grinned. 'It was a close call.'

'I'm pleased for you,' she said. 'You deserve it. As to why I'm here, I've no idea. I had a call telling me to get here and wait for you.'

'Nobody tells me anything, either,' he muttered as he led the way to the hospital entrance.

Chaos reigned inside the reception hall. Four uniformed police officers and three hospital security guards were attempting to control a group of five angry men who were remonstrating loudly. Hospital staff were urging anxious outpatients to move away from the testosterone-charged scrum.

Gordon held up his warrant card and shouldered his way to the front desk. 'You have a patient: Ronald O'Neill? We were told that he was in the Critical Care Unit?'

The receptionist checked her screen. 'That's correct. You'll find it on the second floor. It's the purple zone. You can take the elevators over there, or the stairs around to your left.' She frowned. 'Either way, I'm afraid you'll have to get past that lot.'

'What are they complaining about?' he asked.

'They've just been told that a relative has passed away and they're not allowed onto the ward. We expect this kind of thing on a Saturday night, but never in the middle of a weekday.'

'No guesses as to who the relative is,' said Nick as the elevator doors closed.

'Did either of you recognise any of them?' Gordon asked his officers.

'Not me,' Nick replied.

'Nor me,' said Carly.

'I did,' said Jo.

The three of them stared at her.

'The thickset one with a bald head, wearing a white T-shirt and jeans, that's Steven Yates,' she said. 'He's Ronnie O'Neill's enforcer. A proper Manc hardman. The youngest of them in the shiny blue suit? That's Jason O'Neill, Ronnie's son.'

'How come you know them?' Gordon asked. 'I don't remember our coming across them when you were with the syndicate?'

'I did two spells in South Manchester before I joined CID,' she told him. 'I was stationed at Greenheys and then Wythenshawe. I heard a lot about the O'Neills, and our paths crossed a few times. Jason was a bit of a hothead, but I don't think it ever went beyond him being cautioned.

I remember once we arrested him for GBH following a fight in a pub in Royal Oak. But it never came to anything.'

The elevator stopped and the doors slid open.

'What happened?' asked Gordon.

'Witnesses came forward claiming it was self-defence. The victim refused to press charges.'

'What about CCTV?' said Carter.

'According to the landlord it wasn't working that night. Claimed he'd taken the old tape out and forgot to put a new one in.'

'Was that before or after Yates paid him a visit?' said Gordon.

'How did you guess?' she said.

As they approached the doors that led to the wards a female police officer barred their way.

'I'm sorry,' she began. 'Staff only past this point. You need a lanyard ID . . .'

The four of them simultaneously held up their warrant cards.

She tentatively checked Gordon's ID, ignoring the rest of them. 'I'm sorry, Detective Chief Inspector,' she said. 'We've been told to treat it as a crime scene.'

'You'll need to log us in then.'

She looked flustered. 'I haven't been given a log yet. Someone's supposed to be bringing it up.'

'You could be waiting some time,' said Carter.

'We'll go through then,' Gordon told her. It wasn't a request.

'You can't come in here!' A fierce-looking nurse in a navy uniform trimmed with white strode towards them.

Gordon held up his warrant card again. 'Greater Manchester Police,' he said. 'We're here in relation to Ronnie O'Neill.'

Her body relaxed and her tone morphed from withering to weary. 'Right. We were told to expect you. My name is Mary Marshall, the duty matron. Do you need to see him?'

'Yes please.'

'Very well. Come this way.'

She paused to sanitise her hands using the pump on the wall beside the next pair of doors and waited for them to do the same.

'The unit includes intensive care and high-dependency patients,' she told them. 'There are also isolation beds. There is a significant risk of infection for patients whose immune system is already compromised.'

She entered a code on the key pad, pushed open the door, led them to a side room, and paused.

'I have to advise you not to touch the body,' she said quietly. 'There's a suspicion that a poison of some form may have been administered. Until the exact nature of that poison is known we cannot risk transference.'

'Won't we have to wear gloves or a mask?' Jo asked.

'No. Whatever it is, it's not going to be infectious and it's unlikely to be contagious other than by direct contact of broken skin with the agent itself or with bodily fluids.' She frowned. 'At least, let's hope not, for the sake of those of us who treated him.'

She opened the door, stepped back to let the four detectives enter, followed them in, and closed the door behind her.

The body lay on its back on a hospital bed, surrounded by the paraphernalia of critical care. A ventilator machine had been pushed back into one corner, a trolley with an infusion pump into another. The screen of the patient monitor was blank. The head, shoulders, and arms were visible, but the rest of the body was covered with a thin clean paper sheet.

'We arranged him like this to minimise contact,' she said. 'We assumed that the police and the pathologist would want to see him *in situ* before he was moved to the mortuary.'

Gordon moved to the top end of the bed. O'Neill's eyes were closed and none of the anguish and trauma that he must have suffered was evident in his expression. His lips were swollen and tinged with blue. The whole of his face and his head – bald as a snooker ball – was a sickly yellow. Bruising on his neck and shoulders was less evident on his arms where tattoos vied for attention. His hands were swollen.

'Mr O'Neill was brought in to Accident and Emergency,' she began, 'with a history of bronchial irritation, a dry sore throat, congestion, chest tightness, skin irritation and then, most recently, vomiting and diarrhoea. He was severely dehydrated and had extremely low blood pressure. He had excess fluid in his lungs and difficulty breathing. He was immediately transferred to the Acute Medical Unit for assessment where he began to suffer a series of seizures. It was quickly established that he was going into multiple organ failure, and some form of poisoning was suspected. He was transferred here to the Critical Care Unit where it was possible to treat his multiple needs and isolate him in a side room. Sadly, there was nothing we could do to save him despite the best efforts of a team of four consultants and specialist nurses. His liver, spleen, and kidneys had already stopped working. Finally, his heart gave up and he was pronounced dead at 8.16 a.m.'

'The bruising?' asked Gordon.

'Caused by the liver and kidney failure. The jaundice, too.'

'What is this, Matron?' Jo had moved around to the opposite side of the bed and was pointing to the right side of O'Neill's neck. 'It looks like an entry wound of some kind.'

'The paramedics who brought him in believed it to be an infected insect bite, largely on the basis of what the family told them. We quickly came around to your conclusion. Close inspection led to the hypothesis that this might have been caused by some sort of pellet,' she added.

Gordon and Carter joined Jo to see for themselves. On the side of the neck, two inches below the chin, was an ugly brown and yellow crater, a quarter of an inch in diameter. Surrounding the crusted perimeter, but double the size, was a scarlet circle of inflamed skin punctuated by tiny yellow pustules.

'An air rifle pellet?' said Jo.

'Possibly. At first the assumption was that an infected insect bite or sting had led to sepsis, which was overwhelming his organs. However, there were too many contradictory symptoms and the doctors came down on the side of poison. Samples are still being analysed.'

'Is it possible that the two are separate?' asked Gordon. 'That he was stung or shot and that a poison was administered in some other way?'

'Orally, for example?'

A man's voice from the doorway. He was tall, a little on the heavy side, with thinning hair, and intelligent eyes behind frameless spectacles.

'This is Dr Okafor,' the matron told them. 'He's one of the consultants who treated Mr O'Neill.'

'With ingestion, the initial symptoms would have been radically different,' the consultant explained. 'Gastrointestinal pain, with rapid onset of nausea, vomiting, diarrhoea, and dysphagia – that is, difficulty in swallowing. Intestinal haemorrhages would have resulted in melena and hematemesis.'

'Bloody faeces and vomit,' the matron translated.

'Either way,' said the consultant, 'the end result would have been the same: multiple organ failure.'

'Assuming that this was a poison,' said Gordon, 'is it possible to estimate when Mr O'Neill came into contact with it?'

The doctor shook his head. 'Not without knowing the nature of the toxin. Having said which, it would be reasonable to hypothesise that it would have been when he received that wound on his neck. Matron?'

'The family told us they thought it had happened on Friday morning,' she said, 'while he was playing golf.'

'Three days ago,' said Gordon. 'Might you have been able to save him, Doctor, if he had come in straight away?'

'I'm sorry to have to repeat myself,' Okafor replied, 'but I can't answer that without knowing the exact nature and quantity of the toxin that entered his system. I will say this though. Whoever did it almost certainly intended not only to kill the poor man, but to make sure that he suffered a prolonged, humiliating, and painful death.'

'I can think of a few dozen likely guys in Manchester alone,' Nick muttered. 'Not to mention Eastern Europe, Turkey, and a load of expats in Spain, Cyprus, and the Algarve.'

Chapter 5

They regrouped in the corridor outside the room.

Gordon turned to his detective sergeant. 'I want you to wait here until the pathologist has been. Whoever it is, impress on them the urgency of the situation. We need that post-mortem today. Tomorrow morning at the latest.'

'If it's Professor Flatman, he won't take kindly to being told.'

'He knows the score. This isn't a hit-and-run, it's a time bomb waiting to go off. While you're waiting I need you to get the hospital to email me the results of the tests their forensic lab is running on the tissues from O'Neill's neck. Make sure they understand that the tissues themselves are evidence in a criminal investigation and need to be bagged, sealed, and labelled for collection.'

'What are you going to be doing, Boss?' Carter asked.

'SI Stuart, DC Whittle and I are going to have a word with the son and the enforcer. We need to take the heat out of the situation before they do something they'll regret.'

It was the first time that Gordon had intimated that Jo could have a role in this investigation. Things were looking up. Although it would still mean walking on eggshells.

Order had been restored in the reception area. Outside the main doors a ragtag group of the original protesters stood on the pavement, shepherded by police officers and security staff. A woman, two tough-looking men in their fifties, and a man half their age stood in a corner of reception close to the entrance to the corridors. They were closely supervised by two uniformed police officers, and two detectives both of whom Gordon recognised. One of the detectives noticed Gordon, and walked over to join them. He was tall, dark, and handsome, with an air of confidence that Jo was willing to bet came with senior rank.

'Gordon,' he said, holding out a hand, 'I thought it was you.'

'Good to see you, Nigel,' Gordon replied. 'It's been a while.'

'I've been to the Met and back,' he said. 'What have you been doing while I've been away? Burglary, assault, and public order? I bet you've been sharing your incomparable expertise with rookie detectives hanging on your every word?'

Gordon grimaced. 'FMIT, actually.'

'The Force Major Incident Team,' said Fox. 'I'm impressed. Well, since it's excitement you're looking for, you couldn't have timed it better.' He switched his attention to Carly Whittle. 'Aren't you going to introduce us?'

'This is DCI Nigel Fox,' said Gordon. 'Nigel, this is Detective Constable Carly Whittle.'

'Pleased to meet you,' said Fox, shaking her hand.

'I'm one of those rookie detectives,' she told him, as she removed her hand from a grasp that Jo thought lingered longer than was appropriate.

'And this,' said Gordon, 'is Senior Investigator Joanne Stuart, from the National Crime Agency.'

'Well, hello,' oozed DCI Fox, offering his hand again.

'Hello to you,' she said, all but crushing his hand before swiftly releasing it.

Fox stared at his fingers, watching the blood flood back into them.

Gordon winked at Jo, trying hard not to smirk.

'How come you're babysitting O'Neill's mob, Nigel?' he asked Fox.

Fox looked over his shoulder to where the group was standing. 'And the grieving widow,' he replied. 'The lovely Sheila. I'm deputy commander of the Xcalibre team now. DI Robb over there, she's with Operation Challenger.'

It made sense. GMP's long-standing anti-gun and anti-gang unit, and the organised crime unit tasked with the prevention, disruption, and apprehension of organisations like that of the O'Neill's.

'As soon as we heard Ronnie O'Neill was dead and the circumstances were decidedly dodgy,' Fox continued, 'we knew we had to get right in the faces of this lot before all hell broke loose. The question is, what are you doing here?'

'I'm the Senior Investigating Officer,' Gordon replied, 'until I hear otherwise.'

Fox whistled through his teeth. 'Lucky you,' he said. 'What about you, SI Stuart? What's your interest?'

'Good question,' she replied. 'That has yet to be determined.'

Fox turned back to Gordon. 'In that case I assume you'll want to talk to them?'

'The wife, the son, and anyone who believes they can throw some light on how and when Ronnie O'Neill received a wound on the side of his neck.'

Fox nodded. 'That'll be Jack Reilly and Steve Yates. Unfortunately, Yates left the hospital shortly before we arrived. I've got a team trying to track him down.'

'I'll start with the O'Neills then,' said Gordon. 'Is there somewhere private I can speak with them?

'We've been trying to persuade them to come over to the Bereavement Care Centre. One of their advisers is on her way to collect them, but they're refusing to budge till they've seen the body. Maybe you'll have better luck.'

'I'll do my best,' said Gordon as he led the way across the reception area.

Jason O'Neill's arms were tight around his mother's shoulders. It looked to Gordon as though he was both holding her up and protecting her. He had his father's bullish physique, but without the weight. His eyes, red from crying, were full of suspicion.

'Who the fuck are you?' he snarled.

'Detective Chief Inspector Holmes. My colleagues and I are here to investigate your father's death.'

Jason's eyes widened. 'Finally!' he said. 'Someone who admits he was murdered!'

'I didn't say that, Mr O'Neill,' said Gordon, 'but we do have reason to believe that your father's death was suspicious. I'm here to establish exactly how he died.'

'Reason to believe! Establish how?!' Jason spat out the words. 'I'll tell you how he died. In terrible pain. In fear. In total fucking disbelief. And we had to watch it happen, my mother and me.'

Sheila O'Neill began to sob, every word like a stab to her heart. Her son struggled to hold her upright.

'Leave it, Jason,' said Jack Reilly. 'For your mum's sake.'

'He's right, Jason,' said DI Robb, the Challenger detective. 'We all understand why you're angry, but it isn't helping.'

Jason rounded on her. 'Helping? I'll tell you what'd help – you lot getting off your backsides and finding whoever did it. Because I tell you, if you don't, we will!'

'I'm not going anywhere until I've seen Ronnie,' wailed his mother.

'I'm afraid that won't be possible until the pathologist has seen your husband, Mrs O'Neill,' said Gordon gently. 'You'll be able to see him as soon as he's been moved to the mortuary. While you're waiting, we'd like to ask all three of you some questions. Not here though – somewhere private. Like the Bereavement Centre. It's in the same building as the mortuary.'

'One of the bereavement advisers is on her way,' Robb added. 'She can take you over there, and accompany you to the mortuary as soon it's possible to do so.'

Jason O'Neill looked as though he was about to protest but Reilly put his hand on his shoulder.

'Better there than down the cop shop, Jace,' he said.

Sheila O'Neill squeezed her son's hand tightly. He looked at her and then at Gordon. 'Right,' he said. 'Let's get it over with.'

Nigel Fox drew Gordon aside and whispered in his ear. 'Thank God for that,' he said. 'I'm going to go outside, warn that lot out there to leave it to us, and then send them packing. Then I need to check on where that mad bastard Yates has got to. You will keep us in the loop, won't you?'

'Likewise,' said Gordon.

Chapter 6

They were about to head off to the bereavement centre when Gordon's phone rang.

'I'll have to take this,' he said.

Jo stepped away to give him some privacy. He turned his back and lowered his voice. Nevertheless, she could tell from the way his shoulders hunched and the way he became increasingly animated that this was not good news. He glanced over his shoulder at her with a grim expression that gave her the distinct impression that whatever it was, for some reason he held her responsible. After a minute or so he turned towards her and held out his phone.

'It's Assistant Chief Constable Gates. She wants a word.' He looked and sounded seriously pissed off.

Jo took the phone. 'Joanne Stuart,' she said. 'What can I do for you, Ma'am?'

'You can start by putting this on speakerphone,' Gates said. 'I want DCI Holmes to hear this so there are no misunderstandings.'

Jo pressed the icon and held the phone up between them.

'I've spoken with your Director of Investigations,' said Gates, 'and she's agreed to second you to GMP to head up the investigation into the murder of Ronnie O'Neill.'

Jo glanced at Gordon. He shrugged and looked away. When Gates continued, it was – and not for the first time – as though she'd been reading Jo's mind.

'In case you're wondering, DCI Holmes is comfortable with this. I need him to take over an investigation into an unconnected series of shootings.' She paused. 'At least I hope to God that it *is* unconnected.'

Her tone softened. 'GMP are badly stretched, Jo, and not just by the savage cuts to frontline officers, year on year. Following the Manchester Arena bombing, the Chief Constable has had no option but to transfer a whole tranche of detectives to Serious and Organised Crime and Counter Terrorism Command. Your people have agreed that this investigation may have wider national significance and that the NCA will cooperate in any way they can. You can work out of Nexus House – the home of GMP Major Incident Team and Serious Crime Units – with Syndicate One. DS Carter will be your deputy. I'm sure I don't need to tell you that this needs a firm hand and a light touch.'

'I think you'll find that's an oxymoron,' Gordon muttered.

'I heard that, DCI Holmes,' said Gates. 'SI Stuart knows what I mean and so do you. The press will be all over it. The Mayor and the Leader of the Council will start leaning on the Chief, and she'll be leaning on me. The last thing we need is a gang vigilante war breaking out. A return to the bad old days of "Gunchester".'

'And who will I have to lean on, Ma'am?' Jo asked.

'You've got Carter and the rest of the syndicate. The Operation Challenger and Operation Xcalibre teams will concentrate on de-escalation. That means dissuading the O'Neill organisation from trying to do our work for us and stopping all the other gangs from attempting to take advantage of the situation. All you have to do is catch Ronnie O'Neill's killer.'

Jo placed her hand over the phone and whispered to Gordon, 'Should be a breeze.'

'That's the spirit,' said Gates. 'I knew I could count on you.'

Gordon rolled his eyes.

'I'll handle the press from Central Park,' she continued. 'I'll leave you two to get on. The clock is ticking.'

She ended the call before either of them had a chance to respond.

Jo handed the phone back to Gordon. 'Just like the old days,' she said.

'With half the resources,' he said sourly.

'I'm sorry,' she said. 'About . . . them parachuting me in like this.'

'Don't be. Not your fault. Besides, I'll have my investigation sorted in no time. A couple of wannabe hardmen riding around on scooters, trying to frighten each other by firing popguns through each other's windows? Yours, on the other hand, is shaping up to be a right nightmare.'

'Thanks for that,' she said. 'You always were a ray of sunshine.'

Chapter 7

'Why don't you sit down?' said Jo. 'You could be here a while.'

They were in a family room on the ground floor of the Children's Hospital. Sheila O'Neill, who had proved to be in no state to be questioned, was next door with the bereavement adviser and DC Whittle. Her son was pacing up and down like a caged animal. Jack Reilly stood behind a settee facing the door as though expecting someone armed with a Kalashnikov to burst through it at any moment. Jo and DI Alice Robb were standing just inside the door.

O'Neill glared at them. 'Why don't you two piss off and do your jobs?' he said. His eyes rested on Jo. 'Hang about,' he said, 'do I know you?'

'Our paths crossed when I was based in South Manchester,' she said.

His eyes widened. 'That's it! You and some copper with a broken nose and cauliflower ears tried to pin GBH on me.'

'You were never charged,' she said.

He grinned, exposing a row of crooked teeth and a pair of gold crowns. 'Course I wasn't, cos I didn't do it. What's this then? You coming back for more?'

'This isn't helping, Jace,' said Reilly.

'He's right,' Jo agreed. 'The sooner you answer our questions, the sooner we can get on with our investigation.'

'Go on then,' said O'Neill without breaking stride. 'What do you wanna know?'

'When did your father receive that injury to the right side of his neck?'

Jason stopped pacing, stared at her and then at Reilly. 'What's that got to do with anything?'

'We don't know yet,' she replied.

His eyes widened. 'You saying that's what killed him?'

'As I said, we don't know. What do you think caused your father's death?'

'He was poisoned, wasn't he, Jack?' He looked to his friend for confirmation. 'That's what Steve said.'

'What Steve thought,' said Reilly. 'What we all thought.'

'And when was this poisoning supposed to have taken place?' Jo asked.

'Friday night. We went to an Italian in the city centre, to celebrate Mum and Dad's thirtieth anniversary. It was straight after that he started to get ill.'

'Where was this?'

'Da Rapallo, on Albert Square.'

'How many of you were there?'

'Five tables of eight.'

'Forty then?'

'Yeah, give or take.'

'Was it a private party, or were there other diners in the restaurant?'

'We took up about half the restaurant, but the place was packed all night.'

'DC Whittle will get the details from you when we've finished,' she told him, 'including the names and addresses of everyone who was in your party. But for now, can you tell me when your father received that injury to his neck?'

'Friday morning about . . .'

'11.30,' said Reilly.

'Yeah, half eleven. We were on the golf course playing a two-ball foursome. Dad was driving off the seventh tee when he suddenly dropped his club and slapped the side of his neck. Something stung him.'

'Wasp, he thought,' added Reilly. 'Or a horsefly.'

'Did either of you see it?'

'No,' they said in unison.

'Did you hear anything?'

'Like what?' said Jason with a sneer. 'Buzzing?'

'Anything at all unusual,' said Jo.

They stared at her and then at each other.

'Hang on,' said Jason. 'Are you saying someone shot him? Someone shot my dad?'

'I'm not saying anything,' Jo replied. 'I'm simply trying to establish how he came by that injury.'

But Jason wasn't listening. He was staring wide-eyed at Reilly. 'That's just the kind of thing those bastards would do, Jack.'

Reilly shook his head. 'They'd have made sure. Blown your dad's head off.'

'What bastards would those be, Jason?' asked Jo.

Jason ignored her question. 'He's right,' he said. 'It was only a scratch.'

Neither Jo nor Alice Robb responded.

'What if it was a poison dart, Jace?' said Reilly. 'Like they do to an animal?'

'Animal!?' O'Neill yelled. 'My dad?' His eyes bulged and his fists clenched. 'I'll give them fucking animal!'

Chapter 8

Jo pulled up at the gatehouse, showed her ID, and waited patiently for them to check her out.

Up ahead was Nexus House. From the outside it could easily be mistaken for just another brick and glass office block on the industrial estate just yards from the M60 motorway. In reality, it housed three of GMP's elite teams: the Serious Crime Division, the Economic Crime Unit, and the Cold Case Unit. The Forensic Services team was also here, which in theory meant a much faster turnaround of crime scene samples. It had been opened less than two years ago, a fortnight after her secondment to the NCA.

Jo wondered why they were taking so long in the gatehouse. She was impatient to get going, but also apprehensive. Presumably the syndicate she'd worked alongside on Operation Hound would have relocated here by now. She hoped so, and that it would be the one that she was about to head up. This investigation was going to be challenging enough without having to establish her authority and credibility after being parachuted into an already tight-knit team.

One of the civilian gatekeepers tapped on her window and handed back her ID.

'All good, Ma'am,' he said. 'Follow the road around to the right and park up wherever you can find a space. The entrance is slap bang in the middle. You can't miss it.'

At the front desk she was told that ACC Gates had rung and told them to expect her. She was asked to complete a form giving her details and car reg and then handed a temporary guest pass on a lanyard. A member of the front desk staff led the way to one of the major incident rooms on the second floor. Jo took a deep breath and opened the door.

She had no idea what she'd been expecting, something new and shiny perhaps, but it was more the shock of the familiar. It was like walking into the MIR at Central Park, or even being back at Longsight. Row after row of desks, each with a monitor. The only real difference was the absence of wall space, compensated for by standing whiteboards and interactive screens. Also the number of empty desks, presumably reflecting the steady erosion in front-line staff.

Nobody looked up as she entered the room, but she'd already spotted some familiar faces. Duggie Wallace, a collator and senior intelligence analyst, Jack Benson, senior crime scene investigator, and Detective Constable Jimmy Hulme, the joker of the pack. To her right, Ged, the syndicate Office Manager, was deep in conversation with Gordon Holmes. If this was her syndicate, it was a great start. Ged noticed her for the first time. She smiled and said something to Gordon Holmes. He turned and waved Jo over.

'Don't worry,' he said. 'I'm not here to queer your pitch or tread on your toes. I thought you might welcome my having a few words with this lot to explain my imminent departure and warn them that they'd better give you one hundred per cent or they'll have me to answer to.'

'Thanks,' she said. 'I really appreciate it.'

Which was not what she was really thinking. This was all about him needing to say goodbye, and making sure they knew he hadn't been pushed aside by a woman. As for warning the syndicate to behave for her, it was the kind of patronising male behaviour that still haunted the force despite the best efforts of the Equality and Diversity team.

'Welcome back, Ma'am,' said Ged.

There was no way she was going to call Jo by her given name, and she had always struggled with Ms Stuart. Jo couldn't care less. Having Ged on her side was worth a dozen lapdogs.

Gordon clapped his hands twice. 'Listen up!' he bellowed.

Everyone stopped what they were doing and looked up. Several of them smiled when they saw Jo beside him.

'There's good news and bad news,' he said.

'No change there then,' someone said.

Gordon waited for the laughter to subside. 'The bad news is that I've been reassigned to Syndicate Four to investigate the outbreak of shootings in South Manchester.'

This was met by a few groans and some sympathetic murmurs that left Jo in doubt as to how much he would be missed.

'The good news is that DI Stuart – currently NCA Senior Investigator – has been seconded back to us to lead a new investigation. Her bad news is that she has to do it with you lot.'

Benson and Wallace began to clap. DC Hulme and several of the others joined in. Soon the entire room appeared to be applauding her. Jo had been hoping that the old guard would be happy to see her, but this was embarrassing.

Gordon stepped aside to make way for her. She stepped forward, motioned for those who were standing to sit down, and waited for the applause to fade.

'Thank you,' she said. 'The feeling's mutual. I'm guessing that by now you'll all have heard about Ronnie O'Neill's untimely demise in suspicious circumstances?'

Heads nodded, and there were murmured asides.

'Well,' she said, 'the investigation is now officially ours.'

There were murmurs of excitement and a couple of people even punched the air.

'I'm glad to see you're all up for it,' she said. 'Because this has A-plus priority. That means twenty-four-hour coverage until we have a handle on it. Probably, until we have the perpetrator in custody.'

That was met with a few more groans, but nowhere near as many as she'd expected. But she knew that none of them would have been in this syndicate if they didn't live for moments like this. They would work every hour that God sent them to get the job done, and deal with the domestic fallout when it was all over. Until the next one came along. It was a relentless process – one that cost too many of them their domestic relationships. Hers included.

'So, initial lines of enquiry,' she continued. 'Jack, I need a CSI team down at the Worsley Golf Course. At the moment, it appears to be the nearest we've got to a crime scene. Though God knows what kind of trace evidence they'll get after all the rain we've had overnight and this morning. Then, as soon as we have a list of people who were on the course on Friday morning, I'll need some of you to interview them. There'll also be door-to-door enquiries at some of the surrounding properties. The rest of you will either be collating information as it comes in, sifting intelligence on potential suspects, or analysing passive data – in particular, CCTV from the hotel and golf course parking lots and the surrounding roads.'

'What will we be looking for, Boss?' said Detective Constable Hulme.

'Honestly?' she replied. 'Right now, I haven't a clue. But trust me, by the end of the afternoon I will.'

'What are you calling this investigation, Ma'am?' Jack Benson asked.

'Good question,' she said. 'Duggie, I need a name for a new operation.'

'Right away, Boss,' Duggie Walters replied, turning back to his computer.

The door burst open and DS Carter came barrelling in, closely followed by DC Whittle.

'That was quick,' said Jo. 'Has the pathologist been?'

Nick Carter looked at the sea of faces staring at them.

'It's fine,' she told him. 'I was just briefing the team. You can tell us all.'

'Been and left,' Nick replied. 'It was Professor Flatman. He asked for the patient's notes, took a quick look at the body, and then turned to me. "You can tell DCI Holmes," he said, "that I concur with the findings of the hospital. This man is definitely deceased."' He waited for the laughter to subside. '"I also agree that the cause of his death, which we will not know with any certainty until I've performed the post-mortem, would appear to be decidedly fishy. A non-technical term, Detective Sergeant, which you should not write down and may not quote. And now I am leaving. I have a particularly interesting cadaver to attend to."'

'Did you explain the urgency of the situation?' she said. 'That we need the PM as quickly as possible?'

'I didn't need to,' Nick replied. 'He said we were lucky. He had a particular interest in this one, and he'll do a late-evening PM just for us. To be honest, I got the impression someone had already been on to him.'

Jo nodded.

'Probably the Coroner,' she said. 'I'm not the only one who's being leaned on.'

She turned to Carly Whittle.

'What about you, Detective Constable? I hope you've got some good news?'

'Good and bad, Boss,' she replied.

'Give me the bad first.'

'Jason O'Neill and Jack Reilly were happy to give loads of detail on the night out at the Italian in town, but when it came to suggesting names for people who might have been prepared to murder O'Neill, they couldn't think of a single name.'

'With him being such a saint,' said Nick.

'And the good news?'

'DCI Fox has tracked down Steven Yates, and he's agreed to meet up with you, Jason, Reilly, and a Nathan Burke – the fourth member of their Friday morning foursome – at the golf club this afternoon.' Carly hesitated.

'Go on,' said Jo.

'I hope you don't mind, Ma'am,' Carly continued, 'but I took the liberty of contacting the golf professional at the club to ask him if he'd arrange some buggies to ferry you all out to the seventh tee, and if he'd accompany you.'

'Well done,' Jo told her. 'Feel free to keep taking liberties like that.'

'Until you get it wrong,' quipped Nick.

Duggie Walters rose from his desk. 'Boss,' he said, 'that operational name you wanted? It's just come through.'

'And?'

'Alecto.'

DC Hulme shook his head. 'That computer down at New Scotland Yard has a sick sense of humour,' he said.

'Why? What's wrong with Alecto?' Duggie asked.

'In Greek mythology she was one of the Furies. Her job was chastising humans guilty of crimes such as anger. Like her sister Nemesis did with the Gods.'

'Sounds perfect,' said Jo.

'Not really. She caused one of the Trojan Wars in Book 7 of the Aeneid. I thought we were trying to stop one breaking out.'

'How does he know these things?' asked Carly.

'Because he's a nerd,' said Nick. 'He sees himself as a twenty-first-century Inspector Morse.'

Several of the DCs laughed.

'I don't own a Jag,' Hulme replied. 'I'm not into Wagner or opera, I don't have time to do crosswords, and I don't have a limp.'

'The absence of a limp we can fix,' said Gordon ominously.

Cue more laughter.

Nothing's changed, Jo reflected. *It's just like the old days. Especially those seven years with the Major Incident Team before my secondment. Except this time, I'm the Boss. And now the buck stops with me.*

Chapter 9

'Looks like you're off to a flying start,' said Gordon.

The room was a hive of activity. Everyone appeared to know exactly what to do.

He led Jo to a minimally furnished glass-partitioned interior office at the far corner of the room, closed the door behind them, and perched on the edge of the desk.

'Seems a bit depleted out there,' she said.

'Like Gates said, it's partly cuts, and partly fallout from the Manchester Arena bombing. But what she didn't tell you is that recruitment to CID has dropped off. All of a sudden everyone wants the regular hours, even if it does mean doing shifts.' He grimaced. 'It's a wonder there's any of us left.'

Jo had heard as much. She hadn't realised it was that bad.

'I give it twelve months,' Gordon continued. 'Then there'll be a handful of guys sitting in front of computers going through dashcam footage sent in by members of the public. The only cases going to court will be traffic-related. The burglars, drug barons, rapists, and murderers are going to have a field day.'

She smiled. 'This is the Gordon I've come to know and love – one of life's true optimists.'

He checked his watch and slid off the desk. 'There is a silver lining,' he said. 'Detective Constable Carly Whittle. She's intelligent and very enthusiastic, just like you were when you started.'

'Enthusiastic?'

'Put it this way. Some of the team have started calling her Percy.'

'Percy?'

'As in persistent. She's like a dog with a bone. Twenty minutes in an interview room with Carly Whittle is a lifetime for the toughest criminal mind. She wears them down till they'll admit to robbing their kids' money boxes.'

'Surely the Crown Prosecution Service would have something to say about that?'

'That's where you're wrong,' he told her. 'She's one of our most successful interviewers. Knows where the boundaries are and stays just this side of the red line. Only it's as exhausting for whoever's in there with her as it is for the suspect!'

He opened the door. 'I'm off. Good luck, Jo. You're going to need it.'

Jo followed him out. The energy in the incident room was charged, as though full of static. There was something about a large team of people energised by a sense of common purpose. Not that she didn't enjoy working with the rest of the Behavioural Sciences Unit back at The Quays, but there were only five of them. This was exhilarating. And for the first time she was truly in charge.

Nick Carter was leaning over Carly Whittle's desk, talking to her. Jo was disappointed in him. She could be mistaken, but he seemed to have become more flippant, less respectful, and less supportive of junior members of the team. Tom Caton would never have stood for it. She decided to nip it in the bud. She went over and joined them.

'How did you get back here, DS Carter?' she asked.

Carter seemed momentarily surprised by her formality, but then he grinned. 'I blagged a lift, like DCI Holmes suggested.'

'And you, DC Whittle?' she asked.

'There weren't any patrol cars outside the Children's Hospital,' she said hesitantly. 'Given the urgency, I grabbed a taxi.'

'That'll have to come out of your own pocket,' said Nick. 'Don't expect to claim for it.'

'It's a shame you didn't think to share your ride with Carly then, isn't it?' said Jo.

Nick appeared to have a ready answer to that, but when he saw the look on her face, he thought better of it.

'I'd like a word, DS Carter,' she said. 'In my office.'

Chapter 10

The convoy of electric buggies wound its way between the fairways and stopped below the tees for the seventh hole. Jo was in the first buggy with Dermot Wheaton, the club professional; DC Whittle and Jack Benson were in the second; Jack Reilly and Nathan Burke in the third; Jason O'Neill and a firearms expert followed behind them; and four of Benson's crime scene investigators brought up the rear. Steven Yates had not turned up, was not answering his phone, and his whereabouts were unknown.

'This is it,' said Wheaton.

Yellow-and-black crime scene tape flapped and billowed in a blustery wind. The surface of the pond rippled from right to left, reminiscent of an oncoming tide. Two hundred yards away, a semicircular canopy of trees swayed in perfect harmony with the flag on the green in front of them. The leaves, shimmering russet, gold, and brown in the late autumnal sunshine, completed a scene of beauty and tranquillity. It was an unlikely setting for a murder, although in Jo's experience there was no such thing.

She waited at the foot of the steps for the others to congregate around her. 'We need to get this right,' she told them. 'There are two purposes to what we're about. The first is to establish what happened here on Friday morning. The second is to gather forensic evidence.'

'The forensics will be problematic, Ma'am,' said Benson. 'As I understand it, this hole was only taken out of use three hours ago.'

'That's correct,' said Wheaton. 'As soon as we were contacted, I sent two groundsmen to close this hole and divert people playing the course around it. Your colleagues arrived with the tapes just an hour and a half ago.'

'How many people do you reckon have played this hole since Friday?' Benson asked.

'I thought you might want to know that, so I did a rough calculation. Weekends are always busy, but I'm afraid we also had block bookings for company golf days yesterday and today.' Wheaton shrugged apologetically. 'There must have been close to five hundred people played this green since Friday lunchtime.'

'That need not be such a problem,' said Jo. 'Assuming that Mr O'Neill was struck by some kind of missile while on one of these tees, the only evidence we'd expect to find will be a pellet, or a dart of some kind. Recovering that would be really helpful. But just as important is establishing where the perpetrator fired it from. If we can find out where he laid up, took the shot, and which escape route he followed, that could yield a great deal more useful information. Agreed?'

'Yes, Ma'am,' Benson acknowledged.

'Good. In which case I propose that we begin with the reconstruction and leave Mr Benson and his CSI team to carry out a detailed search.'

She waved forward Jack Reilly, Nathan Burke, and Jason O'Neill.

'I realise this is going to be hard,' she said. 'And especially for you, Jason. But I can't stress enough how important it will be in helping us to catch the man who killed your father. You do understand?'

O'Neill, his hands deep in the pockets of his jeans, nodded while avoiding eye contact. 'Yeah.' He was strangely subdued compared with his outburst in the bereavement centre. He seemed almost as nervous as Jack Reilly, who was anxiously scanning the trees off to their right.

'Don't worry,' she said. 'The officers who set up the crime scene tape are out there guarding the path behind those trees. They've made sure there's no one there if that's what's bothering you.'

'I'm fine,' muttered Reilly, sounding anything but.

'In which case, perhaps we can start. Which of these tees were you on?'

'The back one,' said Burke. 'What d'you take us for? Jessies?'

Jo nodded to the cameraman. He skirted the tee on the left-hand side and waited to see how the players would line up.

'I'm going to ask Mr Wheaton to take the role of your father,' she said. 'You two play yourselves. Jason, please stand where Mr Yates was at that moment. I'm relying on the two of you who were here to make sure everybody is in the right place at the right time, from the moment you start up these steps. Is that clear?'

Burke and Reilly looked at each other and then at her.

'Okay, we get that,' said Burke.

'In which case, let's start. In what order did you climb these steps?'

It took almost two minutes for the two of them to agree this, and then a further five to agree who had been standing where when Ronnie O'Neill had played his shot.

When the tableau was finally in position, the club professional turned to Jo. 'Do you want me to actually play a shot, with a real ball?' he asked.

'Yes please,' she replied. 'I want everything exactly as it was.'

'D'you want me to tell you where the ball ended up?' joked Reilly.

'Shut it!' Jason O'Neill snarled, betraying just how tense he was.

The firearms expert stepped forward. 'Actually, that's not a bad idea, Ma'am. It may give us a better idea of the likely trajectory of the pellet, assuming that this gentleman can replicate Mr O'Neill's swing?'

'Is that feasible, Mr Wheaton?' said Jo.

'It won't be perfect,' he said. 'Everyone's different. But I can give it a go.'

'In that case, yes please,' said Jo. 'So where did the ball land?'

'About three feet from the pin and about a foot to the left of centre,' said Reilly.

'I agree,' said Burke.

'Hallelujah!' said O'Neill. 'Finally, something we can agree on.'

'Do you remember what club he used?' Wheaton asked.

'A seven,' said Burke.

'A six,' said Reilly.

'Here we go again!' said O'Neill.

'It was definitely a six,' said Burke. 'I remember because I used a seven and Ron said I should've used a six. And that's what he used.'

They all stared at Reilly. He conceded with a shrug of his shoulders.

Wheaton went back to his buggy, selected a club, put several plastic tees in one pocket and a handful of balls in the other, and returned. 'Where exactly was your friend standing?' he asked.

That sparked another lengthy squabble.

'For Christ's sake!' said O'Neill. 'It'll be dark soon. He won't be able to see the green, let alone the flag.'

The spot was agreed on. Burke and Reilly took up their positions, behind and to the left of Wheaton, with Jason O'Neill alongside them.

'I need to take this from several different angles,' said the cameraman.

'And I'll probably need more than one attempt,' said Wheaton.

'I thought you were supposed to be a pro,' growled Jason O'Neill.

'That's enough, Jason!' said Jo. 'If you don't stop this I'll have to ask you to go back to the buggy.'

If the look he gave her was meant to intimidate, it failed. She was used to dealing with men who resented taking orders from women.

The mood became sombre as Wheaton began his practice swing. Finally the realisation dawned that a father and friend had been murdered in this very spot. As the professional's swing reached its highest point, his shoulders turned and his neck was exposed. Nobody followed the ball. All eyes were on the woodland off to the right.

The ball had landed six feet from the pin, and three feet or so to the left.

'How was that?' Wheaton asked.

'Not bad,' said Burke grudgingly.

The cameraman gave the thumbs up and began to walk towards the front of the tee box.

'You're taking a hell of a risk,' said the professional. 'If I slice the ball this close up it could kill you.'

'You're not going to though, are you?' the cameraman asked.

'It's unlikely but I can't guarantee that I won't.'

'We can't do it then,' said Jo, remembering the risk assessment she'd signed off back at Nexus House.

'Is it okay on the other side of the tee?' asked the cameraman.

'So long as I don't let go of the iron,' said Wheaton. 'And that hasn't happened in donkey's years.'

'It did to poor old Ron,' said Reilly.

Chapter 11

'What do you think?' asked Jo.

Reilly, Burke, and O'Neill had left with Dermot Wheaton. Jo, Jack Benson, and Carly Whittle were huddled around Manish Jindal, the forensic firearms expert, who was studying the video footage from the camera, propped up on the seat in one of the buggies.

'Comparing the post-mortem photos of your victim with the position of the golf professional's neck today, that shot can only have come from somewhere in those trees to the right of the tees,' said Jindal. 'I'll be able to give you a more accurate estimate when I've analysed them back at the lab. But for the purposes of your initial search today, I can fairly confidently say that the shooter must have been within a twenty-degree sector.' He used his arms to create a segment. 'From there to there.'

They turned to look at the dense wood of beech, oak, and sycamore that curved around the edge of the rough grass.

'That's what?' said Jo. 'A hundred yards or so?'

Jindal took what looked like a pair of blue and black binoculars from his case.

'What are those?' asked Carly Whittle.

'Laser rangefinder. Golfers, archers, rifle and pistol target shooters, and hunters all use them. This pair is perfect for golfers and hunters.

Up to fifteen hundred yards the accuracy is within fifty yards. Back at Claybrook we've got a military version that's accurate to over fifteen miles – that's about twenty-five kilometres.' He raised the rangefinder, trained it on the trees, and moved it slowly from right to left across the sector he had identified.

'Between a hundred and twenty to a hundred and twenty-nine yards,' he said as he lowered them. 'That's a hundred and ten and a hundred and eighteen metres, give or take. And it depends on how far back in the woods he was when he took the shot.'

'That seems a hell of a long way for an air rifle,' said Benson.

Jindal shook his head. 'You'd be surprised. The longest recorded shot with an air rifle stands at one thousand and sixty-five yards. You go on YouTube, you'll find a guy in the States who hit a golf ball on top of a tin can with his second shot at one hundred and fifty yards. He used a .22, eighteen grain ASP pellet.'

'ASP?' said Jo.

'Advanced Sports Pellet. They were specially designed for competitive shooting. Very popular and unfortunately very common.'

'This wasn't a lucky shot then?'

Jindal frowned. 'Can you just run that first piece of footage for me?' he said to the cameraman. 'Only slow-mo it for me so we can see the time lapse.'

When the replay had finished, he stood up. 'He had less than half a second when the neck was exposed. He would have had to anticipate the timing and the trajectory, make allowance for the crosswind – although that was probably coming over his shoulder and not such a problem as it might have been – and know how long it would take that pellet to reach its target.'

'How long might that be?' asked Jo.

'They can travel in excess of the speed of sound,' he replied. 'Up to one thousand six hundred feet per second – but that's with much lighter pellets. With an eighteen grain we're looking at around eight hundred feet per second.'

'And you estimated the distance as around three hundred and sixty-five feet,' said Jo. 'So just about doable?'

Jindal nodded. 'Providing you're a bloody good shot. I'm not sure I could do it first time, and I'm on the range most days.'

'Which tells us that we're looking for someone who's an experienced shooter. With air rifles in particular?'

'Exactly.'

'What kind of air rifle?' asked Benson.

'Now you're asking,' said Jindal. 'There are lots of models you could make that shot with. But if you wanted it more or less silent, and with deadly accuracy, I'd go for one with professional specifications that exceeded the requirements for the task. Something like a Ruger Yukon Air Rifle. It's gas-ram piston driven, one of the least difficult to cock. It has an integrated silencer and fires a .22 pellet at one thousand and fifty feet per second. Either that or the Black Opps Tactical Sniper Air Rifle.'

'Sniper rifle?' said DC Whittle. 'Are you sure we're talking air rifles?'

Jindal nodded grimly. 'I know what you're thinking. You don't need a licence for an air rifle. But trust me, these are basically replicas of the ones used by military special forces. Okay, they're intended to be used for target shooting, and the humane killing of small game, and pest control, but in the wrong hands they can be used to kill humans too.'

Jo stared over at the trees, a rainbow of colours swaying majestically in the wind. 'Like this one did,' she said. 'Maybe not immediately. And certainly not humanely.'

Chapter 12

Forty minutes later, Jo was back at Nexus House. Half of Jack Benson's team were crawling inch by inch over the tee on the seventh hole. The remainder were trying to pinpoint the exact spot from which the gunman had fired. Searching for broken branches, disturbed undergrowth, footprints, traces of cloth snagged on thorns – anything that might provide the slightest evidence that could be used to place the perpetrator at the scene, if and when they caught him.

When, Jo said to herself. *It has to be when, not if. There's enough anxiety out there without having a maniac roaming the city, armed with deadly poison and a sniper rifle.*

She was in her office drinking water from the cooler when her personal phone rang. She checked the caller ID. Abbie. *What the hell does she want now?* She took a deep breath and answered.

'Abbie. What's up?'

There was a pause long enough for Jo to sense Abbie steeling herself.

'I was hoping you could let me know when your sale's going through? Only it's my due date in a fortnight and I was anticipating it would all be sorted by then.'

Jo bit her lip and resisted the temptation to remind her that this was the third time she'd asked in as many days.

'You'll remember that I exchanged contracts with the buyer on Friday,' she said. 'And I'm sure I mentioned that they're wanting completion by the 23rd.'

'Next Monday,' said Abbie. 'And you'll do a bank transfer straight away? I'll email you my bank details this evening.'

'No need,' said Jo. 'I still have them.'

'Actually, you don't.' There was a noticeable shift in tone. She sounded uncharacteristically tentative. Almost apologetic. 'The bank's the same. The account's changed. Make sure you delete the old ones, Jo.'

'I will.'

If only it was as easy to delete the memory of those final fractious months together. And the hurtful things they had said. *How much easier life would be if we could edit out the bad stuff. Like a movie, or an airbrushed photograph.*

'And how are you, and . . . the baby?' Jo asked.

But Abbie had gone. She no longer had time for goodbyes it seemed, or pleasantries. A knock on the door reminded Jo that neither did she. It was Carter. She waved him in.

He hovered in the doorway. 'I'm sorry about earlier, Ma'am,' he said, looking genuinely apologetic. 'The DC Whittle thing. It's not like me. I don't know what came over me.'

'For God's sake, come in and close the door,' she said. 'And stop this "Ma'am" nonsense when we're on our own. How many years have we known each other? It's Jo, alright?'

He relaxed, closed the door and sat down.

'Otherwise I won't be able to call you Nick,' she continued. 'And then I won't be able to fire a shot across your bows by calling you Detective Sergeant Carter.'

It was enough to draw a line under the dressing-down she'd given him earlier that day. Jo knew that he had gamely hidden the hurt he'd felt following her promotion to inspector, when he'd been the longer serving detective. To be fair, he'd never suggested that it was anything to do with her gender and had been one of the first to congratulate her. But that wouldn't stop him feeling aggrieved. Now he was faced with the loss of his pal Gordon Holmes, and to make matters worse, here she was, back as his boss and line manager. They needed each other and she was determined to make him feel as valued as Caton had made her feel.

'Fair enough, Jo,' he responded with a broad grin. 'So, where are we up to?'

'We're pretty certain now where the perpetrator was when he fired that pellet at Ronnie O'Neill. CSI are searching the area. DC Whittle is setting up door-to-door enquiries along millionaires' row on Bridgewater Road. She's making sure they ask for any private CCTV footage.'

'You reckon the perp' may have used that road for his entry and exit?' said Nick.

'Who knows? It's the nearest point to the seventh hole. And there's a wide path behind it that runs between two of those mansions. But he could just as easily have masqueraded as a golfer and joined the course at any point around the perimeter. The forensic firearms expert thought that most likely, because he'd have been able to hide the rifle in a golf bag, provided he'd topped up the gas first. With his baseball cap pulled down low, nobody would have given him a second glance.'

'Still worth getting witness statements from everyone who was playing or working the course that day,' he said.

'We can't afford not to. Problem is that it was a large company's annual two-day conference for employees from all over the UK. And members were also playing that day. I've asked the director of golf, the conference manager, and head of the country club to get me the names of everyone who was there that day. They reckon it'll come to more than five hundred people.'

'That's a hell of a lot of interviews. Don't expect Gates to sanction overtime.'

'ACC Gates,' she reminded him.

You had to set the limits on between-rank informality, Caton had taught her. Otherwise it might come back to bite you.

'ACC Gates,' he acknowledged. 'In case you're wondering, I've set up the incident room for Operation Alecto with Ged, and the murder log. Nobody's going to be able to criticise our information collation, analysis or storage. There's a timeline analysis chart ready and I've brought a management team checklist for your approval. I took the liberty, with you not knowing some of the syndicate, of suggesting names against most of the roles. I can talk you through any you're not sure about.' He handed her the list.

'Nick, you're a genius,' she said. 'And a mind reader to boot. I was dreading having to do that.'

'You're welcome,' he responded. 'And I'm not the only one pulling out all the stops. Just before you arrived back here Jack Benson sent over a couple of files.'

He placed his tablet on the desk and clicked on a folder headed *Alecto CSI SOC 1–3*, then clicked on each file in turn. One was a map of the scene, with photographs and a diagram. The second was a list of crime scene features, again with photographs. The third contained the videos taken of the reconstruction.

'Based on what you've told me,' Nick continued, 'I can get Duggie to construct a map of all the physical search zones, areas for house-to-house enquiries, and passive media recovery. That'll tick the mapping requirements of the Investigation Manual.'

Jo was relieved. Her biggest fear, apart from failing to nail the bastard, was not getting the basics right on her first really major investigation as SIO.

Then Nick grinned and spoiled it for her. 'Just as well,' he said. 'Because we've bugger all else.'

There was no paper on the desk, other than those ominously piled on top of Gordon's in tray. She opened one of the drawers looking for a pad she could scribble some thoughts on. There was only an A4 manila file. She took it out, placed it on the desk, and opened it.

'Who'd have thought,' she said. 'Thank you, Gordon.'

Nick Carter craned forward. 'Is that what I think it is?' he asked.

'If you think it's a super-handy digest of the *Murder Investigation Manual*, you'd be right,' she replied, leafing through the laminated sheets of checklists and diagrams.

'He kept that close to his chest,' said Nick. 'I often wondered how he was suddenly so on the ball when DCI Caton left.'

'Here we are,' said Jo. 'The very thing. Saves me opening my tablet. Bring your chair round here, Nick, where you can see it.'

It was a list of all the key elements involved in investigative strategy – the main focus for any Review team after they'd checked the Fast Track menu. Miss any of this out and she'd be toast. She ran her finger down it.

'Crime scene, that's in hand. Hopefully CSI will find something for Forensics to look at, and we're waiting on the results from the tissue samples taken at the hospital. Post-mortem: do we know when that's taking place?'

Nick looked at his watch.

'Eight o'clock this evening,' he told her. 'Sorry, I should have told you straight off. Professor Flatman pulled rank and pulled out all the stops. Said he'd never seen a case like this one.'

'Nobody has,' said Jo. She pointed to the next one. 'Witnesses – we've three of those, one of whom has done a runner. We've already carried out a reconstruction. Not that it's provided us with much to go on. Victim Care is already round at Mrs O'Neill's, despite her son's protestations. House-to-house enquiries are under way. As for suspects, Operation Challenger is compiling a list of anyone who might have had a grievance against Ronnie O'Neill.'

'Enough to fill a phone directory by all accounts,' said Nick. 'And we can't start any elimination enquiries until we have those names.'

'ACC Gates has insisted that she'll be handling Media,' said Jo, 'which is fine by me. But if it starts to get ugly, I have no doubt that yours truly will suddenly find herself in the firing line.'

'Never been a problem for you in the past,' said Nick.

Jo ran her finger further down the list and paused. 'Community is a tricky one. This isn't like the States where multiple shootings are commonplace.'

'I know,' said Carter. 'Sixteen mass shootings this month alone. It was on the news on Saturday night. Thirteen killed, sixty wounded. An average of four people shot per incident.'

'One person roaming the streets over here with poison pellets is probably going to get more or less the same reaction,' she said. 'It's going to take a concerted effort to reassure the public and I don't want the syndicate to have to spend time on that.'

'Another one for Assistant Chief Constable Gates,' Nick suggested. 'Neighbourhood teams, the force Twitter feed, media statements, they'll all have a part to play. Do you want me to chase it up?'

'If you could.'

She looked at the last three items on the list. 'Between us, I think we've got passive data recovery sorted. Until we have a suspect there's no cause to develop a search strategy other than at the crime scene. That just leaves covert intelligence. I'm assuming that Operation Challenger and Operation Xcalibre must have assets in place helping them to compile that list of names. We need to make sure they keep their ears to the ground and see if there are any whispers about possible motives or, even better, likely suspects.' She put the checklists back in the folder and stood up. 'Time to brief the team before I get over to the morgue.'

'Just a thought,' said Nick, one hand on the door handle. 'About the passive data. What about a public dashcam appeal?'

'Go on.'

'Assuming the perpetrator left on foot, on a bike, or some other vehicle. There are bound to be people with dashboard cameras fitted to their cars who'll have unwittingly captured footage with him on it. Either the vehicle and its number plate, or maybe him crossing the road, or walking to a car with a golf bag. I bet there are as many dashcams out there now as static cameras.'

'Well done, Nick,' she said. 'I should have thought of that.'

'You did,' he said, with a broad grin. 'You just hadn't said it yet.'

She laughed. 'Do you know when I first heard that said?'

'Of course I do. On your first day as a DC at Longsight. I was your DS, Gordon was our DI. Tom Caton was the boss – he said it to you. Like he said it to everyone when they first started. Like you will to DC Whittle.' He opened the door for her. 'When you do, you'll owe me a pint, Boss.'

'You're on,' she said.

Chapter 13

The team briefing was going well and Jo was relieved. It was important to make that first impression – like the brand-new manager of a premiership club about to face its sternest test. Long-standing members like Carter, Duggie Walters, and to his credit even DC Hulme, were playing their part with positive comments and suggestions. The ones she'd not come across before were still weighing her up. She could see it in their eyes and their fixed and watchful expressions. Twenty minutes in, Ged signalled that she needed a word. Jo asked Nick Carter to take over.

'I'm sorry, Ma'am,' said Ged, 'but Mr Benson says there's been a breakthrough. He thought you'd want to know.'

'He has Skype on his tablet, hasn't he?'

'Yes, Ma'am.'

'In which case, tell him to Skype you and put it through to the interactive whiteboard. I'd like everyone to hear what he has to say.'

Ged looked uncertain.

'You know how to do that, don't you, Ged? If not, Mr Wallace can help you.'

'It's not that,' she replied. 'I just wondered how secure it was.'

'Don't worry,' Jo told her. 'All video, voice, and file transfers are encrypted. Only calls to landlines and personal phones over the ordinary phone network are at risk of being eavesdropped.'

Jo rejoined Nick and waited until he'd finished talking the team through the passive data issues.

'Right,' she said. 'There's an update coming through from the crime scene. I've asked Ged to put it up on the screen because I want you all to hear it. It'll be quicker that way than my having to repeat it, and some of you may have questions others haven't thought of. That's the way I intend to run this investigation. Whatever your own particular role, I want each of you to have the same access to information as everyone else. When it comes to solving difficult problems, who's to tell which mind may see the missing piece. There'll be no prima donnas on Operation Alecto – me included.'

That brought murmurs of appreciation and smiles all round.

'Well done, Boss,' whispered Nick.

Everyone turned to watch as Jack Benson's face appeared on the whiteboard, distorted into a ghoulish mask by the harsh lighting from crime scene arc lamps.

'Good evening, Mr Benson,' said Jo. 'Good of you to join us. Please tell me you have some good news?'

'I'll let you be the judge of that, Ma'am. But we have made progress. For example, we recovered this from the tee on which the victim was standing when he thought he'd been stung by a wasp.'

His latex-gloved hand appeared in front of his face. Something was held between his thumb and forefinger. The object was a dull silver colour and he turned it slowly for them to see.

'Is that what I think it is?' Jo asked.

'Yes, Ma'am,' he said from behind his glove. 'It remains to be confirmed, but I don't think there's any doubt that Forensics will identify it as an air rifle pellet.'

A cheer went up in the room and a few people applauded.

'We found it using a metal detector,' Benson continued. 'It's a bit dirty because it had been trampled several inches into the ground, but you can still see the tiny holes drilled into the surface.'

'To contain the poison?' said Nick Carter.

'Presumably. Shouldn't take us long to find out when we get back.'

Benson lowered his hand. 'We also found a spot in the woods from which the perpetrator may have fired the shot. The grass has been flattened and some branches broken off, possibly to provide a better view of the tee. We also have some partial boot prints to and from those places. They're not brilliant, and whether or not they'll be viable for comparison with those on the national database, it's too soon to tell, but I have someone lifting them as we speak. There was also a scrap of fabric on a nearby branch, but we would need something to match it to.'

'Is there any indication of how the perpetrator may have got to and from his hiding place?' Jo asked.

He nodded, revealing the beginnings of a bald patch on the crown of his head. 'Yes. The flattened grass and the footprints lead to a path that runs behind the woods, along the perimeter fence for a row of houses, and then out onto Leigh Road. But also eastwards away from the tee in the other direction. The problem is that loads of people have walked that path since Friday, some with dogs. It's also muddy from the rain, so isolating the shooter's boot prints from the others is going to be tricky.'

'Do your best,' Jo said.

'I will, Ma'am. And we've also taken samples of pollen from the site in case you manage to get approval for palynology in the hope of placing a suspect at the scene.'

'Is that it?' Jo asked.

'Yes, Ma'am. So far that's all we've got.'

'Does anyone have a question for Mr Benson, or helpful comments?' Jo asked.

DC Whittle put her hand up. 'What occurs to me,' she said tentatively, 'is how the perpetrator knew that O'Neill would be playing that day?'

'That's a good one,' said Jo, 'but let's hold that thought for a moment. Does anyone have any queries or suggestions specifically for Mr Benson and his CSI team?'

Lips were pursed and heads shaken but no one spoke.

'In that case,' Jo said, 'well done, Jack. Given the circumstances, you've recovered far more than we might have expected. Give your team my congratulations. Make sure they're properly fed and watered. And don't feel you have to work through the night. The search perimeter has been secured, so you can start again in the morning.'

When the video call ended, she turned to DC Whittle. 'Returning to your question, Carly,' she said, 'you've had time to think about it. What do you think the implications are?'

'That he's either familiar with the victim's habits, or he's been following him. Either way it must have taken a lot of planning.'

'We know that Ronnie O'Neill was a member of the club,' said Carter. 'But we need to find out if he was in the habit of playing on Fridays.'

'He'd only been out of prison for a month,' Jo reminded him. 'That's hardly long enough to establish a pattern. Given the nature of the attack and the preparation required, DC Whittle is right that it must have been planned for some time. Probably while O'Neill was still inside. In which case the perpetrator will have been looking for settings frequented by O'Neill that would provide him with covert cover, ingress, and egress.'

'Would it be too much of a coincidence for the perp' also to have been a member of the club?' DC Hulme suggested.

'Probably,' said Jo. 'But he could have deliberately joined while his victim was inside. That way nobody would view his presence on the course as suspicious. He'd be acting in plain sight.'

'That'd take some balls,' said Carter.

'If the perp' is a man,' someone shouted.

Jo waited for the laughter to subside. 'Not such a daft remark,' she said soberly. 'Statistically, women are more likely to use poison to kill. Female serial killers, for example, are more likely to have been harbouring deep-felt grievances and to have killed in cold blood rather than the heat of the moment. And just because a gun's involved, it doesn't mean that the unsub is a man. Until we know otherwise, this is a gender-neutral investigation.'

She scanned the room waiting for absolute silence and for every eye to be on her before she spoke. When she did, you could have heard a pin drop.

'Make sure you remember that.'

Chapter 14

'You can sew him up, Benedict.'

Sir James Flatman, Home Office pathologist, turned away from the stainless-steel table, ran his gloved hands under a faucet over a sink along the wall and shook them dry. Then he removed his face mask and turned to face the gallery.

Beneath the bright lights signs of his advancing years were cruelly exposed. He had been in his late fifties the first time Jo had met him in this very theatre. Now that he was approaching seventy his hair had turned white. Always on the heavy side, his body was now positively corpulent. Jowls hung beneath his chin. His eyes were hooded and there was a stoop where once he had been the epitome of military bearing. Jo felt sorry for him.

The door behind her opened. Carly Whittle slipped in and took the seat beside her.

'Good of you to join us, Detective Constable,' said Flatman. 'Most of them don't make it back.'

'Don't mind him,' Jo whispered. 'He's like that with all the girls.'

'I heard that, SI Stuart,' he boomed.

Jo leaned into the mic. 'Good,' she said.

He roared with laughter. 'Not lost any of your feistiness then? Rank doth become you.'

Carly Whittle's jaw dropped.

'We go back a long way,' Jo told her. She raised her voice. 'We're in a bit of a hurry, Sir James. Can we just get on with it, please?'

He chuckled and stepped to one side, conscious that he was in the mortuary technician's way. Behind him they could see Ronald O'Neill's violated corpse. The chest flap retracted over the head, ribs split open, the empty cavity where the organs and intestines had been. Jo forced herself to concentrate on Flatman's lips.

'Did I tell you he still had his electronic tag around his ankle when they wheeled him in?' Flatman said. 'I had to wait for someone from the monitoring service to come and remove it. That was a first. So was the modus operandi. Never had poisoning by pellet before, although one of my colleagues had something similar. The Markov case?'

Jo nodded. 'Georgi Markov, 1978. I was one at the time. I had to google it.'

'That's the one. Bulgarian defector. A colleague, Dr Bernard Riley, treated him at the time. The medics and the police hadn't a clue what had happened until he discovered a tiny pinhead-sized pellet embedded in Markov's thigh. The victim thought he'd been bitten by something because there was just a red mark like a pimple on his leg. Unknown to him that pellet was releasing ricin into his bloodstream. He died four days later.'

'And you're saying that's what happened here? That he was poisoned with ricin?'

Flatman shook his head. 'I can't say that. You'll have to wait until the samples have been analysed. Even then you may not be able to establish that.'

'Why not, Professor?'

'Because the ricin, if that's what it was, may no longer be in his system. Your best chance of identifying the foreign agent that killed him is to find the pellet in which it was transported.'

'We have,' Jo told him.

'In which case, don't let your Forensics services near it. Get it straight down to Porton Down. Whatever it was, they'll be best placed to tell you.'

'Shit!' murmured Jo. She pulled out her phone and began to compose an urgent text for Jack Benson.

'What I can tell you,' Flatman continued, 'is that in this case the cause of death was consistent with ricin poisoning. When it's absorbed into the skin, as opposed to being ingested, it has the effect of preventing the body from producing the proteins needed by every cell in the body. I won't bore you with the details. All to do with amino acids and messenger RNAs. The point is that over the course of two to five days it leads to the breakdown of all the major organs and the central nervous system. I also found at the puncture site on the neck evidence of erythema, vesication, ecchymosis, and oedema – redness, blisters, bruising, and fluid retention for the layman – that are symptomatic of an allergic reaction. I am confident that analysis of the samples,' he waved his hand in the direction of the three refrigerators behind him, 'will confirm that this was what happened here. There are other poisons of course that can lead to all of this, which is why you need to see what Porton Down has to say.'

'So, he died of . . .?' said Jo.

'Multiple organ failure and shock.' Flatman shook his head. 'A bloody awful way to go.'

'Thank you, Professor,' she said.

'You could be looking for a fan of *Breaking Bad*,' he said.

'I beg your pardon?'

'*Breaking Bad*. Walter White tried every which way – adding it to an addict's meth, sprinkling it on food, lacing a cigarette, substituting it for artificial coffee sweetener. Pretty far-fetched really. Your perpetrator appears to have come up with a much more effective and dastardly solution.'

'That's because truth really is stranger than fiction,' Jo replied. 'Isn't that what you tell your students?'

Chapter 15

It was gone 10 p.m. when they arrived back at Nexus House. Jo quickly brought Nick up to speed.

'Porton Down?' said Nick. 'How long is that going to take?'

'I have no idea,' said Jo, 'given we're talking about a top-secret government establishment.'

'Does Benson know?'

'I reached him just in time. The pellet is downstairs with the Forensic Science Service. They haven't touched it, thank God. I've arranged for one of our motorcycle officers to take it as far as our boundary with the Cheshire Force. It's going to be motorcycle-relayed all the way to Wiltshire.'

'Like a kidney transplant.'

'And every bit as precious. Except I couldn't get approval to use the Police National Air Service.'

'Welcome to the real world,' said Carter. 'Cutsville. Also known as Austerity City.'

'Have we made any progress while I've been at the post-mortem?'

'Not really. CSI have packed up for the night as per your instructions. I also called a halt half an hour ago to the house-to-house enquiries around the perimeter of the golf course and in the vicinity of Ronnie O'Neill's home. I hope that's alright, Boss?'

'I'd have done the same. They'll have caught quite a few people who work during the day, but then those are the ones who wouldn't have been around on Friday morning either. They can start again tomorrow. It's not as though we're working a golden hour. The shooting was—' she glanced at the clock '—eighty-three hours ago.'

She scanned the incident room. There were close to thirty officers working away at their desks. Heads down, jackets over the backs of their chairs, sleeves rolled up. Cans of energy drinks were in evidence. Three more officers were queuing at the coffee machine.

'I'll give this lot the option of clocking off now and coming in as usual tomorrow,' she said. 'But by the look of it, if they do go home they're not going to sleep till dawn crawls over the horizon.'

'What are you going to do, Boss?' he asked.

'Make a start on Gordon's in tray. Most of it will be GMP stuff that I'll have been out of the loop for. I'll save that for you to deal with. I'm also going to put an email together for my colleagues on The Quays. I'm hoping to enlist some support with Alecto.'

'I thought you said they were tied up with an honour killing operation?'

'They are. But I was assured I could tap into NCA resources. Nobody stipulated which ones. I'm going to ask Andy Swift, our forensic criminal psychologist, if he can put together an initial crime profile for the killer. Just a sketchy one. Something to be going on with. And I'm going to ask my NCA colleagues to work through their databases for anything that might relate to similar offences.'

Nick frowned. 'You don't want Duggie Wallace getting the impression you don't trust him,' he said.

'Don't worry,' she said. 'He won't. Don't forget they worked together on all the other cases where GMP involved both me and the BSU. Duggie's got the HOLMES 2 database. These will be different resources – ones that GMP won't have access to.'

'Sounds a bit clandestine to me,' said Nick.

'That's because you believe in conspiracy theories.'

'Only when they're my conspiracies.'

'Fair enough,' she said. 'Now I suggest you get home to your family, Nick. I'll hold the fort here providing you're back for six in the morning?'

'Are you sure, Boss?'

'Just go, before I change my mind. It's not as though I've anyone to rush back to,' she murmured as she watched him leave.

The next four and a half hours crawled by. She gave up on the in tray an hour in. Every single document related to previous investigations, bean counting, or policy memos. She turned her attention to her own policy file, ensuring that all her key decisions concerning lines of enquiry and resource deployment were up to date. Then she checked on those of the house-to-house manager and Jack Benson, the senior CSI and crime scene manager. Everything seemed watertight.

She left her office and went from desk to desk checking that those officers who had opted to stay behind were okay. Any that looked like nodding off, and the two that already had, she sent home.

'And please don't fall asleep at the wheel,' she told them. 'For your own sake, and that of your kids and partners, if not for mine.'

DC Hulme was by the water dispenser. She went to join him.

'Are you alright, Jimmy?' she asked. Even for her, formality went out of the window at three in the morning.

'I'm fine, Boss,' he said. 'How about you?'

'I'm in the red zone, close to empty,' she admitted, slipping a beaker under the dispenser.

'This one will cheer you up,' he said. 'What's all the rage in the custody suites these days?'

'I doubt I'd have a clue on a good day,' she said.

He grinned. 'Suspects asking if they can have a selfie mug shot.'

'Sorry,' she said. 'You've lost me.'

'Cell-fie?'

Jo forced a weary smile. 'Thanks for that, Jimmy,' she said. 'You've made my night.'

Every team needed a Jimmy Hulme, she reflected as she made her way back to her office. Being a detective was a privilege. Exciting, challenging, sometimes dangerous, and often distressing. But most of the time it was downright boring. You needed someone to keep the spirits up. Even if it was with a well-worn joke or a bit of banter. Jimmy Hulme was their someone. That's why they tolerated him. But when you saw past the joker and the polymath, he was actually turning into a damned good detective.

Chapter 16

Day Two – Tuesday, 17th October

'Are you ready, Ma'am?'

Helen Gates peered over the senior press officer's shoulder into the packed media suite. The room buzzed with anticipation.

'Where the hell have they all come from?' she murmured. 'We were supposed to be keeping the lid on this until we had a better idea of what's really going on.'

'Too many people were aware of the circumstances of Ronnie O'Neill's demise, Ma'am,' Grace McAndrew replied. 'His fellow golfers, the staff at the Royal Infirmary, and at the mortuary. It was inevitable that word would get out and speculation grow.'

'They're not going to be satisfied with what I've got for them.'

'When are they ever, Ma'am?'

'That's true,' Helen replied. She took a deep breath, pulled her shoulders back, and nodded. 'Come on then,' she said. 'Let's get it over with.'

A hush fell over the room as they took their seats. Helen pulled the microphone towards her.

'I am going to read a prepared statement,' she said, 'after which I will be happy to respond to questions before asking you to assist us in appealing to members of the public for information that may assist us with our enquiries.'

She waited for the several murmurs to die down and then began.

'Yesterday morning, my officers were called to Manchester Royal Infirmary following the death of a fifty-three-year-old male. He had been admitted in the early hours following a 999 call from his home. It quickly became apparent that he was suffering from total organ failure. Despite the best efforts of the medical staff, he died at 8.16 a.m. I am now able to confirm, in the light of a post-mortem carried out yesterday evening, that we are treating this death as suspicious and investigating it accordingly. Relatives have been informed and the investigation is ongoing. I will take questions, but I am sure that you realise that at this early stage there is a limit to the amount of information I can share with you.'

A host of hands were raised.

Grace McAndrew selected them in turn. 'BBC *North West News*. Mr Grice.'

'Do you have a name for the victim?'

'The deceased is a Mr Ronald O'Neill, who had been living in Longsight with his wife and son,' said Helen.

The press officer pointed to a female on the front row. 'I'm sorry, I don't have your name?'

'Alex Southgate, *Manchester Evening News*,' she replied. 'How did he die?'

Helen was tempted to say 'horribly' but sanity prevailed. 'He died of multiple organ failure.'

'Yes, but what caused the organ failure in the first place?'

'That has yet to be established.'

The next question came uninvited. 'You must have some idea, or why else would you be treating it as suspicious? Is it true that you believe he was poisoned?'

Helen recognised the voice and tone. He was telling her that he already knew the answer. Testing her to see how much more she was prepared to give away. It was that damned investigative reporter again. What the hell was his name?

The senior press officer read her expression, placed her hand over the mic, and whispered in her ear. 'Ginley,' she said, 'Anthony Ginley.'

That journalist who they'd had down as a suspect in the Operation Juniper serial rapes a couple of years back, and who'd been a thorn in GMP's side ever since. Now he'd presented Helen with a dilemma. Did she give away a little more than she'd intended, or risk him revealing it himself and making her look either ill-informed or evasive?

She leaned into the microphone. 'There is some indication that a foreign substance may have been involved. We're in the process of trying to establish the nature of that substance.'

'Foreign as in Russian?' asked Ginley.

It was clear from the expressions on the sea of faces in front of Helen that most of the other people in the room had no idea what he was talking about.

'Not every unidentified substance has to be about the Russian State,' she said. Regretting it immediately.

'Not even when it comes in the form of a *pellet*?' shouted Ginley over the chorus of questions he had unleashed from those around him.

McAndrew placed her hand over the microphone again. 'Damage limitation,' she whispered. 'Give them something to lessen the speculation and I'll move it on as quickly as possible.'

Helen nodded. At the briefing they had discussed the worst-case scenario, and this was it. She just hoped she could remember the form of words that had been agreed.

'It is the case,' she said, more calmly than she felt, 'that we believe this unknown substance to have been delivered via an air rifle pellet three days prior to Mr O'Neill having been admitted to hospital. Despite this being an unusual mode of attack, we have no reason to believe that the motive is political in any shape or form. On the contrary. We believe it to have been entirely personal. Members of the public should not be concerned and it would be irresponsible to suggest otherwise. I am unable to add any more at this stage as it would prejudice our investigation.' As Helen leaned back a barrage of questions erupted.

Grace McAndrew took hold of the microphone and waited until a modicum of order had been restored. 'We will not take any more questions,' she said. 'However, ACC Gates will make a direct appeal to the public, which we trust you will support by all means at your disposal.'

'We are particularly interested,' Helen began, 'in hearing from anyone who may have seen someone acting suspiciously in or around Worsley Golf Course between the hours of 7 a.m. last Friday morning and twelve noon on the same day. If you believe that you have any information, however small, that may assist us in this investigation, contact us directly by dialling 111, or by speaking anonymously with CrimeStoppers on 0800 555 111, or online at www.crimestoppers-uk.org. Thank you.'

Helen and the senior press officer pushed back their chairs, stood up, and left the room.

'Well done, Ma'am,' said Grace McAndrew.

'I'd save the congratulations till you've seen the headlines,' said Helen despondently. 'This isn't *Children's Newsround* we're talking about.'

Chapter 17

'You look dreadful,' said Andy. 'Like you've been up all night.'

He, on the other hand, looked fresh and laid-back in one of his trademark T-shirts and a pair of cycling shorts. Hugging a cortado, he had chosen a discreet corner seat out of earshot of the handful of customers in the industrial-chic Dockyard bar in the heart of Media City.

Jo dropped her bag on the table, put down her mug, and pulled up a chair beside him. 'That's because I have,' she said. 'As good as. I clocked off at six, grabbed a couple of hours' sleep, and here I am.'

'Very commendable,' he said, 'if it wasn't for the fact that sleep deprivation is totally counterproductive. The brain does its optimum problem-solving while we're asleep. That's why the best solutions tend to come to us in the morning. As William Blake put it, "Think in the morning. Act in the noon. Eat in the evening. Sleep in the night."'

'So how come owls are considered wise, when they do their best work at night?'

He smiled. 'You forget, they then sleep throughout the day.'

'Thank you for slipping away from the office,' she said. 'I didn't want to breeze back in when I knew you were all so busy on the honour killing case.'

'Your email piqued my interest.'

Jo blew across the surface of her coffee. 'I knew it would.'

'Why?' he asked, leaning back in his chair and cradling his head in his hands.

'Because apart from the bizarre modus operandi, there are so many potential motives and, so far, not a single suspect.'

'True,' he said. 'But it's the MO that interests me most. That is what lies at the heart of every behavioural profile. If you had to ascribe a single motive to this killer based on his method of dispatch alone, which one would you choose, Jo?'

'Revenge,' she replied, without a moment's hesitation.

'Why?'

'Because of the unusual and horrific nature of the means he chose to kill his victim. Horrific, both because of the time it took to end O'Neill's life and the nature of the suffering that it caused. Only someone who had reason to really hate him would have gone to the trouble of choosing such a method.'

'Anything else?' he asked.

Jo put her mug down. 'The planning involved. This was not a spur-of-the-moment killing – not in the heat of battle, as it were. Researching the poison, whatever it was; preparing the pellet to transport the poison effectively; choosing the crime scene to avoid detection; knowing the victim's movements. Practice shooting. All of this suggests highly sophisticated planning over time.'

Andy unclasped his hands and straightened up. 'Very good,' he said. 'You should be doing my job.' He removed his glasses and began to polish them.

Jo recognised the signs. 'And now you're about to tell me everything I missed out.'

He smiled and put his glasses back on. 'Not quite everything. Not until I have more information.'

'However?' said Jo, picking up her mug.

'However, I can tell you that there are two possible scenarios here. One of which accords exactly with your analysis. The other does not – at least not in its entirety.'

'Now you're losing me.'

'Bear with me,' he replied. 'If we take your initial hypothesis of a slow-burn revenge killer, what does that look like?'

He placed his hand on the trackpad and opened a file on his computer screen. It was a diagrammatic cross section of a volcano. 'There are a number of metaphors we behavioural psychologists apply to revenge killers. This is my personal favourite.'

He used the cursor to move around the diagram.

'Down here in the depths is the magma. Molten rock bubbling away. Red-hot, desperate to escape. Blocked by the plugs of lava at the surface. It toils away, the pressure building as more and more magma pushes up from the depths. On the surface, there are few if any signs of the turmoil below. The odd whiff of sulphur perhaps. A few tremors. But nothing to indicate with any certainty when the volcano will erupt with violent and unpredictable force.

'Thus it is with the slow-burn revenger. One with a very personal hurt to avenge. He, or she, will be adept at hiding their simmering anger. The longer they do so, the greater the pressure, the frustration, the rage. There will be tiny signs of mental trauma that only those who know them intimately may pick up on. Even then, they're likely to be misinterpreted as bad temper, depression, a minor psychotic episode. However, those who know how to read the runes—'

'Forensic psychologists, like you?'

He nodded, showing just a hint of irritation at the interruption. '—those signs will appear as warning markers. Unfortunately, without access to the perpetrator's psychiatric history, the only time that's going to happen is after the crime has been committed. After he or she has already blown.'

'So you're basically saying you can't help me?'

'I'm not saying that at all. Only that what help I can provide may be of limited value.'

'That's a given,' said Jo. 'You mentioned two scenarios?'

He swivelled his chair to face her. 'The second still includes the one I've just set out, but it also involves a third party – a very different individual.'

'Different in what way?'

'Cold, indifferent, heartless, mercenary, driven by a very different motive: money.'

'A professional hitman.'

'Or an amateur hitman.'

'I'm inclined to discount the amateur,' said Jo, 'given the level and quality of planning involved. The possibility of a paid assassination is already on our radar, because those seem to be the only precedents for this kind of MO. What you're saying is that we could be looking for two perpetrators acting in common. The paymaster with the grievance and the hitman who carried out the killing?'

'Exactly. And if so, that would entail two very different profiles. Even the profile for the person with the grievance would be different because the act was performed at arm's length. Through an intermediary.'

'I get that,' said Jo. She downed the rest of her coffee and stood up. 'I'm grateful, Andy. How soon could you get something over to me?'

'This afternoon,' he told her. 'With the usual caveat: don't set too much store by it. I just hope it helps.'

Chapter 18

Nick Carter waved her over the second she stepped inside the incident room.

'We've made some progress!' He pointed to his computer screen. 'I'll show you.'

'In my office,' she said. 'I need to sit down.'

'Are you alright?' he asked as they weaved their way between the desks.

'I'm fine. Just a bit lightheaded.'

He lowered his voice.

'You need to get your head down as soon as you can. Have a little snooze. I'll cover for you.'

'Like that would go down well. It's a shame Gordon didn't have blinds fitted.'

'They told him he couldn't. Force policy.' He mimed quotation marks with his fingers. 'Openness and transparency apparently. For which read austerity. They couldn't afford them.'

Jo put her bag on the desk and her jacket over the back of her chair.

'It's quiet in there,' she said. 'Where is everybody?'

'Three of them have gone to retrieve passive data identified by the house-to-house team. Two of them I sent to join the door-to-door enquiries. The six who worked through the night with you I told to come in at twelve. No point in having a load of zombies wandering around the place like the living dead.'

Jo woke up the computer screen, entered her password, and clicked on the Alecto folder.

Nick pointed to the Forensics subfolder and then one of the files marked *Ballistics*.

'Before they sent the pellet off to Porton Down,' he said, 'they weighed it inside the evidence bag, took some photographs, and showed them to their ballistics expert.'

A series of photographic images appeared.

'It's an Air Arms Diablo Field Domed .177 calibre, 4.51mm pellet,' said Nick. 'It's all there in the report.'

Jo zoomed in on the first of the images. Despite the coating of dried soil, it was unmistakably an air rifle pellet, although not a standard one. This was a partly flattened, straight-sided metal cylinder with a broad dome at the end. She nodded.

'Higher velocity, with a flatter ballistic curve in flight. Light and powerful. It provides greater accuracy over a longer distance.'

'I'm impressed,' said Nick.

'Don't be,' she said. 'I came across these during my weapon training.'

She moved through the remainder of the images, stopped on one that caught her eye, and zoomed in. It was a close-up of the domed head. She zoomed in closer.

'Look,' she said. 'You can just make out tiny perforations on the surface. Most of them are filled with soil. That must have been how he inserted the poison.'

'They're not much larger than pinpricks,' Nick observed. 'How the hell did he get it in there, let alone keep it there? Surely the pressure would have flushed it out as it flew through the air?'

'I've no idea,' she said. 'That's what I'm hoping Porton Down will be able to tell us.'

She closed the file. 'Is that it, Nick?'

'No, there's more. While you've been catching up on your beauty sleep we've been looking at possible motives.'

She scooted her chair back.

'The obvious one is Benjamin Stanley, the guy Ronnie O'Neill committed GBH on. The reason why he was imprisoned. Where are we up to with him?'

'It was a nasty assault. With a meat cleaver. O'Neill was lucky he wasn't done for attempted murder. Stanley was trying to muscle in on O'Neill's territory. Pushing drugs that he'd allegedly sourced from a mob in Newcastle. O'Neill and Yates paid him a visit at his home. They claimed Stanley picked up a cleaver from the central island in his kitchen – one of those wicked ones the Chinese use for chopping ingredients – and threatened them with it.'

'More likely defending himself,' said Jo.

'That's what he said. What wasn't disputed was that O'Neill wrestled it off him and sliced half his ear off. He claimed it was an accident while they were struggling. Stanley swore that O'Neill pulled it free, then deliberately swung it at him. His wife corroborated his story. Yates stood by his boss's account.'

'I can see why the CPS went for GBH,' she said. 'Either way it seems to me they both had a reason to want to revenge themselves.'

'Maybe Stanley was worried O'Neill would do exactly that when he came out of Belmarsh?'

Jo wasn't so sure. 'Ronnie was perfectly capable of arranging that from inside. And what better alibi than to have been residing at Her Majesty's pleasure? But you're right. We can't afford to ignore the possibility. Do we have any other suspects yet?'

Nick leaned over, slid her trackpad towards him, and selected another folder. Jo was too tired to tell him that she was perfectly capable of managing this herself. That he had only to point to the screen. Maybe she would next time he looked like doing it. Or was she simply being petty-minded?

'DI Robb over at Operation Challenger sent us these details of rival drug gangs, known wholesale suppliers and smugglers, and major dealers he may have ripped off, or inadvertently sold a dodgy supply to. She says your NCA could have sent you the same, given the two of them are working together.'

There were over twenty different files, each codenamed.

'So many?' she said.

'That's just the tip of the iceberg.'

He clicked on the first of the files. A chart appeared, listing names and roles within the criminal organisation, each with a hyperlink attached. Jo reclaimed the trackpad and clicked on the link beside the head of the gang. Four pages of information appeared covering his life story, police record, known and suspected illegal activities, criminal associates, a picture file with mug shots, and covert photographs.

'They're all like this,' said Nick. 'I've got two DCs working their way through, trying to establish any connections with our victim. It'll be a damn sight quicker if you can persuade DI Robb to talk us through it.'

Jo had opened a link entitled *Operation Mandera, Current status*. Whole blank sections within paragraphs of marked text had been redacted.

'What's that about?' she asked. 'I thought we were supposed to be on the same side?'

'Apparently they've done that to protect a CHIS,' he told her. He shook his head. 'Covert Human Intelligence Source – what was wrong with just saying "undercover officer"?'

'Not all covert sources are police officers,' she reminded him. 'They could be using a civilian employee or a paid informant.'

'Whatever,' said Nick. 'That's who we need to be talking to. Someone on the inside who really knows what's going on.'

'That isn't going to happen anytime soon.' Jo had been there. Protecting your asset came before everything else. If not, who was going to be stupid enough to put themselves in such a dangerous position in the first place?

'What about the other line of enquiry I asked you to set up?' she said. 'The possibility that there was an internal feud or takeover brewing while O'Neill was inside? Maybe that's why Steven Yates has gone walkabout?'

Nick stood up and stretched. 'I'm waiting for DCI Fox over at Xcalibre to get back to me. If anyone knows, he will.'

'Well, chase him up for me.'

'Will do.'

'Do we know where Stanley is right now?'

'He hasn't left town if that's what you're wondering.' He pointed to the screen. 'It's all in that file marked *Hippo*.'

'On the heavy side, is he?'

'See for yourself.'

Jo clicked on the file and saved it to her tablet's Dropbox.

'I'm going to pay him a visit, Nick. While I'm gone, see if you can find out where the hell Steven Yates is. He didn't turn up for the reconstruction and no one has seen hide nor hair of him since. If he's hell-bent on revenge for the murder of his boss, we have to stop him before he triggers a bloodbath.'

Chapter 19

'What's this? A halfway house?' said Carly Whittle.

'How d'you mean?' asked Jo, switching off the engine.

'In my limited experience,' said Carly, 'most dealers live in social housing – flats and semis – that mask the size of their enterprise. The Mr Big drug barons live in mansions. That's when they're not living it large on the Costa Del Sol.'

Jo looked out of the window. The 1930s four-bedroom detached in the Stockport suburb of Heaton Mersey had been given a substantial makeover completely out of keeping with its neighbours. PVC windows had replaced the original sashes. Spherical CCTV cameras hung below the eaves at either side of the blue slate roof. A Palladian porch had been added. Stone lions stood on concrete plinths beside the six-foot high electronic gates.

'I see where you're coming from,' she said. 'Not going to win any Design Council awards, is it?'

The gates were open. In the driveway, a man was power-washing the rear of a dark blue Jaguar XJ Portfolio.

'He's not looking to hide his wealth from the tax man, is he, Boss?' Carly commented as they unclipped their seat belts. 'And, assuming that's him, I can see where he got his nickname from.'

The man was almost as wide as he was tall. His bronzed bald head shone like a polished snooker ball. The bottom third of his left ear was missing. As he moved, the flesh around his middle swayed disconcertingly. He heard their feet crunch on the gravel drive and turned around. An off-white, three-inch scar ran from where his earlobe should have been and down across his neck, just short of the jugular.

'Who the hell are you?' he demanded. He registered the IDs they were holding aloft and, with his finger still on the trigger, lowered the pressure washer lance to the ground. Pieces of gravel shot towards them, forcing them to move back.

'I suggest you switch that off, Mr Stanley,' said Jo, 'before I arrest you for assaulting police officers with intent to cause actual bodily harm.'

He smiled thinly as he released the trigger. 'Clumsy of me,' he said. 'I forgot it was still on.' He dropped the lance on the floor, placed one hand on the trunk of the car, and shuffled his legs apart so he could reach down to switch off the power unit.

That's confirmed one thing, Jo decided. *There's no way he could have fired that shot himself. Not unless he drove a mobility scooter through those woods beside the seventh tee.* The thought of it conjured up a smile.

'What are you laughing at?' he demanded.

His face, flushed from all the effort, seemed even more belligerent. Less like a hippo and more like a bouncer gone to seed.

'I was just admiring your Jag,' she said. 'Is that the V6 supercharged version?'

Her quick thinking wrong-footed him. 'Er . . . yeah,' he said. He recovered his composure. 'But you didn't come here to talk motors.'

'You're right, Mr Stanley,' she said. 'I think it's better if we do this inside.'

He folded his arms as best he could, resting them on his bulging stomach. 'Not unless you've got a search warrant.'

Jo turned to Carly. 'Do we have a search warrant, Detective Constable?' she asked.

Carly shook her head. 'No, Ma'am. I didn't realise we'd need one.'

'Me neither,' said Jo. 'Given that it was never our intention to carry out a search. But if Mr Stanley feels we ought to, then you'd better go and get one.'

'Hang on!' said Stanley, looking very confused. 'There's no need for that.'

Jo raised her eyebrows. 'But you said . . .'

'I know what I said. Just tell me what this is all about.'

'We'd like to ask you a few questions about your relationship with Ronnie O'Neill,' she paused. 'Recently deceased. As I'm sure you know.'

He visibly relaxed. So much so that Jo was beginning to think they were wasting their time. But then again, maybe he was a damn good actor. No one whose business was as bent as his could have possibly managed to avoid the Proceeds of Crime Act without having become a very proficient liar.

'I wondered how long it would be before your lot came knocking,' he said. 'I should've guessed. You'd better come in so I can get it over and done with.'

They followed him across the gravel and up the steps into the porch. He shouldered the door open and waddled down the hall ahead of them.

'Close the door after you,' he grunted.

He led them into a kitchen the size of Jo's apartment and turned to face them, his back propped against the central island.

'Go on then,' he said. 'Ask me. Where was I when Ronnie O'Neill was killed?'

'Very well,' said Jo, knowing full well this was too good to be true. 'Where were you when Ronnie O'Neill was killed?'

Stanley spread his arms wide. 'Now how can you expect me to know where I was, when I don't even know when he was killed?'

'Fair enough. So where were you between 10 a.m. and twelve noon last Friday morning?'

He frowned. 'Last Friday? I heard he died yesterday, in MRI.'

'It's Friday morning that we're interested in,' said Jo. 'Where were you, Benjamin?'

His eyes narrowed. 'I'm Benjamin to my wife when she's pissed off with me, and Benjie to my friends. You're neither. So it's Mr Stanley – got it?'

'Last Friday morning, Mr Stanley?' said Carly Whittle.

He turned his beady eyes on her. 'Found your tongue have you, sweetheart?'

'That's it,' said Jo. 'Benjamin Stanley, I would like you to accompany us to the North Manchester Divisional police station to assist with our enquiries into . . .'

'Whoa . . .' he said, holding both hands out in front of him. 'There's no need for that. I was only having a laugh.'

'So, you regard Ronnie O'Neill's death as a laughing matter?' said Jo.

'Come on, that's not fair,' he complained. 'You wanna know where I was on Friday? I'll tell you. I was at Malaga Airport waiting to board a plane back to Manchester. Check with the airline. Check with Border Control.'

'The perfect alibi,' said Jo.

He bristled. 'What's that supposed to mean?'

'What it says. If you were in Spain, there's no way you could have attacked Ronnie O'Neill yourself.'

'There you go then.'

'But someone could have done so on your behalf.'

He placed his hands on the counter behind him and levered himself upright.

'That's it!' he said. 'I'm not saying another word without my solicitor present.'

Jo got the impression that if he could have got away with adding 'before I throw you out myself', he would have done.

As he shepherded them out of the kitchen and down the hall, he was unable to resist a parting salvo. 'Okay, I get it. You think because he chopped my ear off, I owe him one. Well, he got his comeuppance, didn't he? A seven-year stretch in Belmarsh. If anything, there was more of a chance he'd reckon he owed me one. Why d'you think I've got the gates and the cameras?'

Jo turned around on the step. 'Just so long as you don't think you still owe that family a payback,' she told him. 'Because we'll be watching you.'

'Ronnie O'Neill was a mad bastard!' he shouted at their retreating backs. 'Good riddance to bad rubbish. If you find out who did do it, let me know. I'd like to shake his hand.'

The two detectives faced each other over the roof of Jo's Audi.

'What do you think, Boss?' said Carly.

'What do you think?' Jo replied.

'He seemed genuine to me.' Carly grimaced. 'If that's a term you can apply to scum like that.'

'A word of caution, Detective Constable,' said Jo. 'I suggest that you resist referring to any member of the public, however flawed, as scum. Not only is it the beginning of a slippery slope, but, if anyone was to report you, you could be looking at a disciplinary. And don't apologise or look so embarrassed. Of course he's scum – just don't let anyone hear you using the term. That's all I'm saying.'

'Yes, Boss.'

'You drive,' Jo said, throwing Carly the keys.

Carly looked at them suspiciously. 'Are you sure your insurance covers me?'

'What do you think? I'm going let you drive uninsured? Open it up, will you? I need to sit down before I fall down.'

'I hope you didn't mind my asking,' said Carly as she belted up.

'Don't be daft. I'd be worried if you hadn't. As it happens I've got fully comprehensive for third parties, for business use only. You know how it is. In this job you never know when you might need to chase someone on foot and have someone else take over the controls.'

'Are you okay, Boss?' said Carly. 'You look really peaky.'

'I'm fine,' Jo assured her. 'Bugger all sleep and no breakfast, that's all. There's a cafe and sandwich bar on a shopping precinct on Victoria Avenue, just before we join the motorway. Let me know when we're there.'

She adjusted the seat, lay back, and closed her eyes.

Chapter 20

Somewhere a phone was ringing.

Jo jerked awake and sat up. It was her hands-free phone. The screen told her it was Agata, then the ringing stopped. She looked around; they were outside the cafe. The wind had picked up and rain lashed the windshield.

'How long have I been asleep?'

'Just over half an hour,' said Carly. 'You were really gone. I didn't want to disturb you.'

'Next you're going to tell me I was snoring?'

Carly raised her eyebrows and rolled her eyes.

'For God's sake!' said Jo. She opened her bag and took out her purse. 'Here, make yourself useful while I ring this number back. I'll have a double-shot skinny latte and a bacon sandwich. With brown sauce. Plenty of it.'

She watched as her DC bent into the wind and sprinted, head down, until she reached the shelter of the billowing blue-and-white striped cafe awning. Then she returned the call.

'Aggie. You called me.'

'Jo! Thank God. I didn't want to bother you at work, not in the middle of a murder investigation, but I was worried about you. You haven't returned my texts.'

Jo could have kicked herself. It was amazing having someone actually care about her again. And having someone to care about. One more reason why she didn't want to mess this relationship up.

'I'm sorry,' she said. 'I only managed a few hours' sleep last night and it's been full on since I got in. In fact, I've just had a nap in the car, courtesy of the new DC.'

'Good for her,' Agata replied. 'You sound as though you'd benefit from a large strong coffee.'

Jo smiled. 'Mind reader.'

'I'm sorry I wasn't able to help with your packing,' said Agata, 'but I hope to be back in Manchester before you move in to your new apartment. I can help with that instead. And throw you a celebration dinner at mine.'

'I can't wait,' Jo told her. 'I just hope we can wrap up this investigation before then.' *Some hope*, said the little voice at the back of her brain. 'How is your own investigation going?'

There was a short silence.

'"Interesting" is all I can say over the phone. I'll tell you more when I see you.'

Jo laughed. 'You're even more paranoid than I am.'

'With good reason, Jo.'

There was a rap on the passenger window. Carly Whittle stood there with sodden hair, two Styrofoam cups clasped to her chest, and a paper bag tucked under her chin.

Jo lowered the window. 'I'm sorry, Aggie,' she said. 'I'll have to go. Breakfast is here.' She smiled up at her DC and took one of the cups from her.

'No problem,' said Agata. 'I have to go too. Love you.'

'Love you too,' said Jo.

Just saying it gave her a warm glow inside. It was yet another confirmation that she'd been too long in an emotional wilderness.

The driver's door flew open and Carly ducked inside the car. 'Bugger this,' she said. 'Next time it's your turn, Boss.' She wedged her cup between her thighs and handed Jo the bag. Jo opened it up. There were two bacon sarnies, six sachets of brown sauce, and some paper napkins.

'Brilliant,' she said. 'But I can only manage one of these sandwiches.'

Carly mopped her face with a handkerchief, and then prised the top off her coffee cup. 'The other one's sausage. It's for me.'

'Good for you,' said Jo, reaching inside for hers. 'This is just like being on the road with DCI Holmes.'

Carly nodded. 'He's always saying an army marches on its stomach.'

'Don't tell him I said this,' said Jo, 'but you can definitely tell that he does.'

They kept the laughter short and got stuck into their sandwiches.

Hailstones beat a tattoo on the roof and hood, and torrents of water poured down the gutters, pooling in the road where drains were full to overflowing.

Jo wiped her mouth with a napkin, screwed it up, and placed it in the paper bag. 'Where the hell did all this come from?' she asked, peering through the windshield.

'On the radio it said it's the tail end of Hurricane Ophelia. Downgraded to a storm.'

Jo scrunched the bag into a ball and stuffed it in the side pocket on the door.

'Well, if this is the tail end,' she said, 'I'm bloody glad we didn't get to experience the front end.'

Her phone rang. It was Nick Carter.

'Boss,' he said, 'I was getting worried. You've been off the radar.'

'Not really.' She winked at Carly Whittle. 'We've finished interviewing Benjie Stanley. Just about to join the M60.'

'What's that noise I can hear?' he asked.

'"The Ride of The Valkyries",' she told him.

'Can't hear your engine though,' he said. 'Are you at the lights?'

'What is this? The inquisition?' she mouthed to DC Whittle, who raised her eyebrows. 'I stopped to pick up some coffee to keep me awake,' she said. 'We were just about to set off when you called. Why? What's the hurry?'

'ACC Gates used her influence to get permission for us to talk to the guy who was the undercover asset on Operation Mandera. He's currently with the Regional Crime Squad. He's on his way over here now. I knew you'd want to be here when he arrives.'

Jo sat up. 'How long have I got?'

'Fifteen minutes. I've just spoken with him. If you hurry you might just pass him on the motorway.'

'We're on our way.'

She looked across at DC Whittle. 'Have you completed the pursuit course?'

Carly smiled. 'Yes, Boss.'

'Good.' She fastened her seat belt. 'Show me what you've learned.'

Chapter 21

Detective Sergeant Robert Attwood entered the room.

She observed him closely as they shook hands, exchanged greetings, and took their places at the table. He was nothing like she'd expected. Several inches shorter than her, clean-shaven, in a sports jacket, black-and-white checked shirt, and black moleskin trousers. Undercover, he'd stand out a mile. An impression that was heightened when he spoke.

'I know what you're thinking, Ma'am,' he said in a quiet cultured baritone voice, 'but you'd never have recognised me when I was on Operation Mandera.'

'I'm impressed,' she said. 'I didn't think I was that obvious.'

'Reading people, especially their body language and their faces, it's what keeps you alive.'

Jo didn't see any need to tell him that she really did understand. That she'd been there too. It could too easily be misinterpreted as scoring points.

'Thanks for agreeing to come and talk to us,' she said. 'I realise that from your point of view any sharing of information beyond your handler represents a degree of risk.'

He nodded. 'You're right, Ma'am. To be honest, I was surprised when they agreed to let me assist you. It must be important?'

'It is.' She told him why.

'I see where you're coming from,' he said. 'You'd like me to tell you the names of any villains I came across who might have a grievance against your victim, Ronnie O'Neill?'

'Not just while you were undercover,' she told him. 'But also while you've been working with Regional Crime and my NCA colleagues on Operation Titan.'

He frowned, and sucked air through his teeth. 'I can try. The trouble is that most of it is going to be really superficial. I mean, I don't recall anyone actually saying they were going to off him, or even that they wished he was dead. It's more about him being viewed as a difficult customer, a rival, or an obstacle to their plans. Any one of those things might give them a reason to rejoice in his death. But not necessarily to feel they had to eliminate him.'

Jo tried hard to hide her disappointment. 'I understand that,' she said. 'You're saying that there was no one who felt so strongly about him that they'd be prepared to have him killed.'

He shook his head. 'Not that I became aware of. Having said which, I was only a soldier. I never sat at the top table, as it were. What was said behind closed doors remained a mystery to me.' He shrugged. 'And again, even with the talk I was party to, some of these guys are even better actors than I am. Especially the real psychos. Trouble is, with nineteen of the ringleaders jailed on the back of the operation I was involved with, there's a new breed coming up behind them we haven't got a handle on yet.'

'I'll take what I can get,' said Jo. 'If you can just list them in priority order, together with an indication of any potential motive for killing Ronnie O'Neill, that would be brilliant. We can add them to the list that Challenger have just sent us.'

'I can do that,' he said. 'Give me twenty minutes. But I warn you. It's going to be a long list.'

An hour later he had taken them through each of the names on the list, including those now in prison serving lengthy sentences. Combined with those from Challenger, there were over forty names in total.

'And that's excluding some of the foreign gangs beginning to feel their way,' he said. 'Like the Bulgarians.'

Nick Carter sat back and shook his head.

'We had no idea,' he said. 'It's going to be a mammoth task to work through this lot.'

'If you had to go with your gut,' said Jo. 'Who would you put your money on?'

DS Attwood stared at the list of names. 'I don't know about the individuals, but if you're pushing me . . .'

'We are,' said Jo, trying not to sound as though she was pleading.

'Then I'd say there are two motives you could concentrate on. The first one is the Merseyside drug barons – inside and outside prison – who've had their supply lines into Lancashire, Cheshire, North Wales, and the Lake District disrupted by our recent successes. They'll be looking to grab some of the lucrative Greater Manchester drugs market, in particular, the rapidly expanding spice trade.'

He picked up his pen, leaned forward, and ringed four of the names on the list. 'The second is a bloody sight more problematic.'

'In what way?' said Carter.

Attwood pointed his pencil at Jo. 'Your colleagues at the National Crime Agency have just produced a report into a rapidly expanding trend they used to call "going country" but we now term "county lines".'

Jo nodded. 'I read a digest of that report. City gangs sending dealers as young as eleven and twelve to sell drugs in coastal towns all over the country.'

'They've been doing that for years,' said a sceptical Nick Carter. 'We used to call it "going out there".'

'Only now it's exploded,' said Attwood, 'using the motorways and intercity rail network. Across the Pennines into Humberside, up the

M6 into Scotland – all over the place. It's led to a heightening of tension between the local criminal gangs and the newcomers.' He shook his head. 'If your victim had been trying to muscle into that business, he could have fallen foul not just of the Liverpool gangs but rivals here in Manchester, or even some of the far-flung ones – in London, for example, or Bristol.'

'That's all we need,' said Jo. 'It was bad enough when we thought it was localised. I can just see Helen Gates's face when I tell her we're going to have to triple the budget so we can "go country" ourselves.'

Chapter 22

'Needle in a bloody haystack!' said Nick Carter, dropping the folder containing the list of names on the desk.

'He did his best,' said Jo. 'But I agree. If we have to work backwards from every villain that may theoretically have a motive to murder O'Neill, we could still be at it this time next year.'

Nick slumped down in a chair. 'It's not as though we've got any leads.'

Jo sat down opposite him. 'So we go with the rule book,' she said. 'We continue to follow the evidence. Someone was in those woods. Someone who knew that O'Neill would be on that tee. Someone who arrived and left in broad daylight. Who was a skilled marksman with a power air rifle, and who either had the ability to prepare both the pellet and the poison, or who knew people who did.'

'How difficult would that be, I wonder?' said Nick. 'All you'd need is instructions off the internet.' He pulled distractedly at an earlobe. 'Shame they've just locked up that guy who was reactivating all those antique weapons that flooded the market up here. Even made the bullets that went with them. He'd have been my number one suspect.'

The phone rang. Jo picked it up. 'Yes, Ged?'

'It's DCI Fox, Ma'am.'

Jo mouthed the name to her deputy. 'Put him through, please,' she said, selecting speakerphone. 'DCI Fox, what can I do for you?'

'It's more what I can do for you, Jo.' His voice had a smooth, almost oily quality over the phone. 'And it's Nigel. Although my friends call me Nige.'

Jo raised her eyebrows. Nick stuck two fingers down his throat and pretended to gag.

'I have DS Carter with me, Nigel,' she said. 'We're on speakerphone if that's okay?'

'Of course,' he said. 'Absolutely fine.' The change in tone suggested otherwise. 'We've had a bit of a situation, Jo,' he continued. 'I thought I'd better let you know.'

'Go on.'

'The head of one of the drug gangs we've been trying to disrupt walked into my office demanding that we give him protection—' He paused dramatically. '—from the O'Neill family.'

'What's his name, Nigel?' she asked, catching Nick's eye, and pointing to the folder on the desk.

'Ryan Walsh.'

Nick flipped open the folder, stabbed the first page with his finger, and angled the folder towards her. Walsh was number five on the list.

'The Burnage Celtic Crew,' she said.

'You're well informed,' said Fox.

'To be fair, he was one of the names you sent me.'

He laughed. 'Anyway, I listened to what he had to say and sent him on his way.'

'You didn't believe him?'

'Didn't have any reason to. It's not as though someone had made direct threats or actually fired shots through his living-room window.'

'So why is he this scared? It must have taken a lot for someone like him to beg for police protection. It's unheard of, isn't it – a gang boss? Think of the loss of face.'

'Initially, that's what I thought. But I got the impression he was playing with us. Him trying to take off some of the heat we've been applying.'

Nick looked sceptical and shook his head.

'What made you think that?' Jo asked.

'Like I said, there was nothing concrete. He claimed the word on the street is that the O'Neills hold him responsible for Ronnie's death. That they're gearing up to lift him and do unspeakable things to him before they feed what's left to the fishes. And they've been warning the rest of his crew to keep their heads down unless they want to suffer the same fate.'

'If it isn't a game,' said Nick, 'the O'Neills must have good reason to think he was responsible?'

'Walsh nibbled away at some of their territory while Ronnie was inside. Ronnie was starting to claim it back. His death could be interpreted as a pre-emptive strike by the Celtic Crew.'

Jo recalled the discussion she'd had with Andy Swift. 'But the way he was killed . . . the lengths the killer went to, using a slow-burn poison,' she said. 'That sounds personal, not business.'

She sensed a shrug at the other end of the line.

'They'd had words in the past.'

'What happens now?'

'Don't worry,' said Fox. 'I'm covering my back. I've sent a DI to warn off the O'Neills. And I've arranged for our surveillance on Walsh and his crew to be a bit more visible. Whatever the truth of the matter, that's going to disrupt their activities even more. And if I'm wrong and he *is* the target and the O'Neills are stupid enough to go ahead – well, at least I can demonstrate that I went by the book. But let's face it, Jo, that's a hell of a lot of ifs.'

'And if you're wrong and Walsh does disappear?'

Fox laughed again. 'Don't quote me, but that'll be one more massive pain in the arse we don't have to worry about. And look on the bright side: someone will have done your job for you.'

'What do you want to do, Jo?' said Nick, when the call had ended.

'Make Ryan Walsh our prime suspect. If he's telling the truth and the O'Neills are out to get him, they must reckon he killed Ronnie.'

'And if he did, do you really think he'd draw attention to himself by crawling to DCI Fox for help?'

Jo sighed. 'I know. But we can't afford to ignore the possibility. I want to know where Walsh and members of his crew were last Friday morning. The registration of their vehicles. If any of them are known to possess, or have a history of using, air rifles. DCI Fox and DI Robb should have most of that information.'

She stood up. 'If you crack on with that, I'll see if anything has come out of the house-to-house enquiries, the CCTV analysis, and the request for information from anyone who was on the golf course that day.'

Chapter 23

'See yer. Wouldn't wanna be yer!'

Melissa Walsh watched her friends climb on board the bus, took a puff of her inhaler, and put it in her backpack. Grateful for the lull in the storm, she turned to walk down the road, past the sports hall and the sixth form centre, before sauntering through the gate in the railings and into Platt Fields Park.

Her dad was going to be furious, but she'd always been able to wind him round her little finger. He'd sent her a text to say that one of his stooges was going to pick her up from school in the Hummer. The Hummer, for God's sake! That was never going to happen. It was bad enough her being one of the nouveau riche without having to climb into a black armoured monstrosity with tinted windows outside the region's foremost all-girls' private school. Not when everyone else was picking their darlings up in Mercedes and luxury SUVs.

She'd told everyone her dad was a businessman. Like Alan Sugar off *The Apprentice*. One look at that Hummer though, and the tongues would be wagging. Especially if Skanky Morris was driving. In her mind's eye she could see all the images appearing on Facebook and Instagram. A trickle, then a flood. The rumours and the gossip. It'd only be a matter of time before the trolls turned up.

She had to stop while a couple of Canada geese crossed the path in front of her and headed down the bank into the lake, pursued by a honking gaggle of larger white geese. *That'll be me*, she reflected, *if they find out what my dad's really into.*

She paused to take in the beauty and tranquillity of this place. The autumn colours of the trees on the island mirrored in the shimmering water, as ripples from the wake of the waterfowl gently sliced through them. This was her guilty pleasure, walking home through the park.

Her dad thought she always caught the bus home, like she'd promised. Unknown to him, on days like this she'd stroll across Platt Fields and then take a shortcut through Fallowfield. It was less than a mile and a half. She glanced at the clock on the front of the pavilion. It was only 3.38. If she got a move on she'd be home by a quarter past five.

Melissa failed to notice the man in a grey hoodie and sweatpants sitting on the bench behind her, talking into his phone. He waited for her to set off walking, then stood up and followed her.

There were shouts and screams coming from the skateboard park. As she passed the two bowling greens an old guy sweeping sodden leaves looked up and waved. She almost returned his wave but didn't. *You never know*, she told herself. *What if he's a perv or a paedo?*

She paused in front of the gates and stooped to pick up a chestnut with half its shell still attached. Running her fingers lightly over the surface of the shiny reddish-brown fruit, she marvelled at the magic that nature was capable of producing. She placed the chestnut in her coat pocket and walked out onto Mabfield Road.

She failed to notice the white van parked at the side of the exit, until she heard a metal door sliding open. A gloved hand clamped over her mouth and she felt herself grabbed from behind and lifted bodily off her feet. A second pair of hands seized her coat, and she was bundled into the van. The door slammed shut and the van set off. At the corner of Riga Road, the door slid open a fraction and Melissa's backpack was flung onto the pavement. The door closed and the van sped off, turned right onto Wilmslow Road and slowed to match the speed limit.

The van was on the outskirts of the city when Melissa's phone began to ring.

Chapter 24

'Sorry, Boss.'

The detective leading the passive data analysis on the shooting eased back his chair and turned to looked up at her. 'The problem is, we've no way of knowing if he did exit down that track between the big detached houses and onto Leigh Road. The only static cameras are back towards the motorway, and further down the road as it approaches Boothstown.'

'What about the CCTV from the houses?' Jo asked.

He shook his head. 'Waste of time. They're set back from the road, and they're angled on the driveway, the fence, and the gates. You can't see what's on the other side.'

'What about the static cameras? Have you been looking for any significant time lapse between cars entering and then leaving that stretch?'

The second she saw the pained looked on his face she regretted having asked.

'We've been doing that as a matter of routine, Ma'am. The half a dozen we identified as potentially having stopped to pick someone up have all been investigated and eliminated. One was a courier. One a tradesman. The rest were residents.'

She noted the sudden change from 'Boss' to 'Ma'am'. A gentle reminder not to underestimate this team.

'There is another possibility, Ma'am,' said the female detective alongside him. 'What if the perpetrator didn't get a lift, or drive off in some vehicle he parked up? What if he simply crossed the road and entered the fields on the opposite side? He'd only have been visible for a couple of seconds then, at the most.'

'Is that possible?' said Nick. 'I thought there was a wall along there and dense undergrowth.'

'The wall ends immediately opposite where he'd come out,' she replied. 'Look.' She opened Google Earth, clicked on a marker pin she'd set up, and zoomed in.

Sure enough, the wall curved inwards and was replaced by a row of bushes forming a hedge beneath the trees that lined the road. There was a gap less than a yard or so wide between the bushes, through which a gravel and sawdust path was just visible.

He could easily have squeezed through there, Jo realised, *even with a golf bag on his back.*

'Where does this lead to?' she asked.

The female detective exited Street View and zoomed out. On the opposite side of the trees were fields.

'This is the former Worsley New Hall and Gardens Estate, developed by the Earl of Ellesmere,' she said. 'The Royal Horticultural Society have just started clearing some of the grounds in preparation for a new RHS garden.'

'Doesn't that mean there would have been people around on Friday?' said her colleague. 'Volunteers, contractors, or whatever?'

'Possibly. But I understand they've started work on the walled kitchen garden, which is way over here. He'd be hidden by the trees most of the way. They probably wouldn't have taken any notice of him even if they did see him. All he had to do was turn left along the field edge, then join this path here, and follow it for six hundred yards to the motorway roundabout. If he had a car parked at the John Gilbert pub he could head off in any direction and no one would be any the wiser.'

'Good work,' said Jo. 'That gives us another avenue to explore.'

'It could just as easily be another blind alley to go down,' murmured Nick.

'I know,' Jo replied. 'But we can't afford to ignore it, however many person hours it takes.'

The door to the incident room burst open, and Gordon Holmes barrelled in.

'Thank God you're both here,' he said. 'DCI Fox asked me to let you know there's been a development.'

'Why didn't he tell us himself?' said Nick.

Gordon shrugged. 'Search me.'

'A good development or a bad one?' Jo asked uneasily.

'You tell me. Apparently the twelve-year-old daughter of one of your suspects has gone missing. The father thinks she's been kidnapped.'

'Ryan Walsh?' said Jo.

'How do you know?'

'Because Walsh swears that the O'Neill family is out to get him. He begged your pal Fox for police protection. He said no. That's why he asked you to tell me. He's too embarrassed to do it himself.'

'Bloody hell!' said Gordon. 'What a mess.'

'Exactly,' said Jo. 'This is the last thing we need. Where is DCI Fox now?'

'He's on his way round to Walsh's, trying to establish what's really going on.'

'Hoping against hope that it's not a kidnap,' said Nick. 'For his own sake.'

'Come on, Nick,' said Jo, 'get your coat.'

'Why, where are we going?'

'To join them. I'm not leaving it to DCI Fox to handle. For the sake of Operation Alecto, and above all for the sake of that missing girl.'

Chapter 25

'What the hell are you doing here?'

DCI Fox strode across the kitchen and pushed Jo into the hallway. A dog began to bark somewhere in the house.

'You do that again,' she said quietly but firmly, 'and I'll break your bloody arm.'

'Did you just threaten a senior officer?' Fox growled.

'Did you just assault a junior officer?' Jo replied. 'A female one at that?'

'He did,' said Nick. 'I saw him.'

Fox stabbed a forefinger at Nick. 'You stay out of it!'

'Look, Nigel,' said Jo. 'I get why you got DCI Holmes to do your dirty work, but right now only one thing matters. Not your operation or mine. This is all about the safety of that girl.'

'She's only been missing an hour and a half,' he said. 'I'm not convinced she's been kidnapped.'

'The father is.'

'We can't take his word for it. He's paranoid.'

'Look,' said Jo. 'You've already turned down his request for protection. Wouldn't it be safer to assume the worst, just in case?'

He thought about it. 'I'm dealing with this,' he said. 'I'm prepared to let you listen to what he has to say just in case it has a bearing on your investigation. But only on condition that you keep your mouth shut.'

'Whatever you say,' said Jo. Not that she had any intention of doing what he asked.

'So much for Mr Charmer,' whispered Nick as they followed Fox into the kitchen.

A pale-faced, bottle-blonde woman stood by the sink. Her hands were shaking and there was a sound of ice chinking against the sides of the tumbler she clasped in her hands. She'd been crying. A muscular, shaven-headed man, close to six feet tall, stood beside a granite-topped island, the knuckles of his clenched fists white with tension. Fear was etched on his face. A second man, skinny, with the sunken eyes and hollow cheeks of a habitual user, stood near the back door as though hoping to make a swift exit should things turn nasty.

'Mr Walsh,' said Fox. 'This is Senior Investigator Stuart and Detective Sergeant Carter. They're investigating the death of Ronnie O'Neill. I've agreed they can listen to what you have to say.'

Walsh stared at the newcomers, and then back at Fox, his eyes blazing with indignation. 'I asked you here to find my daughter. Not to try to pin that bastard's death on me.'

'That's not why we're here,' said Jo. 'We have as much interest in ensuring the safety of your daughter as DCI Fox.'

Fox turned on her. 'I told you . . .' he began.

'The sooner you tell us,' Jo continued, 'why you believe your daughter has been kidnapped, the sooner we can set about finding her.'

Walsh exploded. 'I don't believe, I bloody *know!*'

'Then why don't you tell us,' said Fox, trying to rescue the situation.

Walsh pointed a finger at the DCI. 'When I told you I needed protection from the O'Neills,' he said, 'it was obvious you didn't believe an f'ing word I was saying. So I sent Melissa a text telling her I was sending Morris here to pick her up in the Hummer. Only when he got there, she didn't turn up.'

'Are you sure she received the message?' Jo asked. 'Did she text you back, for example?'

'She's a teenager. She never texts back. But the message was definitely sent. And she checks her phone as soon as they're allowed to switch them back on at the end of the school day. First thing she does. They all do. Besides, I sent it at lunchtime, so she had two opportunities to read it.'

'How long did he wait for her?' Fox asked.

'Fifteen bloody minutes before he rang me to say she hadn't shown up.'

Squirming beneath his boss's irate gaze, the hapless Morris stared down at the floor. 'I waited another ten minutes,' he said, shuffling closer to the door. 'Then I did go looking for her. But nobody had any idea where she was. All her friends had gone.'

'How did Melissa normally travel home?' Jo asked.

'On the bus,' said Walsh. 'That's what we agreed. If she was staying late for hockey practice or whatever, either I'd pick her up or I'd arrange for someone else to go.'

'Did she ever have something on after school on a Tuesday?' Nick asked.

Walsh looked at his wife. She shook her head nervously.

'Could she have gone back with one of her friends?' asked Jo.

'Not without telling me. Besides, we've rung the ones we have numbers for. They said they got on the bus, and she was still there, outside the school.'

'What time was this?' asked Fox.

'Just gone half three. But you're wasting time. I'll show you how I know she's been kidnapped.' He picked up his phone.

'Melissa doesn't know but I set up a tracker on her handset. As soon as Morris told me she hadn't turned up I checked it. It showed her going south on Palatine Road, just before it hits the motorway.'

About three miles from the school, Jo reckoned. There was no way she could have covered that distance that quickly on foot.

'Why didn't you tell us straight away?' said Fox. 'Where is it telling you her phone is now?'

'It's no use,' said Walsh. 'As soon as I saw where she was I rang her. But she didn't answer. And then the phone went dead so I can't track it.'

'Give me your phone,' said Fox. 'Then we can fix the last known location before it was switched off.'

'No need,' said Walsh cagily. 'They'll have ditched the phone. I've got people down there already, looking for it.'

Fox held out his hand for the phone.

'That's not the point,' he said. 'We need to know the route, as well as where that phone may be, so we can check all the relevant cameras to see if we can spot the vehicle.'

'You're not having this phone,' said Walsh. 'You can take a photo, right? That'll tell you all you need to know.'

'I need it,' said Fox firmly. 'It's vital evidence that can help us find Melissa.'

Walsh put the phone in his pocket.

'Not without a warrant,'

'For God's sake, Ryan!' said Mrs Walsh. 'Give it to him. What if she has one of her attacks?'

'Keep your nose out, Andrea,' he told her. 'I know what I'm doing.'

'What kind of attack, Mrs Ryan?' said Jo.

'Asthma. She's got asthma. Stress can set her off. She had a bad attack before her SATs. They had to call an ambulance. God knows what this will do.'

Walsh's phone rang. 'It's the school,' he said.

'Put it on speakerphone,' Fox demanded.

'Mr Walsh, this is Mrs Harrison, the bursar,' said a cultured voice. 'We have just been contacted by a member of the public. She found a backpack on the pavement outside their front door. When she looked inside, it was full of your daughter's exercise books.' There was a pause. 'And her Ventolin inhaler.'

Andrea Walsh began to wail.

'Where does this person live, Mrs Harrison?' said Fox.

She gave them the address.

'Mabfield Road,' said Carter. 'That's on the other side of Platt Fields Park. It leads onto Wilmslow Road.'

'Melissa probably walked through the park,' said the bursar. 'Quite a few of the girls do if they live close by. I do hope she turns up soon. We're all very concerned, Mr Walsh.'

'Not as concerned as I am,' Walsh snapped.

'Of course. Is there anything we can do to help? For example . . .'

'I'll let you know,' said Walsh, rudely ending the call. He stared at the detectives facing him. 'I told you!' he said. 'There's no way she can have dumped that bag. The O'Neills have got her. If they harm one hair on her head, I swear I'll . . .'

'Best not to tell us,' said Fox. 'And I suggest you hand me that phone, for your daughter's sake.'

Still Walsh prevaricated. Jo guessed that he was processing the cost-benefit analysis. The risk to his daughter of not handing the phone over, as against the risk to himself if the police decided to walk the cat back on some of his shady contacts.

'Please give them the phone, Ryan,' pleaded his distraught wife.

Ryan Walsh ignored DCI Fox's outstretched hand, stepped reluctantly forward, and handed it instead to Jo. 'Just so you can find my daughter,' he said. 'Yeah?'

Chapter 26

'What do you think?' said DCI Fox, staring back at the house. 'She's only been missing an hour and a half. You know what kids that age are like.'

'I'd say he's right,' said Jo. 'Someone has taken his daughter. Whether or not it's connected to Ronnie O'Neill's murder remains to be seen.'

'It could be street robbery,' Fox pointed out. 'Someone grabs her phone then tries to wrestle her backpack off her. She drops it and runs off. Johnny panics, and ditches it when he realises her dad could be tracking it.'

'So why hasn't she rung the police, her mum, or her dad?' said Nick. 'And why didn't she go back to see if her bag was still there?'

Fox snorted. 'Because she's terrified of her dad and her mum's a bleeding wreck.'

'We're wasting time arguing about it,' said Jo. 'I'm going to contact the AKEU.'

'Who the hell are they when they're at home?' Fox demanded.

'The Anti-Kidnap and Extortion Unit is an NCA specialist outfit,' she told him. 'They're on standby around the clock to support UK, EU, and global law enforcement services. They're on a par with their

FBI equivalent, on whom they're modelled. I'm surprised you haven't heard of them.'

'This is a GMP operation,' he told her. 'I'll let you know if and when we need any help. Until then, I suggest you butt out and concentrate on finding your killer. The sooner you do that, the sooner the rest of us can get back to proper policing.' He turned his back on them and stormed off towards his car.

'At least talk to their on-call officers,' she called after him. 'What harm can that do?'

He ignored her, got into his car, and drove off.

'No harm at all,' said Nick. 'Except to his ego. What are you going to do, Jo?'

'What do you think? I'm going to call Harry Stone, and get him to talk to Helen Gates. She's bound to order Fox to cooperate with the AKEU.'

'He won't like it. You know how it is. He'll wind his cronies up and when your secondment to the NCA is over he could make your life a misery.'

'As though I care,' she said. 'There's a girl's life at stake right now. What's that compared with male pride?'

'What do we do now?' he asked.

'You get a lift back to Nexus House. I'm going to pay Jason O'Neill a visit. Hopefully I'll beat DCI Fox to it. He'll only get his back up. I can speak to my boss on the way.'

'You're sure about this?' Harry Stone sounded wary.

'Absolutely, Boss.' Jo replied. 'It's too much of a coincidence for that girl to go missing immediately after her father pleads for police protection. What is it we always say? Trust the parents' instincts. Nine times out of ten they'll be right. For all his bluster the father is terrified and so is the mother. And there's no other explanation for what happened with her school bag and her phone.'

She sensed Harry's hesitation and pressed on. 'Besides, if there is a connection, finding out who's abducted her and why can only help with Operation Alecto.'

She gave him time to think it through.

'Well,' he said at last. 'There's no conflict of interest. On the contrary, we're working with Titan, and they have an ongoing interest in all your potential suspects. I suppose I could have a word with ACC Gates. Or even ask the Director to talk to the Chief Constable.'

'That would be brilliant, Boss,' said Jo. She said a silent prayer. 'There is just one other thing.'

'There always is with you, Jo,' he said. 'Go on, spit it out.'

'When the AKEU are looking for Senior Investigators to work with them, could you suggest Max Nailor? Only I desperately need someone I can trust to work with both me and DCI Fox.'

Harry sighed. 'Leave it with me,' he said. 'No promises, but I'll see what I can do.'

Chapter 27

'This is crazy,' Jo muttered to herself.

The avenue leading to the O'Neill house was crammed with vehicles. Dozens of cars had their wheels on the pavement to each side. A monster SUV was blocking the entrance to the drive. She was forced to reverse all the way to the end, park around the corner, shrug on her NCA cagoule, and then walk back up the street.

Thirty yards from the house she reached an unmarked car with two bored-looking detectives slumped in the front. The windows were steamed up, and as she approached there was a single burst from the windshield wipers as they flicked away the rain. She stopped and knocked on the window. The man on the passenger side stared up at her suspiciously. She showed him her ID. He lowered his window a third of the way, forcing her to bend lower.

'Sorry, Ma'am,' he said. 'I didn't recognise you with your hood up.'

The driver leaned across. 'I saw you on the telly, just after you shot that serial rapist.' He grinned. 'Nice one, Ma'am.'

It sickened Jo that men like this always assumed that she'd taken pleasure in firing that shot.

'Where are you stationed?' she asked.

'Wigan, Ma'am,' said the passenger politely, sensing her irritation.

'And what are you supposed to be doing here?'

He shuffled uncomfortably in his seat. 'Keeping an eye out for trouble.' He pointed to the image of Steven Yates on the screen in front of them. 'And looking for this villain.'

'And what do you think he'd have done if, like me, he'd come up unseen behind you and seen his face staring back at him?'

The driver sat back and pretended to look out of the window.

His colleague had the grace to look embarrassed. 'Legged it, Ma'am,' he replied. 'Sorry, Ma'am.'

'I suggest you switch that off,' she said, pointing to the iPhone on his lap. 'Then you can keep your eyes on the wing mirror, while your colleague watches the house.'

'Yes, Ma'am.'

'Carry on,' Jo said. She straightened up and walked off.

She could well imagine what they'd be saying to each other now. *Three bags full, Ma'am.* And a hell of a lot worse. God, she was sounding more and more like Helen Gates. She shouldn't have let them get to her. He couldn't be expected to recognise her. Even after the cuts, they still had six thousand frontline officers. And the driver had meant well. It was too late now. Word would fly round Wigan, and then across the force. *That Joanne Stuart, she's a stuck-up bitch. Promotion's gone to her head – same as all the others.* She could just hear Gordon's advice. *Man up, Jo,* he'd say. Just before she punched him.

To her surprise, the SUV turned out to be an armed response vehicle. Two riflemen sat in the back. The driver gave her a cool, hard appraisal as she walked past.

She showed her ID to the officer on the door of the house, pushed back her hood, and had a shake to dispel some of the water, before entering. Jason O'Neill was standing by the fireplace in the lounge. Jack Reilly was at his side.

'Not you as well!' said Reilly. 'I wondered when the cavalry was gonna turn up.'

The tall, broad-shouldered man standing with his back to Jo turned around. She recognised him as Detective Superintendent Ellis, the North West Regional Crime Unit's Titan commander.

'You'se wanna sort yourselves out,' said O'Neill. 'Decide who's running this shambles.'

It was obvious from his expression that Ellis was thinking much the same thing.

Jo decided to get in first. 'SI Stuart, NCA, seconded back to GMP as Senior Investigating Officer for Operation Alecto, Sir. The murder of Mr O'Neill's father.'

'I see,' he replied. 'So this is your show?'

'Yes, Sir.'

'Well, I'm here to make sure that things don't get out of hand – that they don't escalate. I was hoping to convince Mr O'Neill that it would be in his best interest to leave everything to us.' He tipped his head in a show of deference. 'To you, that is.'

Jo watched Jason O'Neill to see what his reaction would be. 'At this moment I'm here in relation to the disappearance of the daughter of someone known to Mr O'Neill,' she said.

If Jason knew what she was talking about he was hiding it well. 'Missing kid? What the hell's that got to do with my dad? You're supposed to be looking for the bastard that killed him, not flitting round after someone else's brat.'

'The child in question is twelve years old,' said Jo. 'Her name is Melissa. She's the daughter of Ryan Walsh.'

O'Neill shared glances with Jack Reilly. Both of them seemed genuinely surprised. 'Walsh?' said Jason. 'His daughter's gone missing and you think it's got something to do with me?'

'He claims he's been receiving threats. Threats related to your father's murder.'

Jason took a pace forward. He shook his head wildly. 'If I thought he killed my dad I wouldn't bother with threats. He wouldn't know what hit him.' He turned to his colleague. 'I'd never touch a kid, would I, Jack? You tell 'em.'

'He wouldn't,' said Reilly. 'No way.'

'Maybe not,' said Jo. 'But Steven Yates would. And there's something else you should know. She suffers from asthma. Whoever took her threw her bag away. Her inhaler was inside. If she has a major attack, without it – or immediate medical attention – she's likely to die.'

O'Neill paled. *Either he's involved*, Jo decided, *or he's coming round to the view that his enforcer is.*

'Where is Steven, Jason?' she said.

'That's what I want to know,' DS Ellis began.

A woman's voice cut him off. 'You've got to stop it, Jason!'

Sheila O'Neill had entered the room from the hall unseen. Jo stepped aside so she could go to her son. Her hair was unkempt, her face drawn, her eyes bloodshot. 'She's only a child,' she said. 'Your father wouldn't have wanted this.'

'I've got nothing to do with this, Mum, I swear,' said Jason. 'And I cannot believe that Steve would either.'

'Even so,' she said. 'You could try to help them get her back.'

'Listen to your mother, Jason,' said Jo. 'Before it's too late.'

'I told you,' he retorted. 'I've got nothing to do with it. But I'll put the word out, okay? See what I can find out.'

'Make sure you do,' said Ellis.

'So long as your lot—' O'Neill hurled at Jo's back as she headed for the door, '—get on with finding out who murdered my dad!'

In the drive, Nigel Fox was remonstrating with the driver of the SUV, trying to get him to back out so he could get his own car in. His face turned another shade of red as he spotted Jo crunching towards him.

'And you!' he bellowed. 'I thought I told you to butt out? What the hell are you doing here? Please tell me you haven't spoken with O'Neill.'

'Don't worry,' she replied. 'He's got the message. And by the way, Detective Superintendent Ellis is with him at the moment. I should hurry. You wouldn't want him to queer your pitch.'

She brushed past him and hurried back down the avenue. *I don't care if it does come back to haunt me,* she decided. *It was worth it just to wipe that look off his face.*

Chapter 28

It was 7 p.m. when she got back to Nexus House.

Carter was hard at work allocating tasks. 'How did O'Neill react,' he asked, 'when you told him about the missing girl?'

'All innocent.'

'Did you believe him?'

'I think so. At least about the kidnap. Although I'm still inclined to think he put out those threats towards Ryan Walsh. He's probably been putting pressure on everyone and anyone he thinks might have had a grudge against his dad or might know something about it.'

'I wish we had his criminal intelligence network,' said Nick. 'Make life a damn sight easier than having to rely on Twitter.'

'When I asked him about Steve Yates,' said Jo, 'if he could have used his own initiative to snatch Melissa, he scratched behind his ear, looked down at the floor, and said that he could not believe he would do it.'

'There you go then,' said Nick. 'Three different tells: avoiding eye contact, having a good scratch, and suddenly using contraction-free Queen's English. That's as good as a confession.'

Jo shook her head. 'Not a confession as such, but it means he knows that Yates is well capable of pulling off a stunt like that. It's exactly the kind of misguided loyalty that could get them both locked up.'

Ged was waving her phone at Jo. 'It's Mr Stone,' she mouthed.

Jo went over and took the handset. 'Harry?'

'Jo. I went straight to the Director. She spoke with the Chief Constable. It's been agreed. GMP have officially asked for the AKEU to provide them with expertise and advice. They'll also be able to call on our rapid response team if it turns out there's a siege situation.'

'DCI Fox is going to hate this,' she said.

'Don't blame me, Jo. It's what you wanted. Senior Investigator Arran Bailey will head up the AKEU team, and Max will join them so he can make sure you're kept in the loop.'

'Thank you, Boss,' she said. 'That's a great weight off my mind. It means I can concentrate on Alecto without having to worry about Melissa Walsh.'

'Knowing you, you'll still worry,' said Harry. 'But my advice is to try and put it out of your mind. For all we know, it may have nothing whatsoever to do with your investigation.'

'You're right,' she said, 'and I will.'

Jo didn't believe that for a minute. It wasn't just that the timing was such a coincidence, it was also the lack of any contact between the kidnappers and the Walsh family. No instructions, no warnings not to tell the police, no ransom demands. Nothing. Just a big, fat, empty silence. She handed the phone back to Ged and rejoined Nick Carter.

'Where are we up to?' she asked.

'We're up to our necks in CCTV, and witness statements from witnesses who saw san fairy Ann,' he said gloomily.

'San fairy Ann? Do you even know what that means?' she asked.

'It's a Franglais play on words,' said DC Hulme, arriving to hand Carter a sheaf of statements. 'A corruption of "*ça ne fait rien*", which means "it doesn't matter".'

Nick grunted. 'Like most of the pointless facts stuffed inside your head.' He waited for the DC to drift back to his desk. 'Have you eaten today, Boss?' he said. 'I don't know about you but I'm starving.'

Jo realised that she hadn't had so much as a cup of tea since the coffee and sandwiches in the car that morning.

'Now you mention it,' she told him, 'I'm starving too.'

'What's it to be? Canteen or the McDonald's on Snipe Way?' He grinned. 'Silly question. I'll nip down to the canteen and see if they've got any salads left.'

He returned twenty minutes later carrying five small carrier bags. Jo opened the office door for him and stepped back as he dropped everything on her desk.

'Canteen was out of salads,' he told her. 'So I nipped down to McDonald's specially for you.'

'It wouldn't have anything to do with your own dietary requirements then?'

'You're turning into a cynic.' He started unloading the contents. 'You're lucky. Christmas has come early. There's a grilled chicken salad for you, a double chicken burger for me, an apple-and-grape fruit bag to share for dessert, a latte for you, a double espresso for me – and a special treat to welcome you back!' He produced it with a magician's flourish and lobbed it in her direction.

'What is it?' she asked.

'A bag of reindeer treats.'

She turned it round. A pouch full of carrot sticks.

He grinned. 'You can keep it in your pocket and have a nibble whenever you need a boost.'

⌣

Jo was updating the policy book when her phone rang.

It was Max Nailor. 'I thought you might appreciate an update on Melissa,' he said.

Her heart skipped a beat. It was impossible to tell from the tone of his voice if it was good or bad news. Then she realised. If it had been either this wouldn't be an update.

'You haven't found her yet?' she guessed.

'Not yet, Jo. We're making some progress though. Her phone has been recovered from the putting green on Northenden golf course. It was right beside the road, so our assumption is that as soon as they discovered it they threw it out of the window.'

'That'll have been when her father rang,' she said.

'We also retrieved footage from cameras on Wilbraham Road that enabled us to identify five potential suspect vehicles.'

'Why suspect?'

'Because of the nature of them – four are vans, one's an SUV with tinted windows – and because of the timing. We're trying to locate both the vehicles and their owners.'

'The odds are they'll have used a stolen vehicle and changed the licence plates,' she said.

'I know. But we have to try.'

'Have the kidnappers made contact with the father yet?'

'No,' he replied. 'So the decision's been taken to hold a press conference that includes an appeal from the parents. It's timed to go out as part of the ten o'clock newsfeeds, with repeats in the morning.'

'That's going to be tricky,' said Jo. 'From what I've seen, the mother is likely to crack up and the father's hardly the kind of person people will empathise with.'

'We don't have an option,' he said. 'It's not just about getting the public onside. It's more about the kidnappers realising she needs that inhaler or they'll be facing a murder charge. We've already made that clear on all the local radio channels.'

Jo didn't respond. The silence mushroomed.

'I know what you're thinking,' he said at last. 'But while there's life there's hope.'

'We don't know that she's alive,' Jo said.

'AKEU believe she is, and they're the experts. Experience tells them that there has to be a major payback from taking a risk like this. Revenge doesn't cut it. Nor does killing a child fit the organised crime profile. That falls way outside their twisted code of honour.'

'Tell that to the Mafia,' said Jo, 'and the relatives of all the children they killed, albeit as collateral damage.'

'How did you get on with – what was his name – your victim's son?' said Max, deliberately changing the subject.

'O'Neill. Jason O'Neill. I think it came as much of a surprise to him as it did to us.'

'In which case, it's unlikely whoever's taken her will do anything stupid without his agreement. Especially if it's this Yates person, his enforcer.'

'Let's hope so.'

'Where are you up to with your investigation, Jo?'

'Treading water. Waiting for a lifeboat to come along.'

'Or a bottle with a message in it?'

'Yeah. Like, "I did it, and my name is . . ."'

Their laughter was the kind that only people with the darkest shared experiences would understand. Firemen, paramedics, social workers.

And members of a murder squad.

Chapter 29

Melissa turned onto her back. Her wrists and ankles chafed from the ties that bound them. Her mouth was dry because of the gag. Her nose was partially blocked and, with the hood pressing against it too, she was worried that if it got any worse she'd not be able to breathe at all. Even more terrifying was the possibility that she might have an attack. Just thinking about it brought the gradual feeling that an elephant was slowly lowering itself onto her chest. The tortuous sensation of drowning followed. Gasping, gasping for air. She dug her nails into the palms of her hands, drawing blood in an effort to stay calm. And forget that she no longer had her inhaler close to hand.

She had desperately tried to tell them when they threw her bag out of the van, and again when the tall thin one brought her food and water, but he just told her to shut up. She'd tried to tell the short dark one who stood in the doorway and watched, but he didn't seem to understand. And he never spoke either. He reminded her of those men in the hand car wash where Skanky Morris sometimes took the Hummer on the way home from school.

Because of the hood they'd put back over her head she had no idea what time of day it was. Or how long she'd been here. But she had discovered that when she moved her head against the pillow in a certain way she could dislodge the hood just enough for a chink of light, or the absence of one, to tell her whether it was night or day.

She tried to remember the sounds she'd heard since arriving here. The howling wind. The drone of planes passing overhead. Vehicles arriving and leaving. Doors being slammed shut. The murmur of voices, all male and indistinct. Every now and then there was a noise like the microwave at home when it had finished cooking.

Earlier that evening she'd heard raised voices and what sounded like an argument, cut short when someone with a deeper, older voice told them to be quiet. Twice she'd heard a dog barking. She thought it must be late in the evening. Perhaps they put the dog outside to do its business and it was barking to be let in again. That's what her own dog, Freddy, did. The thought of him brought tears to her eyes. They pooled beneath the hood and slowly seeped out, leaving tracks down both cheeks.

She'd tried to recall everything that had happened because she knew it would help the police to catch the people who were holding her. She remembered the moment when she was grabbed, lifted off her feet, and thrown into the van. Apart from the skinny foreigner who she'd christened Gollum, the one she'd seen most clearly was of medium height, well built, wore a black hood, and a scarf over the lower part of his face. He was The Boxer. She could still see those eyes, hard and mean. They reminded her of Skanky Morris, when the slimeball wasn't off his head.

How can Dad do that, she wondered? *Put my safety in the hands of a druggie? What kind of a father does that? And why does Mum let him? Because she's scared of him, that's why. Terrified, more like. He even frightens me sometimes. But at least he'll be looking for me. And he's always saying he knows people who know people. What if he finds me and catches these kidnappers before the police do?* She shivered at the thought of what might happen.

She remembered them forcing the gag into her mouth and pulling the hood over her head. She knew she'd bitten one of them because she heard him squeal and curse her, and there was that metallic taste of blood in her mouth that you get when you bite your cheek. Her hands had been tied and her bag was ripped from her back. Then the van had slowed down. She'd heard the door slide open and close again. Then it sped up and braked again, so suddenly that her head banged against something hard and metal. It hurt like mad.

She could still feel it a bit, and she'd had a headache ever since. Her phone had rung in her pocket and one of them had sworn and scrabbled to find it. Then she'd heard the door slide open again and then close. She knew he must have thrown it out into the road. Her heart had sunk, because it would be harder for her dad to find her now. He'd put a tracker app on her phone. He thought she didn't know, but she did. Sometimes, when she wanted to go somewhere he wouldn't approve of, she'd leave the phone at the house of one of her friends and pick it up afterwards. If only she'd switched it off when she put it in her pocket. Too late now.

At one point, she thought, the van must have come off the road, shortly before it arrived where she was now. She knew that because it went over a bumpy surface like a cobbled street, making it bounce from side to side and up and down, like her dad's Hummer when she went to the riding school to ride her pony. *Maybe it's a farm*, she thought. But she hadn't heard any farm noises. No animals, no tractors, nothing like that.

She remembered the damp musty smell in the hallway. A mixture of wet dog, cigarette smoke, and fried food. Them carrying her up the stairs, tying her feet together, and dumping her on the bed. The thin duvet, the rank smell of sweat on the pillow that made her want to heave.

She was pleased with herself. When her captors released her, the police would be really impressed when she told them everything she'd remembered.

She shivered again because it was cold in here. Wherever here was. And because she needed to wee. God, how she needed to wee. She'd been holding on ever since they'd brought her some kind of metal bucket and forced her to squat on that. And they wouldn't let her up until she'd been. She couldn't see the bucket, but she'd felt it, hard and thin against her thighs and bum. And all the time she'd known they must be watching her. Making faces at each other. Silently laughing. She blushed at the memory.

She'd give anything for that bucket now, but it was on the floor somewhere. Out of reach. Not that she could have managed it, tied up like this. Thinking about it had been a mistake. Her body decided for her. It was almost a relief as her muscles relaxed and a gush of wet warm pee spread in a circle and seeped into the mattress beneath her.

Melissa turned onto her side to escape the damp patch, buried her head in the pillow, and began to cry.

Chapter 30

A cruel wind swirled around the shopping precinct, scooping up discarded burger trays and plastic cups. Tiny tornadoes deposited detritus in neat piles at the base of planters and in the angles where buildings met.

The centre ground was held by half a dozen youths on mountain bikes, their faces lit by the glow from smartphone screens, the silence punctuated by their laughter. A car approached. Blue-tinted headlights swept the area. The youths turned to see who the intruder might be, their faces ghoulish, half-lit beneath their hoods. When the passenger door opened they mounted their bikes in unison and rode away. One of them raised a finger in the air as he performed a wheelie in futile protest at this disturbance.

Sean Roche, huddled in the doorway of Poundland, watched as the headlights of the BMW were extinguished. Slamming the door behind him, a large man in a dark bomber jacket and black jeans walked purposefully towards him. Sean shivered. It was the not knowing that got to you. Never knowing the why or wherefore. Or where it was going to lead.

The man stopped just short of the doorway, looked left, then right, and stepped closer. He loomed over Sean.

'You got the message then?' he said.

Sean nodded, like a spaniel eager to please. 'Yeah.'

The man held out his hand. 'Go on then.'

Sean began to take his hand out of his pocket, then stopped half-way. 'What if I need it?'

'You can get another one,' the man growled. 'Say you lost it. Now give!'

Sean placed the inhaler into the man's outstretched hand. 'Where am I going to get one at this time of night?' he asked.

'Asda's started doing them. We checked.' The man grinned. 'Your welfare is important to us, Sean. There's a pharmacy in their all-night superstore on the retail park.' He took his other hand from his pocket and held out a small roll of notes. 'There's fifty quid for your trouble.'

Sean reached out and took the money. As he did so, a massive hand closed over his, squeezing it like a vice.

'You'd better be right about there being plenty of doses left in this.'

'There are, honest,' said Sean. 'I've only used it a couple of times since I got it.'

The vice tightened. 'Careless of you to have lost it so soon then?'

'Yeah . . . it was.'

'Where did you lose it, Sean?'

'I think I must've left it on the bus.'

'Which one?'

'Number 18. I was going from Wythenshawe to the Trafford Centre.'

'Did you report it missing to the bus company?'

'No.'

'Why not?'

'Because I wasn't sure that's where I'd left it. And it's easy enough to get another one with me prescription.'

'Nice one,' said the man. He relinquished his grip and patted Sean on the side of his face. His hand rested on Sean's cheek. His thumb curled beneath Sean's jawline and tightened around his neck. 'You know what happens if you breathe a word of this to anyone?'

Sean attempted to nod. 'Yeah,' he croaked.

'Good man,' said the man, releasing his grip. He placed the inhaler in his pocket and zipped it up, then pushed back his sleeve to check his watch.

'That pharmacy,' he said. 'It closes at eleven. So you'd better get a move on, but don't run.' He chuckled. 'We wouldn't want anything to happen to you before you get there.'

Chapter 31

Day Three – Wednesday, 18th October

There were footsteps on the wooden staircase. The door opened. A hand found the switch. Light seeped beneath Melissa's hood.

'Christ!' A voice exclaimed. It was Gollum. 'She's only pissed herself!'

'Get on with it!' said The Boxer, pushing him into the room.

Embarrassed beyond words, Melissa pretended to be asleep.

Gollum grasped the duvet and pulled it back, revealing Melissa curled up in a foetal position, her back towards him. He prodded her with a bony finger. 'Wake up!' he demanded.

She slowly rolled over. He reached down and yanked the hood up onto her forehead.

'See what I've brought you,' he said.

Melissa's eyes slowly adjusted to the light. Her heart skipped a beat. In his hand he held a Ventolin inhaler.

'We'll have to take the gag off or she won't be able to use it,' Gollum observed.

'You don't say,' said The Boxer. 'Well, I never!'

He entered the room and approached the bed. He leaned down so close that Melissa could smell stale tobacco and beer through the balaclava.

'We're going to have to take that gag off,' he said. 'But the same rules apply as when we bring you food and drink. You don't speak and you don't call out. Do you understand?'

Melissa stared into those cruel eyes and nodded.

'Good girl.' He lifted her head with one large hand and untied the gag with the other. 'Nobody will hear you even if you do,' he said, 'so you'd be wasting your breath. And if you do call out, my friend here has a way of making sure you'll never call out again. Nod if you understand.'

Melissa nodded.

The Boxer stood up, took the inhaler from Gollum, and placed it between Melissa's bound hands, and pulled the duvet back over her.

'Don't lose it,' he said.

The two men walked to the door. The Boxer turned.

'That rule,' he said, 'there's one exception. When you need the bucket.' Then he switched off the light and closed the door.

Melissa's fingers closed over the inhaler. She had no idea if the canister contained the right level of dose for her. She didn't really care. Whatever it was it had to be better than not having it at all. She wondered what this meant – them bringing it to her. Somehow they must have found out she needed it. And surely it meant they didn't want her to die? At least . . . not yet.

The cold made her shiver. She pulled the duvet closer, wincing as the cable ties bit into her wrists. She turned back to face the window, shuffled as far as possible from the patch of damp, closed her eyes, and prayed for sleep to envelop her.

Less than twenty miles due north, Jo dreamed she was on a deserted beach on the Isle of Skye. Her parents had first brought her here. But now they were gone. It was dusk. The cliffs rose sheer behind her. The tide had turned, threatening to cut her off. She picked her way across rocks and boulders, slick with mounds of seaweed. Several times she fell and grazed her knees. Gulls wheeled and spiralled overhead. Like parchment shadows, ghostly white against a steel-grey sky, they mocked her with their calls. By the time she reached what she had hoped was the safety of a shingle spur the tide had cut her off.

In desperation she scanned the beach, the cliffs, and the empty expanse of sea. There was no help at hand, no prospect of rescue or escape. How had it come to this? Lost, alone, and abandoned. The last rays of the sun shimmered gold across the incoming waves and came to rest on her face, before dipping beneath the horizon. Darkness fell. And as the freezing wind chilled her to the bone the cries of gulls grew ever louder.

Jo rolled over and reached for the phone. 'Oh no!' she whispered. 'Please no!'

It was 3.32 a.m. Only bad news came in the hours before dawn. She pressed the little green symbol and waited with baited breath.

'Yes?'

'Is this SI Stuart?'

'Yes. What is it?'

'I'm sorry to disturb you, Ma'am. Detective Superintendent Ellis told me to let you know that there's been an incident on Merseyside which he has reason to believe may be connected to Operation Alecto.'

'An incident? On Merseyside? What kind of incident?'

'I don't have any details but, as I understand it, a shooting of some kind. The victim is critically ill in the Royal Liverpool University Hospital. On the Critical Care Unit. He advises that you get there as soon as possible if you want to speak with the victim.'

'Who do I ask for?'

'Morris Arthur Grimshaw.'

'Thank you,' she said. 'Please tell Detective Superintendent Ellis that I'm on my way.'

Articulated lorries trundled along the inside lane of the M62. A steady stream of white delivery vans joined the motorway at each of the successive slip roads, rear lights shimmering in the early morning mist. Jo had the outside lane almost entirely to herself. Occasionally she had to use her blues and twos to clear the way.

She flitted between two trains of thought: interpreting the dream and trying to second-guess what lay ahead. The first was the easier to compute. She'd been to Skye with her parents when she was eight or nine, and then again in her teens. That second time they'd gone walking in the foothills of the Black Cuillin mountains and enjoyed memorable scrambles to several of the peaks. It had been a magic time. On both occasions, they had visited beaches, one of which could easily have featured in her dream. But she'd never lost contact with her parents, and certainly never been left alone by them.

On the other hand, she had been abandoned by Abbie, hadn't she? And now she had the trauma of leaving the apartment they had so lovingly furnished together. Jo gripped the steering wheel tightly.

And then there was Melissa Walsh. Twelve years of age. Snatched from the pavement. Fearing for her life. Lost and alone.

A yellow van veered from the centre lane into the outside one, forcing her to brake. She swore, flashed her lights, and gave him a burst of her siren. It took another hundred yards before the driver finally pulled back into the middle lane. Jo looked across as she sped past. A young woman clutched the steering wheel with her left hand and was texting on her phone with her right. Jo gave another burst of her siren, made eye contact with the startled face in her rear-view mirror, and accelerated away. It took her less than half an hour to cover the thirty miles.

Her heart beat a rapid tattoo as she raced across the parking lot and into the hospital. Two uniformed officers stood guard in the corridor outside the Critical Care Unit. One had a Heckler & Koch semi-automatic slung across his chest. The other held a log on which he entered Jo's name, before punching a code into the keypad beside the doors.

A tall thin woman with mousey brown hair cut into a short bob stood at the foot of the bed, her back towards the door. It was Detective Sergeant Teresa Coppull from Merseyside's Major Crime Unit. At the sound of the door closing she turned and smiled wanly at Jo.

'We should stop meeting like this,' she said.

'Terry,' said Jo. 'How are you?'

'Better than him.' She nodded towards the figure in the bed.

It was impossible to tell if this was a man or a woman. The head was bandaged. The mouth and nose covered by a mask attached to a ventilator. Tubes taped to both arms snaked upwards to IV drips hanging from portable stands. On the far side of the bed a nurse anxiously watched the battery of digital monitors.

'His name is Morris Arthur Grimshaw,' said Teresa. 'He's a major player in the North West drug scene. Liverpool-based. We netted all of his gang in a major bust. Eighteen of them are banged up on remand. He's the only one that got bail.' She shook her head. 'Poor sod. He'd have been safer inside.'

'What happened?' said Jo.

Teresa looked across at the nurse and raised her eyebrows. The nurse checked the monitors, leaned over her patient, straightened up, and shrugged.

'Let's take this outside,' said the Liverpool detective.

When the door was closed she positioned herself so that she could keep her eyes on the bed. 'I'm not supposed to leave the room,' she said. 'But I doubt whoever did this to him had the foresight to get to a nurse on the CCU. Not that there would have been any point. He isn't going to make it.'

'That's official?' said Jo.

'It's what the doctors say. The prognosis is that he'll be dead within twenty-four hours.'

'Will I be able to speak with him?'

'You can speak all you like, Jo, but it's going to be a one-way conversation. That's what I was checking with the nurse just now. He may or may not be able to hear you, which is why I brought us out here, but he won't be able to reply. They've put him in an induced coma.'

'Bugger!' said Jo.

'Don't worry,' Teresa told her. 'Detective Superintendent Ellis and I got to talk with him before they put him under.' She opened her shoulder bag, took out a notebook, and handed it to Jo. It was Teresa's official PNB. 'If it's a list of names you're looking for they're all in there. Obviously I need it back but I'll email you them from my tablet.'

Jo turned to the most recent entry. Timed and dated at 2.45 a.m. that morning, it was a record of a brief conversation between Ellis and Grimshaw. It ended with a list of names. There were twenty-seven in all. She didn't recognise any of them. 'Why have you underlined some of them?'

'They're all associates of his.'

'If they're his pals, why would they want him dead?'

'Because he's the only one who got police bail? And that's because he's the only one the CPS reckon we don't have enough evidence against to prosecute. He got lucky. But his mates don't know that. Or if they do, they may find it highly suspicious. They'll have worked out we had someone on the inside. It wasn't him but they're not to know that.'

'They'd have had to get a message out. Arrange for someone else to do this?'

Teresa laughed. 'Every other day there are drones delivering phones, SIM cards, and drugs over the walls of Her Majesty's prisons. Not to mention bent screws supplementing their meagre salaries by ferrying messages to and fro. You know that.'

Of course she did.

'Why aren't you inside the room?'

They turned to find Ellis, the Titan commander, striding towards them.

'I came outside to brief SI Stuart, Sir,' said Teresa. 'Thought it best the nurse wasn't party to that. Don't worry, I haven't taken my eyes off them.'

That seemed to satisfy him.

'Where is he up to?' he asked.

'No change. He's in a coma and he's slipping away. Irreversible multiple organ failure. They didn't have a clue what it was.' She turned to Jo. 'They thought it might be sepsis from the wound on his neck until we told them it could be ricin poisoning. It was too late by then.'

'I'd assumed,' said Jo, 'that the reason you thought there was a connection with my investigation was something to do with how he came to be like this. Now I know.'

Ellis gave Teresa a dirty look. 'You haven't told her?'

'She didn't have a chance,' said Jo quickly. 'I've only just got here.'

'Best do it now then,' said Ellis. 'I've no doubt SI Stuart will want to see the crime scene. Why don't you show her while I get someone else to babysit him?'

Chapter 32

'When did this happen?' said Jo.

They were travelling in her car because Teresa had arrived at the hospital with Detective Superintendent Ellis.

'Sunday afternoon.'

'Two days after Ronnie O'Neill was shot. Today's Wednesday. When was he taken ill?'

'On Monday evening he first realised something was wrong. He told his wife he thought he was going down with the flu. Dosed himself with painkillers and over-the-counter remedies.'

'He didn't associate it with what happened on Sunday?'

'Apparently not. He knew he'd been shot because the pellet lodged in the back of his neck.'

Jo glanced across at her. 'Why didn't he go straight to the hospital?'

'It wasn't that deep. Played the hardman, like they do. Just pulled it out when he got home, swabbed it with TCP, and put a plaster over it. He assumed it was some kid messing around. And he knew if he went to hospital they'd have to report it to the police. He didn't want the aggro, especially with being on bail.'

Twenty minutes later Teresa instructed her to turn left off the tree-lined avenue of detached houses into a driveway.

'What is it with this guy and golf clubs?' Jo asked as she pulled up outside the white-walled red-roofed clubhouse.

'I take it that's a rhetorical question?' said Teresa, unbuckling her seat belt.

'I thought this was the Royal Birkdale,' said Jo. 'Home to the British Open Championship? That's what all the signs were saying.'

'That's just a bit further on. There are quite a few courses on this stretch of the coast.'

Teresa led the way to the professional's shop.

'I'm terribly sorry,' the professional told them, 'but I'm afraid that all the golf carts are already out on the course. Your colleagues have requisitioned them. I can get one of the ground staff to come back and pick you up but you may have to wait ten minutes or so.'

'In that case,' said Teresa, 'I think we'll just head on out there.'

'I can show you the way if you like?'

'No need,' Teresa replied. 'I know where I'm going. And it's only, what, half a mile?'

'Just over,' he said. 'Keep your eyes open. And if anyone shouts "Fore!" . . .'

She finished it for him.

'Duck down and cover your head. What do you take us for? Just because we come from the city doesn't mean we're complete numpties!'

The sun was rising as they set off. Set among undulating sand dunes, covered with windswept grass straw-bleached by the sun, and dotted with stands of pine, Jo found it stunning.

'How does someone like Grimshaw get to play at a club like this?' she wondered.

'They pride themselves on an inclusive policy,' said Teresa. 'I guess that means so long as he can afford it and he wears the right gear, he has the same opportunity as anyone else. He may even be a member for all we know.'

'Can you find out for me?' said Jo. 'If he is, it would help to explain how the unsub knew to choose this place as his kill site.'

'Strictly speaking, he didn't though, did he? Kill him here? That's the clever part.'

When they reached the fourteenth tee it was deserted.

'That's because he was shot on the green, down there,' said Teresa. 'Just as he was putting for a birdie.'

Jo followed her gaze. The beautifully manicured fairway stretched straight as a die in a valley between grass-covered dunes, before swinging gently to the right, where she could just make out the edge of the green, a cluster of golf carts, and people clad from head to foot in white and blue. In the distance, beyond the green, above a wide expanse of pine trees, rose the fells that marked the western outpost of the Pennine Hills.

'That's Blackpool Tower,' said her colleague, pointing northwards. 'And those mountains beyond it, that's the Lake District. And if you turn around you can just see the mountains in North Wales. I can think of worse places to die.'

'Only he didn't die here, did he?' said Jo. 'Strictly speaking.'

'Touché,' said Teresa. 'Very droll.'

Chapter 33

'There were seventy-six golfers on the course at the time your victim was here,' the crime scene manager told them. 'And another forty either in the clubhouse or waiting to start. God knows how many have tramped their way through here since then. Plus there must have been hundreds of locals and dog walkers using the rights of way across the course and over the dunes.' He eased his hood back from his forehead a little and scratched his head. 'I don't like to admit that we're wasting our time here, but the chances of finding anything useful are pretty remote, I'm afraid.'

'So why have you roped off the green?' said Jo.

He pulled a face. 'Just to stop my lot trampling all over it.' He pointed to his right. 'Our search is concentrated on those trees over there, and over there.'

They were two clumps of pine trees. One on a dune about fifty yards away, another closer to a hundred and thirty yards.

'Why there?' asked Jo.

'Because,' said Teresa, 'we know that he was struck by that pellet in the back of the neck, and according to two of the witnesses who were with him at the time he was standing with his back to those dunes.'

Jo could see that it made sense. They were the only places that offered cover for a shooter.

'It's more likely to have been the ones that are furthest away,' she said.

'Why do you say that?' asked Teresa.

'Because there's very little likelihood that anyone would strike a ball so hard and so badly that it might end up among those trees. Whereas with the other ones it would be a distinct possibility.'

'You play then, do you?'

'I don't have time, but I dabbled when I was at uni.'

'For what it's worth, I agree with you,' said the CSI. 'But you know how it is: we have to cover all the angles. Now we've got some daylight we'll see if your marksman left any trace for us to find.' He scratched his head again. 'Though I think we've more chance of spotting a pair of those red squirrels mating. And they're notoriously shy.'

'If you do, I suggest you respect their privacy,' Teresa called after him, 'or you're likely to have the Green Party coming after us.'

She took her tablet from her bag and switched it on. 'It was still dark when I came out here earlier,' she said. 'The boss wanted to make sure that the course was closed today and a cordon set up around this area.' She grimaced. 'Case of closing the stable door after the horse has bolted. But, like the man said, we have to cover the angles . . . and our backs.'

Her fingers whizzed across the keys, then she handed the tablet to Jo. 'Here's an aerial view. She pointed with her finger. 'This is us. As you can see, if someone was in those trees, his best escape route would be to drop down behind the dune those trees are on and follow the valleys either straight out onto the Shore Road or carry on across it into the dunes on the other side.'

'Wouldn't that risk his being seen by people walking in the dunes or on the beach?' Jo asked. 'He's going to look a bit suspicious carrying a golf bag to hide his air rifle.'

'He could disguise it as one of those stunt kite bags. Nobody would give that a second glance on this coast. Of course, the other choice would be to circle round to the left and come out in this estate over here. There are four different access points from these paths that run across the golf course and around the backs of the houses. Once he's on that estate he gets in his car, then he's got the choice of the Shore Road or Kenilworth Road. If he goes that way he's across the rails, and off down any one of these lanes across the fields, none of which have cameras on them.'

'It's a nightmare,' said Jo. 'Two more or less identical crime scenes, thirty miles apart, under two different police jurisdictions, both of which are basically stone cold. How the hell am I supposed to manage this?'

'You're in luck,' Teresa told her. 'Detective Superintendent Ellis and my bosses are concerned that Grimshaw's death could trigger another set of gang wars across Merseyside. They're prepared to pick up the tab for all the resources needed in the short term in relation to Grimshaw, but I wouldn't hang about if I were you. If it turns out this is an isolated event this end of the Ship Canal, they'll bounce it back in your direction like a hot potato.'

'I'll take what I can get,' said Jo. 'And since there's nothing I can do here I'd like to get back to Manchester as soon as possible.'

'I'll grab one of these golf carts,' said Teresa. 'I've always wanted to drive one.'

Jo hung on for grim death as the Liverpool detective attempted a slalom turn on a tricky sloping corner.

'Why would anyone want to kill both Ronnie O'Neill and Morris Grimshaw?' Jo asked. 'That has to be the key.'

'Who knows?' said Teresa. 'I can tell you that our intel has found no links between them in any capacity whatsoever. As suppliers, customers, or rivals.'

'Not even in relation to this new trend they used to call "going country" but we now term 'county lines' where they're using teenage dealers to invade other people's territory?'

The cart tilted ominously as it veered off the sandy track.

'Watch out, Terry!' Jo yelled, throwing her body to the left to counterbalance them.

Teresa regained control and continued as though nothing had happened. 'Not as far as we're aware. Although I admit it would be strange if the kids they're sending out to establish new customer bases hadn't become aware of each other's presence. Although I suppose one of the existing local gangs might want to send a message to the city dealers to stay away from their patch?'

That made perfect sense, Jo decided. It would also fit with the nature of the attacks, at least in relation to their resembling assassinations. But why take all the risk and trouble of using ricin as the agent of death? If Andy Swift's assessment was correct, this bore the hallmarks of a personal revenge crime, not a crime syndicate settling scores.

The golf cart came to a halt beside the pro's shop and Jo alighted. Teresa remained sitting there, looking at her phone.

'Come on, Terry,' said Jo. 'I'll drop you back at the hospital.'

Teresa put her phone back in her pocket and climbed out of the cart. 'Make that the St Anne Street nick,' she said. 'Grimshaw just passed away. Detective Superintendent Ellis is dealing with that end of things. He wants me to chase up the passive media analyses. See if we can identify some potential suspect vehicles.'

'Let's hope you have better luck than we've been having,' said Jo. 'I'll get my team to send you a list of car registration numbers – see if we can't find a match. Right now, that's the best hope we have.'

Only hope, was what she was really thinking as she opened the car door.

Chapter 34

Jo was queuing to come off the M62 and onto the M60 when a call came through on her hands-free.

'Sorry, Max, I'm driving,' she said. 'Can we keep this short?'

'No problem,' he replied. 'It's not as though there's a great deal to tell, I'm afraid. A burned-out vehicle matching one of our suspect vans has been found on waste ground in Wythenshawe. No sign of Melissa or her captors. We're combing the area for CCTV footage to see if we spot a change of vehicle, but if they're canny, they'll have done that somewhere else. Forensics are trying to identify the van. Odds-on, it'll have been stolen specifically for the job.'

'What about Jason O'Neill?'

'His house and Steven Yates's house are both under observation and subject to digital and telephonic surveillance. We've seen and heard nothing suspicious from either of them. On the contrary. Jason O'Neill has been busy ringing round issuing orders to his people to look for Melissa, and warning all and sundry to let him know if they hear any whispers about who might have done this. Failure to do so, he says, will result in severe retribution.'

'Did he sound genuine?'

'Put it this way. If he wasn't, then he's a bloody good actor.'

No sooner had she ended the call than another came through. This time it was Helen Gates.

'Where are you?' Gates demanded.

'I've just joined the M60 at Worsley, Ma'am. I'm heading clockwise to miss the traffic queuing for the Trafford Centre. I should be at Nexus House in about thirty minutes.'

'Forget that,' said Gates. 'The Chief Constable wants a face-to-face with the two of us. I'll expect you at Force HQ in twenty minutes' time. Don't keep us waiting.'

Make that thirty to forty minutes, Jo thought as the traffic began to slow ahead of her.

She took a deep breath and entered the GMP Headquarters fourth-floor meeting room. There were only three people at the table, but the sense of gravitas seemed to fill the whole space. In the centre sat Robert Hampson, the Chief Constable, with Charlotte Mason – the Mayor of Greater Manchester – and Assistant Commissioner Helen Gates on either side. They had their backs to the window, forcing her to take a seat facing them. It felt like an interview, or an interrogation.

Hampson looked pointedly at his watch.

'I'm sorry, Sir,' said Jo. 'There was a tanker broken down in the roadworks.'

'Well, we're all pushed for time,' he replied. 'You know everyone here, so let's get straight to the point. What is the status of Operation Alecto? And keep it brief.'

How the hell did she answer that? *You want brief*, she decided, *I'll give you brief.*

'Ongoing,' she said, 'and complicated.'

He nodded. 'By this killing on Merseyside, I presume. Is it connected?'

'That has yet to be confirmed,' she replied. 'But it certainly looks that way. The MO is identical. A pellet loaded with poison – presumably ricin – like the one here in Manchester. Even the setting chosen was the same. A golf course.'

'Were the victims connected?'

'Again, we have yet to establish that. They were both involved in the same criminal enterprise, so it's likely that they would at the very least have been aware of each other. The Merseyside Force and the Regional Organised Crime Unit have agreed to handle their end for the time being. We've already set up a direct comms system connecting our two investigations.'

'I've already spoken to the Mayor of Liverpool,' said Charlotte Mason. 'He's totally on board with this. This is precisely why we've both been demanding resources to fight the drug problem in our cities and pressuring the Home Secretary to scrap his supposedly new drugs strategy and listen to those of us who know what's happening on the ground. Is this all about spice, do you think?'

Jo was aware that she was in favour of decriminalising cannabis for medical use, highlighting the appalling impact of supposedly legal highs like spice on the homeless and other vulnerable people in the city centre, and the massive waste of police time in dealing with it.

'It is one line of enquiry,' she told the Mayor, 'but it's too early to tell.'

'Do you have any leads at all?' asked the Chief Constable.

'We have an exhaustive list of names of those who might have a grudge against either of the victims. Unfortunately, none of the names appear on both lists. We do have partial boot prints and a piece of fabric from the Manchester crime scene, together with hours of passive media to work through, principally from fixed-speed and ANPR cameras. Work is proceeding with regard to all three.'

'But no suspect?'

'What about the ricin?' said the Mayor. 'That sounds sufficiently unusual to give you something to go on, I would have thought?'

'That's why I've arranged to visit the Porton Down military science park tomorrow,' Jo said.

'Military science park?' the Mayor said. 'Is that a euphemism for secret arms research establishment?'

'You're going to Porton Down? That's the first I've heard about it,' said Helen Gates, raising her eyebrows. 'Who's going to lead the investigation while you're away?'

'My deputy, DS Carter,' said Jo. 'We'll be in constant communication, and if I leave before six in the morning I can be back by three in the afternoon.'

'Not if the M6 has anything to do with it,' muttered the Chief Constable.

'Is there anything resource-wise we can get you that might speed things up, SI Stuart?' asked Helen Gates.

'Don't you think we should approach the National Crime Agency first?' said the Chief Constable, forestalling Jo's response. 'Before we start to use our own extremely stretched resources?'

Jo raised her hand but didn't wait to be invited to speak. 'Sir, if I may? The NCA are already heavily involved in supporting the operation to find Melissa Walsh.'

'Is there a link between this missing schoolgirl and Operation Alecto?' asked the Mayor.

'I believe so,' Jo said. 'A tangential connection.'

'In what sense?'

'We think that she may have been taken by people close to the first victim, who suspect that her father may have been responsible for his death, or at the very least know something about it.'

'Which is exactly the kind of escalation we're trying to prevent,' said the Chief Constable. He turned to address Helen Gates. 'Helen, my fear is that as soon as the news breaks about this latest incident, gang bosses across the entire region are going to be looking over their shoulders, wondering if they might be next. Trying to work out who might be behind it, and if they should make a pre-emptive strike. It has the potential to become a nightmare scenario.'

'We're on top of that, Robert,' said Gates. 'Challenger and Titan are both involved. If there's the slightest hint of any of that, they will know and step in before the gangs get a chance to act.'

'Like they did with this kidnapping?' he replied.

Gates was about to protest that this was unfair, but the Mayor got in first. 'There must be something the Northern Powerhouse can do to support this,' she said.

'We both know, Charlotte,' said the Chief Constable bitterly, 'that until the Government puts its money where its mouth is, this is a powerhouse without any gas in the tank.'

'Thanks to the Mayor they have finally agreed to pay the full cost of the Arena terrorist attack,' Helen Gates pointed out.

'Only because of the public outrage when it looked as though they were not going to,' said the Mayor.

This isn't getting us anywhere, Jo decided. *And I need to get back to Nexus House.* She raised her hand. 'If I might suggest,' she said. 'If either the Merseyside Force or the Regional Organised Crime Unit could be persuaded to continue to run the investigation into the killing over at Ainsdale until we at least identify the perpetrator, that would make it much easier for my syndicate to cope.'

There was silence while they thought about it.

'I'm sure that between us we can make that happen, Robert, don't you?' said the Mayor.

'Since we don't have anything left in the budget to throw at this, I don't see that we have any option,' the Chief Constable replied.

'There'll have to be another press conference,' said the Mayor.

'But we've only just had one, about the kidnapping,' said Helen. 'Can't we just issue a press release?'

The Mayor shook her head. 'A second shooting incident involving a toxin that you suspect to be ricin? They're bound to want answers.'

'That we don't yet have.'

'Granted. But the speculation that this might be connected to terrorism has to be knocked on the head. Always assuming that you're sure there's no connection?'

The three of them stared at Jo.

'There is absolutely nothing to suggest that there is,' she said.

'Unless it's a dry run?' the Mayor suggested. 'A terrorist, or terrorists, conducting live trials prior to some form of assassination attempt?'

'You've been reading too many crime thrillers, Charlotte,' said the Chief Constable.

'I hope you're right,' the Mayor replied, 'because you and I are going to have to reassure the Prime Minister following this meeting.'

She addressed herself directly to Jo. Slowly and deliberately. Her gaze was still and penetrating. 'Specifically, SI Stuart,' she said, 'the Prime Minister wants to know if she should convene COBRA. As the Senior Investigating Officer, are you telling me that she has no reason to contemplate that?'

The Cabinet Office Briefing Room A, where the heads of security, police, and armed forces meet with the Prime Minister and Home Secretary to plan their response in times of national crisis. Woah! thought Jo. *If I get this wrong they'll never let me forget it.*

'At this moment,' she began, 'there is nothing whatsoever to suggest that the two attacks are in any way connected with terrorism. Our working hypothesis is that it's in some way connected with the victims' involvement in the supply of illicit drugs.'

The Mayor held her gaze for a few moments, then said, 'At this moment?'

'Yes,' said Jo.

The Mayor nodded. 'Then that is what we shall tell her,' she said.

'In that case,' said Jo, easing her chair back, 'if there's nothing else?'

The Chief Constable looked at her for a moment, as though about to reprimand her. He relented and waved her away with a sweep of his arm. 'No, you'd best get on with it. And make sure you keep ACC Gates updated of any developments, however small. She has a press conference to prepare. Do you hear?'

'Yes, Sir,' she said. 'And thank you.'

'Thank you, SI Stuart,' said the Mayor as Jo stood up.

It's nice to feel appreciated, Jo thought as she closed the door behind her.

Chapter 35

Day Four – Thursday, 19th October

It was 9.25 a.m. when Jo pulled up outside the gatehouse of the Defence Science and Technology Laboratory. Thanks to an early start, she'd made better time than expected. But the fact that she'd been at Nexus House until close to two o'clock last night meant she had had less than four hours' sleep. She had no idea how long she could keep this up.

Somehow the facility seemed less sinister than she had imagined. Apart from the KEEP OUT, MOD PROPERTY, and DANGER! HAZARDOUS AREA! signs on the fences and the two Ministry of Defence police officers she had spotted armed with MP7 semi-automatic sub-machine guns.

She showed her ID, signed the visitors' book, and was escorted to the reception building. This single-storey, red-brick and glass structure looked more like the reception centre of a Royal Horticultural Society property than one of the most advanced and secret military facilities for research into chemical, biological, radiological, and nuclear defence measures on the planet. It didn't make her feel any less nervous.

'Your host will be with you shortly, Ma'am,' she was told. 'Please take a seat. And do help yourself to a drink from the machine while you're waiting.'

She'd only taken a few sips of a much-needed coffee when a man in his forties wearing a smart blue suit and carrying a small black briefcase arrived at the front desk. He moved like someone who kept himself fit. His eyes regarded her with curiosity behind frameless spectacles, and he had a broad smile on his face.

'Please don't stand up, Ms Stuart,' he said. 'At least finish your drink.'

They shook hands, and he sat on the couch opposite her.

'My name is Reg Laxton,' he said. 'I'm a molecular biologist and team leader. I've worked here for fifteen years, and I haven't had a day off work for sickness in all that time. I hope you find that a little reassuring?'

Jo grinned sheepishly. 'Is it that obvious?'

'No more than most,' he replied. 'You'd be surprised how many visitors imagine that they're at imminent risk of contracting some deadly virus, being struck down by a nerve agent, or leaving lit up like a beacon by nuclear radiation.'

'You can't blame people,' she said, 'given the stories that circulate and the secrecy.'

'Let me set your mind at rest,' he said. 'For a start, we're only one of a number of establishments on this science and technology park and elsewhere, working to ensure the security and defence of the United Kingdom. Secondly, research into chemical and biological weapons ceased back in the 1950s. Since then we have not, I repeat *not*, engaged in the development of any chemical or biological weapons. This is a defence establishment. Our work is all about staying one step ahead of those who may already have, or wish to develop, such weapons so we can put in place countermeasures to the threat they may represent. Obviously, this work involves the production of very small amounts of these agents so we can develop means to counter them such as prevention, speedy detection and identification, preventative treatment, and decontamination. However, the safe storage and disposal of such samples is of paramount importance to us.' He grinned. 'As I'm sure you'll appreciate, our concern is not only for the wider public, but for those of us who work here too.'

'And ricin is one of the substances that you test?'

'Among others. There is sarin, for example, and other organophosphorus agents. Then there are the pathogens such as ebola, anthrax, smallpox, and the plague bacterium – to name but a few. In studying these, we have become a major centre for research on behalf of the National Health Service, and one of the world's leading authorities on viral inoculations.'

He leaned closer, using his hand to indicate that she should do the same. Then he looked cautiously over each shoulder before whispering in her ear. 'And, just for the record, we have never had the body of an alien brought here, or to any of our other establishments. Unless you include politicians.'

Evidently pleased with his performance, he sat back and laughed. Jo joined in. It was, after all, a half-decent joke. Or was it, she wondered, a double bluff?

He placed both hands on the coffee table. 'I see you've finished your drink, so I think we'll crack on. They've booked a room for us to use. You can get another cup and take it through with you if you like?'

'I'm fine,' said Jo, picking up her bag. 'And I'm on a really tight schedule.'

'Aren't we all?'

Jo had the feeling that he didn't really mean it.

Chapter 36

Laxton led her to a small room at the end of the reception area. Inside were two chairs with a desk between them. He opened his briefcase, removed a manila folder and an A4-size brown envelope, and placed them both on the desk in front of him.

'Before we begin,' he said, adopting a serious tone, 'I'm afraid I have to ask you to sign a copy of the Official Secrets Act.'

'I've already done that,' she said, 'as part of my role with the National Crime Agency.'

He shook his head. 'I'm afraid that won't be sufficient for our purposes. You'll need to sign this one, asserting that you will not disclose any of the information that you receive today that is marked as, or otherwise identified as, classified.'

Jo felt distinctly uncomfortable. 'What if it proves essential that I do so,' she said, 'in order to progress our investigation? Or to prosecute the perpetrator, for example?'

He smiled benignly. 'I can assure you that it won't be.'

'But what if it is?'

'Then you'll have to refer that back to us so that a determination can be made in relation to that which you wish to disclose, and the specific context in which you wish to disclose it.'

It was a well-rehearsed form of words. Jo could see no way around this, but it left her wondering what it was they could possibly have to hide? 'Very well,' she said. 'On that basis, I'm happy to sign.'

He handed her a single sheet of paper headed with an MOD logo and the company logo. She read it carefully, signed it, and handed it back. He placed it in his briefcase, smiled, and picked up the brown envelope.

'Now let me see,' he began. 'You sent us this potential exhibit for identification and analysis.'

He opened the envelope and used his forefinger and thumb to slide out a transparent evidence bag within which was a second transparent bag containing the air rifle pellet retrieved from the seventh tee at the Worsley golf course. She could see that the original evidence record was still attached to the internal bag, and that the continuity label had been updated by the staff here at Porton Down to maintain the chain of evidence. Both bags had been sealed, and then resealed with forensic tape. The scientist opened the folder, removed some photographs and a sheet of typed paper, and placed them on the table.

'The pellet itself was identified by your own ballistics experts,' he said. 'Our task was to discover if the pellet had been modified to deliver a toxic substance, and if so the nature of that substance.' He picked up the sheet of paper and studied it.

Jo's impatience got the better of her. 'And have you?'

He smiled and handed her the report. 'Yes,' he said. 'And, yes, this pellet has been modified and impregnated with a toxic substance. We have identified that substance as ricin. A highly toxic substance that if injected, inhaled, or ingested has the potential to be fatal. In the case of injection or inhalation the equivalent of less than a few grains of salt would be sufficient to kill an average-sized human being.'

'But not if it's ingested?'

'In that case a significantly higher dose would be required because the process of digestion tends to mediate the pathology of the toxin.'

'And this pellet could have contained sufficient amounts of ricin to explain the death of the person at whom it was fired?'

'On the basis of the post-mortem findings that you sent us, I can say categorically that they're consistent with ricin poisoning and, given the deceased's body weight, a fraction of the amount of ricin that this pellet was designed to transport would have been sufficient to explain his death.'

That was all that Jo needed to hear. She scanned the report and it was obvious that although full of scientific jargon, the gist of it was that the poison would have broken down the protein in Ronnie O'Neill's body and inexorably caused his death.

'How easy would it have been for someone to acquire ricin?' she asked.

'In its pure form, impossible, unless one happened to access it in a research establishment such as ours. Even then, security would be such that it would be incredibly difficult and risky to do so.'

'Which is presumably how the agent who killed the Bulgarian defector, Georgi Markov, sourced it. From a State laboratory?'

'Exactly. We know that the poison-tipped umbrella used to inject a pinhead-sized impregnated pellet was designed for the assassin by the KGB. It's a reasonable assumption that they also supplied the ricin.'

'But there's nothing to suggest that my investigation involves a political assassination,' said Jo.

'Quite.'

He reached into his briefcase and pulled out a small brown envelope. He smiled and with a flourish tipped onto the desk six small, shiny, chocolate and coffee mottled beans. Jo half expected him to add, *Hey presto!*

'Ricin is produced from the beans, also known as seeds, of *Ricinus communis* – the castor oil plant to you and me. The seeds themselves are poisonous. This number of seeds, if ingested in this form, is likely to prove fatal, but only if chewed. A packet of ten seeds can be bought online or in nurseries for less than a pound. They're also available in larger quantities on the dark web. Occasionally as much as two kilograms. And of course, anyone in this country with a greenhouse and a conservatory could grow their own plants and have a continuing supply of beans.'

Similar in size and colour to the pinto beans used to make burritos, they looked so harmless sitting there on the desk. Jo picked one up and examined it. With its oval shape and two small yellow protuberances at one end it was not unlike a beetle. This was what had led to Ronnie O'Neill's sudden demise.

'Deceptively pretty, isn't it?' said the scientist. 'But it's a very simple process to extract the poison in a concentrated form in one's own kitchen, using a similar process to that used to produce cyanide from almonds. In the last forty years there have been close to thirty publicly recorded incidents involving the illicit purchase, manufacture, and intended or actual use of ricin with the intention of committing murder. The bulk in the USA, including envelopes containing ricin powder sent to President Obama and certain senators. Here in the UK there was evidence of its preparation on one occasion in Liverpool, and also following a raid on a flat in London. There has also been one report of a Sunni militant Islamist group carrying out trials on animals, and possibly on a human.'

Jo raised her eyebrows. 'Publicly reported?'

'There have been others, but they're not currently in the public domain, and for your purposes I'm afraid that they remain classified.'

'Even though I've signed your form?'

'Yes. But I can assure you that they have no relevance whatsoever to your investigation.'

'With respect,' she said. 'You can't be sure of that.'

He shook his head. 'I'm sorry, you'll have to take my word for that.'

She decided to let it go. 'And the process is simple?'

'And, like most things, whether desirable or undesirable, readily available on the internet.'

'And presumably the killer copied the idea of using a pellet to deliver the poison from the Markov case?'

He shrugged. 'That's for you to discover. But I'm sure you're right. In the Markov case the pinhead-sized pellet was an alloy of platinum and iridium. It was drilled with holes 0.016 of an inch in depth: invisible to the human eye. The ricin was inserted in powder form and sealed over with a wax designed to dissolve under the skin to release the toxin.'

He selected two photographs and slid them across the table. 'These are images of the pellet you sent us.'

They were magnified photographs showing the head of the pellet protruding above the flattened skirt. The dirt had been removed, and nine holes the size of the tip of a biro were visible.

'The pellet is of standard construction – in this case, lead with a small amount of antimony to increase its hardness and reduce oxidation. It's a soft metal and easy to drill. The holes you see are 3 millimetres in depth, and 0.5 millimetres in width. In three of them we found subcutaneous tissue, soil, the residue of ricin in powdered form, and honey.'

'Honey?'

'One of the more solid forms of honey. From New Zealand. In two other holes we found undisturbed ricin powder beneath a layer of beeswax. Once he'd loaded the ricin powder, your killer used beeswax to seal the holes prior to firing the pellets. Beeswax hardens at normal temperatures but softens at body temperature.'

'How would he know that was going to work?'

'He'll have read that the Bulgarian assassin used some form of wax to seal the pellet used to kill Markov. Presumably he experimented, using trial and error? On simulated targets? Or on animals perhaps – stray dogs or cats? That's what I would have done.'

He retrieved the photographs and slipped them back into the folder. 'Ricin doesn't have the longevity of other potential biological weapons such as botulin, anthrax, or sarin,' he said. 'It tends therefore to be used exclusively for close-up attacks such as assassinations and domestic poisonings. Your case represents an interesting new dimension of that.'

'Interesting.' *That's not how Ronnie O'Neill's or Morris Grimshaw's families would describe it,* Jo reflected. 'There's been a second fatality,' she told him. 'The attack took place last Sunday. The victim died yesterday.'

He raised his eyebrows. 'With the same methodology?'

'Identical. Right down to the fact that a golf course was chosen as the crime scene. Unfortunately, the victim removed the pellet himself and threw it away.'

He shook his head. 'That's a shame. Also, from your point of view, I suppose it's a very worrying development?'

'That's an understatement,' she said.

He placed the report back in the folder. Then he put the evidence bags on top of the folder and slid them across the desk towards her. 'That's it, I'm afraid. It's all I have for you.'

'To what extent are those who come in contact with any of these victims of the poison pellets at risk themselves?' she asked. 'Medical personnel, first responders, CSI, for example?'

He smiled. 'None from contact with the victims. They're neither infectious nor contagious. Any ricin that enters the body will be broken down very quickly, hence the reason it is difficult, if not impossible, to identify after a matter of hours. The only risk would come from careless handling of the pellet if, as in the case of the one you sent me, some of the ricin is still sealed beneath a layer of the beeswax.'

'Is there an antidote for ricin poisoning?'

His smile was almost smug. 'As it happens, there is. Developed right here in our laboratories. I'm proud to say that I've been involved for the past two years in bringing it into production.'

Jo was finding it difficult to retain her composure. She had the impression he regarded it as interesting from an academic and professional perspective. For her, it was one of life and death.

'In view of these two attacks,' said Jo, 'is it possible you could let us have a batch for use in the event that any more victims come to light?'

He sat up and his grin widened. 'I did wonder when you were going to ask – we'd anticipated that you would. There's a toxicologist at the Manchester Royal Infirmary who is a registered member of the National Poisons Information Service. A batch of a dozen antidotes was dispatched to him this morning by courier.'

Jo felt a surge of anger that he had been deliberately holding back from telling her, as though it was some kind of game. Two people dead already, yet he was treating their discussion like a competition. On the other hand, at least he was ahead of the game.

'There is a caveat, however,' he continued. 'Currently the efficacy of this antidote is limited in most cases to the first twenty-four hours after the poison has entered the body. For most people, after exposure to lethal doses for more than four hours, the effects are irremediable, even though it may take up to five days to kill them. If there are any more victims, I hope they come forward pretty smartish.'

Jo placed the folder and the evidence bags in her own document case and stood up. 'Thank you for this,' she said. 'And for not drowning me in technical terminology.'

He stood and held out his hand. 'Not at all. It was a pleasure and, as I said, of great interest to us. If you have anything more you need to know, don't hesitate to contact us.' Jo shook his hand and he opened the door for her.

She turned in the doorway. 'I have one last question,' she said.

He folded his arms. 'When people say that it usually turns out to be the most important one.'

'It has just occurred to me to ask if you also happen to have developed a vaccine against ricin?'

Both his expression and his voice became guarded. 'That, I'm afraid, is something that I'm unable to answer.'

'Unable or unwilling?'

He shrugged. 'Both.'

'Which I assume means that it is highly classified information?'

'That's correct.'

'But surely I've just signed a declaration that would cover this?'

He shook his head. 'There are different levels of access according to the different classifications, and I'm afraid that this particular piece of information is way above yours.'

'Let's assume,' said Jo, 'that I receive information that one or more persons are likely to be targets of our unidentified subject? If a vaccine exists wouldn't it be prudent to make it available to them? That's a simple duty of care.'

'If there were such a vaccine,' he said, choosing his words with great care, 'and such an occasion was to arise, I would suggest that you let us know immediately and I would of course pass your request on to the relevant authority.'

'In which event,' said Jo, 'let's hope the relevant authority is capable of making a speedier decision than most government departments.'

'Hypothetically,' he said.

Chapter 37

Black clouds rolling in from the south-west promised more heavy rain. As soon as Jo reached the motorway she called Nick Carter on the hands-free. He answered within seconds.

'Boss?'

'Flatman was right,' she told him. 'The pellet retrieved from the seventh tee at Worsley contained ricin: Ronnie O'Neill died of ricin poisoning. Almost certainly Morris Grimshaw did, too.'

'Then it's a bloody good job you got us started on contacting suppliers of castor oil seeds for the names of anyone who made multiple purchases.'

'How is that going, Nick?'

'Slowly. They're not a proscribed substance, so none of the retailers have lists of purchasers. They have to wade through their credit sales data. Anyone who paid cash is going to be virtually untraceable. Sounds like it should be a proscribed substance, like arsenic.'

'In that case almonds would have to be proscribed too,' she pointed out. 'And cherries and apples and pears, because their kernels, pits, and pips contain cyanide.'

'When you put it like that,' he said.

'Perhaps our best bet would be GCHQ?' said Jo. 'They look and listen for keywords and phrases in digital and analogue communications that might indicate possible terrorist activity. I'd be surprised if the word ricin wasn't one of those triggers.'

'Which is fine if the unsub or the person he contacts is already on their radar. Otherwise it seems pretty random, like finding a needle in a haystack.'

'People carrying out internet searches or going on the dark web looking for places to purchase ricin is hardly random.'

'Point taken. Aren't you best placed to approach them through the NCA?'

'I'll do that as soon as I get back to Manchester,' she told him. 'I got a bit of good news while I was here, but it's best I share that in person, however secure this phone is supposed to be. Now it's your turn. What progress have we made?'

His sigh told her everything she needed to know. 'If you go by volume of data, time, and effort,' he said, 'a hell of a lot. If you're talking about leads or genuine suspects, none at all.'

'He can't have just parachuted onto those two golf courses, taken those shots, and then been airlifted out. What about the vehicle licence plates?'

'We've tracked down the drivers of half of the ones we're interested in. The Merseyside Force have got seven licence plates they're still pursuing.'

'Membership of gun clubs? Purchases of that particular make of pellet?'

'We're still on it. If and when we get a match to the driver of one of those vehicles with either the gun clubs or the pellet purchases, then we'll have ourselves a prime suspect. You know how it is. We just have to grind it out.'

'Oh hell,' she said. 'I forgot to ask. Have they found Melissa yet?'

'You've obviously not been watching the news. They've done an appeal for any sightings of her and her photo is out there on Facebook and Twitter. So is Steve Yates's latest mug shot, even though there's no evidence he's actually involved.'

'Still nothing then? No contact with her parents? No demands or threats?'

'Not a sniff. I spoke with Max Nailor twenty minutes ago. I got the distinct impression they're getting desperate.'

Jo felt a jolt of unease. She'd assumed the girl had been taken as a means of putting pressure on her father, that there was no intent to do her harm. Now she was not so sure. Large globules of rain began to splatter the windshield, and for a moment her vision was obscured until the automatic wipers came on. 'I'm sorry, Nick, I'll have to go,' she said. 'I should be back with you in about three and a half hours. Keep me posted.'

'Will do, Boss,' he said. 'See you soon.'

The journey was as frustrating as she had feared. It was plain sailing all the way to Stafford, and then the traffic began to slow. By the time she reached Sandbach it had come to a standstill. *Here we go,* she told herself, *you have now arrived in Britain's Bermuda Triangle. Abandon hope all ye who enter here.* It took an hour to crawl the twelve miles to Knutsford Services, before things picked up. Just when she was beginning to think she might make it before sunset, another call came through. It was Nick again.

'Boss,' he said, without preamble, 'where are you?'

'Coming up to the M56 turnoff. Why?'

'Good.' He told her, 'You need to go straight to the Royal Bolton Hospital.'

Her stomach lurched. 'Melissa?'

'No,' he said. 'There's been another one. Like Ronnie O'Neill and Morris Grimshaw.'

'Who's the victim?'

'I haven't got the details. Only that it's a male. I'm already on my way.'

'I'll meet you there.'

She killed the call, swore, switched on her blues and twos, and floored the accelerator.

Chapter 38

Carter was standing under the canopy outside the entrance to Accident and Emergency nursing a cardboard cup. He shook his head. 'You needn't have rushed, he was DOA.'

'Bugger!' she said. 'Did anyone get to talk to him?'

'He was still alive when the paramedics got to him but he was incoherent. He passed away in the ambulance.'

'Who is he? Anyone we know?'

'I doubt it. Not unless you've been kipping in doorways or keeping company under railroad arches.'

'He was a rough sleeper?'

Carter drained the cup and crushed it in his hand. 'It doesn't get much rougher than the doorway of an abandoned chapel in the middle of a cemetery.'

'Where is the body now?'

'In the mortuary, waiting for you, CSI, and the pathologist. I left him in the capable hands of DC Whittle.'

Jo stared at him. 'Not on her own, I hope?'

'Course not.' He lobbed the cup into the wastebasket. 'She's got a uniformed officer with her. Although, of the two of them, he's looking the worse for wear.'

The young PC standing beside Carly Whittle looked distinctly queasy.

'Are you alright, officer?' Jo asked.

'Yes, Ma'am,' he replied. 'I've never been good around dead bodies.'

'When did you pass out?' she asked.

He smiled weakly. 'I haven't, Ma'am, not yet.'

'You wally!' said Nick. 'She's asking when you completed your training.'

'Oh, yes, of course. Easter this year.'

'Then it's about time you got used to it. "The dead are always with us."'

'Isn't that ". . . the poor are always with us"?' asked Carly Whittle.

'You don't get poorer than when you're dead,' Nick responded. 'And by the sound of it you've been spending too much time with DC Hulme.'

'When you two have quite finished,' said Jo. She turned to the mortuary manager. 'I'm sorry about that.'

The mortuary manager was used to graveyard humour. Her smile was forgiving, her manner composed. 'As we were alerted to the fact that this was a suspicious death, with an unknown level of risk of contamination, I ensured that the full protocol was followed,' she said. 'The body has not been cleaned. It was lifted and transported inside a biohazard containment body bag. The clothing removed to enable emergency treatment has been bagged and sealed in a biochem-hazard property bag. Your colleague here has possession of that.'

'And his personal effects?'

'I have them, such as they are, Ma'am,' said Carly Whittle holding up another evidence bag.

'Michael here will assist you,' said the mortuary manager. 'I'll be in my office if you need me.'

The mortuary technician handed each of them a face mask and then led them past two stainless-steel autopsy tables to a gurney, on which lay a large black body bag. Jo and Nick positioned themselves on one side, with the technician on the other. On Jo's signal, he unzipped the first layer from head to toe, peeling it back sideways to reveal a transparent window beneath which the body was visible.

'Can you unzip this one too, please?' said Jo.

The technician hesitated. 'I understood he was a hazard?' he said. 'That's why he's in this pouch.'

'I'm assured that there's no risk,' Jo told him. 'And we do need a photograph so we can identify him.' Still he hesitated. 'I'll take full responsibility,' she continued. 'Besides you're the only one with gloves and protective clothing.'

He reluctantly unzipped the transparent cover and stepped well back.

The familiar odour of smoke, sweat, and urine, mingled with that of death. Blank rheumy eyes stared up at them. Sticky matter had formed in the corners. The sclera was yellow and bloodshot. The face was gaunt and lined, with sunken cheeks. Parted lips exposed blackened teeth, and one missing canine. Dark, lank, greasy grey-flecked hair stuck to the scalp and forehead. Most startling of all was the contrast between face and hands, weathered the colour of mahogany, and the lily-white skin stretched tight across his emaciated body, peppered with irregular brown and yellow bruises.

'Looks like he's taken a beating or two,' Nick observed. 'Recent, but not within the past few days.'

'The pathologist will be able to give us a better fix on that,' said Jo. 'What I don't see is where he was shot?'

'Nothing on this side,' said Nick.

'It's towards the back of his neck,' said the mortuary technician. 'The reason you can't see it is that it's under his hair.'

'Can you show me, please?' Jo said.

The technician went over to a bank of stainless steel drawers and returned with a plastic spatula which he used to lift the hair away from the left-hand side of the victim's neck. Jo leaned closer. Nick came to see for himself.

Where the trapezius muscle joined the neck was a wound with the appearance of a large, badly infected boil. At the centre was a crater with a black necrotic crust surrounded by a shiny yellowish substance, and beyond that the telltale reddish blush of sepsis.

'That's horrible,' Nick observed.

Jo stood up, stepped back, and removed her face mask. 'Thank you,' she said to the mortuary technician. 'I'll just take a couple of headshots with my phone and tablet, and then we'll be on our way. Our crime scene investigators will also want to take some photographs before the autopsy takes place and collect the clothing and property evidence bags. This officer will remain here until then.'

She turned to look at the young policeman standing beside DC Whittle. The blood had drained from his face. 'You might want to bring him a chair,' she said.

Photos taken, Jo and Nick joined Carly.

'Is there anything in there,' said Jo, pointing to the property bag, 'that might help us identify him?'

'There's a photograph of a woman with a teenage boy and girl,' she said. 'Could be his family, I suppose. Other than that, there's just some loose change, seventy-five pounds in new and used five-pound notes, and two bags of pills that look suspiciously like spice to me.'

'He's been dealing drugs,' said Nick. 'That figures.'

'If you're after a name, you might want to start with the council's Street Life team, Ma'am,' said the young constable. 'They're your best bet. I'll give you the address for Urban Outreach. It's only ten minutes away from here.'

Chapter 39

'Mumbles,' said the Urban Outreach manager, staring at the image on Jo's phone taken in the mortuary. 'That was his street name.'

'Mumbles?' said Nick Carter. 'He came from up by the Mumbles Reservoir?'

The manager frowned. 'No. Apparently, it's because he used to mumble.'

'Why was that? Because he was intoxicated, or high on drugs?'

'Again, no. I gather it was a mental health thing.'

'Do you know his real name, or where he came from?' Jo asked.

'I don't. He only came a few times. But I remember the second time was on a Tuesday. I persuaded him to have a word with the BiDAS team.'

'BiDAS?'

'Bolton Integrated Drugs and Alcohol Service. There's no one in today, but you could try Beth. She's one of our Homeless and Vulnerable nurse practitioners.'

Beth had a client with her, but they only had to wait a few minutes. Jo showed her the image.

'Oh dear!' she said. 'Poor man. What happened to him?' She saw the look on their faces. 'No,' she said, 'of course. I shouldn't have asked.'

'His street name was Mumbles,' said Jo. 'We understand that he had at least one session with the BiDAS team. Would there be a record of that?'

'There should be.'

'Under section 29(3) of the Data Protection Act 1998,' said Nick Carter, adopting an authoritative tone, 'we have a right to see such information, given that it is in pursuit of both the prevention and detection of a crime, and the fact that in this case the patient is not in a position to give or refuse consent.'

The nurse practitioner smiled sweetly. 'I'm aware of that,' she said. 'And furthermore, paragraph 22 of the General Medical Council guidance on confidentiality gives me the right to disclose such information if the client's right to confidentiality is outweighed by the public interest.'

'Bravo,' said Jo.

'I'm sorry,' said Nick. 'I shouldn't have assumed.'

'We need, as a matter of urgency, to be able to identify this man,' said Jo. 'A name would be a start.'

The nurse practitioner went over to a bank of filing cabinets, unlocked the drawers, and slid one open.

'Initial records tend to be paper-based,' she said. 'It's more informal and less likely to cause anxiety than using a computer. Ah . . . here we are.' She withdrew a thin brown folder and walked over to her desk.

'His name is Anthony, or Tony, Dewlay. Also known as Mumbles. Forty-seven years of age.' She looked up. 'That's the average life expectancy of a homeless person.' She continued to read the notes. 'Originally from Preston. He confided that he worked for a big insurance company, in their main offices, erm . . . as an actuary. His wife ran off with his divorced brother. He became depressed and started drinking, lost his home in the divorce settlement, moved into a rented terraced house, lost his job, couldn't pay the rent, got evicted. Ended up on the streets seven years ago. He's been living as a homeless person ever since – Bolton,

Salford, Manchester, Bolton again. A couple of squats, but mainly as a rough sleeper.'

She looked up, sighed, and handed Jo the folder. 'Very sad, but all too common. And it will continue to be so, unless someone can magic up the resources we need for counselling and mental health.'

'What's this scribbled in pencil at the bottom?' Jo asked, handing the sheet back.

'It's querying drug abuse as well as alcohol dependency and booking him a BiDAS appointment for the following Tuesday.'

'And did he turn up?'

'I don't know. I'd have to check the computer.'

'If you could,' said Jo, 'that would be really helpful.'

Chapter 40

'How far to the cemetery?' asked Jo.

'Half a mile. Just the other side of the A666,' said Nick.

They stood in the entrance, staring out through a determined drizzle at the wall of a fire-surround factory on the opposite side of the street. Carly Whittle, having handed over to the CIS team, had joined them after cadging a lift from a patrol car. The computer confirmed that Anthony Dewlay's only appointment had been with death.

'Right,' said Jo. 'You get back to Nexus House, Nick. I'll take DC Whittle with me. I want you to find out everything you can about the deceased. Especially what he's been doing since his marriage broke down seven years ago – shortly before Ronnie O'Neill was sent down. If he has been dealing drugs there may well be a link to either O'Neill or Morris Grimshaw, or both.'

'I'll see what the Bolton Neighbourhood Team and the Drugs Squad can tell us first,' he replied. 'And once we know where he tended to hang out I'll sent some DCs to begin questioning other rough sleepers. There's no point in wasting resources until we've got a handle on when and where he was shot.'

'Resources? What resources?' asked Jo ruefully.

'Don't worry,' he responded. 'Now we've officially got a serial killer on our hands they'll have to cough up.'

Jo grimaced. 'Don't hold your breath.'

Her phone rang.

'Speak of the devil,' she said. 'It's ACC Gates. You'd better get going. We'll catch you up.'

She accepted the call. 'Ma'am?'

'Is it true?' Gates demanded. 'There's been another one?'

'It looks that way, Ma'am. Pending confirmation by a Home Office pathologist.'

'He's dead already?'

'On arrival, Ma'am.'

'Did anyone get to speak with him?'

'Unfortunately not. We have no idea where or how long ago he was shot.'

'Do you have a name?'

'Yes. And he's not on the system.'

'So you don't know if he's connected to either of your previous victims?'

'No, Ma'am. But we're running a full background check. I'm sure we'll find something.' She managed to stop herself from adding 'eventually'.

'This is a nightmare,' said Gates, more to herself than to Jo.

'Yes, Ma'am.'

'How did the hospital know to contact us?'

'Because immediately I had the pathologist's report on the first victim I put out an alert across all the NHS Trusts, not just those in the North West, referencing the symptoms they need to look out for and the number to ring.'

'Well done,' the ACC replied grudgingly.

'I'm just off to have a look at the place where he was found, Ma'am, to see if there are any clues as to where he might have been attacked.' Jo looked at Carly and raised one eyebrow. 'My driver has just arrived.'

'Yes, yes,' said Gates. 'You'd better get off then. I'll have a word with the Press Office, see if we can put together a statement that'll keep the wolves at bay.'

'Yes, Ma'am. If there's nothing else?'

'Just keep me updated.'

'Yes, Ma'am.'

'Whatever progress you make, however small, I want to hear about it immediately. Do you understand?'

'Yes, Ma'am.'

'I don't want to have to call you first.'

'No, Ma'am.'

The ACC ended the call.

'Three bags full, Ma'am,' Jo muttered as she put the phone back in her pocket. She caught the expression on Carly Whittle's face. 'You didn't hear that.'

Carly smirked. 'No, Ma'am.'

Jo shook her head. 'Just get in the car,' she said.

Chapter 41

Heather Rand parked her Golf in the one remaining space outside Ye Olde Cock Inn, applied the handbrake, and let her head drop back against the headrest.

What a day – stressful didn't cover it. Dropping her granddaughter off at school in all that wind and rain. Then having to rush back to her daughter's house to collect the pull-up poster that Rose needed for the conference she was organising at the university and had forgotten to take with her. Doing the fortnightly shop at the food store. Then preparing a one-pot meal for their dinner that evening before going back to pick up Poppy, take her home, and keep her occupied until her mum came home. Finally, she had some time to herself.

It had never been like this with her parents. She'd never have dreamed of asking her mother to drop the children off, let alone provide after-school care and full-time cover for most of the school vacation. The one time that she had asked, the response had been brutal and conclusive.

'You shouldn't have had them if you can't look after them yourself. When I had you and your brothers I made sure I put you first. That's why I put my career on hold, and then went part-time when you were all back in school. That's the trouble with your generation. You want it all. You're not prepared to make sacrifices like we were.'

She told herself that it was because her parents had lived through both the Great Depression and the Second World War. She, on the other hand, was one of the golden generation with free higher education, full employment, a National Health Service, straight onto the housing ladder, final salary pension. Maybe this was payback time and the reason her own generation was such a soft touch: guilt.

A succession of barks from the rear of the car jolted her from her reverie.

'I'm coming, Jake!' she said. 'Hang on in there, there's a good boy. I'm coming.'

She kept him on his lead as they wound their way along the paths through the rock garden, and down past the pond. Despite the storm that had only just abated, leaves clung stubbornly to the acers, creating a stunning panoply of russet, orange, yellow, and lime above the emerald splash of water marginals.

Jake hurried on, nose to the ground, tracking the familiar scent of dogs and their walkers. Once past the formal rose garden, its forlorn naked bushes denuded by the storm, she let him off his lead. He set off, golden brown behind swaying from side to side, plate-sized ears close to the ground as he nosed his way towards the River Mersey.

Heather loved the peace and solitude of this charming part of the city's green lung. It felt a thousand miles away from the stream of traffic on Kingsway. She had been retired less than six months, but that seemed an age ago. The stress of a high-profile occupation long forgotten, and certainly not missed.

She called the cocker spaniel and put him back on his lead until they had negotiated the wooden slatted walkway across the bog. She let him go again when they entered Stenner Woods, and stopped to admire a crimson maple, backlit by the late afternoon sun. A flash of green off to her left, close to the edge of the woods caught her eye. She turned to look. The upper branches of a larch, its leaves already turning yellow, were populated by a dozen ring-necked parakeets. She stopped to watch them.

For over a year she'd been hearing rumours that a flock of thirty or so of these exotic birds had made their home here, but it was the first time she'd sighted even one of them. Was this more evidence of global warming, she wondered? That North West England was now considered a suitable habitat by birds whose true home was the foothills of the Himalayas?

Three minutes passed as, content to let her watch, they chattered and groomed one another's wings. Heather suddenly realised that Jake had disappeared and called him back. He came bounding through the trees, tail wagging furiously. She took a treat from her pocket and bent to greet him.

The pellet struck her hard. The sudden shock and pain caused her to stumble and topple to the ground. Jack began to circle, barking furiously.

The birds rose as one and flew into the sunset, squawking their displeasure as they went.

Chapter 42

'What a place to die!' Carly Whittle observed.

Standing facing the abandoned chapel, surrounded by gravestones, Jo found it hard to disagree. They were alone, it was dark, and a hard rain had begun to fall.

'Where the hell are the CSI?' she said. 'This area hasn't even been taped off.'

'We don't know for certain that he was shot here,' said Carly, in an attempt to be helpful.

'We don't know that he wasn't!' Jo snapped back. She saw the fleeting look of disappointment on her DC's face. 'I'm sorry,' she said. 'I shouldn't be taking it out on you.'

'It's okay, Ma'am.' Carly held up her phone. 'Do you want me to ring Nexus House? Find out where they are?'

Jo wiped a raindrop from the end of her nose and shook her head to displace the rest from the hood of her cagoule.

'Thanks, Carly,' she said. 'I'm going to have a poke around.'

She shone her tactical spotlight torch on the chapel doorway. A sodden bundle of cardboard on the stone steps marked the spot where Anthony Dewlay had spent his last night on this earth. When she lifted it with the toe of her boot a tartan blanket was revealed and what looked like the strap of a bag of some kind. She bent, lifted the blanket aside, and pulled out a backpack of the kind favoured by motorcyclists. It looked relatively new. She crouched, unzipped the neck, and tipped the contents onto the blanket. Beneath a sweatshirt with a Preston North End logo lay a towel and a zip-up polythene bag containing a toothbrush, a battery-operated shaver, a washcloth, a bar of soap, a comb, and a half-squeezed tube of toothpaste. In a second polythene bag were three phones.

'Bingo!' she said, taking one out and switching it on. It took thirty seconds before the screen lit up and invited her to enter a password. 'Bugger!' She'd have to wait for the techies to mine whatever treasures might be hidden inside.

'CSI are en route,' Carly Whittle declared, tucking her phone into a pocket. 'Should be with us shortly. What have you got there, Ma'am?'

She leaned forward, covering them both with her umbrella.

Jo showed her the phone. 'Basic model, password-protected, almost certainly prepaid – essential technology for the modern pharmaceutical entrepreneur.'

'Come again?'

'Drug dealer.' She held up the bag. 'There are two more in here. Odds-on, we'll find scores of text messages from people he's given his number to so they can contact him when they want to score, and he can give them a location where they can collect. If we're lucky, we may be able to identify the number of his supplier, though I doubt it. Even if we do, that one's almost certain to be either prepaid or a single-use and throwaway burner.'

She rooted around among the remainder of the contents of the backpack with a gloved finger. 'Two pairs of thick woollen socks, all dirty. And . . . ugh . . . likewise, three minging pairs of jockey shorts.' She sat back on her heels. 'What I don't get, is what he was doing sleeping rough?'

'If he goes to a homeless hostel he'll either need to be claiming benefits, or have a referral from social services, the council, or an advice centre,' said Carly. 'And if he's known or suspected to be a dealer, there's no way they'd take him.'

'True,' said Jo. 'But he's got seventy-five pounds in his wallet. There are plenty of places offering a bed for the night at thirty pounds or less. Better still, he could do what most itinerant dealers seem to be up to these days and stay rent-free in some desperate drug addict's council flat in exchange for a daily score.'

'Maybe he was hiding from someone. The same someone who killed him?'

Jo pursed her lips. 'Except that, as far as we can tell, neither of the other victims were expecting their killer. Why should he be the exception?'

'You said it, Ma'am,' said Carly. 'As far as we can tell.'

A car horn sounded. They turned to watch the lights of a van as it led a quartet of cars down the semicircular tarmacked path towards them. Jo flashed her light in its direction. It was a Ford Transit with blue and yellow markings, emblazoned with the CRIME SCENE INVESTIGATION logo.

'That's a lot of people,' Whittle said.

'It's a lot of ground,' said Jo. 'Not to mention the woods all the way around the perimeter.'

'There was a time when I fancied myself as a CSI,' said the detective constable. 'It's on days like today that I thank my lucky stars I'm not.'

The lead van came to a halt. The passenger door opened and Jack Benson climbed out. He pulled up his hood and came to join them.

'He certainly picks his places, your killer,' he grumbled. 'Is this where the victim was found?'

Jo pointed to the chapel doorstep. 'Over there. But we think he was shot several days ago, so there's no telling if it happened here or not.'

'Bloody hell!' Benson responded. He turned through 360 degrees. 'It's going to take an army to search all this, and you're saying it could be a waste of time?'

'Not necessarily,' said Jo. 'If this was where he was sleeping on a regular basis it could still be where he was shot. And we believe that's his rucksack. You may get something from that if the perpetrator searched it.'

DS Miller, the Forensics search team manager, joined them, accompanied by a civilian in a high-vis jacket and trousers.

'Have you heard this, Dave?' said Benson. 'The victim was found in that doorway, so we're going to have to search all of this, including the woods, on the off-chance the killer was here.'

'It's not as bad as it looks,' said Miller. 'If he was shot here, with all these trees dotted around the chapel, there's a limit to the number of places from which the killer would have had a clean shot.'

'Is this going to take long?' asked the civilian. 'We've got three interments booked in for tomorrow.'

'And you are?' said Jo.

'Harold Farnworth, Cemeteries Maintenance Supervisor.'

'Well, Mr Farnworth, it'll take as long as it takes. But there's no reason why your burials can't still go ahead. Tell me, were you aware that there was a man sleeping rough in this cemetery?'

'We have had some signs of that over the past week or so,' he replied. 'Bits of cardboard and newspapers.' He pointed to the chapel doorway. 'Like that stuff there. Trouble is, the council's got seven cemeteries and one crematorium. With all the cuts, I haven't got the personnel to send someone out to check every night.'

'There you go, Jack,' said Jo. 'It sounds like our victim has been making a habit of dossing down here. Maybe it won't be such a waste of time after all.'

'Well, there's a limit to what we can do tonight,' he said. 'I suggest . . .'

Jo's phone rang. She held up a hand. 'I'll have to take this.' She turned her back to the wind and rain and checked the screen. It was Nick Carter.

'You're not going to believe this,' he said. 'We've got another one!'

Chapter 43

It was 7.50 p.m. when they finally emerged from the rush-hour crawl around the M60. A firearms officer armed with a Heckler & Koch semi-automatic stood outside the main reception doors of Wythenshawe Hospital. He directed them to the Acute Medical Receiving Unit where Nick Carter was waiting for them.

'The victim was walking her dog in Fletcher Moss Park,' Nick told them. 'Name of Heather Rand. Sixty-four years old. Single. Lives in West Didsbury.'

'Rand?' said Jo. 'Where do I know that name from?'

'She was a Manchester Coroner. Just retired.'

'That Heather Rand,' said Jo. 'I must have been to loads of her inquests.'

'You and me both.'

'What's her condition?'

'Stable. Only because our friend made a mess of this one.'

'A mess? How?'

'His aim was off for once.'

He held up a clear polythene evidence bag containing a small plastic polypot sealed with biohazard tape, in which nestled a bloody, flattened pellet.

'This went through her parka and a woolly sweater and embedded in her upper arm. Unfortunately, she then fell over and dislocated her other shoulder. She's a tough old bird though. She got back to her car and drove herself here.'

'With a dislocated shoulder?'

He grinned. 'I know. Lucky she wasn't pulled over by a traffic car, not that we can afford them anymore.'

'I need to tell them to get onto the Manchester Royal,' she said. 'Have them send over a dose of the ricin antidote Porton Down delivered this morning.'

'Sorted,' he told her. 'As soon as I heard she was here, I rang them and told them about the antidote. It was couriered over straight away. They've already administered it.'

Jo collapsed onto a chair and let out a sigh of relief. 'Thank God for that,' she said. 'We've finally got a live one. How soon can we talk to her?'

'Right now, if you want. They've just moved her into a private room on one of the wards.'

They showed their ID to the uniformed constable sitting on a chair outside the entrance to the ward and headed to the ward front desk.

'How is Heather Rand doing?' Jo asked the ward sister.

'Very well, considering. A&E knew what they were dealing with thanks to the police alert we received earlier in the week. The pellet was removed immediately under local anaesthetic, and the wound was thoroughly flushed out. Then her shoulder was reset. The antidote was administered half an hour ago. Now all we can do is monitor her and wait to see if there are any complications.'

'And pray,' muttered Nick Carter.

'That too. Although I understand that the prognosis with such early treatment, irrespective of the antidote, is generally favourable.'

'Are we able to speak with her?' said Jo. 'It's extremely important that we do.'

'Of course. I gather that she's understandably anxious to talk to the police herself. Just don't tire her out. Follow me, please. And one of you will need to bring a chair from the day room. It's just down there.'

Heather Rand was sitting up in bed with her right arm in a sling. A stand supported two IV bags that fed a catheter inserted in her left forearm. A bank of screens monitored her vital signs. There was colour in her cheeks, and she seemed remarkably calm and collected. She regarded them with bright steely intelligent eyes.

'I know you two from the Coroner's Court,' she said, once introductions had been made.

'Indeed,' said Jo. 'More times than any of us care to remember, I guess.'

Heather pushed with her left hand on the bedclothes in an attempt to lever herself up, wincing with pain as she did so.

'Allow me,' said Jo, hooking an arm under her left armpit, and lifting her gently at the same time as she plumped the pillows up behind her back with the other hand.

'Thank you,' said the former coroner. 'That's much better.' She smiled. 'When I retired I thought that was the end of police officers, medics, and expert witnesses. How wrong was I?'

'The doctor said you're doing really well under the circumstances,' said Jo.

'Some circumstances,' she frowned. 'Ricin. What the hell is that all about?'

'They've told you then?'

'They had to. In order to get my permission to administer the antidote. I thought I'd misheard. I'd assumed they meant mycin – that it was a simple antibiotic. But ricin? As far as I'm aware that's a weapon of choice for political assassins and terrorists.'

'There have been recent incidents of its use in domestic murder attempts,' Nick told her.

'Attempts?' There was a hard edge to her voice. 'Don't you mean actual murders?'

Jo and Nick glanced at each other. Carly Whittle turned her attention to the screen of the tablet on which she was waiting to take notes.

'Come, come,' said Heather. 'Just because I've retired doesn't mean I'm not capable of watching the news and putting two and two together. Two deaths following shooting incidents with air rifles in less than a week. One here in Manchester, one in Southport. All the panic about possible Russian involvement. And now here's me. Bit of a coincidence, don't you think?'

'Keep this to yourself,' said Jo, 'but it's actually three. There was another one earlier today. You're the fourth to have been shot – the only one to have survived.'

'Bloody hell!' The colour drained from the former coroner's cheeks. The pitch of one of the bleeps from the monitor rose and accelerated momentarily, before falling back close to its former levels. 'This is a spree killer?'

'Or a serial killer,' said Nick. 'Depending on how you read the intervals between each attack.'

'Whatever,' said Heather. 'He's clearly on a rampage of some kind.'

'We don't think so,' said Jo. 'Rampage and spree imply someone frenzied and out of control. These attacks involve careful planning and preparation. There is method behind them.'

Heather sank back into the pillows. 'Method in the madness,' she said.

'If you like.'

Heather raised her left hand, trailing wires across the bed, as she tucked it under her right elbow to provide extra support. 'But why me, for God's sake?' she asked.

'That's what we need to find out,' said Jo. 'I need to ask you some questions. Not all will make sense but I'd like you to bear with me. Is that okay?'

Chapter 44

'Fire away.' Heather Rand grinned ruefully. 'Whoops – that was a Freudian slip.'

'At least you can joke about it,' said Nick. 'That's a good sign.'

Jo gave him a dirty look. He just shrugged.

'I'm going to throw some names at you, Miss Rand,' she said. 'Then ask you some questions about your movements today, and finally explore the possibility that some person or persons may have a grudge against you. Detective Constable Whittle will be taking notes. Is that alright?'

'That's fine,' the former coroner replied. 'And, please, call me Heather.'

'Very well, Heather. Let's start with those names. I'll run them past you. You tell me if any of them mean anything to you. Let's start with Ronald O'Neill, also known as Ron or Ronnie O'Neill?'

She thought about it, then shook her head. 'No, sorry. That doesn't ring any bells.'

'In his fifties. Short, stocky, muscular, shaven-headed?'

'Still no, I'm afraid. Sounds like a bit of a bruiser.'

'How about Morris Arthur Grimshaw? In his twenties. Scouse accent. Thin, with a pinched face, sharp nose, small eyes, and protruding teeth?'

Her eyes moved to her left, and then up towards the ceiling. She shook her head. 'The name doesn't mean anything to me, although I've seen a fair few young men like him in the public gallery over the years. Usually when one of their mates has come to a violent and untimely end.'

'And finally,' said Jo, 'Anthony, also known as Tony, Dewlay. That's D, E, W, L, A, Y. In his late forties and a homeless rough sleeper. Before then he worked in insurance in Preston.'

Once again, Heather shook her head. 'No. I've never heard of him either, I'm afraid.' Her eyes widened. 'Hang on. These are the other victims, aren't they? Three more, you said.'

'I'm sorry,' said Jo. 'I can't confirm or deny that.'

'Don't worry,' Heather replied, 'you don't have to. I can check that out online on my phone, or as soon as my neighbour brings me my tablet in the morning.'

'About today, Heather,' said Jo. 'I understand you were walking your dog in the park?'

Alarm flooded the patient's face. She attempted to sit up and winced with pain. 'Oh my God!' she said. 'Jack! How could I forget Jack?'

'It's alright, Miss Rand,' said Nick. 'Jack's fine. Our first responder called one of our dog units. One of the dog handlers has taken him home with him.'

She sank back into the pillow. 'Poor Jack,' she said. 'He must be worrying as to what's going on. He's a real fretter.'

'By the time you get out of here,' said Nick, 'you'll probably find he's been taught a few more tricks.'

'How often do you take him to Fletcher Moss?' Jo asked.

'Twice a day, early morning and early evening. At weekends, we go later in the morning. It's funny really, but although I've retired, I seem to be sticking to the old routines. Weekends are every bit as special even though I no longer work.'

'Do you always follow the same route?'

'Invariably. There are two ways round, but I always end up going through Stenner Woods.'

Jo nodded. 'That's where the incident occurred?'

'Where I was shot? Yes.' She shook her head. 'If I hadn't stopped to admire those parakeets . . .'

'Tell me about your movements prior to arriving at the park, Heather,' said Jo.

'You think whoever attacked me may have been following me?'

'I have no idea, but it is something we have to check out.'

'Of course. Well, I left home at seven this morning.'

'Where is home?'

'On Fog Lane in West Didsbury, about half a mile away from the park.'

'Were you in the car, or on foot?'

'On foot.' Heather paused. 'We did our usual tour of the park. Got back about ten to eight. I had some cereal, then drove to Northenden to pick up my granddaughter, Poppy. I dropped her off at her school on Beaver Road and then, as I was driving back home, my daughter texted to say she'd forgotten a poster display she needed urgently, so I had to go back to Northenden to pick up the poster and take it to the university.'

'Which university,' asked Jo, 'and which building?'

'Manchester University, the Department of Chemistry. Rose was waiting for me outside the entrance on Brunswick Street.'

'Chemistry?' said Nick.

'That's right. She's a senior lecturer in biochemistry.'

'After you'd dropped off the poster?' said Jo. 'What then?'

'I drove to the Tesco Superstore on Parrs Wood Lane – realised I'd left my list on the fridge door. Drove back home, collected the list, then back to Tesco's. I did a major shop. Went home. Unpacked everything. Had a bowl of soup and a coffee. Prepared a casserole for Poppy and Rose. And then set off to pick up Poppy from school. I took her back to her house. Popped the casserole in the oven, and kept her occupied until her mum came home. I got back home at about 6 p.m. Jack was desperate for a pee, so I took him straight to the park.' She smiled. 'Don't worry, I had my pooper scoop bags with me. Then we wandered down through the rock gardens, round the pool, through the rose garden, and across the fields to the Mersey. Then we followed it round and headed into the woods – that's when I was shot.'

'Did you get a sense that anyone may have been following you at any time during today?'

'No.'

'Did you see anyone behaving suspiciously in the park?'

She shook her head. 'Not unless you include the young man with a Staffordshire terrier who allowed his dog to defecate against the rose arbour, pretended to pick up the resultant mess, and then scurried off?'

'Did you observe anyone carrying a large bag?' said Nick. 'A kitbag, for example, or something that might hold golf clubs or fishing tackle?'

'Long, rather than wide,' Jo added.

Heather thought about it, then shook her head. 'Sorry. Nothing like that. It was mainly dog walkers, a few couples, people walking alone, and a small group of joggers.'

'Joggers?'

'Male and female, mixed ages. They were all wearing the same tops – yellow and blue, like they were members of a club.' She was beginning to look tired. Every now and then she grimaced at the pain in her shoulder as she tried to make herself more comfortable.

'Would you like me to call a nurse?' said Jo.

'No,' Heather replied. 'It's okay. Let's just get it over with, shall we?'

'Very well,' said Jo. 'Now I need you to think about anyone who might harbour a grudge against you, however remote you think it may be.'

'I've been lying here trying to do exactly that,' she replied. 'It's surprising when you put your mind to it how many people in your life you realise that you've pissed off one way and another. Take my sister and me. We always had a pretty robust sibling rivalry right from the outset, and when our parents died it got worse rather than better, but she lives in California now with her third husband. Not that she'd have the imagination to try to kill me like this – a knife in the back's more her style.'

She registered the expression on their faces and smiled. 'Only joking,' she said. 'Well, half joking. There are one or two colleagues I've rubbed up the wrong way over the years, including one who was eventually fired for sexually harassing me. Don't get excited though. He committed suicide a few years back. Nothing to do with me. Well, not directly. His wife walked out on him when his peccadilloes brought him to the attention of the police. He took the coward's way out. Jumped off Barton Bridge with a couple of dumb-bells tied around his neck.'

Nick Carter shuddered. 'I couldn't do that,' he said. 'Too much time to regret it on the way down.'

Jo nudged him with her elbow. 'What about inquests that you've been involved in, Heather?' she said. 'There must have been some where relatives or people who were subsequently charged with homicide were deeply unhappy with the outcome of the inquest? I can remember several where people displayed almost uncontrollable anger.'

'Me too,' said Nick.

'There were,' said Heather Rand. 'Of course there were. When you've lost a loved one, especially in tragic and avoidable circumstances, and it turns out that nobody was really responsible – at least not in law – or that there is simply insufficient evidence to reach a verdict, that must be unbearably painful. So yes, I've had threats made against me in court. Malicious and threatening emails and letters. The occasional disgusting package sent in the mail. Several resulted in injunctions having to be taken out against the perpetrator by the Office of the Chief Coroner. I'm afraid I can't give you chapter and verse on them all, but they were all logged and stored, so you shouldn't have any trouble accessing them.'

'Do any of them, say within the past six years, stand out as particularly bitter and unresolved?' Jo asked. 'Especially ones that happened six or seven years ago?'

The former coroner sighed. 'There is one that would fit those parameters,' she said, 'but I hope I'm wrong.'

'Go on.'

'It was the spring of 2011. A woman was killed outside her children's primary school by a hit-and-run pensioner. The distraught driver handed himself into the police the same afternoon. Following evidence from other mothers, the lollipop lady, and the police, the verdict the jury arrived at was accidental death. The husband was serving in Helmand at the time and was flown back on compassionate leave. He took it really badly and had to be restrained in court. He yelled threats at me and at some of the witnesses outside. He made an official complaint that came to nothing. I heard that he subsequently had a breakdown. He was discharged from the army on medical grounds. I think his children were being looked after by his wife's parents.'

'When was the last time you heard from him?' said Jo.

'I haven't, not directly. The injunction put paid to that. But I was shown a newspaper piece a couple of years back. One of those bleeding hearts articles in which he was interviewed about this terrible miscarriage of justice and how it had affected him. Teesdale, I think his name was – Aaron Teesdale.'

'A couple of years back,' said Nick. 'So why do you still think it might be him?'

Heather Rand's expression softened, and her voice was tinged with remorse. 'Because I think he was right. At the very least the finding should have been causing death by careless driving.'

'How so?' said Jo.

'It hinged around whether or not the pensioner was driving when knowingly suffering from a physical condition that significantly and dangerously impaired his driving.' She slid her left hand up her arm and began to massage her shoulder. 'It all came down to that word, *knowingly.*' She slowly shook her head. 'I made the fateful decision to call a jury. Not out of cowardice, you understand, but because this had a high profile in the press and had developed into a public interest case. I'm afraid that despite my attempt to direct the jury, they found in the driver's favour.'

'Why do you think that was?' asked Nick.

'I can't be sure,' she said. 'But there is a tendency for juries, not just in the Coroner's Court but in Crown Court too, to be less willing to convict in cases of manslaughter by negligence if they believe that the likely sentence arising from a guilty finding would be disproportionate.'

'But this wasn't a criminal court?' said Jo.

'No, but they probably feared that a verdict of causing death by careless driving would lead to the police and the CPS reviewing their position and taking him through the criminal courts.' Heather sighed. 'In my experience, in those cases where the family is left feeling an immense sense of injustice, the pain and the bitterness never go away – if anything, they deepen.' All of her earlier positivity had faded. She looked pale and exhausted. 'Now, if you don't mind,' she said, 'I'd like to rest.'

'Aaron Teesdale. He has to be favourite?' said Nick Carter. 'I wonder what he did in Helmand. Perhaps he was a sniper?'

'Let's not get ahead of ourselves,' said Jo. 'There's no connection between his grievance and any of the other victims.'

Nick shrugged. 'Perhaps he's turned into a vigilante? Avenging injustices right, left, and centre?'

'There's only one way to find out,' she said. 'We're all going to head off back to Nexus House. Once we know where Heather Rand was standing when she was shot, Jack Benson's team can have a look at Stenner Woods. But if the last three crime scenes are anything to go by, we're not going to learn anything new from Forensics. Best we concentrate on witness sightings and vehicle licence plates around the time of the shooting. Can you progress that, Nick?'

'What are you going to do, Ma'am?' he asked.

'A quick background check and a risk assessment on Teesdale. See if I can get a magistrate to issue a search warrant, and then pay him a visit.'

'What about me, Ma'am?' asked Carly Whittle.

'I'd like you to print off your notes and get them into the system. Then I want you to contact the Coroner's office and arrange to go through that harassment list she mentioned, and any complaints made against her. You can contact them tonight, but I doubt you'll be able to get them started before the morning.' She unlocked her car. 'The other thing you can both do is warn me if you see ACC Gates entering the building. You'll know it's her by the steam coming out of her ears.'

Chapter 45

'Do we have to do this here?' Aaron Teesdale held the door to the office open in the vain hope that she would say no.

'Yes, I'm afraid we do,' Jo replied. 'For the time being.'

'What does that mean?'

'That it depends on the answers you give to my questions. If I'm not satisfied with them, then I'll have to arrest you and ask you to accompany me to a police station for a formal interview.'

He closed the door, walked over to the desk, and sat down. 'You'd better get on with it then,' he said.

Jo had brought DC Hulme with her to take notes, having first warned him not to say anything unless it was through her. The last thing she needed was his brand of irony. While Hulme prepared himself, she scrutinised the ex-soldier, now assistant manager of a food store. He was shorter than her, much more so than she'd expected for a former Royal Marines Commando sergeant. But he still had the buzz-cut hair, upright posture, and cool wariness in his pale-blue eyes. If his taut, muscular figure was anything to go by, he still kept himself fit.

'So,' he said. 'What's this all about?'

Best to hit him with it straight away, Jo decided, and see what she could gauge from his reaction.

'Do you recall the name of the coroner at the inquest into the death of your wife?'

Teesdale's face clouded over, and he folded his arms across his chest. 'So that's it,' he said. 'I've spent seven years of my life grieving, then trying to move on. And now, just when I thought I'd put it behind me as much as I'll ever be able to, you two come crawling out of the woodwork.'

'I'm truly sorry for your loss, Mr Teesdale,' said Jo, 'but I do need you to answer the question.'

His left leg began to pump up and down. 'You tell me why you need me to answer, and I'll decide if I'm going to.'

'Very well,' said Jo. 'The person to whom I refer has been the victim of an assault.'

He looked incredulous. 'And you think I was responsible?'

'I'm sure you understand that I have no choice other than to investigate that possibility? So please, answer the question?'

'Of course I remember her name – Rand, Heather Rand.' He shook his head in disbelief. 'She was about as much use as a chocolate teapot.'

'Meaning?'

'Meaning that she knew full well that it wasn't simply an accident. That stupid, selfish old git got behind the wheel knowing he wasn't fit to drive. He lied on the self-disclosure form he had to fill in for the Driver and Vehicle Licensing Agency, he lied to his insurance company, he lied to the police, and he lied in the Coroner's Court. Rand as good as admitted that when she summed up for the jury.'

'Then you can hardly blame her for their decision?'

'Why not? She should have made it plainer. She should have directed the jury to deliver a verdict of manslaughter.' He thumped the desk with his hand, causing the monitor to sway perilously. 'Slaughter's the right word. My wife wasn't the victim of an accident – she was mown down in cold blood. She was murdered. Simple as.'

If he's like this now, what must he have been like seven years ago? Jo wondered.

'I understand you were in Helmand province at the time,' she said. 'In Afghanistan?'

He nodded. 'Sangin.'

'That must have been hard?'

'Hell on earth.'

Jo had meant his receiving the news about his wife's death while he was away on active service. But he had misunderstood and was already replaying the nightmare in his head.

'Operation Herrick. Our last tour. We were supposed to be handing over to the Yanks. Should have been a simple holding operation but the Taliban had other ideas. They sent their best men to take us on. They blended in with the locals, so you could never be sure who you were dealing with till it was too late. Never mind the Charge of the Light Brigade, every single time we went on patrol it was like walking into the valley of death. Bombs to the right of you, semi-automatics to the left of you, snipers all around.'

DC Hulme had stopped making notes and was listening intently. The veteran caught his eye and spoke directly at him.

'I suppose you think IEDs were just something they put by the side of the roads to blow up our vehicles? Well, they weren't. They were everywhere. There were tripwires. IEDs at the base of walls that they triggered with a radio command or a simple phone call. It got so the only way we could patrol an area was down the drainage ditches. When we did, the cunning bastards set up ambushes.'

Teesdale switched his attention to Jo. 'Do you know how many men we lost on that tour?'

Jo shook her head.

'Fourteen. Out of six hundred and seventy men. Plus another forty-nine wounded. Not to mention the ones whose wounds didn't count.'

'Post-traumatic stress disorder?' said Jo.

The fingers of his right hand drummed a tattoo on the top of the desk. 'The thing about PTSD,' he said, 'is that you never know when it's going to hit you or what's going to trigger it. With me it was Mel's death that brought it on. After the funeral, the slightest sound of a car braking, a door slamming, I'd break out in a cold sweat, my heart would start pounding, I'd be in a blind panic, looking for escape routes. I couldn't go within a mile of my kids' school – had to get one of the other mums who lives nearby to drop them off and pick them up. I couldn't fall asleep at night. When I did, I'd be back in Sangin trying to put a field dressing on a bloody stump while bullets flew all around.'

He looked up, his eyes appealing for understanding. 'I couldn't even hold a conversation with the kids. They took them off me.'

'They?' said Jo.

'Social Services. Handed them over to Mel's mum and dad. Had to. I had a complete breakdown. I was in hospital for over three months.'

'Where are they now?'

'Still with their grandparents. I have regular access – see them three or four times a week – but they're better off with them.'

'And how are you now, Aaron?' she asked. She could tell from his expression that he wasn't fooled by the use of his given name.

He scowled. 'Managing, till you came along. I'm on a daily dose of Paroxetine. Plus talking therapy when I feel I need it. Which after today is likely to be tomorrow.'

'Just a few more questions then we'll leave you in peace.'

He laughed, as though he thought that highly unlikely. 'Go on then.'

'Where were you, Aaron, between 6 p.m. and 7 p.m. yesterday evening?'

His brow furrowed. 'That's easy. I was right here. Didn't get away till gone ten.'

'You won't mind if I check with your boss?'

'Be my guest. You can check with the time and motion guy too.'

'Time and motion?'

He pointed to the small glass dome on the ceiling. 'The CCTV. It's everywhere. I wouldn't be surprised if there's one hidden in the loos.'

'If I were to give you a series of dates and times,' she said, 'do you think you could tell me where you were on those dates too?'

He smiled thinly. 'No problem.'

Jo nodded to Jimmy Hulme, who handed Teesdale a sheet of paper. He studied it. 'I can tell you now, I was working on every one of these dates,' he said. 'It's all I do these days.'

'If you could just double-check, complete the form, sign it, and let me have it back before we leave,' she said.

'Will do.'

'Do you own or rent a garage or a lock-up?' she asked.

'Only the one attached to the house.'

'And would you have any objection if we were to search your house, Aaron?'

He sat up. 'You don't have probable cause,' he said. 'And I'm guessing you don't have a search warrant?'

'What are you all of a sudden?' said Jimmy Hulme. 'A barrack-room lawyer?'

Both Jo and Teesdale gave him a dirty look.

'You're right,' said Jo quickly, 'we don't, but if you've nothing to hide a voluntary search would help eliminate you.'

The veteran stood up. 'I finish at ten,' he said. 'I'll be home by quarter past. Meet me there and I'll show you round. He arched an eyebrow. 'I take it you know the address, what with you being detectives?'

Chapter 46

'What do you think, Ma'am?' said Jimmy Hulme, as they climbed into the Audi.

'I think you should think about what "don't say anything unless it's through me" means.'

'Sorry, Ma'am.' He managed a half-decent impression of sheepish.

'You will be if you do it again.' Jo fastened her seat belt. 'You've been watching too many TV detective series. This isn't *Life on Mars*.'

She switched on her phone and checked for messages. There was one from Nick Carter saying he had an appointment with the Coroner's clerk at 8.45 in the morning. One from Helen Gates wanting an update. And two identical ones from Max Nailor: *Call me*.

He answered on the second ring. 'Jo. I've been trying to reach you.'

'I know. I've been interviewing a suspect.'

'Any luck?'

'Too soon to tell. I take it you've no news of Melissa or you'd have told me straight away?'

There was a short pause. 'Have you activated your jammer?'

'It comes on automatically,' she told him, 'whenever the phone is active and hands-free.'

'In which case, I'm afraid the answer is no. We know that the van was stolen the day before yesterday from a builder's yard in Trafford. We even have images of the thieves who took it on the firm's CCTV. Two teenagers – one we think is female. But they both wore hoods and the picture quality is terrible.'

'How did they get to the yard?'

'By car. They were dropped off in the neighbouring street. And guess what?'

'The car was stolen?'

'And fitted with cloned plates. So now we're trying to track that, and wade through thousands of hours of CCTV from the Wythenshawe estate – but it's unlikely that's where she's being held. The odds are there was a switch to another vehicle, or she was taken somewhere else, and the van driven to the spare ground where it was torched by one of their mules.'

'Still no communication between the people who are holding her and the Walshes?'

'No. Nothing.'

'That's not good.'

'No.'

There was a long pause.

'That's why I rang you,' he said. 'Do you think you could have another go at Jason O'Neill? He's still our favourite suspect.'

'I'm assuming the Anti-Kidnap and Extortion Unit have facilitated elite surveillance?'

'Of course. But it took all day. Both ISDN secure machines failed twice, so the request had to be couriered down to the surveillance commissioners for approval. It's only been in place since midday.'

'And?'

'And nothing. If anything, he appears to be using his best efforts to find her. One minute he's checking with his minions to see if they've heard anything, the next they're calling or texting him to say they haven't.'

'Any mention of Steven Yates?'

'Not once. And that's the strange thing. It's almost as though locating his right-hand man is the last thing he wants to do.'

'It sounds as though O'Neill suspects you're listening in?'

'In his shoes, wouldn't you?'

Jo checked the time on the console. 'I've got exactly an hour before I need to be somewhere else,' she said. 'That gives me just enough time to get to O'Neill's and back, with a brief conversation in between. That's the best I can do, unless you're prepared to have me knock him up at midnight or wait till the morning?'

'Now would be good.'

'I'm on it,' she replied.

'Elite surveillance?' DC Hulme asked as they set off.

'What it says on the tin. The best of the best.'

'Listening devices. Computer intercepts? That sort of thing?'

'Much better than that.'

'I tried to get on the College of Policing communications data seminar,' he said, 'but there was a massive waiting list.'

'Which one?'

'The Evolving World of Communications Data. Challenges for Investigative Teams.'

'Good for you,' she said. 'But even if you'd been front of the queue you'd have been out of luck.'

'Why's that, Ma'am?'

'It's only for senior investigating officers and above.'

She glanced across at him. He looked genuinely disappointed, not at all like the office joker he pretended to be.

'Don't worry,' she said. 'That course wouldn't have covered what I'm about to tell you, so consider yourself privileged.'

He angled his body towards her. 'I'm all ears, Ma'am.'

Jo grinned. 'How very appropriate.'

'How's that?'

'You've heard of the Smurfs?'

He nodded. 'Little blue Belgian cartoon gnomes. I watched the film with my niece and nephew. Please don't tell the others, Ma'am. I'll never hear the last of it.'

'Our secret,' she said, 'providing you continue to do my bidding.'

'Blackmail's a criminal offence,' he said.

'Extortion, Detective Constable, extortion. But only if you can prove it. Now, where was I?'

'Smurfs.'

'Among the Government Communication Headquarters' numerous techniques is a special set of programs known as the Smurfs. In essence, they're secret intercept tools. Three of them are fairly common knowledge, ever since the Edward Snowden leaks revealed GCHQ had been sharing smurfed information with the US National Security Agency.'

She paused as she braked at the third set of lights on Princess Avenue and waited until they'd come to a stop. 'There's Dreamy Smurf, Nosey Smurf, and Tracker Smurf.'

'You're having me on, Ma'am.'

'I wish,' she said. 'Dreamy Smurf remotely turns on phones that are off. Nosey turns on the phone's microphone. Wherever the phone is, they'll be able to listen in to everything that's going on.'

'And Tracker Smurf?'

'Does exactly what it says.'

'Geolocates the phone?'

The lights changed to green and Jo set off. 'Even more accurately than the normal triangulation from cell-phone towers.'

'Blimey,' said Hulme. 'Next you'll be telling me it'll take photos on demand.'

'Correct. Once GCHQ has sent the exploit SMS and gained control of your phone, they can access your contacts list, see your call and text record, and where you've been. The lot.'

'And that's what they've been doing with O'Neill's phone?'

'Probably. But only after the surveillance commissioners had given their approval. And the same with any other phone he uses that they know about.' She shrugged. 'But then who's to say he hasn't got one they don't know about?'

'They will if they're listening in.'

'Only if he's got a smurfed phone nearby when he calls on a burner. From what SI Nailor told me, either O'Neill is wise to all this, or he had nothing to do with Melissa's abduction.'

She checked her rear mirror and glanced across at him. 'Now do us both a favour and give it a rest. I need to think about how to tackle this. Melissa's life may depend on our not messing it up.'

Chapter 47

'That's odd,' said Jo.

'What is?' asked Jimmy Hulme.

'No watchers and no Armed Response. It looks as though DCI Fox has decided to throw him to the wolves.'

The avenue was deserted, unlike the last time she'd been here. The dark-blue Jag was still in the drive. The house was in darkness.

'What about the van parked up on the left just before we turned into this street?' said Hulme.

'Well spotted.' Jo unfastened her seat belt. 'That'll be one of the AKEU surveillance backups. Can't just rely on the Smurfs.'

As they crunched their way to the front door unchallenged, the driveway was flooded with light and a front curtain twitched in the right-hand bay window. DC Hulme rang the bell. A light came on in the hall. A shadow approached, growing in size until it filled the glass panels and the door opened.

'I might've guessed!' Jason O'Neill growled. He turned his back on them and walked towards the light. 'Close the door after you.'

They followed him into the kitchen. There was a darts match on the television. The volume had been muted. A cell phone, and a landline handset lay side by side on the central unit. The only sounds were the ticking of a wall-mounted clock, and a spluttering coffee machine.

O'Neill switched off the machine, topped a mug up with coffee and milk, and turned to face them. 'I thought you'd given up on me.'

'Not while Melissa Walsh is still missing,' said Jo.

He shook his head. 'I'm sick of telling your lot. That was nothing to do with me.'

'Maybe not. At least, not directly.'

He arched an eyebrow. 'What's that supposed to mean?'

'Where's Steve Yates, Jason?' she asked.

He shrugged. 'Search me.' He blew across the surface of the coffee and took a sip. 'I've been trying to locate him myself. He took it bad when Dad was murdered. You never know how grief's gonna affect someone, do you?'

'How has it affected you, Jason?'

His fingers gripped the mug more tightly. His eyes betrayed a flash of irritation. 'I'll let you know,' he said.

'The thing is,' said Jo, 'there's been another incident.'

'Incident?' He looked surprised, and wary. 'What kind of incident?'

'Someone else has been shot. Just like your dad and the other two victims. Only this person, as far as we can tell, had no connection with your father whatsoever. Nor for that matter did the previous victim.'

'Is he dead?'

'She. And no, she isn't dead, and she is expected to recover completely.'

He placed the mug down on the central island and thrust his hands into the pockets of his jeans. 'Lucky for some. Who is she?'

'I can't tell you that.'

He scowled. 'You give me her name and I'll tell you if she had anything to do with us.'

Jo felt DC Hulme staring at her. She knew he was thinking what she was thinking: the three of them were not alone. There were others listening. Recording every word. She weighed it up. Heather wasn't dead, nor was she likely to die. There were no relatives to inform. Plenty of people knew about the attack. It wouldn't be long before the press would be all over it. There was just one problem. If the perpetrator discovered that she was likely to recover, might he try again? But he was going to find out anyway, once she was released from hospital.

'You'll find out soon enough,' she said, for the sake of the listeners. 'But I want you to promise not to share this information until it's public knowledge, otherwise you could be putting her at further risk.'

Jason smiled broadly, but his eyes remained cold. 'You can trust me, officer,' he said. 'I always keep my word.'

'Heather Rand,' Jo said. 'She's a retired Manchester Coroner.'

'Rand?' He chewed the name over, then shook his head. 'Can't say I've ever heard of her. Mind you, Dad might have done. There'll have been a fair few inquests over the years he'd have had an interest in.'

The silence was shattered by a loud and insistent ringtone. O'Neill took a cell phone from his back pocket, shook his head, and looked around the room. Jimmy Hulme pointed to a chunky black and silver phone resting beside a large air fryer.

O'Neill crossed the room and picked it up. ''Ello?' He listened for a moment and then turned to look at the two detectives. 'Hang on,' he said, 'I'm putting this on speaker.' He touched the screen and held up the phone. 'It's Burke,' he said. 'Go on, Nathan, tell 'em what you just told me.'

'We've been all over Wythenshawe, Sharston, and Newall Green,' said the voice. 'No one's seen owt or heard owt. I've got people sniffing around on the Sharston and Roundthorn Industrial Estates. I swear down, I've never seen so many bizzies on the streets. We're tripping over them everywhere we go. I tell you what, if she's here, they've got her well hidden.'

'What about Steve Yates, Nathan?' said Jo. 'Have you heard from him?'

The phone went silent. O'Neill gave her a dirty look. 'Go on, Nathan, tell her,' he said.

'Nothin' to tell, Jace. It's like you said. Looks like he's gone to ground. Knowin' Steve, he'll be in touch when he's good an' ready.'

'Cheers, Nathan,' said O'Neill. 'Keep me posted.'

'Will do, Boss.'

O'Neill ended the call and put the phone down. 'Satisfied?'

'How's your mum?' said Jo.

'How d'you think?' He walked back round the island and picked up his mug. 'Been skriking her head off non-stop since Dad died. The doctor gave her some sedatives. They knocked her out, thank God.'

'I'm sorry for your loss, Jason,' she said. 'I'd hate to think of Mrs Walsh going through what you and your mum are going through, only worse. If that's possible?'

He lifted the mug, took a sip, pulled a face, and threw the contents in the sink.

'Time you left,' he said.

Jo knew they were wasting their time, but at least she'd tried. 'Come on, Jimmy,' she said.

They were halfway down the hall when O'Neill called after them.

'You talked about me not putting that woman at risk. What about me and my mum? Why's our protection been pulled?'

Jo turned to face him. 'They're probably out there looking for Melissa Walsh. Along with the rest of the officers your men keep bumping into. I'm sure that once she's back home, safe and sound, DCI Fox will consider redeploying them.'

'And pigs'll fly!' he said.

The floodlights came on as they stepped onto the drive.

'Do you think he set that up for us? The phone call?' said Jimmy Hulme as he paused by the passenger door.

'He didn't know we were coming,' she reminded him.

'Maybe one of his cronies – the one who was watching us from the bay window – sent Burke a quick text to call in – make it look legit?'

'I'm impressed,' said Jo. 'There's more to you than meets the eye.'

She could have sworn the harsh light had caught him blushing.

'Thanks, Ma'am,' he said.

'I hadn't finished,' she said and got in the car.

He joined her and began to buckle his seat belt. 'Sorry, Ma'am,' he said. 'What were you going to say?'

'Thank God, DC Hulme.' She grinned. 'Thank God there's more to you than meets the eye.'

It took him a moment or two to work that one out, by which time she was reversing out of the drive.

'By the way, Ma'am,' he said, 'I've been thinking. What with our theory about the unsub being a revenge killer?'

'Go on.'

'Well, I've just recalled that one of the names for the castor oil plant, on account of the shape of the leaves, is *Palma Christi.*'

'The significance being?'

'The Hand of Christ,' he said. 'That'd make a great moniker for a psycho, don't you think?'

She glanced across at him. He was gazing through the side window, looking really chuffed with himself. *Jimmy Hulme,* she reflected, *you never fail to surprise me.*

Chapter 48

Close to midnight, Jo switched on the light, slumped down on the sofa, and contemplated the jumble of crates.

They summed up where she was in her life right now. In limbo. Not really here, and not yet there. Wherever there was? That was true not just of a physical space that she could truly call home, but also the state of her love life, and her work. Abbie would continue to haunt her emotional life until Jo was gone from here and settled into the apartment at The Quays. And, in all likelihood, not even then until she'd made it hers, and Abbie's baby had been born. As for her nascent relationship with Agata, it was far too soon to tell where that was heading.

A sudden pang of guilt made her put the pizza box she was carrying down on the nearest crate, and fish her phone from her bag. She switched on and scrolled through the texts. There were two from Abbie, both of which she deleted unread. There were four from Agata, each one increasingly anxious. Jo checked the time. It was far too late to call, but the least she could do was text her back. Her thumbs skimmed across the screen.

Aggie . . . I'm SO sorry!!! It's been a hell of day. I've driven four hundred mules, been to two crime scenes – one was another murder – interviewed one victim and loads of witnesses. Just got in after fruitless search of home of suspect. AND to top it all, that young girl still missing! Had to keep phone on mute, haven't even had time to read messages. I know it's no excuse, but I hope you'll forgive me. Will call in the morning, I promise. Love you. Jo XXX.

She pressed send, and picked up a slice of pizza. It was still in mid-air when the phone rang. It was Agata.

'Jo, thank God you're alright. You are alright, aren't you?'

'I'm fine,' said Jo. 'Just tired and hungry.'

'Don't tell me you've been too busy to eat? You've got to eat and drink, keep your strength up – even more so when you're under stress.'

Jo smiled to herself. Agata was beginning to sound like her mum. The real one. The one who had adopted and raised her.

'Thanks, Aggie,' she replied, 'but I picked up a pizza on Stevenson Square. I was about to eat it when you rang.'

'Don't let me stop you, Jo. It'll get cold. You eat, I'll do all the talking.'

Jo laughed. 'I'm going to take you up on that. I'll put you on speaker. Don't worry, there's no one else here, just me and a load of crates.'

'Oh, Jo. That's so sad. Never mind, you'll soon be over here, on The Quays—' There followed a nervous pause as Agata weighed the impact of her next few words. When they came, it was in a rush, on the outbreath. '—with me.'

'Can't wait,' spluttered Jo through a mouthful of tomato, spinach, goats cheese, and basil.

'It sounds like you've had an awful day,' said Agata. 'Bad enough there were two more victims but having to cope with all those mules as well.'

'Mules?' said Jo. 'What mules?'

Agata laughed. 'Check your text. The four hundred you drove?'

Jo smiled, wiped her mouth with the back of her hand, and licked off a smear of goats' cheese. 'I was in too much of a hurry to check. I felt guilty because I hadn't got back to you.' She picked up another slice.

'Never mind about that,' said Agata. 'I wanted to tell you that I'm heading back north to Manchester.'

Jo's spirits lifted. 'When?'

'In the morning.'

'You finished the story you were working on?'

'No, not exactly. It's on hold at the moment. It's complicated. I'll explain when I see you. What I wanted to tell you is that I've been asked to cover the story of the missing girl. Melissa Walsh?'

Jo's heart sank. She had no idea how to respond.

'Jo?' said Agata. 'Are you still there?'

'Uh huh,' Jo managed.

Agata picked up on the change in vibe. 'Look,' she said. 'I realise this could be tricky, but I'm sure we can work around it. We did with your last investigation, didn't we, even though we were not in a relationship at that time? After all, it's not as though you're leading the investigation?'

Jo's mouth had dried up. The piece of pizza she'd been chewing was stuck to the roof of her mouth. She poked at it with her tongue and tried swallowing.

Agata ploughed on. 'I'll pursue my own sources, I promise not to ask you for any information, and I won't use anything you tell me that you don't want me to.' There was still no response. 'Of course, if you think there's a conflict of interest, I'll just tell them no. That's one of the advantages of being freelance.'

Jo swallowed again, this time successfully. 'You don't need to do that,' she responded. 'Like you said, I'm sure we'll be able to work it out.'

'That's brilliant,' said Agata, as though it was already a done deal. 'Look, Jo, I'll let you finish your pizza and get a good night's sleep. I'll ring tomorrow when I'm back on The Quays. I'll help you shift your stuff and fix you dinner at mine. Then I'll know you're getting some decent food down you. We can catch up properly over a bottle of wine.'

She sounded so young and enthusiastic that it made Jo feel even more exhausted. Old, even.

'Let's see how tomorrow pans out first,' she said, immediately regretting her lack of positivity. 'I can't wait to see you, Aggie,' she added. 'I really missed you.'

'Me too.' There was an awkward pause. 'Good luck with the investigation. And remember, Jo, you've got to start taking care of yourself.'

'I will.'

'Tomorrow then?'

'Tomorrow.'

'Love you.'

'Love you too.'

Jo switched off her phone. Suddenly, the three remaining slices of pizza had lost their appeal. She closed the box, picked it up, and went through to the kitchen. She wrapped the leftovers in foil and placed them in the fridge. Then she poured herself a glass of milk, took it into the bedroom, and undressed.

She turned on the shower, closed her eyes, and imagined herself under a waterfall in a tropical rainforest as the cascade of water swept away eighteen hours of sweat, stress, and frustration.

Agata threw her phone on the bed and lay down beside it. She was beginning to regret not having been totally honest. She told herself she was simply being sensitive to the pressure Jo must be under right now. But deep down, she knew that she'd really been worried about herself. About how Jo might react if she knew the truth. About how that might damage their fragile, embryonic relationship.

What would it have cost for her, she wondered, to have admitted that she was not in fact freelance at this moment? That she'd taken on a lucrative six-month contract, and that when the small print had been pointed out to her, after she'd signed up, it turned out to be far more flexible from her employer's point of view than she had anticipated.

'Ah, Agata,' the commissioning editor had crooned. 'How are you getting on with the honour killing story?'

'It's early days,' she'd replied, 'but I've made some useful contacts and I have some very promising leads.'

'Good, good.' He had turned and looked out from his twenty-first-floor eyrie on Canary Wharf, across the Thames towards Greenwich. 'Only we'd like you to put that on hold for the moment.' He had swivelled to face her. 'We'd like you to pop back up north and see what you can dig out on these serial ricin attacks.'

Agata remembered blushing at the time, just as she was doing now. 'I'm afraid that won't be possible,' she'd said.

'Why not?' he'd demanded. There had been something about his expression that told her he already knew the answer.

'Because there's a conflict of interest,' she'd told him. 'I'm in a relationship with the Senior Investigating Officer.'

His smile was lizard-like. Fixed and contemptuous.

'Which is, of course, precisely why we chose you, Ms Kowalski.'

'I'm sorry,' she'd replied. 'I can't do it. It's a question of ethics.'

The smile faded. 'Since when did ethics have anything to do with journalism?'

She'd been tempted to remind him of the five core principles of journalism, and how the second of them – independence – included matters of conflict of interest but she could see she was wasting her time.

Faced with her obdurate silence he had picked up the contract from his desk and waved it at her like a headmaster with an end-of-term report.

'In which case,' he said, 'your refusal amounts to an immediate termination of your contract and will require the return of such monies as have been paid to date, or alternatively, copies of all the data you have compiled on the project commissioned by us, including the names of contacts you have established.'

Before she had a chance to reply his expression softened. His tone conciliatory.

'There is an alternative. The case of the missing schoolgirl. What was her name again?'

'Melissa. Melissa Walsh.' She mentally kicked herself for having been sucked into a reply.

'Melissa. That's the one. Well, if you tell me you're prepared to get us an exclusive on that – without compromising your commendable principles – then I'm sure we can find someone else to pick up the ricin affair.'

Agata kicked off her shoes and lay back on the bed. She felt certain that this had been his endgame all along. That he had been playing her. Perhaps he knew how much she had depended on this contract for the final payment on her apartment on The Quays?

Jo would have understood, she felt sure of that. But it wasn't a gamble she was prepared to take. Not yet. Perhaps not ever.

Chapter 49

Melissa held her breath and strained to hear above the howling wind. There it was again. An owl hooting. She'd heard it twice the night before. She guessed that meant they were holding her somewhere in the countryside, on the outskirts of the city.

On the other hand, those planes low overhead must mean that the airport was close by. To relieve the boredom, she'd started counting the intervals between them. She'd worked out that it depended on the time of day. Sometimes they were as little as thirty seconds apart, one following close on the heels of the next. But at night-time they seemed to stop completely, starting again in the early hours of the morning. Because of the engine noise that grew steadily louder but never changed in tone, she felt sure they were inbound, slowly losing height as they prepared to land. Not the sudden deafening roar of take-off she was accustomed to on their twice-yearly flights to Majorca, that slowly faded as the plane gained height. That was a clue, wasn't it?

And then there were the clues she'd picked up about the men who were holding her. There were three of them. And they were all men; she could tell by their voices. Only two of them ever spoke in her presence but she heard them talking to each other downstairs from time to time. Mainly first thing in the morning and again in the evening. There was a high-pitched squeaky voice that she felt sure must belong to the tall thin one. She'd christened him Gollum because sometimes he sounded like a cat sicking up fur balls. Then there was the shorter one, about the same height as her dad, with a broad chest, powerful arms, and mean eyes. He was The Boxer – the one with the Manc accent, the one who did talk to her. If growling commands qualified as talking. The last of them, she'd only caught glimpses of in the doorway behind the others. She was beginning to think he must be a foreigner. He had the look of one of those travellers who put their vans on the spare land by the Apollo.

She felt pleased with herself. Surely all this would help the police to identify them when she was released.

She shuddered involuntarily. They were going to release her, weren't they? They had to. They wouldn't dare keep her here much longer. They must know what her dad would do when he got hold of them. Well, maybe not him personally, but Skanky Morris and Dad's other 'associates'. And the police would be looking for her too.

She opened and closed the fingers of both hands to relieve the cramp. They'd taken the plastic ties off her wrists and ankles that morning but had replaced them with what she thought was nylon rope and tied that to the bed frame, top and bottom. It meant she had less movement, but at least the pain wasn't so bad now. The worst had been when they'd cut the ties off. The blood rushing back into her fingers and toes had hurt so much it made her scream, and one of them had clamped his hand over her mouth. She'd tried to bite him and received a slap across the face that stung for ages. The funny thing was, the pain, it had made her feel alive. Made her angry. Shaken her out of the pit of self-pity she'd fallen into.

A new noise caught her attention. It reminded her of their ride-on lawnmower back home. Except that this was overhead and getting louder. A helicopter! That's what it was – a helicopter. It must be the police searching for her. Her heart began to thump uncontrollably. She struggled to free her hands and legs, straining at the rope, ignoring the pain as the nylon bit into her skin. She tried to shout but it came out as a muffled croak.

The helicopter was right overhead now, hovering. They must know she was here. They'd see the vehicles. Wonder what they were doing here. They'd send someone to investigate.

She imagined men, dressed all in black, automatic rifles slung across their backs, abseiling down from the helicopter to rescue her. She willed them to come and get her.

The sound changed as the helicopter climbed, turned, and moved away. Steadily receding, until all that was left was the howling of the wind, the patter of rain on the windowpanes, and the sobbing sound as she cried herself to sleep.

Chapter 50

Day Five – Friday, 20th October

'Ma'am.' Phone in hand, Nick Carter waved to her from across the incident room, covering the microphone as she approached. 'It's the Manchester Coroner's Service Manager,' he said. 'A Mrs Janice Westwell. We may have a lead.'

'She's in early,' Jo replied.

'I got her number last night and texted her. Told her that her former boss had been attacked and we urgently needed her help.'

He took his hand away and spoke into the phone. 'Thanks for holding, Janice. I've got my boss, SI Stuart, with me. I'm going to put you on the speakerphone. Can you please tell her what you just told me?'

'Of course.' She had one of those cultured accents that was impossible to place. 'Mr Carter asked me if I could think of any inquests held by Ms Rand that were followed by serious threats or harassment. There were several that sprang to mind, but I checked our record of restraining orders just to be sure. There were two that stood out. One Mr Carter tells me you were already aware of . . .'

'Aaron Teesdale,' said Jo, willing her to get to the point.

'That's right. The other one followed a particularly distressing case. A fifteen-year-old girl, Elaine Clements, who was found dead in her own bedroom by her father. The post-mortem found she'd died from an overdose. The finding of the inquest was misadventure. Death from a self-administered opiate. In essence, drug misuse.'

'What was the opiate?'

'Cocaine.'

'And the father was unhappy with the verdict?'

'The father was distraught, angry, and abusive. He made wild threats when the verdict was read out and had to be restrained and led from the court. I remember it well because I had to apply for a restraining order on Heather's behalf. It didn't stop him sending vile anonymous letters to the office and to her home. Anyone else and she'd have reported him to the police.'

'But she didn't?'

'No. She felt sorry for him. That was typical of Heather – too soft for her own good.'

'When was the inquest?'

There was a pause while she checked.

'Six years ago. January 2011.'

'The same year O'Neill was put inside,' Carter observed.

Jo flashed him a warning look.

'I beg your pardon?' said the service manager.

'Nothing,' said Jo. 'It was just an aside. Tell me, was there a jury, or did Ms Rand handle it alone?'

'It was a Coroner's inquest. There was no jury.'

'How long did the threats and harassment go on for?'

'Several months, on and off. But for several years afterwards we'd receive a card in the mail on the anniversary of the inquest.'

'What kind of card?'

'A remembrance card – like the ones people distribute at funerals? I have in front of me the last one that we were sent, back in 2015. It has a photograph of the young woman on the front, her name, the date on which she died. Underneath that is written: MUCH LOVED. GREATLY

MISSED. NEVER FORGOTTEN. And then there's a drawing of a heart with a large hole in the centre.' She paused. 'It's really rather sad.'

'Do you have the father's name and address to hand?'

'Yes, of course.'

'I'd appreciate a copy of your file and of the inquest proceedings,' said Jo. 'Could you arrange that for me?'

'Certainly. I'll do it straight away.'

'In that case, I'll send someone over for them later this morning.'

'I can email them right now if that would help?'

'That would be brilliant, Mrs Westwell. Thank you for all your help.'

'Not at all. I hope you catch whoever it was who attacked poor Heather.'

'Don't worry,' said Jo. 'We will.'

The email arrived two minutes later. Jo spent the next five minutes speed-reading the attachments, then stood up, caught Nick's attention through the glass and beckoned to him.

'Did you find anything interesting?' he asked, closing the door behind him.

'It's as she said,' Jo replied. 'The verdict of misadventure was inevitable. Had it been a listed company I've no doubt the CPS would have brought a corporate manslaughter charge, but it was a self-administered Class A drug and neither the supplier nor the dealer had been identified. Besides, who's to say if it was the size of the dose she took, or the purity of the cocaine that was responsible?'

'What about the forensic analysis?'

Jo shook her head. 'She went up to her room at nine-thirty the evening before she died. The father didn't find her until eight in the morning. We know that cocaine has a half-life of an hour and given that there was no telling when she took it, they were unable to come up with a reliable estimate of how much she took. The whole thing was complicated by the fact that she was clearly new to drug-taking, which meant that whatever dose she took, her body was always going to react in a more extreme way than if she'd been a habitual user.'

Nick dragged a chair away from the desk and sat down heavily. 'Russian roulette!' he said. 'That's what they should be teaching the kids in school. That every time they decide to experiment with drugs they're gambling with their lives.'

'They do tell them,' Jo reminded him. 'But did you ever pay attention to what your teachers or your parents told you when you were a teenager?'

'When it came to drugs I did.'

She cocked an eyebrow. 'What about fags and alcohol?'

'They don't count. It's like comparing nursery scissors and sushi knives.'

'More people die from—'

He finished it for her. '—Cirrhosis and lung cancer than drug abuse. I get that. But not the very first time they take a drag or knock back a gin and tonic.'

'Moving on,' said Jo. 'I've got the details for the dead girl's family. I want you to get someone to find out where they are now, then we can decide how to proceed.'

'Was she right?' he said. 'Does the father look like a goer?'

'Put it this way,' said Jo. 'She didn't exaggerate his reaction, or his ongoing threats against Heather Rand. I can only assume that allowances were made, both by her and the police, for the fact that he was grieving. Otherwise he'd certainly have been given a custodial sentence. But let's not lose sight of the fact that he wasn't the only one affected – just the most visible.' She handed him a sheet of paper. 'Quick as you can, please, Nick.'

Chapter 51

The wind and the rain showed them no pity, exposed as they were out here in the open.

Jo rang the bell again and pounded on the door. Just as she was beginning to think there was no one home, the door opened. A tall, statuesque woman in her late forties blocked the opening. She frowned at them.

'You're wasting your time,' she said.

'I beg your pardon?' said Jo.

'I'm a confirmed atheist,' the woman replied. 'Beyond persuasion. Impervious to faith-based arguments and believe me, I've heard them all. You'd be wasting your time and mine. Good day.'

She stepped back and began to close the door. Jo lifted her hood with one hand and held up her ID with the other.

'Police!' she said.

The door opened again. The frown deepened.

'Police? Why didn't you say so?'

'Mrs Clements?' said Jo.

'Yes. Only it's Wilkins now. I reverted to my maiden name.'

Jo put her card away. 'Could we come in, please, Miss Wilkins? It's regarding your daughter, Elaine.'

Helen Wilkins's eyes stared blankly back at her. Jo wondered if she'd even heard what had been said. Then her face seemed to collapse in on itself, and her shoulders sagged. Suddenly she seemed years older. She turned away, leaving the door open behind her.

They wiped the soles of their shoes on the doormat, then debated whether or not to remove their soaking wet Avenger jackets and hang them over the newel post.

'We could always give ourselves a shake instead?' whispered Carly Whittle. She pointed to the black Labrador, head cocked to one side, watching them from the kitchen doorway.

'Best not,' said Jo. 'Not without an invite.'

They found their host seated in a leather armchair, staring into the flames of a roaring wood burner.

'Miss Wilkins?' said Jo.

She turned her head to look up at them. 'What the hell do you want after all this time?' She looked and sounded more weary than angry.

'Is there somewhere we could hang our jackets?' said Jo.

Helen Wilkins cast her eyes over their dripping apparel as though registering it for the first time. 'There are hooks in the downstairs loo. It's just off the utility room.'

'The dog . . .?' said Carly.

'Buster? He's harmless.' She turned back to face the fire. 'More likely to lick you to death than take a chunk out of you.'

Jo took off her jacket and removed from the pockets her phone, pocketbook, and warrant card. While she waited for her DC to return, Jo decided to take a seat on the sofa.

'That's it, make yourself at home,' said Helen Wilkins, without turning her head. Her tone was unreadable. She picked up a poker, unhooked the glass door, and stabbed at the fire. Logs crackled and shot out sparks in all directions. After a few seconds she closed the door, replaced the poker, and carried on staring into the stove.

Jo wondered what was going through the woman's mind. The last time she'd seen her daughter alive? The moment she was told that her daughter was dead? The hopes she'd harboured for her daughter and the future they would never share going up in flames at the crematorium?

Carly sat down beside Jo clutching her tablet, pocketbook, and a biro.

'I'm going to record this,' Jo whispered. 'You take whatever notes you feel appropriate. Key points. Thoughts that occur to you. Questions that arise. Okay?'

'Yes, Ma'am,' Carly replied.

Jo cleared her throat. 'Miss Wilkins?'

The woman flinched as though someone had slapped her across the face or disturbed a vivid dream. She looked up, saw them sitting there and slowly sat back in her chair.

'You didn't answer my question,' she said. 'Nobody gave a damn at the time, so why now? After all this time.'

When Jo had finished telling her, Helen Wilkins pushed herself out of her seat and walked over to the window. She stood with her back to them looking out at the storm. A streak of lightning zig-zagged in front of her right shoulder. She began to count slowly, out loud. 'One, two, three, four . . .' When she reached eleven there was a loud rumble of thunder. 'Two and a bit miles away,' she said. 'I wonder if it's coming or going.'

Carly Whittle nudged Jo with her elbow. 'Is she alright, Ma'am?' she whispered.

Jo shrugged. It was impossible to tell.

Miss Wilkins turned to face them. 'So,' she said, 'it isn't about Elaine at all, is it? Not really. You want me to help you solve another case.'

'A case that may concern what happened to her,' said Jo. 'To be honest, we don't yet know. That's why we need your help.'

Helen Wilkins walked back to her chair, and sat down.

'This is about James, my first husband, isn't it?' she said. 'The way he reacted to Elaine's death. The threats he made against the Coroner.'

'I'm really sorry to be doing this,' said Jo. 'I'm sure the last thing you need is for someone to bring it all back.'

'Bring it all back?' she replied. Her back stiffened and with it the tone of her voice. 'Bring it all back? It never went away. It never will.' She stared at them. 'Do either of you have children?'

They both shook their heads.

'Well, when you do,' she continued, 'and God forbid you lose one, then you'll understand.'

Jo wanted to tell her that she'd sat with more bereaved parents than she cared to remember, but she knew that empathy simply wouldn't cut it. Experience told her to let silence do the heavy lifting. After a long minute Helen Wilkins began to talk again.

'It takes everyone in different ways, you know?' she said. 'Grief. At first, I retreated into myself. I was in denial, I suppose. But I had another child to think about and a husband who was incapable of looking after himself. We wives don't have the luxury of being able to wallow in self-pity or embark on grand campaigns for justice. I don't blame him though, James. All that hell and fury, it was just a way of shifting the blame. Of not having to face his own feelings of guilt. The overwhelming sense that he had failed in his duty to protect our daughter.'

She searched their faces, to see if they had any sense of what she was talking about. Jo nodded to show that she did. Beside her, Carly picked up the cue and followed suit.

'There was nothing I or anyone else could do to convince him otherwise,' she continued. 'He was obsessed with finding someone to blame. In the end all that self-loathing, anger, and frustration proved impossible to live with. Not just for me, but for our son too. I told my husband to leave.'

'How did he react?' asked Jo.

'He went upstairs, packed a couple of bags and left. I think he was relieved.'

'Why relieved?'

'Because he was finding it impossible too. Living in the house where our daughter had died. Sleeping next to the bedroom where he had found her in a pool of sick. Living cheek by jowl with two people who didn't feel the same way that he did.'

'You separated?' said Jo.

'And then divorced.'

'How long ago was this?'

'When he left, or when the divorce absolute came through?'

'Both.'

'He moved out in December 2012, two years to the day that Elaine passed away. The divorce became final the following September.'

'Where did your husband go when he left?'

'At first he rented a flat in town. Once the house was sold and he had enough to buy somewhere outright, he moved into a terraced house in Rusholme.'

'You didn't keep the house as part of the settlement?' said Jo. 'I'd have thought you would have done, with it being the marital home and you having a child to raise?'

'I couldn't bear to stay there either,' she replied. 'And it wasn't healthy for Darren, our son.' She shook her head slowly. 'Too many memories. I gave my husband £40,000 from the sale. It wasn't part of the divorce settlement, but I felt sorry for him and I had some money of my own from my parents.'

'Did you stay in touch?' Jo wondered.

'Not really.' She looked up. 'Not my choice, you understand – his. I think that just seeing us, Darren and me, was too painful a reminder for him,' she said. 'But in any case, I wouldn't have let Darren see him after the breakdown.'

'Breakdown?'

'That's right. One of his work colleagues rang to tell me. He'd developed severe depression. He was hospitalised for a while and never returned to work.'

'When was this?'

'The spring of 2013, I think. He moved away that autumn.'

'Do you know where he is now?'

'North Yorkshire, I think. Somewhere in the Wolds. But I haven't heard from him since then. Neither, to the best of my knowledge, has Darren.'

'How did all this affect your son?' said Jo.

'Darren?' She seemed genuinely taken aback. 'How is that relevant?'

'It must have been very difficult for him?' said Jo, swerving the question.

Helen Wilkins got up, picked up two small logs from the pile in the hearth, opened the glass door and placed them inside. She gave the fire a few prods with the poker and sat down again.

'He was seventeen, his sister was fifteen. They squabbled all the time, like all teenagers do. Darren had it in his head that Elaine got all the attention. He teased her mercilessly about her clothes, her hairstyles, the fact that she'd declared herself vegan. He decided early on that she was spoilt because she was the youngest and because she was a girl.' She looked up and made eye contact with Jo. 'It wasn't true, of course, but that didn't stop him thinking it. Elaine, on the other hand, resented the extra freedom he was given because he was older. But for all that, they loved each other. So yes, it was difficult for him.'

'I don't suppose the fact that your husband was so angry helped?' said Jo.

'No, it didn't, which is one of the reasons I told James to leave. Darren had become even more moody than before. And introverted – he'd take to his room for hours. Headphones on, crouched over his laptop. I was really worried when he went away to university in London. I needn't have worried, because the first time he came home it was obvious that his mood had shifted. It was a pleasure to have the real Darren back.'

'What did Darren read at university?'

'English Literature.'

'Where is he now?'

'He rents a nice little terraced house in Walkden, just a couple of miles away. He's a freelance copywriter. He also does copy-editing and proofreading for publishing houses.' She smiled. 'He's doing well for himself.'

Jo couldn't think of anything else to ask. 'Well, I think that's everything,' she said. She turned to Carly Whittle. 'Unless . . .?'

The detective constable leaned forward. 'Did either your husband or your son have any interest in air rifles?' she said.

Helen Wilkins frowned. 'Air rifles?'

'Or guns of any kind?'

'Certainly not. Nor would I have encouraged that. James was an avid Rugby League supporter – the Salford Red Devils. And he loved his bowls and snooker. Darren had his Scouts and his books.' She shook her head. 'There were never any guns in this house.'

Chapter 52

'Looks like someone's at home.'

Jo followed Carly's gaze. Although the rain had ceased and the storm clouds had begun to lift, it was still heavily overcast and gloomy. The two-storey red-brick terrace was in darkness, apart from a light shining from a Velux window in the roof space.

'I've been thinking,' said Carly as they walked up the flagged path to the front door, 'the inquest must have been about the time Ronnie O'Neill was sent to prison.'

'And?'

'Well, it's a bit of coincidence, don't you think?'

Jo rang the bell. 'I'm not sure I follow? No link has been established between Heather Rand and O'Neill, or any of the other victims.'

'Maybe not yet, Ma'am. But there is a common factor. Drugs.'

Through the glass panel in the door Jo could see a shadow approaching. 'Mmm,' she said. 'Remind me later.'

The door opened. A young man in his twenties stood there with a bemused expression on his face. He had unfashionable shoulder-length hair, two days' growth of stubble above a chunky white turtleneck, faded jeans ripped at the knees, and Jesus sandals.

'Darren Clements?' said Jo, holding her ID up in front of her.

'Oh God!' His hand flew to his face. 'It's not Mum, is it?'

'No, it's nothing like that,' said Jo. 'We've just come from your mum's, Darren, and she's fine. We need to ask you a few questions, that's all.'

Relief flooded his face, but he was still blocking the doorway.

'Could we come inside, please?' she prompted.

'Oh, yes, right. Of course,' he said. 'Come in.'

There were stairs in front of them and a door to the right. He led them through into an open-plan room that served as a lounge and dining room. Beyond that she could see a small minimally furnished kitchen and UPVC doors leading to a yard at the rear. The dining table was covered with books. Ceiling-height shelves on either side of the fireplace were stacked with paperbacks. There was no sign of a television, but an Amazon Echo shared a wall-mounted shelf with a pile of vinyl records and a turntable.

Darren pointed to the two black leather chairs. 'Would you like to sit down?'

He waited until they were seated, then dragged a massive grey beanbag across the wooden floor and slumped into it.

'What's this about?' he said.

'Does the name Heather Rand mean anything to you?' said Jo.

He pursed his lips, then shook his head. 'No. Sorry.'

'Did you attend the inquest into your sister's death?'

He seemed genuinely surprised. 'Elaine? No, I didn't. Why?'

'Are you sure you don't remember that name?' Jo pressed.

'I told you, no. Why? Who is she?'

Jo watched him closely.

'The coroner at the inquest into Elaine's death.'

His brow furrowed. He ran his hand over the stubble on his chin. Then he leaned forward and his eyebrows shot up.

'Oh God!' he said. 'My father hasn't gone and done something stupid, has he?'

'What makes you say that?'

'You know.' He looked from one to the other of them. 'He was obsessed with her. Made all those threats about her?'

'How do you know about those?'

'Because we had the police round, didn't we? More than once. And he and Mum were always rowing about it.' He paused and slumped back. 'That's why she threw him out.'

'So how come you didn't recognise her name?'

'Because I only knew her as this woman he was angry with. I knew she was the coroner, but I don't recall the name.'

'Have you seen your father recently?'

He shook his head. 'Not since he left. He had a breakdown, you know.'

'Yes,' said Jo. 'Your mother mentioned it.'

He waited for her to say something else. When she didn't, he decided to speak. 'Can you please tell me what this is all about? To be honest, it's spooking me out.'

'Someone has attacked Miss Rand,' she told him.

'That's awful,' he said. 'How was she attacked?'

Jo decided there was no point in keeping it from him, because her next question was going to give it away. 'She was shot.'

He sat up again. 'God, that's terrible. And you think my father has something to do with it?'

'We're just trying to eliminate everyone who may have had a grudge against her,' said Jo.

'Shooting someone,' he said. 'That's some grudge. How is she?'

Jo paused, to make absolutely sure that she had eye contact. She was looking for the slightest pupillary response. Beside her, Carly had also stopped writing and was also watching him.

'She'll live,' she said.

His face was expressionless. There may have been the slightest constriction of his pupils but, if so, it was followed by a gradual dilation. And then he nodded his head gravely. 'That's good,' he said.

'Do you own a gun, Darren?' Jo asked.

He looked surprised and then affronted. 'Me? You can't seriously think it was me?'

'Do you? Own a gun?'

'No, I don't. And I never have.'

'Not even an air rifle?'

'No. Look, I thought this was about my father?'

'Like I said, Darren, we have to eliminate everyone, however unlikely.'

He seemed to relax a little.

'Your sister's death must have come as quite a shock?' she said.

He sat back. 'It did. It doesn't mean I wanted to kill someone.'

'Even the mildest person might feel like wanting to do that at the time,' she said. 'Needing someone to blame. Having somewhere to focus all the anger. It's nothing to be ashamed of.'

'I had someone to blame,' he replied softly. 'Only she was already dead.'

Jo sensed that exploring his feelings for his sister would take them down a cul-de-sac.

'Do you own a car?' she asked.

He shook his head. 'I passed my test at uni, but it's a luxury I can do without. It's not as though I need one for work.'

'How do you get around then?'

'Public transport. There's a guided busway into the city. And I have a pushbike if I need to go to the shops.'

'What is it you do exactly?'

'I'm a copywriter.' He recognised the blank expression on her face. He was used to having to explain. 'I write advertising and marketing copy – anything and everything. For adverts in magazines, newspapers, brochures, billboards, and websites too. I also help with scripts for radio and TV commercials. About thirty per cent of my work is copy-editing and proofreading for publishing houses.'

'Would you mind if we had a look around?' she asked. 'Then we can leave you to get on.'

The threat was implied. Although she knew she'd be pushed to get a search warrant given how little they had. But he didn't seem the slightest bit fazed.

'Help yourself,' he said. 'If you like, I'll make you both a drink while you're at it?'

It was okay to let a witness or a victim make you a drink, but definitely not a potential suspect. That's what Caton had taught her. More as a matter of principle than anything else, he'd told her, unless of course the perpetrator's MO was poisoning. Which in this case, she reminded herself, it was.

'I'm fine, thank you,' she said.

He rolled sideways off the beanbag and stood up. 'Then do you mind if I get myself one?'

'Feel free,' she replied. 'It's your house.'

He smiled thinly. 'How very ironic,' he said.

Chapter 53

'You know what we're looking for,' said Jo, slipping on a pair of blue nitrile gloves. 'If you find anything, don't touch, just give me a shout.'

They started in the lounge. Jo concentrated on the books, checking titles and leafing through the pages. There was nothing that related to guns or poisons, although there were a number of crime, thriller, and mystery novels, and one on forensics. Nothing out of keeping with the job he did.

She checked the understairs storage cupboard and found a typical urban bicycle, in black, with flat handlebars and eight gears, together with a vacuum cleaner and a row of three hooks, on one of which hung a red-and-black windcheater.

They moved upstairs. On the landing was a pull-down ladder leading up into the loft space. She decided to leave that till last. There were two bedrooms. Jo pointed to the smaller of the two. 'You take that one,' she said.

The master bedroom was not much bigger. Twelve foot long by eleven foot wide, it held a standard double bed, a chest of drawers, a pine wardrobe, and a radiator. On a bedside table lay a Kindle, an alarm clock and a lamp. There were framed football prints on the wall and a framed university degree. A UPVC double-glazed window looked out onto the street below. The bed was unmade. Jo lifted the sheets and the pillows. She peered under the bed and then rooted through the chest of drawers. In the wardrobe hung a blue suit, a donkey jacket, and a smart black leather jacket. On the rail below were a number of jeans and chinos. On the bottom were two stacks of shoe boxes. She pulled them out and examined them. They contained shoes and sneakers. She put them back and went out onto the landing.

'Anything?'

Carly shook her head. 'It's just a spare room. A bed and storage.'

The fully tiled bathroom held a panel bath with a shower over it, a vanity handbasin, a low-level WC, and a heated towel rail. Jo tried the panel on the side of the bath. It was firmly in place and the seal did not appear to have been tampered with. She lifted the top of the WC cistern. There was nothing concealed inside.

Carly was waiting at the foot of the pull-down ladder.

'D'you want to go first, Ma'am?' she said.

'Feel free,' said Jo. She waited till Carly was halfway up, then added, 'There could be anything up there. Spiders, rats, a snake.'

The DC looked over her shoulder and poked her tongue out. 'I'll pay you back,' she said.

The compact loft had been converted into a study fourteen feet long and twelve feet wide, with Velux windows front and back. A desk, five feet long, had been placed under the rear window. It held a MacBook Pro laptop, an HP printer, and all the usual accessories. The lighting came from a desk lamp and three LED spotlights fitted to the ceiling. Both sets of eaves had been boxed in to provide storage.

Jo lifted the lid of the laptop and pressed the space bar. To her surprise, the screen lit up. There was no password requirement. 'That's a bonus,' she whispered. 'I'll have a little look at this while you check under the eaves.'

She sat down and began by clicking the Finder icon and entering the word 'ricin' in the search bar. There were no results. She tried again with 'air rifle'. This time there were seven. They all seemed to have the same source PDF. She opened the document. It appeared to be a teen fiction story by an author whose name she didn't recognise about a boy who lived on a farm in Somerset. She brought up the search results in a side panel and read through them. They all appeared innocuous. She made a note of the title and author, closed the document, and searched for recent files instead. Again, there was nothing that caught her eye.

Now she searched the browser history. Most of it seemed to be connected with his work. There were a lot of Google and Wikipedia searches for definitions and dictionary entries. He also seemed to have a passion for American country music. She heard footsteps on the staircase.

'Are you alright up there?' he shouted.

'We're fine, thanks,' she shouted back. 'Nearly finished.'

Jo hurriedly exited the programs and the screen, closed the laptop, and stood up. She could hear him climbing the ladder. She pretended to be staring out of the window onto the street. His head appeared at the top of the steps.

'Find what you were looking for?' he asked.

'No,' she told him. 'Which is good news for you.'

He grinned. 'Sorry to disappoint you.'

'You haven't,' she said. 'Eliminating people is every bit as important as finding the perpetrator. If we can't show that we've done that, it may cost us a conviction.'

'Glad to have been of service then,' he said.

'Do you keep a diary?' she asked.

'I do, as a matter of fact. I have to. With so many different jobs and all the deadlines, if I didn't I'd be in a right mess.'

'Can you show me?'

'Sure. It's right there on my laptop.'

Jo kicked herself mentally for not having spotted it.

He climbed the remaining couple of steps, opened his laptop and then his diary. If he'd noticed anything suspicious he didn't show it.

Although Jo knew that he'd soon find out when he opened Recent Files and saw the one she'd opened at the top of the list.

'Here you go,' he said. 'What dates are you interested in?'

Jo opened her own tablet and pulled up the table DC Hulme had compiled, listing all the key dates and times relating to the four attacks. As far as she could tell he had an alibi for none of them. In every case he was working from home which, given the nature of his work, was not in itself suspicious. She took a photograph of each of the relevant pages of his diary. If it came to it, analysis of his laptop would show if it had been active at the times shown. Unless, of course, he'd reset the time.

'Thank you,' she said. 'Have you finished, DC Whittle?'

Carly crawled out from the eaves, stood up and dusted down her knees, 'Yes, Ma'am,' she said.

'Sorry about that,' he told her. 'It's a mess, I know. And it's hardly something I'm likely to clean.'

'It's fine,' she replied, although she didn't sound it. 'All part of the job.'

'Are you still in contact with your father, Darren?' said Jo.

'No.' He looked uncomfortable. 'Apart from cards at Christmas and on my birthday. And they're usually a couple of days late.'

'You have his address then?'

'Sure.'

He opened the letters folder on his laptop, found the address and pressed print. Jo was impressed by how quickly it appeared. He handed it to her.

'Is that it then?'

'There's just one last thing,' she said. 'I'd like to have a look out back.'

It was a typical and unremarkable backyard of a terraced house. Stone flags, four walls, and a gate to the alley that ran between the two rows of back-to-back houses. The former outside loo was long gone and had not been replaced with a shed. Jo walked to the gate, opened it and looked out. There was nothing of note, except that tall wrought-iron gates had been installed at both ends of the alley. She assumed these would be locked at night, but the residents would have keys. She closed the yard gate and scanned the back of Darren's house and those of his neighbours for CCTV cameras. There were none. She went back inside the kitchen.

'That's it,' she said. 'We're done here. Thank you for your time, Darren. And for being so cooperative.'

'You're welcome,' he said.

As they walked to the car he called after them. 'That woman . . . Helen Rand . . .'

'Heather,' said Jo.

'I hope she'll be alright.'

'I'm sure she will,' said Jo.

She and Carly got in the car and waited until he'd closed the door. 'What do you think?' said Jo.

'He seemed plausible enough,' said Carly. 'I liked him.' She blushed. 'Not in that way, obviously. For a start he's way too young and secondly I doubt my husband would approve.'

'I didn't realise you were married,' said Jo. 'You never seem in a hurry to get home.'

'That's because he's a fireman. He's been on nights. Next week will be a different matter. He'll have a few days off, then he's on days.'

'In that case,' said Jo, 'you won't mind being a bit late tonight.'

'No. Why?'

Jo held up the address. 'Because we're going to pay a call on Mr Clements senior.'

Carly looked back at the house. 'I was wondering, Ma'am. How likely is that? Him never having heard her name. Not when the police came. Not even when his parents were shouting at each other.'

'Maybe he had his headphones on, like she said?'

'Maybe. When you told him she was going to live, I thought he seemed relieved? Like anyone would be.'

'I agree,' said Jo. 'He comes across like an open book.'

Carly grinned. 'Very appropriate for a copywriter.'

Jo was already calling Nick Carter. He answered after only two rings.

'Jo,' he said. 'At last.'

'I want you to check if there are any vehicles registered or insured in the name of Darren Clements – either as owner or keeper.' She gave his date of birth and address.

'Will do,' said Nick. 'Are you coming straight back?'

'No, we're off to North Yorkshire, to interview the father.'

'That's a bugger,' he said.

'Why?'

'Because I've just had ACC Gates in here with steam coming out of her nostrils. She wanted to know what's going on, where you were, and why your phone was turned off.'

'What did you tell her?'

'The truth. That you were questioning potential suspects.'

'What did she say to that?'

'That you'd better have read them their bloody rights. And, as soon as you broke cover, to tell you to ring her.'

'Good job you haven't heard from me then,' said Jo as she started the engine.

Chapter 54

They chased the storm across the Pennines. Swollen streams, replenishing drought-starved reservoirs, cascaded down the hillsides. The windshield wipers fought a valiant battle against the spray from passing vehicles. When the screenwash finally gave out, Jo pulled in to the services at Hartshead Moor. While she topped up the Audi, Carly went to buy them lunch.

Jo got back in the car and checked her phone. There were two missed calls. One from ACC Gates and one from Carter. He had also sent her a text. Short and to the point.

No vehicle of any kind registered, taxed, or insured to that name or address.

She decided to leave the phone on, because not to have done so would have been regarded as highly suspicious and meant that she risked missing important calls. From Max, for instance.

Melissa still preyed on her mind. Not least because the abduction was almost certainly connected with Operation Alecto. Max and the AKEU team would be doing everything possible to find her, but Jo couldn't help imagining how it must be for that twelve-year-old child.

Alone, confused, terrified. Held prisoner in some dark, dilapidated, rat-infested building. Hoping for the best. Fearing the worst.

In Jo's case, it had been a forty-minute ride into the forest and a further fifteen bargaining for her life. It had taken her months to get over it. And she was a grown woman. A professional, trained in hostage negotiation. What chance did Melissa have of ever recovering from this? Assuming she was found alive.

The passenger door opened. Carly climbed in and handed Jo a paper bag. 'I got you a baguette,' she said. 'Breakfast egg and avocado. And a single-shot latte, like you asked.'

'Cheers,' said Jo. She opened the bag and took out a smart black beaker with a ceramic lid. There was a band around the middle proclaiming SAVE THE PLANET. 'What's this?'

Carly grinned and held up a matching one in green. 'They were on special offer. They're reusable. The beaker's bamboo. When you decide to replace it you just crush it, pour boiling water on it and put it in the green bin. The lid goes in the recycling bin. What d'you think?'

'Didn't they have any other colours?'

'I thought you'd appreciate black, Ma'am,' said Carly. 'What with it matching the NCA logo.' She took a bite out of her burrito. 'I could always go back and get you a pink one.'

Jo bit back the smile, put the beaker in the central cup holder and reached for her baguette.

'Don't push it, DC Whittle,' she said.

'This doesn't look right?' said Carly.

Jo had pulled up on a deserted road a mile and a half outside the town of Malton in the Yorkshire Wolds. Neatly trimmed hedges, interspersed with trees, bordered fields of grass. There were no houses to be seen. Jo pointed to the text on the satnav screen:

You have reached your destination.

'It must be around here somewhere.'

'What about the farmhouse and stables we passed a third of a mile back?' said Carly. 'We could ask there.'

They retraced their steps. The farmhouse in question looked more like a stately home to Jo. Or a small estate. The size of three detached houses, it had clearly been modernised. There were three other dwellings, essentially cottages, and over to the right she counted two dozen stables. She drove up the drive and stopped at the first of the cottages. Before she'd even had a chance to unbuckle her seat belt a man emerged from the cottage, bent down and peered in. She lowered the window.

''Ow do?' he said. 'You look lost. Can I 'elp?'

'We're hoping you can tell us where we'll find James Clements?' she said.

He cocked his head sideways a little so that he could see Carly Whittle in the passenger seat.

'Who wants to know?'

Jo reached for her bag so that she could show him her ID. Carly beat her to it.

'Police,' she declared, leaning forward and showing him her warrant.

'Police,' he repeated slowly. 'What's Jimmy gone and done?'

'I didn't say he'd done anything,' said Jo. 'Only that we would like to speak with him.'

'Right,' he said. 'Only we've got a bit of a soft spot for Jimmy. He's had a raw deal, tha' knows?'

'We do,' said Jo.

He nodded. 'Good. Only we get some queer folk pitching up here from time to time. An' you can't be too careful. Not when it comes to racehorses. Lot of money ridin' on them, if you know what I mean?'

'So,' said Jo, 'can you tell me where we'll find him?'

'Aye,' he said. 'I can that. He works on the gallops and he lives on 'em too. You can turn yer car round by the big house and then turn right at the end of the drive. The gallops are half a mile on yer left. Follow the lane and you'll come to a small red-brick cottage with a wooden porch.'

He looked at his watch. 'He's normally there this time o't day. If not, he'll be on't gallops.'

'Thank you,' Jo said.

He nodded and stepped back from the car.

'Go gently with him,' he said.

Chapter 55

The cottage was exactly as described. Faded white paint on the wooden porch and window frames was flaking off in places and the grass surrounding the building was overgrown. At first sight one might think it abandoned, but for the trail of grey smoke curling up from the single chimney. On either side of the lane stood a pair of sturdy posts in need of a gate.

Jo knocked on the front door three times with the iron fox-head knocker. The sound echoed inside. She tried again. This time there was another noise from within. It sounded like a child softly crying.

'What the hell is that?' said Carly.

Jo peered through the window on her right. Logs smouldered in the grate of an open fire, surrounded by an ancient fireguard. The two armchairs on either side were empty. The only door she could see was shut. Carly was looking through the matching window on the left.

'Anything?' said Jo.

Carly stood up and shook her head.

'Nope. Just a wooden table with a pile of clothes on it and a clothes horse.'

'You go that way,' said Jo. 'I'll meet you round the back.'

She followed the stone-flagged path to a high wooden gate that opened into a fenced backyard. Five large turkeys advanced menacingly towards her, fanning their tails and gobbling manically. She hurriedly closed the gate and backed along the cottage wall towards the rear door. Carly Whittle appeared around the opposite corner.

'You're alright, Ma'am,' she said. 'They're harmless. If they start pecking at you, shout at them and wave your arms.'

'Easy for you to say,' Jo replied. The long curved beaks and tiny jet-black eyes imbued the birds with a strange malevolence.

'Shoo!' shouted Carly, advancing on them with a hoe she'd found propped up against the wall. The turkeys scattered, complaining as they went. 'They'll be back,' she said. 'Persistent little buggers. But at least they're not geese – then we would have a fight on our hands.'

Jo's heart stopped racing. 'How come you know all this?' she asked.

Carly put the hoe down and grinned. 'Grandad had a smallholding in Urmston. A bit like this, but three times the size.'

Jo rubbed the grime from the only window with the back of her sleeve. It was a country cottage kitchen that had failed to move with the times. In the centre of the quarry-tiled floor stood a wooden table with a butcher's block and wooden chairs set around it. Behind it loomed a wall-to-ceiling stained pine dresser, with open shelves and cupboards beneath. On the left, a black kitchen range. On the opposite wall, a large brick fireplace containing an unlit wood burner. There was no sign of a child.

'Pass me that pail,' she said, pointing to a galvanised bucket upended beside the gate.

Carly picked it up and handed it to her. Jo stood on it and rubbed the window again.

Immediately below her was a Belfast sink and a draining board piled high with dirty pots. But what drew her attention was the basket between the sink and the table and the little puppy that stared back at her with sad innocent eyes.

'There's your child,' she said, stepping off the bucket.

Carly took her place. 'Aaah,' she crooned. 'She's gorgeous. So cute.'

'How do you know it's a she?' said Jo.

Carly stepped down. 'Because she's gorgeous.'

Jo turned and took in the whole of the yard. It was roughly an eighth of an acre and backed onto a small wood. The section closest to the house held a large shed and acted as a free run for the turkeys and half a dozen ducks. The next section consisted of a mixture of raised beds and open plots, some of which were bare, but most of which contained herbs and vegetables in various stages of development. The final section housed a greenhouse, a large hutch, and a covered chicken run. She estimated there were close to two dozen hens and two roosters.

'Impressive,' she said. 'Looks like he cares more about this than he does the house.'

'Grandad would have loved this,' Carly declared. 'Only he'd have had some goats as well.'

The turkeys had regrouped and were looking in their direction.

'It's time we got out of here, I think,' said Jo, heading smartly for the gate.

'He must be around somewhere,' said Carly, closing the gates and following her down the path.

'The man said if he wasn't here he'd probably be on the gallops,' said Jo. 'Presumably we just carry on down the lane and we'll come to them.'

They decided to go on foot. After more than three hours in the car it was a relief to stretch their limbs and enjoy the fresh country air. After less than a hundred yards they rounded a corner and came upon a large turning circle at the bottom of a grassy hill down the centre of which ran a broad sandy track enclosed by curved plastic-covered railings on either side. From somewhere beyond the hill came the distinctive sound of a tractor.

'That's probably him,' said Carly. She strode towards the sandy track and tested it with her foot. 'Come and look at this, Ma'am,' she said. 'It's like nothing you've ever walked on before.'

Jo went to join her. With each step she took, her foot sunk in a few inches and then bounced back a little.

'It's dead dry,' Carly observed.

'That's because most of the rain falls on us over in the west. By the time it's crossed the Pennines there's beggar all left.'

The sound of the engine rose in pitch and volume. They turned and looked up the track. A large blue tractor appeared on the brow of the hill and came towards them. The driver poked his head out of the cabin and waved his arm furiously.

They could barely hear him above the sound of the engine.

'Get the hell out of there!' he yelled. 'Go on, get out of the road!'

'I get the impression,' said Jo, 'that he's not very happy.'

'I don't see what the problem is,' said Carly. 'He's almost a hundred yards away and he's doing what, two miles an hour?'

They retreated to the sandy turning circle and watched as the tractor approached, dragging a harrow that left behind a perfectly smooth and level surface.

'Hasn't exactly got us off to a good start though, has it?' said Jo. 'I reckon we'll have some ruffled feathers to smooth.'

The driver raised the harrow, took the slipway off the gallop, brought the tractor to a halt and killed the engine.

Carly lowered her voice. 'Good job he's not one of those turkeys then.'

Jo bit her lip and waited as the driver climbed down from the cabin. He turned to face them. Despite the flat cap, the weathered face and unkempt hair, the family resemblance to his son was obvious.

'What the bloody hell did you think you were doing?' he said. 'Silly buggers. Could have got yourselves killed.'

Right on cue, a trio of horses crested the hill at speed and galloped, nose to tail, down the track towards them. Black-visored riders, out of their saddles, backs parallel to the horses' spines, stared fixedly ahead. It was a majestic, mesmerising sight. Two bays and a grey, their flanks slick with the sheen of sweat, emitted rhythmic puffs of steam from their nostrils. With the muffled drumbeat of twelve hooves pounding the sand, they swept around the bend and away.

The man shook his fist at the riders as they passed by. 'See what I mean?' he growled. 'If you'd started walking up the gallop, they could have been upon you before you had a chance to get out of the way. Not that they should have been coming down at all. It's supposed to be one way, and that's up,' he grumbled. 'Worse still is the damage you could have done to man and beast if they suddenly had to slow down. There'd be no avoiding you.' He pointed to the rails. 'There's nowhere else for them to go.'

'We see that now,' said Jo. 'We're very sorry.'

'I've had to sit there,' he said, 'with a horse's head in my lap, trying to comfort her while we waited for the vet to come and put her out of her misery. All because she stumbled coming down there and broke her leg.' His voice was softer now and the anger had been replaced by the remembered emotion of the event.

'We're truly sorry, Mr Clements,' said Jo. Leaving it up to him to decide if she was referring to the present or the past.

His head jerked up and his eyes narrowed as he stared at her. When he spoke, his tone was heavy with suspicion. 'Who are you?' he said. 'And how the hell do you know who I am?'

Chapter 56

'You'd best sit down,' he said, pulling out a chair for himself. 'I suppose you want a drink?'

Jo looked at the pile of dirty pots and sink full of greasy water.

'It's alright,' he said. 'I've got some clean mugs on the dresser. You've come all the way from Manchester, you'll need something.'

'Thank you,' she said. 'Whatever you've got will be fine.'

'Yorkshire tea it is then,' he said. 'What about your mate?'

Jo could tell from Carly's expression that she was thinking about what she had said about accepting drinks from suspected poisoners. In this instance, however, they would be able to watch his every move. Jo gave her a reassuring smile.

'Tea would be great,' said Carly.

He took a sturdy kettle from the range, filled it with water from the faucet, and then plugged it into a socket beside the sink. 'I rarely fire the range up before the end of November at the earliest,' he explained. He took a caddy from one of the shelves on the dresser and plonked it on the table together with three mugs and a china teapot from one of the cupboards. He put three teabags in the pot and then sat down while the kettle boiled.

The puppy was sitting at Carly's feet staring up at her with saucer eyes and an air of anticipation.

'Come away, Sandy!' he said. 'Leave the lady alone.'

'It's fine,' said Carly, bending down to pet the dog. 'She's adorable. What breed is she?'

'A Norfolk terrier,' he told her. 'I got her to help me catch the vermin and tell me when the foxes are sniffing round the chickens. She seems to have taken a fancy to you. You'd better watch out though. She'll ladder your pantyhose and start nibbling your shoes if you give her half a chance.'

Clements pointed to a basket in the corner of the kitchen. The puppy turned reluctantly away from Carly, climbed into the basket, and curled up, head on paws, his mournful gaze following his master's every move.

Jo had been using the time to observe Clements closely. Facially, he appeared a good ten years older than his chronological age and he had a hangdog look about him. His left eyebrow drooped such that his eye looked permanently half closed. He also had a slight tic that caused his nose to twitch ever so slightly every thirty seconds or so. But out there on the gallops and back here too, he moved with a degree of ease more appropriate to his actual age, fifty-one. Despite being determined to remain objective she couldn't help feeling a little sorry for him. She could see what that man back at the big house had meant about them going gently with him.

'So,' he said, 'you haven't told me what it is you want.'

'I'm sorry to be dragging this up, Mr Clements,' she said. 'But it's to do with the former Manchester Coroner. Miss Heather Rand.'

He put his elbows on the table and bowed his head in his hands. His shoulders began to shake and Jo had the impression that he was sobbing. She looked at Carly, who raised her eyebrows and shrugged. Neither of them moved or spoke. The kettle began to spit and then emitted a piercing whistle.

Head still bowed, he stood up, causing his chair to fall backwards and land with a clatter on the tiles. He stooped to right it, then busied himself switching off the kettle and filling the teapot. He stood staring out of the window silently while he waited for the tea to brew. The puppy crawled out of her basket and padded towards him. Several minutes passed. The silence became oppressive and Jo became aware of the ticking of a clock somewhere in the house. Finally, he wiped his face with the back of his sleeve, gave the pot a gentle swirl, and then turned to face them.

There were blotches of red across the whites of his eyes, and the skin had puffed up beneath them. Jo sensed that he might burst into tears again at the slightest provocation.

'I'm sorry about that,' he said, as he filled each of the mugs in turn. 'I take mine black. I suppose you want milk?'

'Please,' they said in unison.

Even when the milk had been added it was still a deep, dark chocolate colour. He sat down, blew across the surface, took a sip, and set down the mug.

'I'm sorry about that,' he said for a second time. 'I wasn't ready for it. Thought I was, but I wasn't.'

He lapsed into silence and, as though by some kind of unspoken agreement, neither Jo nor Carly attempted to prompt him. He took a longer sip and savoured the tea before swallowing.

'Once you said you were police I guessed why you'd come. That it was about her. Not that I knew why. Just that . . . well . . . why else would you come all this way to see me?'

Jo took it to be a rhetorical question. She waited.

'But that wasn't why I was upset, was it?' he said. He picked up his mug, took a deeper draught and cradled the mug in his hands. He shook it gently with tiny circular movements and stared into the whirlpool he had created.

'You can only bang your head against a brick wall for so long,' he said, 'before all that matters is the headache. That's why I came here. To get away from everything that reminded me of why I was angry. Of the real pain I was trying to avoid.' He put the mug down and ran his fingers through his hair. 'When I found Ellie lying across the bed like that my life turned upside down. I couldn't sleep, because when I did I had these vivid horrible dreams. I was angry all the time. On edge. I didn't lose my appetite like my wife did. I had this terrible need to gorge myself. I thought if I didn't get to the bottom of why she died I'd go mad.'

He stared straight at Jo, willing her to understand.

'There were a hundred and thirty-nine deaths from cocaine alone that year. The death rate's going up year on year. They told me it was down to an increase in the purity of cocaine flooding the market. So even people who were used to taking it may not realise that the same dose could be fatal. My Ellie, experimenting with it for the first time, how was she supposed to know? She never stood a chance. And what do the dealers care? I tracked one down. He laughed in my face.'

He spat the words out. 'Said he was sorry for my loss. "I'm just a businessman," he said. "Just like any other supplier. I respond to demand. They ring me up, not the other way round. Buyer beware," he said. "It's up to them to make sure they take the right dose. Use it responsibly. It's not drug use that kills, it's drug misuse. Same with people who eat or drink themselves to death. It's not the food or the alcohol that's to blame, or the shops that sell it."'

'You tracked down a drug dealer?' said Jo. 'Do you remember his name?'

'I never knew his name. I was always asking around. Trying to find out who might have supplied my Ellie. He was just a person someone else I'd come across told me about. A dead end, as it turned out.'

'Where was this?'

'In the city centre. Near the Dale Street parking lot. I gave up not long after that. It was obvious I was wasting my time. Besides, even in the state I was in I knew it was stupid. Dangerous.'

He sighed, put the mug down and looked at Jo. 'Being here. This place. It's been like a medicine to me. Another world where none of that ever existed. Where I can live every day in the present. Not worry about the future. Above all, bury the past. You coming here, it's dug it all up again. That's what upset me.'

The last sentence was delivered as a challenge. As though he was daring her to contradict him.

'I can see that,' she said. 'Which is why I said we were sorry to be dragging it all up again. But when I explain, I'm sure that you'll understand we had no option.'

The dog was now jumping up, trying to attract Carly's attention as she tried to make notes.

'Sandy! Get down!' he shouted. The puppy sank to the floor. He pointed to the basket. 'Get in!' he said. The puppy slunk on her belly across the floor, ears flat to her head. She climbed into the basket and curled up, with her head between her front paws, observing them with sad black eyes.

Clements turned his attention back to Jo. 'Go on then,' he said. 'Explain.'

'Someone shot Miss Rand while she was walking with her dog in Manchester.'

If he was surprised, it didn't show. 'And you want to know if it was me?'

'Was it?'

'No. I didn't shoot her. Though I'd be lying if I said I was sorry that someone else did. But I'm not glad either. Like I told you, I'm beyond all that. I finally realised that nothing is going to bring my Ellie back.'

'You didn't ask how she is.'

'How is she?'

'She'll live.'

He nodded and finished the tea in his mug.

'Do you possess a gun, Mr Clements?' Jo asked.

His expression told her he considered it a stupid question. 'Everyone round here has one. I've got two. A shotgun and a .22. I told you, I'm surrounded by foxes and vermin. When it comes down to it, nothing beats a gun.'

'Could we see them, please?' she said. 'And your shotgun licence and your firearms certificate?'

He returned, carrying over the crook of his left arm a side-by-side double-barrelled shotgun, with the barrels safely broken. In his right hand he held a matt-black rifle that Jo was pretty sure was a .22 LR rimfire. He laid the rifle down on the table and then handed her the shotgun, stock first so she could see it was empty. Then he took the licences from his back pocket and placed them on the table.

He watched her examine the shotgun and then lay it aside and pick up the rifle.

'This is a .22 CZ 455 rimfire,' she said for Carly's sake. 'With a 5-shot detachable magazine.'

'You know your guns then?' he said with begrudging admiration.

She examined the end of the barrel where it had been screw-turned. 'Do you use a sound moderator?' she asked.

'Only at night,' he replied.

'What do you use these guns for?'

'I get to do some beating for the driven shoots around here. Mainly pheasants and partridge,' he said. 'In return, in season they let me shoot a couple of brace a month for myself. I also join rough shoots for hare and rabbits. And when the larder's getting low I go out after them on my own, and for those damn wood pigeons. But most important of all are the foxes. If they get in among the livestock I have to start all over again.'

Jo hefted the rifle.

'Have you ever used air rifle pellets in this?' she asked.

'What kind of a daft question is that?' he said. 'What would be the point, apart from the risk of damaging a perfectly good rifle?'

'But it is possible?'

He frowned. 'It's possible. I've heard of people using nail gun powder blanks with hollow-point pellets. But those are going to make a mess of anything you might be thinking of eating. Like I said, what would be the point, apart from proving you can do it?'

'Because it's cheaper than using bespoke .22 ammunition?'

He sneered. 'Not in the long run. Not if you bugger up the rifle.'

Jo put the rifle down and examined the shotgun certificate and the firearms licence. They had been issued three years previously, within months of each other. Both had another two years to run.

'And you don't possess an air rifle?'

'No. And I never have.'

Jo looked around the room for evidence of a calendar. The kitchen was where most people kept them unless they had a study or used one on their phone.

'Do you use a calendar?' she asked.

He shook his head. 'No need. I'm here seven days a week. Never go anywhere unless it's part of a routine. Like weekly shopping.'

'What about doctor's appointments? Dentists? That sort of thing?'

'I note them down, up here.' He tapped the side of his head.

'So if my colleague were to give you a few dates could you tell me where you were?'

'Try me.'

Carly handed him a typed sheet. He perused it and handed it back. 'I was here,' he said.

'On every one of those dates?'

'I told you, didn't I? Look,' he said, 'my job is to maintain these gallops. And let the trainers know if conditions make any of them unsafe. That's why I live right by them. This time of year you can never tell when someone's going to be out on them. Most of the runs are over by lunchtime, but there are always a few in the afternoon. Horses not part of the stables, or ones that are coming back from injury. Like today. And there's work I can only do before the horses are on them, like mowing the grass gallops, making sure the all-weather ones are safe, checking the rails. The only times I can get away from here are between five in the evening and five in the morning.'

'And there are people who can verify that?'

'All the racing grooms know me. There'll be plenty of them who can tell you if I was out and about on a given day. Any outsiders who want to use the gallops have to rent a slot, so there'll be a record of them. Then there's the other guys who maintain the gallops next to ours. We see each other every day. Sometimes stop for a chat if there's time.'

Jo was beginning to sense that they had been wasting their time. Except that they had had no choice but to definitively rule him in or out.

'When did you last see your son?' she asked.

The question took him by surprise.

'Darren?' He scratched his head distractedly. 'Not since the divorce. In fact, the last time would have been about six months after I moved to Rusholme.'

'Why is that?' said Jo.

'Because it was too hard for the both of us. It brought back too many memories. And to be honest, I think because he blamed me for the break-up with his mother.'

He looked at her with a mournful expression. 'He was right too. Him and his mum, they wanted to put it behind them. Move on with their lives. I couldn't let it go. There was no way we could carry on like that.'

Jo had run out of questions. 'That's about it then,' she said. 'If you could just let me have contact details for your employer, we'll be on our way.'

For the first time he looked concerned rather than upset.

'What d'you want this for?' he asked.

'So that I can check that you were here on those dates we gave you. You do realise that I can't just take your word for it?'

'I suppose,' he said reluctantly. 'You don't have to tell him about the trouble I had, back in Manchester?'

'The restraining order against you in relation to Miss Rand?'

He nodded.

'I take it you haven't told him then?'

'I didn't think it was relevant. He did a criminal records check and it came back clear.' He sounded belligerent all of a sudden.

'That's because it was a civil order, not a matter of criminal record,' she told him. 'You're right – you weren't obliged to tell him.'

'There you go then,' he said. He pushed his chair back and stood up. 'If there's nothing else?'

'Only to ask if you'd be prepared to surrender your passport? Just while I'm checking what you've told me?'

She expected him to object. But he surprised her.

'Not a problem,' he said and left the room. The dog climbed out of its basket and padded after him. He returned in no time at all and handed the passport to her.

'Couldn't have used it if I'd wanted to,' he said. 'It expired four years ago. Never had a reason to renew it.'

He paused and waited for her eyes to meet his.

'And I still don't.'

Chapter 57

They called at the stables and checked Clements's alibi with the owner and those of the grooms who were still around and about. It became clear that Clements couldn't possibly have fired any of the shots, unless he'd had access to a helicopter. When the owner asked why they wanted all this information, Jo went out of her way to give the impression that she was sure it was a case of mistaken identity. In her book, Clements had suffered enough already. What was the point, she asked herself, of destroying the bolthole he had made for himself?

It was 6.45 p.m. when they finally set off back to Manchester. The bad weather conditions earlier in the day had led to several accidents and lengthy delays. The backlog had run over into the rush hour period and they faced a disheartening stop-go journey ahead.

'Can I ask a question, Ma'am?' said Carly. 'Why didn't you take the rifle away for forensic comparison with the two pellets we've retrieved?'

Jo glanced at her. It was a fair question. Deserving a fair response. 'We didn't have a warrant,' she said. 'Although I grant that I could have asked him to volunteer to let me take it. The main reason is that I very much doubt we'd have been able to get a match. It's difficult to establish any kind of pattern a pellet picks up from an air rifle, especially one that's likely to stand up in court. And before you remind me that his was not an air rifle, although his rifle would leave distinctive lands and grooves and rifling marks on a normal bullet, that's much less likely on a pellet with a much smaller surface area in contact with the surface of the barrel. Having said which, if his alibi hadn't stacked up, I'd have been straight back there to collect it.' She pressed the phone switch. 'Now, if you'll excuse me, I'd better ring DS Carter. He'll be wondering how we got on.'

He answered straight away. 'Jo!' he said, forgetting that Carly Whittle would be listening in. 'Thank God for that. I was beginning to think you'd come to harm.'

'DC Whittle and I decided we deserved a day at the seaside,' she told him. 'Finishing off with a fish-and-chip dinner in Scarborough.'

He chuckled. 'Go on then,' he said. 'Tell me you've got our prime suspect handcuffed in the back.'

Jo gave him a potted version of the day's events.

'That's a shame,' he said. 'Must feel like you've wasted the best part of a day.'

'Not entirely. We've as good as eliminated a significant person of interest. The defence won't be able to accuse us of being sloppy. Have you made any progress?'

'Not yet,' he said. 'Since the only trace evidence we've got is those two pellets and a few footprints with no one to match them to, our best bet is still finding common vehicle sightings in the vicinity of two or more of the crime scenes. I've got teams working on that for all three of our victims and Merseyside are doing the same for their one.'

'I hesitate to ask,' said Jo, glancing sideways at Carly, 'but have you heard anything about Melissa?'

'Sorry,' he said. 'I spoke with Max an hour ago. He said they're chasing shadows. Either nobody knows anything, or if they do they're too scared to say.'

'What about the surveillance on the O'Neills?'

'I got the impression that's not thrown anything up either. Though I heard on the grapevine that DCI Fox has his work cut out stopping

Ryan Walsh from going "round there and trying to beat seven bells out of Jason O'Neill".'

'You can hardly blame him,' said Jo. 'I'd want to do the same if it was my daughter.'

'Have you contacted ACC Gates?' said Nick. 'Only . . .'

'I know,' she said. 'I'll do it now.'

'Good luck with that.'

It was Helen Gates's PA who answered. 'Ah, SI Stuart,' he said, in a tone that did not bode well. 'ACC Gates has been hoping that you might return her calls. Unfortunately, she is currently in conference with the Chief Constable and the rest of the Command Team. I was given strict instructions not to disturb them. But I'll be sure to let her know that you called as soon as she returns.'

'Patronising git,' said Jo, after she'd terminated the call.

'Sounds like a reprieve to me,' said Carly Whittle.

'Except that in this case that's called delaying the inevitable,' Jo replied. 'In the meantime, I think we should just enjoy ourselves, don't you?'

She switched to Media and the haunting sound of k.d. lang's 'Constant Craving' filled the car as they sped along the A64.

They were approaching Leeds when Gates rang.

'Where the hell are you?' she demanded.

'On the M62 approaching the Leeds exit, heading west, Ma'am.'

'Where the hell have you been? I've been trying to contact you since mid-morning.'

'Interviewing potential suspects, Ma'am. In Manchester, and then over in the Yorkshire Wolds. They were sensitive interviews so I had my phone on silent.'

'No, you didn't. You had it switched off.'

'I'm sorry about that, Ma'am. I must have done that by accident.'

Jo glanced at her DC. She was staring studiously out of her side window.

There was a brief silence while Gates decided if there was any point in challenging her further. There clearly wasn't. 'So, these potential suspects,' she said, 'please tell me you have some good news?'

'In a way I have,' said Jo. 'All three are connected with the most recent victim – Heather Rand.'

'The Manchester Coroner,' said Gates. 'I worked with her for years. She didn't deserve that. How is she?'

'Getting there, the last I heard.'

'Thank God. You were saying, about the good news?'

Jo was already regretting having implied there was any. She was also aware that Carly had suddenly taken an interest and was listening intently, with the hint of a smile on her lips.

'A person of interest came to light,' she said. 'Someone who had lost a daughter to drugs and after the inquest bombarded Miss Rand with threats. I interviewed his now-divorced wife and his son, and then went over to Yorkshire to interview him.'

'And?'

'I've ruled the wife out. The son looks unlikely, but we'll run the usual checks.'

'And the father?'

'Seems to have put it behind him. But he did get very emotional when questioned and possesses a shotgun and a .22 rifle.'

'A similar calibre to the poisoned pellets!' said Gates excitedly. 'So you've arrested him on suspicion?'

'Unfortunately,' Jo replied, 'it's not an air rifle, it's a different calibre, and he has a cast-iron alibi for every one of the attacks.'

'Shit!' said Gates. 'Where the hell is the good news in that?'

Jo was aware that Carly Whittle's smile had widened considerably and that she was looking forward to the reply almost as much as the ACC herself. 'Well, it's one less person of interest to worry about,' said Jo, as confidently as she dared.

It was clear from the Assistant Chief Constable's reply that she was not aware that there was a junior officer present in the car.

⌒

The incident room had an air of despondency about it. Nick Carter had left for the evening leaving another Detective Sergeant in charge. Two teams of officers were still reviewing CCTV footage from the crime scenes. DC Hulme was still at his desk. While Carly Whittle entered her notes in the system, Jo went to see what he was working on.

'Statements from people living close to Fletcher Moss, and some of the ones who were in the park when the Rand woman was shot.'

'Heather Rand,' she said. 'You wouldn't say "the O'Neill man" now, would you?'

There I go again, she told herself. *Doing a Caton.*

'Sorry, Ma'am,' he said. 'Heather Rand.'

'And have we got anything, Jimmy?' she said, using his given name to take the edge off the situation.

'There is one that came in an hour ago,' he said, 'in response to the request for information boards we put up at the entrances to the park.'

He clicked a file on the screen and brought up the statement. Jo leaned in to read it.

'A sighting of someone carrying what looked like a fishing rod,' Hulme explained. 'Walking away along the path by the River Mersey shortly after she was shot. The informant was one of the regular dog walkers who was there at the time but wasn't aware of what had happened until he turned up as usual this afternoon.'

'He was heading towards Kingsway,' she said. 'We need one of the passive media teams to focus on those cameras and on the ones on the motorway.'

'I've already briefed them,' he replied. 'But he could just as easily have stayed off the roads and carried on into Heaton Mersey or Heaton

Norris. He could even have taken the underpass and gone towards Cheadle.'

Jo turned and looked at the officers working on the passive media screens. 'They're looking there too?'

'Yes, Ma'am.'

She straightened up. 'Well done, Jimmy,' she said. 'Well done.'

Jo went over to brief the officers working on the passive media to call her immediately if they found a definite pattern emerging between the various crime scenes or were able to track the unidentified man with the fishing tackle to an end destination. At the very least either of those might throw up the elusive vehicle that the unsub was using. She'd just finished when Carly Whittle approached.

'I've entered my notes on the system, Ma'am,' she said. 'What would you like me to do now?'

'Go home to your husband and get some proper food down you.'

'What are you going to do, Ma'am?'

'Much the same, as soon as I've brought the Policy Book up to date. I'll see you in the morning. And Carly . . . thanks for today.'

'I quite enjoyed it, Ma'am,' she replied. 'Just a pity we've not a lot to show for it.'

'You'll get used to it,' said Jo. She watched the DC pick up her bag and walk towards the door. 'Actually,' she muttered, too quietly for anyone to hear, 'you won't. You never do.'

Chapter 58

'Jo!'

Agata threw her arms around Jo, stood on tiptoe to kiss both cheeks, and hugged her hard. It was exactly what she needed. Someone to bring her back to a totally different reality. To remind her that there was more to life than murder, mistrust, and misery.

Agata released her. 'Come on through,' she said. 'Dinner's ready.' As Jo followed her into the apartment, Agata held out her hand. 'Give me your coat,' she said. 'I'll put it on the bed.'

The curtains were open. Jo walked across to the window and found the doors to the balcony unlocked. She opened them and stepped out into the cool evening air.

Up here, on the nineteenth floor of Imperial Point, the view was breathtaking. Two hundred feet below, the floodlit bowstring arches of the Millennium Bridge morphed from midnight blue to emerald green and back again. The Manchester Ship Canal shimmered with reflections from the lights along the sweeping curve of West Quay, all the way down to the dark brooding presence of the Imperial War Museum North. Clouds were scudding from west to east. Here and there, in the gaps between them, the sky was studded with twinkling diamonds.

She felt a presence behind her. An arm curled around her waist; a head rested on her shoulder.

'Beautiful, isn't it?' Agata whispered. 'So quiet and peaceful. It feels like a retreat. Where the rest of the world ceases to exist and no one can touch us. I like to imagine it as my mountain hideaway, only without the trees.'

Jo knew exactly what she meant. It was one of the main reasons she'd chosen to move to The Quays. The other one being its proximity to her NCA office. A sudden breeze caused her to shiver.

'Come on,' said Agata, 'let's eat.'

It was only when the first dish appeared that Jo realised how hungry she was. 'This is amazing,' she said, between mouthfuls of creamy cucumber soup. 'Why have I never tasted this before?'

Agata smiled. 'It's one of my favourite Polish appetisers, with a twist. I add an avocado to give it depth.'

Jo tore off a hunk of rye bread. 'I need the recipe. Email it to me.'

'I thought it would be good to make a traditional Polish meal,' Agata told her. 'Partly as a nod to my own heritage, and partly because it's so well suited to autumn and winter.' She shrugged. 'Not so good for the rest of the year. I'll let you have all three of the recipes if you like?'

'Absolutely,' said Jo, 'if the others are as good as this.'

Agata cleared the soup bowls, topped up their glasses, and returned with new bowls and then a large black cast-iron casserole dish. She lifted the lid to reveal a thick brown stew packed with meat and a hint of vegetables.

'Wow!' said Jo.

'*Bigos*,' said Agata. 'You'd probably call it hunter's stew.'

'It smells amazing,' Jo declared. 'What's in it?'

Agata began to ladle the stew into Jo's bowl.

'What isn't in it?' she said. 'Pork, venison, veal, Polish sausage, beef, mushrooms, cabbage, sauerkraut, stock.'

Jo ate voraciously. Thoughts of Operation Alecto and the missing schoolgirl evaporated, together with the physical tension that had accompanied them. There was only room for conversation about the food itself and its preparation.

Just when Jo was beginning to feel sated, Agata presented with a flourish a plate of exquisite crescent-shaped, iced pastries, sprinkled with flaked almonds.

'St Martin's Day Croissants,' she said proudly. 'Also known as *Marcinki* after the region they come from. Traditionally they are eaten on St Martin's Day which is November 11th, and which marks Polish Independence Day. It's only a couple of weeks off, so I thought I'd get in some practice.'

'They look scrumptious,' said Jo. 'What are they filled with?'

'Poppyseed and almonds, corn syrup, sugar, and starch.'

Jo's face fell. 'What's the matter?' said Agata. 'Do you have an allergy?'

'It's not that,' said Jo. 'It's the poppyseed. You do know they're the primary source for heroin?'

Agata laughed. 'Of course,' she said. 'Everyone knows that. But at such a small level as this they're completely harmless or you wouldn't be able to buy them in the shops.'

'But they'll still register as heroin and morphine in a standard drugs test,' said Jo. 'We've been specifically warned about it. I'm sorry, Aggie, but I can't risk it.'

Agata sat down. 'You're serious, aren't you?' she said.

Jo reached across and squeezed her hand. 'I'm sorry,' she said, 'but I am. You know the TV presenter – Angela Rippon?'

'*Rip-Off Britain*,' said Agata.

'Well, she tested positive on the show after eating some poppyseed bread. She did it after hearing about the power-station worker who was sacked for failing a routine workplace test after doing the same. And there's the Swiss national who was given a four-year sentence in Dubai after he was found to have a few poppyseeds on his clothing after eating a poppyseed roll at Heathrow Airport.'

Agata put her other hand on top of Jo's. 'Did you drive here?' she said.

'No.'

'So you can either stay here tonight or go back on the Metro. And what are the chances of you having a random workplace drugs test tomorrow, a Saturday? In the middle of a major investigation?'

Jo smiled. 'A billion to one?'

'There you go then.'

'But there's always a chance of an accident when I'm in the car tomorrow,' Jo reasoned. 'And that might result in a roadside drink and drugs test.'

'So be careful. Or better still, get one of your minions to drive you.' Agata could see that Jo was beginning to waver. She squeezed Jo's hand tight. 'Life's too short,' she said. 'And you know they'll let you off when you explain. It'll not be the biggest risk you've ever taken.'

Ain't that the truth, thought Jo. It was possibly the largest under-statement she'd ever heard. She stared into those big blue eyes, the slightly darker shading of one giving Aggie an air of mischievous intent.

'What the hell,' said Jo, releasing a hand and reaching for a bun.

Later, the table cleared, they sat side by side on the sofa, nursing a Slivovitz plum brandy apiece.

'A nineteenth-century recipe,' Agata explained, 'passed down through the generations by the Jewish inhabitants of Stryków. It even survived the Holocaust, which is more than ninety-nine per cent of those inhabitants did.'

'Are you Jewish, Aggie?' said Jo.

'No. Neither am I Polish. I was born here. I'm a British citizen with a British passport. It is true that because both of my parents are Polish

I'd automatically qualify for Polish citizenship, but it has never crossed my mind. Until now.'

'Why now?'

'Because we Brits have decided to divorce ourselves from the rest of Europe. Poland included. I have always regarded myself as both British and European. I do not want to have to choose. So, if we do leave I shall take up my Polish citizenship.' She nudged Jo with her free arm. 'You realise that means that if we ever go on vacation to Europe together, I'll be able to speed through immigration and customs in both directions, while you have to queue with all those other people from outside the European Union. Don't worry though, I'll wait for you in baggage collection.'

'I know so little about you,' said Jo. 'And with your obvious affinity to Poland, I just assumed . . .'

'That's because my parents wanted me never to forget my roots, or theirs.' Agata swirled her brandy and took a sip. 'When France fell in 1940 the Polish Prime Minister took his Government-in-Exile with him to London. With him came nearly 20,000 members of the armed services. Did you know that during the Battle of Britain and beyond, the Poles made up the largest non-British contingent of pilots and airmen in the RAF? My grandfather was one of them – a war hero. After the war he was given British citizenship. He returned to Poland to try to help rebuild it, but ten years later, disillusioned and certain that the Soviets would never loosen their grip, returned, bringing my father and his two sisters with him. But in 1997, after the Russians had left and Poland was beginning to re-establish itself as a nation, my father and mother took us to live in Poznań and sent my sister and me to Saint Mary Magdalene High School. We both went on to the university there.'

'What did you read?'

'English and Journalism. As you can imagine, the English came easily.'

'What is it like, Poznań?'

'It's a fascinating place. One of the oldest and largest cities in Poland. The Renaissance Old Town survived the German occupation, as did the cathedral, which is the oldest church in the entire country. The Imperial Castle and the Town Hall are really impressive. In summer there are beaches along the River Warta, like in Paris. The city has one of the highest standards of living in Poland.' She raised her glass. 'Oh, and I almost forgot – an exceptional standard of education.'

Jo clinked glasses with her. 'One has only to look at you.'

'I'd love to take you and show you round some day, perhaps?' said Agata.

'I'd love that,' Jo replied. 'I've never been further east than the Rhine.'

Agata adopted a serious tone. 'Did you know,' she said, 'that Winston Churchill promised that the British people would never forget the debt they owed to the Polish troops who fought alongside them, and then, at the Yalta Conference, he agreed to let Russia keep whole swathes of Poland and displaced over a million Poles, including many of those selfsame troops? Many of the troops refused to return home to Poland, and thirty of them committed suicide rather than do so.'

'That must have been dreadful,' said Jo.

'My grandfather said it felt like the ultimate betrayal. That's why the British Government passed the Polish Resettlement Act allowing the troops and their families, and others affected by the annexation to stay in Britain or come to live here.' She shook her head sadly. 'How times have changed,' she said.

The evening had taken a more sombre turn. Jo wasn't sure how to respond. She put her glass down. 'I need the loo,' she said.

'In the bedroom,' said Agata.

On her way back, Jo spotted a laptop open on the bed. Perhaps it was the drink, but she was tempted to take a peek. She tapped the space bar and a document appeared. The headline screamed out at her.

'Melissa Still Missing. What are the police doing to find her?'

A rush of mixed emotions threatened to overwhelm her. Her initial reaction was to feel disappointment and betrayal, but a more insistent voice broke in. *Don't be a fool,* it said. *This is Aggie's job. She did warn you. And, to be fair, she hasn't raised this case, or Alecto, all evening. Stop being so precious, and for God's sake don't mess this one up.*

She quickly put the laptop into sleep mode, praying that Aggie wouldn't notice. Then she picked her coat and bag up off the bed and walked into the lounge.

'You're not leaving already?' said Aggie. She stood up. 'I was hoping you might . . . stay the night?'

'I'm sorry,' said Jo. 'But I'm really bushed. I desperately need a good night's sleep.' She saw how crestfallen Agata looked. 'Seriously,' she said, 'and there's a lot preying on my mind. The investigation. The missing girl. I wouldn't be any fun. And there'll be plenty of other occasions.'

Before Agata could reply, Jo gave her a big hug.

'Thank you, Aggie,' she said. 'It's been a wonderful evening. Exactly what I needed.'

'How will you get back?'

Jo looked at her watch. 'If I leave right now, I'll get the last tram to Victoria. Then it's just a two-minute walk to the apartments.'

Agata followed her to the door. 'Be careful,' she said.

Jo gave her a reassuring smile. 'I'm a big girl,' she said, 'and it's a Friday night. The city will be buzzing.'

There was an awkwardness about their kiss that reflected the conflicting emotions going on in their heads. Jo had no idea what was stopping her from fully committing. And she knew that Aggie couldn't fathom why such a promising evening had suddenly headed south. She stepped out into the corridor.

'My turn next,' she said, 'just as soon as I've got the place straight.'

'Don't forget I promised to help you with that,' said Agata.

'I'll call you tomorrow,' said Jo. 'And thanks again – it really was a lovely evening.'

The elevator doors opened. As Jo stepped inside she looked back towards the apartment. Aggie was still standing in the doorway. Her ash blonde hair framed a sad pale face. She looked nothing like the hard-boiled reporter. More like a little lost doll. Jo felt a pang of guilt and was tempted to run back, hold her close, and tell her there was nothing to worry about. A moment's hesitation and then the doors slid to and the elevator began to descend.

Chapter 59

DAY SIX – SATURDAY, 21ST OCTOBER

Jo moaned. Her temples throbbed, her mouth was bone dry, and there was an insistent ringing in her head. She opened her eyes and quickly closed them against the searing bright light around the edges of the shutters.

The ringing stopped.

She turned her back to the window, warily opened one eye and then the other. She focused on the phone lying on the bedside table. She reached out and picked it up. It was off. She switched it on again. The time said 9.25 a.m.

She cursed and levered herself up until her back was against the headboard, closed her eyes again and took stock.

She didn't remember going to bed, but she knew that her sleep had been populated by the weirdest of dreams. She couldn't remember any of the details, but it had felt like fleeing from one nightmare to the next. From the very hounds of hell.

She put it down to the plum brandy and the poppyseed. *My God*, she thought, *have I just experienced what it's like to be on heroin?*

As the phone came alive, it began to alert her to text after text. She held it up and checked them through bleary eyes. There was one from

Helen Gates. The others were all from the same number. There was one she did not recognise. She opened the first of them, timed at 9.02.

Ms Stuart. We are all here. Where are you?

'Shit!'

She pushed back the bedclothes and swung her legs over the side of the bed, triggering a hammer blow inside her skull. She'd missed the completion of sale they had arranged for this morning. In the open-plan lounge the landline began to ring. She hurried through and picked it up.

'I'm so sorry,' she told the solicitor. 'I had a really bad night and slept through the alarm. Am I too late?'

'Not if you can get here within the next half hour. Mr and Mrs Roberts have to be away by 10.15. I'll get them a coffee. But please hurry. I have another appointment myself at ten.'

Jo splashed her face, cleaned her teeth, threw on her clothes, grabbed her phone, bag, and keys and left.

Forty minutes later she stood on the pavement outside the solicitors, took a deep breath and exhaled slowly. The atmosphere had been frosty and she'd felt dreadful, both physically and emotionally. But the deed was done. Now she could move on.

Her phone pinged. It was a text from Abbie.

All done and dusted?

Jo shook her head. 'You couldn't wait, could you?' she murmured. She kept the reply short and to the point.

Yes. Cheque to follow.

She'd barely pressed send when another text appeared. It was Nick Carter.

Got some good news, Ma'am. Are you coming in?

She replied straight away.

Be with you in fifteen.

In the event, it was more like ten. Jo hated to think what might have happened had she been stopped for speeding. She kept an alcohol self-test kit in the car, so she knew for a fact that she'd been on the amber/green boundary when she set off. But God knows what her opiate level might be. There was no telling how St Martin's Day Croissants would go down as an explanation before an NCA disciplinary enquiry. *Like a lead balloon,* came to mind.

Nick hurried across the room to meet her. He viewed her with surprise and a hint of concern. He lowered his voice. 'You look like shit,' he said.

'Like shit, Ma'am,' she replied.

'Sorry, Ma'am,' he said. 'Are you okay?'

When it was evident that she was not going to elaborate, he launched into a rapid update.

'The hospital's given Heather Rand the all-clear, but they still want her to stay in for a few days just to be on the safe side. Firearms forensics have confirmed what you already knew about it being possible to fire pellets from a long rifle using powder-activated nail gun blanks. But, they say there was no evidence of rifling marks on the recovered pellets. Nor was there any gun powder residue on the pellets. They also say the noise, even with a suppressor fitted, would have been much more evident. Their view is that we're looking at either a standard air rifle, or a target air pistol.'

Jo nodded. 'All of which rules out the rifle I saw at James Campbell's cottage.'

'Exactly. That was a good call, Ma'am. But the really exciting news is that a Nissan Micra was caught on CCTV in the vicinity of two of the sites on the days in question.'

'Which crime scenes?'

'Ainsdale and Bolton. I can show you on the computer,' he said.

'I'll take your word for it,' she said. 'Was it possible to identify the driver?'

'Not from the cameras. He had the sunshield down and a baseball cap low over his face.'

'How do you know it was a he?'

'An educated guess. We were able to get the licence number. The registered owner, keeper, and insured, are one and the same. Duggie Wallace wasn't in, so I got on to your man, Ram Shah, and asked him to get us everything he could on this guy.'

'And?' she said, impatiently.

'He lives in Trafford. He's unmarried, but with a male partner. He works in Manchester for a major insurance company, as a departmental manager. Claims investigation branch. No previous convictions.'

'Does he have a name?'

'Jordan Springer.'

'Get your coat, Nick,' she said. 'Let's go and hear what Mr Springer has to say for himself. And by the way, you're driving.'

Chapter 60

'Poppyseed-filled croissants?' Nick Carter glanced across at her. 'Are you sure you should be telling me this?'

'Why?' she replied. 'Are you going to grass me up?'

'No.'

'Good. The reason I'm telling you is that I thought you'd find it interesting. And just in case I need someone to back me up.'

'Won't Agata do that?'

Jo looked out of her side window, avoiding his gaze. 'Hopefully.'

'Sounds like you did have a rough night,' he said.

'This is it,' said Jo.

The pre-war semi-detached was straight off Barton Road. There was a grey VW hatchback in the drive. Nick pulled in and stopped behind it.

'No sign of a Nissan,' he observed, releasing his seat belt.

They walked side by side up the gravelled drive. The door opened before they had a chance to ring the bell.

The young man standing in the doorway was in his mid- to late-twenties. He was of medium height, slim, dressed in a sweatshirt and jeans, and sported a short black beard. 'How may I help you?' he asked in a surprisingly bass and confident voice.

'Jordan Springer?' said Jo.

'Yes. And you are?'

Jo held up her ID. Nick followed suit. 'Police officers. Could we come in and have a word, please?'

'What's it to do with exactly?' he said.

'It would be better for all of us if I could explain inside,' she persisted.

With great reluctance, he stepped aside and let them in. 'All the way down the hall,' he said.

'Who is it, Jordy?' said a male voice.

'Police,' he replied, shutting the door behind them.

'Police?'

A second man stood as they entered the kitchen. Of African-Caribbean heritage, he looked older than Springer and taller. He wore sweatpants and a tight-fitting cut-off tank top that showed his well-developed muscles to the full. Springer went to stand beside the other man and the two of them exchanged looks.

'This is all very mysterious,' Springer said. 'Are you going to tell us what this is about?'

'My name is SI Stuart,' said Jo, 'and this is Detective Sergeant Carter. And this gentleman is . . .?'

'Adam Sealy. I'm Jordan's partner.'

'We're interested in the whereabouts of this car, Mr Springer,' said Jo, 'registered in your name.'

Nick Carter handed him a photo taken from one of the traffic cameras. The two of them stared at it in disbelief.

'I don't own a car,' said Springer. 'And I've never seen this one before in my life.'

'Do you drive?'

'Not cars, no. I own a mountain bike. I work in the city. I have no need of a car.'

'How about you, Mr Sealy?' said Jo.

'I own a Mercedes SUV, a mountain bike, and a racer I use for my triathlons,' he replied. 'The Merc is being serviced right now.'

'Then how do you explain the fact, Mr Springer, that this car is registered in your name, shows you as the keeper, and is also taxed and licensed in your name?' said Nick.

Adam Sealy looked concerned.

His partner smiled and shook his head as though expressing disappointment. 'I'm sure I don't need to explain this to you both,' he said, 'but it'll probably save us all time if I do. I'm in insurance. I see vehicle fraud like this all the time at work. Fraudsters using false addresses, including email addresses, and easily obtainable cards such as retail store cards to build up a plausible electronic picture of credit activity, which banks, DVLA, insurers, and landlords take as evidence that they're dealing with a genuine applicant. In this case someone must have decided to use my details. All he'd have to do is inform them of a change of address. Probably one he's got on a short lease, in Trafford, using the same information. You must be aware that there have been whole areas of some cities in the UK where over 60 per cent of vehicles are uninsured?'

Jo did, as did Nick. The minute it became clear that Springer didn't even drive, let alone own a car, they had feared exactly this scenario. Tracking down the fraudster would be near on impossible. At best, time consuming.

'Do you know why anyone would decide to use your name and details, Mr Springer?' said Jo.

He shrugged. 'Why do they pick anyone's? Probably just choose one at random from the metaphorical phone book. Or check out a few profiles on social media.'

'You do understand that I'll have to ask one of my officers to check what you've told me,' she said.

'I've nothing to hide,' he told her.

'Good, because just to be absolutely certain, for your sake as much as ours, the officer will also ask you both about your whereabouts on certain days and at certain times.'

'No problem,' they said in unison.

'Have you ever received any official-looking documents, brown envelopes, that sort of thing, addressed to someone else, but with your address?' she asked.

'No,' replied Jordan Springer. 'I'd have certainly remembered if I had.'

'There was one about a year ago, Jordy,' said Adam Sealy. 'I'm sure I told you about it?'

Springer looked surprised. 'You can't have done. Like I say, I'd have remembered.'

'What did you do with it?' asked Jo.

'Wrote "Not known at this address" on it and put it in the mail on the way to work.'

'No!' his partner exclaimed. 'You must never do that.'

'What was I supposed to do with it? Open it?'

'Exactly. Then, if it's legit you can reseal it and send it back to the Post Office. Because there's every chance that someone's using your address to gain credit or official documents.'

Sealy appealed to the two police officers. 'I thought it was illegal to open any mail not in your name?'

'It is,' Nick told him. 'Under the Postal Services Act 2000, a person commits an offence if, intending to act to a person's detriment, and without reasonable excuse, he opens a postal packet which he knows, or reasonably suspects, has been incorrectly delivered to him. The penalty is a fine, or up to six months' imprisonment.'

'Ah!' said Springer. 'But in this case, there would be a reasonable excuse. Namely, making sure someone isn't trying to impersonate me!'

'It's a moot point, Sir,' said Nick. 'You'd be safer returning it to the post office and reporting your concerns to them.'

'I think that's about it,' said Jo. 'If we could just have a look in your garage before we leave.'

'Sure, I'll show you,' said Springer.

They were walking back down the hall when something caught Jo's eye. A framed university diploma in the name of Jordan Springer. He had been awarded a 2:1 honours degree in Economics.

'You were at UCL?' she said.

'That's right. 2010 to 2013.'

'While you were there, did you come across a student named Darren Clements?'

He looked surprised.

'Darren? We shared a house during my last two years. There were five of us in a rental property off Russell Square. He was a year below me, on a different course.'

'Two years?' said Jo. 'You must have got to know him pretty well.'

'I guess so. Not that we were bosom friends. Why are you asking?'

'Hang on!' said his partner. 'Are you saying you think this guy is the person who has been impersonating Jordan?'

'I'm not saying that at all,' she replied. 'It's just that the more information we have, the better we'll be able to pursue appropriate lines of enquiry. Are you still in contact with Darren, Mr Springer?'

'No. I haven't seen or spoken to him since I left university.'

'Is it possible some of your other friends may have done?' asked Nick.

'I suppose so. But if they did, they never mentioned it.'

Jo handed him a card containing her contact details. 'I'd be obliged if you could check and then let me know,' she said. 'Now, the garage?'

Chapter 61

.

'It's got to be Darren Clements,' said Nick as he started the engine. 'Unless he sold the car on to someone else. But it's too much of a coincidence – him having both a motive, and fraudulently obtaining a vehicle spotted in the vicinity of several of the crime scenes.'

'I agree,' said Jo. 'But there's a yawning gulf between believing it and proving it. And we don't know for certain that Ronnie O'Neill, or any of the other victims of these attacks had a role in his sister's death, as suppliers or dealers. It's a pity the original investigation didn't try harder to establish where the drugs she took came from.'

'Once they had a verdict of death by misadventure I suppose they didn't see the point?' said Nick.

'Darren Clements certainly would have done,' Jo replied. 'We need to find that vehicle – preferably with him in it. That means the ANPR database, live and historical searches. And a close look at any passive media footage we can get our hands on within a mile radius of his home. For all we know he may be parking it nearby and using his bike to go to and from it. And I want him under twenty-four-hour personal surveillance.'

'Trouble is, now he knows we're looking at him, he's going to be extra careful. And what's the likelihood he's going to keep using the same car?'

'He doesn't know that we know about the car. Or that we've established a possible link between that and him.'

'Why don't we get a Section 8 warrant to thoroughly search his home? We've got reasonable cause. And there's no way we can obtain the evidence we need without it.'

Jo shook her head. 'You said it yourself, Nick. He knows we regard him as a suspect. I've met him. He was smart, calm, and confident. Arrogant even. He was happy for us to have a good look around. We didn't find anything at his house that could connect him to the attacks, and if there was he's going to have either destroyed it or moved it by now.'

He checked his mirrors and then glanced at her. 'Come on,' he said. 'How many times have you come across a villain who was all of those things, but was so arrogant he didn't bother to cover his tracks?'

Jo thought about it. 'You're right,' she responded. 'There's too much at stake. If it is him and he's been smart, at the very least we'll likely force him to back off. To slow down. Maybe save a life while we're gathering more evidence. If we don't bring him in and he does strike again, how's that going to make us feel?'

'Exactly my thinking,' said Nick. 'And if we're wrong and it isn't him there's nothing lost. And it'll look like we're actually doing something. If you'd seen this morning's shambles you'd know how important that's become.'

Jo's heart skipped a beat. 'What do you mean, this morning's shambles?'

'I hate to be the one to tell you this, Jo,' he said, 'but while you were sleeping off last night's hanky-panky, Helen Gates was being grilled about Operation Alecto on *BBC Breakfast* news. And I have to tell you, it wasn't pretty.'

'Oh hell!' she said. 'There was a text from Gates on my phone but I didn't read it. I was late for the solicitors. I bet she was wanting me to do the interview.'

'That'd be my guess,' he said. 'Or at the very least she'd have wanted you to brief her.'

'Go on,' she said. 'Tell me the worst.'

'She was giving it the usual "Investigations are ongoing . . . A number of lines of enquiry are being followed . . . We are hopeful of a speedy resolution . . ." but the presenters were having none of it. You should have heard them going at it. "Why has no one been arrested? Why has so little information been made public? Is it true there's a random killer on the loose firing pellets laced with ricin? Is Counter Terrorism Command involved? What can members of the public do to protect themselves?" You should have seen her face. It's not easy to look both embarrassed and wrathful at the same time.'

Jo grimaced. 'No prizes for guessing who all that wrath was aimed at.'

'That wasn't the worst of it,' he said. 'One of them asked her if there was any truth in the rumours that the abduction of the missing twelve-year-old girl was connected with the shootings.'

'What did she say to that?'

'The only thing she could say. That the operation was being handled by the National Crime Agency and all enquiries should be directed to them.'

'Apart from the fact that it's not strictly true, it must have come across as a massive cop-out?'

'It did. And when that was pointed out she decided she'd had enough. A technician had to rush on to stop the throat mic ripping her blouse as she walked off.'

Jo leaned forward and banged her head rhythmically against the fascia. It started that hammer going again, but the pain was a comforting diversion. *I suppose this is why people self-harm,* she told herself.

'Poor Helen,' she said. 'She's never going to forgive me.'

'Cheer up,' said Nick. 'You're not alone. She tried to get me too, but I was in the shower. By the time I returned her call she was already in the studio. Don't worry, it'll all be forgotten as soon as we nail this bastard.'

The Airwave radio burst into life. It was ACC Gates. Her voice teetered on the edge of fury. 'DS Carter,' she said, 'is there the remotest possibility that you happen to know the whereabouts of SI Stuart?'

Jo pulled a face, took a deep breath, and sat back. 'I'm right here, Ma'am,' she said.

'Hallelujah!' said Gates. 'The wanderer returns!'

'I'm sorry, Ma'am,' said Jo.

'Sorry? I should bloody well think you're sorry. Are you aware of what I had to endure this morning?'

'Yes, Ma'am. DS Carter briefed me.'

'Lucky you. I had no one to brief me. Because you two appeared to have gone walkabout. Again!'

'I'm sorry, Ma'am.'

'Where were you?'

'I had an appointment with my solicitor, Ma'am. I forgot to switch my phone back on.'

'Something that appears to have become a habit.'

'Sorry, Ma'am.'

'Will you stop apologising and shape up. This is an ongoing multiple murder investigation with unparalleled national interest. I need to be able to contact both of you at any time, night or day. Is that understood?'

'Yes, Ma'am,' they chorused.

'My God!' she said. 'It's Tweedledum and Tweedledee.'

They exchanged glances.

'We have a prime suspect, Ma'am,' said Jo, seizing the initiative.

There was a pause.

'Are you serious, or are you just trying to humour me?'

'I'm serious, Ma'am. Darren Clements.'

'I thought you'd ruled him out? Him and his father?'

'Not entirely. We had nothing to connect him to any of the murders other than a possible motive. But because he lives alone and works from home, he had no concrete alibis for any of the attacks.'

'So what's changed?'

'Despite his motive, he never acted upon it in the way that his father did,' said Jo. 'But now we have evidence that he stole the identity of a former student friend and used that to buy, license, tax, and insure a car that has been placed in the vicinity of two of the crime scenes at times relevant to the shootings.'

'Motive and opportunity,' said the ACC. 'That's too much of a coincidence. All you need now is the means. You have to find that air rifle.'

'I'm on my way to Nexus House to fill out a Section 8 application for a warrant to search his house and put a team together,' said Jo.

'Leave the warrant to me,' said Gates. 'It'll be quicker. I'll give you a call as soon as the magistrate has signed it. You can pick it up from Central Park HQ.'

They both heard the click as she ended the call.

'Well, that went well,' said Nick Carter.

Jo wasn't sure if he was being serious or sarcastic.

He turned off the engine and began to unbuckle his seat belt. 'Tweedledum and Tweedledee?' he said.

'It could have been worse,' she replied.

'Like what?'

'Cagney and Lacey,' she said. 'I know which one I'd be.'

Chapter 62

'There's no response, Ma'am,' said Maguire, the search team leader. 'And no sign of life, as far as we can tell.'

Jo was unsurprised. The surveillance team hadn't observed any movement since they'd arrived an hour earlier. A female officer in plain clothes had just made the initial approach because Jo had been hoping to keep it as low-key as possible. Just in case they'd got it wrong. Some hope.

'Very well,' she said. 'Send them in.'

They watched Maguire return to the lead van and climb into the passenger seat. The van set off, followed by a Land Rover Defender and a sedan, both containing members of the Firearms Unit, then Jo, Nick, DC Whittle, and a loggist from Central Park. A marked Forensics van, a dog unit, and an unmarked van brought up the rear.

The lead vehicles turned left into the suspect's street. The sedan car carried straight on, accelerated, and then turned sharp left towards the rear of the property.

The first of the vans parked broadside across the road. The rear van copied the manoeuvre. Roadblocks in place, three officers in full riot gear ran up the drive, the doors of the BMW flew open and four armed officers came forward and took up positions in the yard, covering the windows with their weapons. Jo walked towards the house, her colleagues beside her.

'So much for softly, softly,' muttered Nick.

The search team leader turned towards them. Jo nodded her head. The foremost officer swung his tubular steel Enforcer, exerting close to three tons of force against the lock. The door flew open. More armed officers, wearing respirators beneath their masks, ran up the drive and straight into the house adding their shouts to those of their colleagues: *Armed Police! Stay where you are! Armed Police! Stand Still!*

By the time the detectives had reached the gate the firearms commander had received the all-clear.

'There's no one in there, Ma'am,' he told her. 'Nor in the yard out back. Looks like the bird has flown.'

The firearms officers had begun trooping back down the flagstone path. Jo stepped back to let them pass.

'Any sign of chemicals? Or potential booby traps?' she asked.

He shook his head. 'They were briefed to look out for both. They'd have told me if they'd spotted anything.'

'Better to be sure,' she said, waving forward the two dog teams.

They watched as a springer spaniel was carried over the broken glass by his handler and set down in the hallway. The handler of a golden retriever found it more challenging as he followed suit. A further seven minutes passed, during which more than a dozen neighbours had appeared in windows and doorways and been told in no uncertain terms to close them and to stay indoors. The handlers returned, both shaking their heads.

Jo's Airwave radio squawked. It was Helen Gates.

'Gold Command. Report, please, Bronze Command.'

'Initial searches complete, Gold Command,' Jo replied. 'All negative. There is no sign of the suspect. According to the dog handlers there was no trace of weapons, drugs, or the specific substance about which we're concerned. I'm just about to send in a biohazard Forensics team.'

'Is that really necessary, Bronze Command? Given the dogs have already been in?'

Nick raised his eyebrows. Jo managed to keep her expression neutral.

'I believe so, Gold Command,' she calmly replied. 'Mistakes happen. Forensics have their own highly sensitive detection equipment. When they're happy we'll carry out a full search of the premises.'

'Have you started door-to-door?'

'Yes, Ma'am. And I've received confirmation that the all-ports warning has been sent.'

There was a long pause.

'The search for the vehicle is ongoing?'

'Yes, Ma'am.'

'In which case, Bronze Command,' said Gates. 'In the absence of the suspect and any immediate threat, I'm handing all operational command of this operation over to you. Keep me informed of any developments.'

'Acknowledged, Gold Command,' said Jo.

'Just find your suspect, SI Stuart,' Gates added, 'before he does any more damage.'

'Thoughtful of her to put that last bit on record,' Nick observed when the exchange was over.

Jo tutted and turned to the loggist. 'You're not making a note of that, are you? My colleague's comment?'

He shook his head. 'As if I would. It was hardly a decision, was it?'

'Thank you,' she said.

Jack Benson, the senior CSI officer, approached with his visor up. 'It's safe for the search team to go in, Ma'am,' he said. 'Free from hazards and as far as we can tell, anything else besides. If pressed, I'd say he's sanitised the place.'

'I'm pressing you,' she said.

He shrugged. 'In that case, in my professional opinion, someone has sanitised these premises.'

Jo turned to the loggist again. 'You can write that down.' She stepped onto the path and headed towards the door. 'Come on, you two,' she called over her shoulder. 'Let's go.'

It was immediately obvious what the CSI leader had meant. Compared with their previous visit everything was neat and tidy and all the surfaces had been dusted. The pile of paperbacks on the dining-room table had disappeared. The vinyl records had been placed in a wicker basket beside the turntable. The kitchen looked as though a professional cleaner had worked on it.

Jo had a look under the stairs. The bicycle was missing, as was the black-and-red windcheater that had hung from one of the hooks. She kicked herself for not having taken a photograph of the upstairs.

Jo found Carly in the study in the loft space. She was standing by the desk, holding a pair of black power leads.

'If I remember right,' she said, 'the last time we were here, they were attached to a laptop and a printer.'

'A MacBook Pro,' said Jo, 'and an HP printer, copier, scanner.' She pointed to the multidrawer filing cabinet. 'See if you can find anything in there or anywhere else that might link him to the Nissan. Maybe an insurance certificate, or a fraudulently acquired driver's licence in Jordan Springer's name.'

She climbed back down the ladder and went into the master bed-room where she found Nick Carter lying flat on the floor, peering under the bed.

'Anything?' she asked.

Taken by surprise, he banged his head on the bedframe, swore, and emerged rubbing the back of his scalp vigorously. 'Not a dicky bird,' he moaned. 'Not even a porn magazine.'

Jo was staring at the bedside table. 'Any sign of a Kindle?' she said. 'It had a red cover on it.'

He followed her gaze. 'No. I've finished in here, except for under the mattress.'

Together they raised one side of the mattress and then the other. 'That's it then,' she said. 'He's taken everything.'

Nick had left the wardrobe doors open. She went over and studied the contents.

'There were definitely more clothes in here,' she said. 'There's a black leather jacket missing and at least two pairs of jeans.' She started opening the shoeboxes. 'I can't be certain,' she said, 'but I think there's a pair of walking boots and at least one pair of sneakers missing.'

'Ma'am?' The senior CSI officer was standing in the doorway. 'We're ready when you are, Ma'am,' he said.

Jo stood up, holding a shoe. 'We're done here,' she told the CSI. 'Photograph everything and then take this place apart. You know what you're looking for.'

'Yes, Ma'am.' He disappeared onto the landing.

'I doubt they're going to find it though,' said Nick.

She threw the shoe at him. He caught it and lobbed it back. 'Misery guts!' she said.

'You know I'm right,' he told her.

'Course I do.' She dropped the shoe on top of the boxes. 'Only you're here to raise my spirits, Nick, not dampen them. Can you try to remember that?'

They reconvened back at the car. The loggist was still with them, recording every decision.

Jo was briefing the search team leader. 'Make sure the officers working the door-to-doors understand we need every bit of CCTV data that any of these other houses might have. That includes dashcams. And when they're taking witness statements, make sure they ask if Clements has been seen driving, or getting into, any vehicle at all. If so, I want the make, colour, time, and description of any other occupants. There's no way he could have left here with his laptop, printer, shoes, clothes, and whatever else he may have needed, on a bicycle.'

He listened patiently, his expression suggesting that he'd already briefed them to do exactly that, but his voice demonstrated that he understood that she was under pressure to be seen to be in charge. That the written log was a way of doing that.

'Yes, Ma'am,' he replied. 'I'll see to it right now.'

They watched him walk briskly away.

'What now?' said Carter.

Jo suddenly thumped the steering wheel. The others stared at her. 'I've been so desperate to find him,' she said, 'that I've taken my eye off the ball.'

'How d'you mean?' said Carter, watching out of the corner of his eye as the loggist scribbled away in the back seat.

'If,' she explained, 'he's been systematically working through a list of people he blames – either directly or indirectly – for his sister's death, then we have to assume there are other names on that list. We've just spooked him. What if he decides he has to speed up his crazy mission before we can stop him?'

'In that case he's more likely to make mistakes,' Nick pointed out. 'The less time he has to plan, the more visible he's going to be.'

'Tell that to his next victim,' said Jo. 'We have to work out who the rest of his targets might be and warn them. Their lives depend on it.'

Chapter 63

'Well?' said Jo.

As Andy Swift raised his head, the image on the screen blurred and then came back into focus. 'From what you've told me,' he said, 'both scenarios are still valid.'

Jo nodded impatiently. 'The slow-burn revenge killer and the professional hitman,' she said.

'But only because you have no evidence relating to Darren Clements other than the hypothesis that he stole a former acquaintance's identity in order to be able to purchase a car that has subsequently been spotted in the vicinity of two crime scenes.'

'There is also the fact that he has a clear motive,' she protested. 'And no one to verify his whereabouts at the times in question. And now he's left the house, sanitised it, and removed everything that might have incriminated him.'

'All grounds for reasonable suspicion,' he said, 'but a long way from evidential.'

He was infuriating when he was playing devil's advocate. She knew why he was doing it. He didn't want her to close her mind to other possibilities. To go racing down a track that turned out to be a dead end.

'I get that, Andy,' she said. 'You've made your point. Can we please move on to your professional opinion on what he's likely to do next?'

He leaned his elbows on the desk and steepled his fingers. 'All the indications are that he's fled his home?'

'Correct.'

'To what end?'

'Come on, Andy,' she said. 'Help me, please. I'm doing all the work here?'

His smile was irritatingly paternal. 'Just answer the question, Jo,' he said.

'To evade capture, or to complete his mission.'

'Precisely. Now, if he had already completed his "mission", as you call it, then experience of such killers leads me to believe that he would either have waited for you to come and get him or taken his own life.'

'So he definitely has other targets out there? More people he needs to kill.'

'Good choice of words,' he said. 'He needs to kill them.'

'And now that he knows we suspect him, how will that affect his behaviour?'

'Does he know? Or does he just suspect that you're looking for him?'

'If he didn't before, he will very soon. There's an APW out on him, and the fourth floor are insisting that we release his photo and description to the media.'

'Ah.' Andy removed his glasses and began to clean them. He put them back on and adjusted them. 'In that case he'll be even more desperate to complete what he sees as his mission. Nothing will be allowed to stand in his way. That makes him incredibly unpredictable as well as even more dangerous.'

'If he's cornered, will it be possible to negotiate with him?'

'That depends on whether or not he's completed his mission. If he has, then yes. If not, then I very much doubt it. He'll see himself as a failure. I think it likely that he would attempt suicide.'

'Not easy with a .177 air rifle,' observed Jo. 'Even if it is firing pellets laced with ricin.'

'In which case, you could be looking at a jumper, or suicide by cop. Either way, not very pleasant.'

'I've had my fill of both,' she said. 'Every time, I was the one left feeling like a failure.'

'Sorry I couldn't be more help, Jo.'

'You have been – if only by confirming what I suspected.'

'Good luck,' he said. 'And be careful. You're the face of this investigation. The closer you get to him the more he'll see you as an obstacle. Remember that.' He sat back. His face receded from the screen. The video link ended.

Jo stood up and went out into the body of the incident room. The energy in the place was electric. Knowing that they finally had a prime suspect and that more lives were at risk had a way of focusing minds. Eyes fixed on screens, fingers scurrying across keyboards. Nobody looked up as she walked between the desks. Nick Carter, his back towards her, was deep in conversation with Ged, the office manager.

'Anything?' she asked.

'Yes, Ma'am,' he said. 'He's still off the radar, but we've just this second identified two potential targets.' He seemed less excited than she might have expected.

'Who are they?' she said.

'One of them's a CPS officer I've come across a few times. Henry Mwamba.'

'What's his connection to Clements?'

'He was the officer who made the decision that no final action should be taken regarding the death of his sister.'

'After the inquest or before?'

'The father appealed to the Senior Investigating Officer, claiming the inquest didn't have to be the final word. When she told him that the case was closed he went straight to the CPS.'

'How did he know who to approach?'

'Mwamba gave evidence at the inquest.'

'And the SIO?'

His expression was grave. It was as though he was reluctant to tell her.

'Just tell me,' she said.

'It was Sarah. Sarah Weston.'

Jo's heart fluttered. Throughout the time that she'd been part of Caton's team, Sarah had been a mentor and a friend, despite the difference in rank.

'Do we know where she is?' she asked. 'The last I remember she was with Child Exploitation and Online Protection.'

'I lost touch,' he said. 'But you shouldn't have any problem finding out. Didn't CEOP become part of the National Crime Agency?'

'Of course,' she said. 'CEOP Command. Bugger! That means Vauxhall Bridge Road. I'm not going all the way down to London. Not at this stage in the investigation.'

'Why not just give her a ring?'

'Because this is something that needs doing face to face.'

'That's what you've got video links for,' he reminded her.

'Right,' she said. 'I'll get straight on to it. You find out where Mwamba is and go and see him. Take him an Osman warning. Tell him to be careful and if anything does happen, to ring us direct and get to Manchester Royal Infirmary ASAP.'

'Will do,' he replied. 'Incidentally, you know you mentioned about a vaccine, and the guy at Porton Down waving Highly Classified at you?'

'What about it?'

'Well, DC Hulme decided to do an online search, and guess what?'

'I haven't time for guessing games,' she told him.

'He's discovered it's commercially available.'

'In which case let's hear what he has to say before we talk to Sarah and Mwamba. Where is he?'

Hulme saw them coming and stood up.

'You can sit down,' said Jo. 'What's this about a commercially available vaccine?'

He looked uncomfortable. 'I didn't actually say it was available,' he said. 'Only that it exists and has been registered by a drug firm.'

'The distinction being?'

He shrugged. 'It's an Orphan Drug.'

Jo was becoming increasingly impatient. 'Meaning?'

'It's the status the US gives to drugs deemed to be safe, effective, and important, but which aren't likely to affect many people and therefore aren't likely to be commercially profitable.'

'I get that,' she said. 'But what I want to know is that if it's a US drug and not commercially available, how the hell do we get our hands on it?'

'As I understand it,' he said, 'it was developed by one of their universities and they're continuing to refine it with this drug company and a number of undisclosed bodies around the world. You can bet that Porton Down is one of them.'

'Which would explain,' said Nick Carter, 'why your guy was so cagey about it. He'd have to get permission from the Yanks to make some available. And I bet it'll cost a fortune. ACC Gates won't like the sound of that.'

'What are two lives worth?' said Jo. 'Well done, DC Hulme. Carry on.'

'Yes, Ma'am.' He looked more relieved than pleased. They moved away from the desk.

'You'll need approval from a Superintendent or above,' said Nick, 'for the Osman.'

'I'm well aware of that,' she said. 'I'll get Ged to prepare the paperwork while I'm trying the Duty Super. If he's not available, I'll have to speak with ACC Gates. But we know they'll both agree. We're talking a credible, real, and immediate threat to life. If you haven't got the letter within fifteen minutes, I want you to warn him anyway. I'll handle any flak.'

'Aren't you going to talk to Porton Down?' asked Nick.

'As soon as we've spoken to Sarah and Mwamba. Let me know when you're done.'

'Right,' he said. 'I'm on it.'

Jo wasn't big on praying, but this time they had a good idea of who the next victims might be. She knew that she'd never forgive herself if Clements got to them first.

Chapter 64

'I'm sorry, Ma'am, but she's not here right now.'

It had taken Jo five minutes to get through the security checks and finally be put through to CEOP Command. It would have been much quicker, she realised, if she'd been a member of the public, reporting online abuse.

'Can you tell me exactly where she is and give me a contact number, please?'

'Is it urgent?' he asked.

'It's a matter of life and death!' She realised that she'd raised her voice and must sound pretty threatening herself. 'I'm sorry,' she said. 'But I'm serious. I have to speak with her.'

'Very well,' he said. 'She's actually in your neck of the woods, doing some CEOP Ambassador training in Stockport. I only have her phone number. We're not supposed to give it out.' He heard her sharp intake of breath and hurried on. 'But under the circumstances . . .'

Jo wrote it down, thanked him, and grabbed her car keys.

Seventeen minutes later she was shown into a small office in a health centre on the outskirts of Stockport. No sooner had the door closed than it opened again. In walked Sarah Weston. Four years older, but hardly changed. She was still the cool, glamorous woman who looked more like a business executive than a police officer.

'Jo,' she said, 'it's good to see you again. But what's this all about and why the urgency?'

'You'd better sit down,' said Jo. She waited until Sarah was seated and then handed her the letter.

'Now you're freaking me out,' said Sarah.

She read the one side of A4 and looked up. Jo thought her remarkably calm.

'I'm used to writing these out in my present role,' Sarah said, 'but I've never been on the receiving end before. How good is your intelligence?'

'You've not been following the news, have you?' said Jo.

Sarah shook her head. 'I've been in Brussels all week at an international symposium on child protection. What news are we talking about?' Before Jo had time to reply, Sarah's pupils dilated. 'The madman with the ricin pellets!' she exclaimed. 'Are you serious?'

'Deadly,' said Jo. 'We have a prime suspect, whereabouts unknown, with a connection to you and a clear motive.'

Sarah let the letter drop onto the seat beside her and sat back. 'You'd better tell me all about it,' she said.

When Jo had finished, Sarah actually smiled. 'So as long as I stay away from golf courses and parks,' she said, 'I'll be fine.'

'You really need to take this seriously, Sarah,' said Jo. 'Now that he knows we're looking for him it's likely that he'll want to kill everyone on his list before we catch up with him. He'll take risks he's never taken before. He may even change his modus operandi.'

'I can see that,' said Sarah. 'More so if he hears that at least one of his victims has survived. What surprises me is that you're sure that it's him. The son. I could have understood if it was the father. He was seriously out of control.' She shook her head. 'Grief and an overwhelming sense of injustice makes for a volatile combination.'

'That's what his latest victim said. Heather Rand.'

Sarah sighed and nodded. 'The Coroner. She made the right call. We all did.'

'Unfortunately, that's not how Darren Clements sees it.'

'So how do you propose that I keep myself safe? I can't just put my life on hold and I don't suppose you're going to give me close protection?'

'I would if it was up to me.'

'But it isn't?'

'No.'

'Don't worry. It's the same with us. We hand out these notifications of threat to life like confetti, but unless we happen to know the exact time and place that the perpetrator is going to strike, there's nothing we can do – strike that – there's nothing we're *allowed* to do, beyond telling them to stay away from their abuser and keep their heads down.'

She looked Jo straight in the eyes. 'Is that what you're going to tell me?'

'I think I can do better than that,' said Jo. 'But you've got more years in than me, so it'll feel like being told how to suck eggs.'

'Don't let that stop you.'

'Very well. For a start, I suggest you don't go home while you're up here.'

'Home is London now. We've separated.'

'I'm sorry.'

'Don't be. I'm not. I married for all the wrong reasons and it's come back to bite me. I'm booked on the 20.17 train to Euston.' She smiled grimly. 'I'll be perfectly safe. I'm in First Class. They'll never allow anyone in there carrying an air rifle.'

'Secondly, don't assume that he hasn't found out where you live and where you work. Is there anywhere else that you can stay until we sort this?'

'Are we talking about the same person? Darren Clements? Mouse of a boy?'

Jo wasn't sure if it was denial or false bravado. But this wasn't the Sarah Weston she knew. 'A mouse on a mission,' she said. 'With a gun and poison pellets. It's a terrible way to die, believe me.'

Sarah sighed. 'Fair enough,' she said, dropping the pretence. 'There are several people I can call. Failing that, I'll book into a hotel under an assumed name. I'll vary my journey to work. And I'll let them know what's going on. The place is a fortress, cameras everywhere, and I'm sure NCA Command will come up with something if he's still on the loose tomorrow.'

'That's better,' said Jo. 'And there is one more precaution that we can take.'

Sarah picked up on Jo's hesitation. 'Why do I get the impression that I'm not going to like this?' she said.

Jo explained about the vaccination. Sarah listened without comment, eyebrows raised throughout.

'And how often has this miracle vaccine been used on humans?'

'I don't know,' Jo admitted.

'But it has been rigorously tested?'

'I assume so.'

'Have you taken it?'

The question took Jo by surprise. 'I'm not one of his targets. Not part of his mission.'

'How do you know that?'

'Because . . .'

'You've met him. He's aware that you're heading the investigation. Who's to say who he'll add to his list?'

'But . . .'

Sarah was now on the edge of her seat, her questions relentless. 'He'll do whatever it takes to complete his mission. That's what you said?'

'More or less.'

'And right now, you stand in his way.'

'I suppose . . .'

'No suppose about it. So, are you going to take this vaccine?'

'I . . . I haven't considered it.'

'Consider it now.'

Jo found it impossible to hide her uncertainty and confusion.

Sarah sat back and slowly shook her head in disbelief. 'So when you said "precautions we can take", you actually meant "precautions *you* can take" . . .'

Jo was out of answers. 'It's your decision, Sarah,' she said.

'This antidote they gave Heather Rand. You said it seems to have worked?'

'Yes.'

'In which case,' said Sarah, 'stuff the vaccine. Back home I'm never more than twenty minutes from the best hospitals in the UK. I can walk to Guy's and St Thomas's from work in less than ten minutes. You get some of the antidote to one of those, and I'll take my chances. Even better, why don't you give me some to take back with me?'

'It'll probably need to be refrigerated,' said Jo.

'They've been using picnic coolers filled with ice bags for organ transplants – pop it in one of those.'

'You're serious, aren't you?' said Jo.

Sarah stood up. 'Damn right I am,' she said. 'Now, are you going to make that call?'

Chapter 65

As Jo drove into the Nexus House parking lot, she saw Nick walking towards the glass-fronted entrance. She called out to him and he waited for her. He looked uncharacteristically glum and somehow drained, like a deflated balloon. They went into the building together.

'How did you get on?' she asked.

He pulled a face. 'I tracked Mwamba down to his local church. He's doing some lay preaching now he's retired.'

'And?'

'He took it surprisingly well – too well. He told me, "God will provide, young man, God will provide."'

'What did you say to that?'

'I was tempted to point out that God hadn't done a brilliant job for Ronnie O'Neill, Morris Grimshaw, and Tony Dewlay.'

Jo pushed open the fire door. 'You didn't?'

'Course I didn't. I merely suggested that it wouldn't do any harm to give God a helping hand.'

'How did he take that?'

'He laughed.'

'You told him about the vaccine?'

'He didn't want to know. Said if it came to it, he'd get himself along to the Royal and place himself in their hands, and God's. How about you? How did Sarah react?'

'Much the same, but without the God bit. How did Mwamba respond to the standard advice about keeping himself safe?'

'He nodded sagely, but I had the distinct impression it was going in one ear and out of the other.'

Jo held her pass up to the pad on the door to the incident room.

'We've done our best,' she said.

'Covered our backs, you mean,' he replied gloomily.

Jo pushed the door open and stepped inside.

'Ma'am!'

Jimmy Hulme and Carly Whittle were leaning over the desk of one of the DCs who had been drafted in to strengthen the squad. Hulme was waving them over. His excitement was encouraging.

'We think we've found out where he stashes his car,' he said, pointing at the screen: a row of identical lock-up garages stood beside a broad unmetalled track.

'Where is this?' Jo asked.

The detective constable zoomed out. Jo could see the rail track behind the garages, substantial residential properties, and the Abraham Moss Academy and Leisure Centre. Three virtual pinboard pins had been inserted on the map as place markers.

'Crumpsall,' said Carly Whittle, 'between Moss Bank and Crescent Road, immediately north of Abraham Moss.'

'That's some way from where he lives,' said Nick.

'Four miles,' said the detective. 'Less than ten minutes if he uses the motorways.'

'One way only,' Carter pointed out. 'He'd have to use his mountain bike on the way back.'

'My guess is he avoids the motorways altogether,' said Jo. 'Too many cameras. We'd have picked him up long before this if he didn't. How do we know this is the place?'

The DC used his cursor to move from place marker to place marker.

'These are where a Nissan Micra car matching the details of the one licensed to Jordan Springer was pinged, Ma'am. I tracked it back towards the suspect's address in Walkden and found these.'

He zoomed out a fraction. A further three place markers appeared.

'When were the most recent sightings?' Jo asked.

The DC split the screen in two. On the right-hand side was a three-column table of matched coordinates, dates, and times. 'As you can see, Ma'am,' he said, 'the most recent were yesterday morning, here and here.'

The cursor moved across the map picking out one place marker two miles west of the lock-ups, and one on Moss Road a few hundred yards away.

Jo checked the table and turned to Nick Carter.

'That was shortly after we left him,' she said. 'He'll have just had time to grab what he needed, clean the place up, and get out of there. The trouble is it looks as though he's left the car there. Which means he must have another vehicle.'

'Unless he's still inside that lock-up?' said Jimmy Hulme.

'Get real,' said Nick. 'He'll be long gone.'

'He could have strapped his mountain bike to the Nissan and then used that?' said Carly Whittle.

'Good thinking,' said Jo. 'Check for live footage from those cameras. See what that gives us. Nick, you stay here and see if we can spot him on any of the passive data from around that area. We need to know if he has alternative transport. And I want a drive-by surveillance on Henry Mwamba. It's not personal protection, but it's the next best thing. And see if you can find out who owns these lock-ups. They look like rentals to me. Oh, and tell Jack to have a Forensics unit on standby. Jimmy, Carly, you're with me.'

'Be careful,' said Nick. But she was already halfway to the door.

Chapter 66

'Where do we start?' asked Jimmy Hulme.

It was a good question. The rough unsurfaced road was deserted. Twelve identical lock-up garages. What looked like brand-new roofs and up-and-over doors. Much larger than they had appeared on the satellite image. Small native deciduous trees and shrubs crowded the bank above the railroad cutting. A dark grey sheet of cloud advanced across the Cheshire plain. Where the sunlight broke through, showers could be seen over Warrington and Wigan. A train rumbled past as they stood there wondering what to do next.

'We'd better start knocking on doors,' said Jo. 'Someone in one of these houses may have seen the Micra outside one of the garages. They might even be renting one right next door to our suspect.'

'We could do with a few more bodies, Ma'am,' said Carly.

'Let's see how we get on,' she said. 'You start at the bottom end, Jimmy, you take the top end, Carly, and I'll start in the middle.'

They were ten minutes in when Jo's phone rang. It was Nick.

'You were right,' he said. 'They were built as a unit by a rental business. The landlord is on the way out to you.'

'Any idea how long?'

'They're in Middleton, so fifteen minutes tops.'

Ten minutes later a black Porsche Cayenne rounded the corner and bumped its way slowly towards them.

'I know what I'm going to do when I retire,' said Jimmy. 'Rent out garages.'

'He's probably got it on one of these rental deals, just like his garages,' said Carly.

'She,' said Jo.

The Porsche pulled up ten yards away, just short of a particularly nasty pothole. A large bottle blonde in a red leather biker jacket – part apprentice sumo wrestler, part drag act – climbed out and walked unsteadily towards them on six-inch heels.

'Person,' muttered Jimmy Hulme, playing the gender-neutral card. He saw Jo's expression and immediately regretted it.

'I don't care,' said Jo, 'just so long as that's a key she's holding.'

'You'se the police?' said the woman in a strong Mancunian accent.

'No, we're having a picnic,' said Jimmy Hulme.

Jo showed her ID. 'And you are?' she said.

'Sharon Osborne.'

'Really?' said Hulme.

She glared at him. 'Yeah! Really. Different spellin', if you must know.'

'Thank you for responding so quickly,' said Jo. 'We really appreciate it.'

Osborne dangled the keys just out of reach. 'Have you'se gotta warrant?' she asked.

'I didn't have time,' said Jo. 'But under the circumstances, which I'm not at liberty to share with you, the alternative is that we break into each of these garages in turn until we find the one that we're looking for.'

The woman scowled. 'No need for that. I was just askin'.' She handed over the key. 'Number 11,' she said. 'Down the end.'

'Thank you,' said Jo.

Osborne followed them as they hurried towards the garage in question. 'It's him, isn't it?' she said.

'Who?' said Jo.

'The guy on the telly. The one you're looking for. Darren somethin'?'

'Darren Clements,' said Jo. 'What makes you think that?'

'I recognised him. It was me that give him the keys.'

Jo stopped and stared at her. 'So why didn't you ring the police straight away?'

'Because that wasn't the name he give me, was it?'

Jimmy Hulme rolled his eyes. The three of them carried on walking.

'It wasn't the name on the direct debits either,' she added, as though that made any difference.

'What name did he give you?' Jo asked.

'Springer – like the dog. Jordan Springer.'

They stopped outside number 11. Jo hesitated. What if it was booby-trapped? Why the hell hadn't she thought of that before – a small explosive device, airborne ricin. Perhaps that was what Nick Carter had meant when he'd told her to be careful.

'Are you thinking what I'm thinking?' said Jimmy. 'That he might have booby-trapped it?'

Osborne's hand flew to her face. 'Booby trap! Fuckin' hell! I'm out of here.'

Jo turned on her. 'Pull yourself together, Sharon,' she said. 'Go and sit in your car. And don't you dare move till I tell you to.'

'What are you going to do?' said Carly as they watched her totter off.

'I can't see him having had time to put it all together,' she said, 'given Clements left straight after we'd been to see him.'

'But he could have had everything he needed right here,' said Carly. 'There was nothing in the house. Odds-on, this doubled as his workshop.'

'Carly's right,' said Jo. 'If we thought someone was trapped inside and their life was at risk, I might chance it. But no one is going to accept a risk assessment based on little more than wishful thinking.'

It began to rain. She pulled up her hood, turned her back to the wind and called Nick Carter.

Chapter 67

'They didn't waste any time,' said Carly Whittle, nodding towards the cameras.

'Hardly surprising, is it?' Jimmy Hulme responded. 'A circus like this? And you can bet it was on every social media channel going before they even arrived.'

Both ends of the road had been taped off and blocked by police vans. Beyond them, press and paparazzi jostled for the best pitches. In every other second bedroom window of the houses opposite the garages at least one person stood with a phone trained on number 11.

'I wish they'd hurry up,' said Jo. 'I can think of better ways to spend a soggy October afternoon.'

Right on cue Jack Benson turned and gave a thumbs up. The three of them walked towards him, passing the two dog handlers and their charges heading back to their van.

'Thank you, guys,' said Jo.

'Our pleasure, Ma'am,' said the older one. Raindrops dripped from his helmet like slow-motion bullets.

It reminded Jo fleetingly of Deer Tick's 'Twenty Miles'.

The dog handler grinned. 'Beats chasing villains over broken glass.'

Jack Benson was waiting beside the transparent polytunnel now surrounding the open door of garage number 11.

'I didn't ask for Bomb Disposal,' Jo said. 'I assumed you'd wait until the dogs had done their work?'

'Not our call, Ma'am,' he said. 'One mention of ricin and device in the same sentence and this is what you get.'

'What about all these Armed Response officers?'

He shrugged. 'They come as a package.'

'Tell them they can go home, dry off, and get some rest,' she said. 'We may need them again when we catch up with Darren Clements.' She peered inside the tunnel. 'Is it okay to go in?'

'Yes. But remember, you can look but you can't touch. Just make sure you kit up. It's the full Hazguard suit, I'm afraid.'

'Is that really necessary?'

He nodded grimly. 'You'll see. There are only two respirators. You'll have to decide who stays out here.'

She turned to Jimmy Hulme. 'Knocking on random doors didn't get us anywhere. I need you to find out from Sharon Osborne if any of the residents around here rent these garages. If so, show them the pictures of Clements and the Micra. Do they recall seeing him with a different vehicle? It's a Saturday. Some of them are bound to be home.'

'If they're not at the Etihad watching the City v Burnley game,' he replied.

'You'd better hope they're not,' she told him, 'or you'll be back here again this evening.'

'Yes, Ma'am.' He cut a forlorn figure as he set off through the slanting rain.

Jo helped Carly Whittle suit and boot, and then the roles were reversed. She hated the protective goggles, the N95 respirator, and the second pair of high-risk gloves. In a bizarre way, they heightened her sense of vulnerability. They also made her feel claustrophobic. To make matters worse, her headache had returned.

She lifted the rear flap of the polytunnel and the two of them stepped inside the garage. The red Nissan Micra was immediately in front of them. The trunk was open, as were all four doors.

'The sniffer dogs?' said Carly, her voice muffled by the respirator.

Jo nodded. 'I'll take the trunk, you check the insides.'

A wheel brace and a carjack lay in the trunk. A spare can of engine oil in a protective jacket had been Velcroed to a side panel. Jo lifted them out and raised the false floor panel. In the well were three environmentally friendly bags from the supermarket. The first contained an Apple Mac Pro laptop computer, a USB lead, and a charger unit. The other two contained notebooks and three phones.

Carly appeared at her side. 'Either he didn't expect us to find this place,' she said, 'or he isn't bothered if we do.'

Jo nodded. 'My thoughts entirely. Did you find anything?'

'No, Ma'am, but you should come and see what's down the other end.'

The bottom half of the garage had been turned into a workshop. A full-width workbench, complete with electrical sockets, held a vertical drill clamped to the wall, two vices, a variety of boxed power drill sets, a large granite mortar and pestle, and a kettle. Along one wall was fixed metal shelving. The shelves were empty. Against the other wall stood two floor-to-ceiling metal lockers, like the ones used in GMP staff changing rooms. Jo tried the doors. The first was locked. The second opened. An all-in-one white biohazard suit, not dissimilar to the one that Jo was wearing, hung from a hook.

'It is him, isn't it, Ma'am?' said Carly excitedly.

Jo had given up believing in coincidence years ago. But the time for excitement was when he was in custody and not before. She turned her attention to what was under the workbench. A grey fireproof safe, a foot wide and eight or nine inches deep. She knelt and tried the lid. It was locked. As she shifted her weight to stand up, she felt something dig into her knee. It was an oval object, less than half an inch, or around a centimetre long, the colour of grey marble mottled with brown markings. A protuberance at one end gave it the appearance of a harlequin ladybird. With some difficulty, she picked it up between thumb and forefinger and examined it.

'What is it, Ma'am?' said Carly.

Jo held it up for her to see. '*Ricinus communis*,' she said. 'This is what a castor bean looks like. If you chew five and then swallow them, they'll likely kill you. But then, how are you going to get your victim to do that? They're far more versatile in the powdered form our unsub favours.'

She placed it down in a space on the workbench and gestured to Carly.

'Come on,' she said. 'We're out of here.'

When they emerged from the polytunnel the rain had ceased. Jimmy Hulme was waiting for them with Jack Benson.

'I got a hit, Ma'am,' he said. 'Person who rents number 7 reckons the guy who uses this one also has a bike and a motorbike.'

'A motorbike? Did he see the make and colour?'

'Negative to both, Ma'am. He just caught sight of it when he was walking past. Possibly red or maroon, but he can't swear to it. Says the guy pulled the door down sharpish. Like he was trying to hide something.'

'Perhaps it was a one-off.' Carly suggested. 'Maybe he normally parks it somewhere else and uses the mountain bike to reach it?'

'If he's using a motorbike it would explain why the Micra hasn't registered at all the crime scenes,' added Jimmy Hulme.

'We need to let DS Carter know that they should also be looking for a motorbike,' said Jo.

'I've already done that, Ma'am,' said Jimmy Hulme, sounding nervous and contrite. 'I didn't think you'd want to be disturbed while you were in there.'

'No need to apologise,' she told him. 'Well done.'

She turned to Jack Benson. 'All yours,' she said. 'There's what looks like a ricin bean on the workbench that needs bagging immediately. When you've done whatever you need to do to the notebooks and the laptop in the trunk, get them over to Nexus House ASAP. We also need that locker forcing and the safe opening. Are you sure Bomb Disposal has passed them both?'

'That's what they said,' he replied. 'Let's hope to God they were right.'

Amen to that, thought Jo. Poisoned pellets was one thing, but an explosive device packed with the stuff was something else entirely.

Chapter 68

Max Nailor was briefing a search team in Royal Oak when the call came through. Steve Yates had been observed entering O'Neill's house.

'If he tries to leave, arrest him,' he said.

'You don't want us to follow him, in case he leads us to the missing girl?'

'No. He knows we're looking for him. He wouldn't be that stupid. If he's come out into the open, there'll be a reason for it. Just do as I say. Wait and watch. And if he leaves, arrest him. I'll be with you as soon as.'

Twenty minutes later he pulled in behind the watchers and knocked on the rear door of the van. It opened, and he climbed inside.

Two operational support assistants wearing headphones sat intently watching a bank of screens. Another sat beside them, also wearing headphones. She was busy transcribing notes into a tablet. The AKEU investigator who had opened the door for Max bade him take a seat on the bench beside her.

'He's still in there?' said Max.

'Yes, Sir.'

'Any mention of Melissa Walsh?'

'No, Sir.'

'What have they been talking about?'

'The weather. How they've been since they saw each other last. City's prospects tonight against Blackburn.' She shook her head.

'The negative impact of cuts to police funding. How we're all run off our feet and chasing shadows.'

'Basically, they know we're listening and they're taking the piss?'

'Yes, Sir. That's the impression we get.'

'Right,' said Max. 'Best not to keep them waiting.'

⁀‿

Jason O'Neill opened the door. He had a sour smile on his face. 'We've been expecting you,' he said. 'Or someone like you. Steve's in the kitchen. You'd better come on through.'

Steven Yates was leaning against the centre island, a bottle of lager in his hand. His tight white T-shirt and bulging biceps suggested that he had spent much of his time away working out. The blue jeans and shiny Dr Martens boots looked brand new. The logo across his chest read *NORA: The North Will Rise Again.* He raised the bottle in salute.

'Come and join us, officer,' he said. 'Take the weight off your feet and have a beer. You look bushed.'

'I don't have time for this,' said Max. 'Where have you been?'

'Course,' said Yates with a show of concern, 'you've been looking for me.'

'Where have you been?' Max persisted. 'We can do this here or at a police station. Your choice.'

Yates took a swig of beer. 'Fair enough,' he said. 'I choose here.'

'Then answer the question.'

'I've been at a mate's. I needed some time away. To grieve over Ronnie – you remember him? My boss and very good friend—' He waved the bottle. '—and father to Jason here.'

'You went away to grieve?'

'Got it in one.'

'And where does this mate live?'

'Dobcross.'

'Saddleworth?'

'Like I said, I needed to get away.'

'You must have known from the television that we needed to speak with you?'

He shook his head. 'We didn't bother with the telly – too busy training in his mini-gym. Running on the moors. Hanging out.'

'The radio?'

He laughed and turned to Jason O'Neill. 'D'you hear that, Jace? The radio! Who listens to the radio these days?'

'What about social media? And phone calls? I know for a fact that Jason and your colleagues tried to get hold of you.'

He grinned. 'D'you see me having a Facebook page? Snapchatting the guys? Instagramming Mr O'Neill's customers?'

'The phone calls?'

'I mislaid my phone.'

'On the moors?'

He shrugged. 'I've no idea. It's a bugger. I'll have to go and get a new one.'

'Your SUV,' said Max. 'We've been trying to trace it in the hope of finding you. Where is it?'

'In the BMW service garage. I asked them to give it a good going-over while I was away.'

'So how did you get back here?'

He raised his eyebrows and took another swig of lager. 'That mate I told you about? He brought me. Soon as we found out you were wanting a word with me.'

'And I suppose he'll vouch for you having been with him all this time?'

'Course he will. Addicted to the truth is Benny.'

'And where can I find Benny?'

'He's right behind you.'

Max turned. A clone of Yates, slightly shorter, ten years his senior, leaned against the doorjamb. He smiled in amusement.

'Say hallo to the officer, Benny,' said Yates. 'He's got some questions for you.'

'Hallo, officer,' said the clone. 'How can I help you?'

'I suppose that you're going to tell me that Mr Yates has been with you since Monday?' said Max.

Benny grinned, revealing teeth that would have benefitted from an orthodontist in his teens. 'Hole in one,' he said. 'And to save you the trouble of asking, we've been joined at the hip ever since. Never left his side, have I, Stevie?'

'Bloody embarrassing when I needed a pee,' said Yates.

That set the two of them off laughing. Max waited for them to recover.

'Did you pick him up or did he come to you?' he asked.

'I picked him up outside the BMW garage in Stretford,' Benny replied. 'Sounded in a right state. Ronnie's death really cracked him up.'

'And you drove straight to Dobcross?'

'Like it was an emergency. You might even have caught me on a speed camera or two.'

'Which route did you take?'

'Oldham. Then the A669 and A670.'

'And today?'

'The same.'

'What's your car registration number?'

Benny told him.

'Stay here,' said Max. 'All of you. I'll be back shortly.'

Benny had to step aside to let him pass. As he did so, he thrust an SD card into Max's hand.

'What's this?' said Max.

'Footage from my CCTV at home. Me and Stevie coming and going. Me and Stevie in the gym.'

'You have CCTV in your home gym?'

That crooked grin again. 'Can't be too careful,' said Benny. 'It's a nasty world out there, officer. There are people who'd steal the froth off your beer.'

Max hurried back to the van. This time the doors opened before he'd had time to knock.

'Did you get all that?' he asked.

'Clear as a bell,' said the investigator. 'Amir is checking the CCTV logs for the 669 and the 670.'

Max handed her the SD card. 'Show me what's on this,' he said.

She stood up and slipped the card into the slot on the side of the computer. The antivirus program confirmed that it was safe and asked for an admin code for permission to open it. She tapped in the code. There were a series of files, each of them timed and dated.

'Which one would you like me to open, Sir?' she asked.

He pointed to the first one. Monday at 3.15 p.m.

She double-clicked it and the screen came to life. It showed the car Benny had claimed to own pulling into a drive and coming to a stop. Max watched as the driver door opened, Benny got out and walked towards the camera.

'Must be over the front door,' observed the DS.

Max had his eyes focused on the passenger door. Five seconds passed, then the door opened and out got Steven Yates. He stretched, went to the trunk, opened it, removed a large holdall and a kitbag, closed the trunk, and followed in Benny's footsteps.

'Try the next one,' said Max.

The two men were both in T-shirts and shorts. Yates on his back on a bench, performing bench presses with an impressive set of weights. Benny stood above him, ready to guide the bar back onto the cradle. The time was 7 p.m. on Monday evening.

'Show the last one,' said Max.

'Sir,' said the furthest of the operational support assistants, lifting his headphones. 'We've got a hit for today on the A669 heading west, at 16.25hrs this afternoon.'

'Okay,' he replied. 'Keep looking.'

He turned his attention back to the investigator. 'You can stop that now,' he said. 'We're only going to see what they wanted us to see.'

'Doesn't mean that he couldn't have directed it all from up there on the moors,' she said. 'All he'd need was a phone we don't know about.'

Max nodded. 'You're right,' he acknowledged. 'It's all too pat and too carefully orchestrated. He's up to his neck in her disappearance. I'd bet my job on it.'

He reached across and touched the second of the OSAs on the shoulder. He turned and lifted his earphones.

'Anything?' Max asked.

The OSA shook his head. 'Chit chat. Totally innocuous, Sir. Too innocuous, if you know what I mean?'

'The fact he's turned up means that's he's up to something,' Max told the investigator. 'I want eyes and ears on all three of them, twenty-four seven.'

'What if they try to leave?'

'I want them followed. It's time those mobile surveillance teams had something to do.'

'Covert or overt?' she asked.

He stood up. 'Overt. They know we're watching them. Better we don't lose them rather than keep up the pretence.'

Max opened the van door and stepped out into the cool evening air. He stood there for a moment staring at the O'Neill house. The shadowy shapes of the vehicles behind the metal gates. The front windows lit, the rooms uninhabited. Like a ghost ship.

'What the hell are you playing at?' he murmured. 'And where on earth is Melissa?'

Chapter 69

Somewhere in the house a phone rang.

Now there were voices. One hollow, on the inbuilt speaker, the other more familiar. Short and missing vowels, guttural, aggressive. Manc on steroids. The one she'd christened The Boxer. Melissa raised her head, straining to hear above the sound of the rain on the windowpane.

She caught the ebb and flow, the shifting emotions, a sense that the power lay with the caller. At this remove, their conversation was as incomprehensible as the Cant language the traveller children had used at her primary school.

Another voice now. Higher pitched, wet and squeaky, like her cat sicking up. Gollum. It sounded as though they were arguing. She strained to see if she could make some sense of it, but the words were fragmented and indistinct.

'Ju . . . do it!' The Boxer?

'But Stee . . . said.' This was Gollum.

' I know wa . . . St . . . said. An . . . m tellin' you . . .' The Boxer again.

A plane approached, drowning out the voices. When the sound of the engines faded the voices were still there, but faint and remote. She guessed they had moved to another part of the house. She let her head drop back onto the pillow and lay there, staring at the ceiling. Now that they had removed her hood, confident in their own disguises, all of her senses were restored. She'd not decided if that was good or bad. The hood had made it easier for her to get to sleep, whatever the time of day. Lying here on her back, she was acutely aware of the sores on her bum and the back of her thighs, where her captors had left her to lie in her own pee until it seeped into the mattress and dried on her skin. She turned onto her side as best as she could and prayed for the night to come and the dark to envelop her.

Sleep stubbornly eluded her. The light and that bloody dog yapping every time a plane flew past conspired to add to her tortured captivity. Melissa no longer had the consolation of being able to cry. She was all cried out. She no longer railed at her father and his cronies for failing to rescue her. Nor her mother for failing to love her. Anger, frustration, and hate for them and her captors had slithered seamlessly into self-reproach and guilt. She realised now that she'd never been worthy, never lovable. She'd failed time and time again to come up to their expectations. Her parents had left her in no doubt that her score on the Common Entrance – enough to gain her access to a private school, but not enough to convince them that it was worth the annual fees – had been a great disappointment to them both. Perhaps that was why they hadn't bothered to come for her? To pay a ransom? To do whatever it took to get her back? The realisation finally hit her, like a blow in the pit of her stomach. It would be best all round if she was dead.

There were footsteps on the stairs. The sound of the key turning in the padlock. Bolts being withdrawn. She turned her head to watch. Her heart thumped in her chest. Her fingernails bit into the palms of her hands. The door opened inwards.

The Boxer entered the room. In one hand he held a plastic pop bottle, in the other a transparent disposable bag like the ones her mother's cleaner put in the trash at home. He threw the bag and bottle down beside her and sat on the end of the bed.

From his right-hand pocket he withdrew a box-cutter – what her dad called a Stanley knife. He held it up so that she could see it. Slowly and deliberately, he first revealed and then retracted the blade several times.

In, out.

In, out.

In, out.

It was a routine to which Melissa had become accustomed. She nodded to signal her compliance. He sat back and waited. His eyes were like empty pits behind the balaclava he now wore. Black holes, within which there was the faintest hint of movement and occasional flashes of reflected light.

He leaned forward, his weight causing the bed to dip and the mattress to rub against her bum. She bit her lip to suppress a gasp of pain. He bunched the pillows up behind her to support her back, then sat back out of reach.

Melissa opened and closed her hand to relieve the stiffness. She painfully manoeuvred herself into a semi-sitting position and picked up the bottle. He watched soundlessly as she struggled to open it with her wrists bound together. Finally, she placed the cap between her teeth and turned the bottle. A small explosion of gas and cola splashed her face and dribbled down her neck. She spat out the cap, gulping several greedy mouthfuls before the gas rising back up her gullet forced her to stop. She examined the bottle. It was some kind of nasty cheap cola. It tasted like heaven. She clamped the bottle between her knees and turned her attention to the bag.

A packet of barbecue crisps and a burger. A large beef patty, topped with cheese, and sandwiched between iceberg lettuce, tomato, and toasted bun. Melissa burped. She could feel her gastric juices beginning to flow.

'I told you,' she croaked. 'I'm vegetarian.'

He made a sound that could have been a growl or a laugh, reached out, grasped her arm with one hand, and removed the patty with the other. He let go and sat back. He shoved the patty through the slit in his balaclava, took a bite, and began to chew contentedly.

When she'd finished eating the crisps, he waited for her to drink the remainder of the cola. Then he took the bottle, roughly tugged the pillows away, restoring them to their original position, and got up. He stood in the doorway for a moment, staring back at her. Something in the angle of his head, and the glint in his eyes, sent a chill up her spine.

'Don't get too comfortable,' he growled. 'It'll soon be time to say goodbye.'

The door closed. Melissa lay back on the pillow. She realised that the rain had stopped. There were muffled voices. Outside the house this time. A van door slid open, the sound of metal on metal setting her teeth on edge. There was a dull thud as something was thrown inside the van. Her heart began to pound. They were getting ready to go. That must be what he'd meant. They were leaving her behind. A sudden belch carried with it undigested food. There was a sickening taste of bile at the back of her throat. She was terrified she would choke and began to cough.

Suddenly, her chest began to squeeze as though unseen hands were tightening a broad belt around her. In a panic she turned on her side and scrabbled desperately beneath the pillows. Her fingers found the inhaler. She closed her lips around the mouthpiece, pressed the canister down, drew in a long slow breath, and began to count to ten.

Melissa expelled her breath and gulped a mouthful of air. And another. And another. Told herself that she had to relax. Lay on her side clutching the inhaler just in case. Her heart was racing and she felt dizzy. But she was still alive.

Chapter 70

Day Seven – Sunday, 22nd October

'No! Please, no!'

A phone was ringing. Shrill, insistent.

Jo opened her eyes, rolled over, and picked up her handset. 'Aggie?'

'Jo? Are you alright?'

Jo's throat felt like sandpaper, her mouth dry, her lips parched. Encouraged by the sense that finally they were getting somewhere, she'd worked all night, along with most of the team. She'd left for home as dawn was breaking, intending to shower, change, grab a bite to eat, and go straight back in. The mistake she'd made was to lie down on the bed for a moment. She had woken . . . she stared at the phone . . . two hours later.

'I'm fine,' she said. 'I just woke up.'

'I'm sorry,' said Aggie. 'If I'd known . . .'

Jo levered herself upright, her head against the wall. 'Don't worry,' she said, 'it's good to hear your voice.' There was a long pause. Jo wasn't sure if they had been cut off. 'Aggie?' she said. 'Are you still there?'

'Yes, Jo, I'm here. I was just plucking up the courage to tell you.'

Jo sighed. *Here we go*, she told herself. *I knew I'd blown it on Friday night.* She steeled herself. 'Tell me what?' she said.

'That article I was writing? About Melissa's disappearance?'

'And the total incompetence of the police?' Jo sensed Aggie reeling at the other end of the line, as though she'd slapped her in the face. 'Sorry,' she said. 'That was a cheap shot.'

'No more than I deserved. It's in this morning's *Observer*. Actually the police don't come out of it too badly. It's more about getting the public onside. Humanising Melissa. Getting them to care. Encouraging them to report anything suspicious, look in outhouses and sheds – that sort of thing.'

Jo was too tired to care. She had bigger fish to fry. 'I'm glad to hear it,' she said. 'But you needn't have worried. I'm not the SIO on that case.'

'I know, but . . .'

'Seriously, Aggie,' said Jo, swinging her feet off the bed, 'I'm fine with it. Let it go.'

'Thank you so much,' said Aggie. Her relief was palpable, even over the phone. 'I was worried sick about how you'd take it.'

Jo stood up and stretched. 'When you get to know me better,' she replied, 'you'll realise I have a thicker skin than that.'

'How is the hunt for Clements going?' Aggie asked. 'It's all over the media. On the NCA and GMP Twitter feeds. There's a photo of him in most of the Sunday papers.'

Jo was glad to hear it. She couldn't fault Helen Gates for the way she was managing the Press.

'We're making progress,' she replied, conscious that she was deliberately giving as little away as possible. And what did that say about the trust in this relationship? 'But I won't be happy until we've caught and charged him.'

'Do you want me to come over and help you move the rest of your stuff out?' said Aggie. 'Aren't you supposed to be out of there by midday tomorrow?'

Jo cursed. She'd lost track of what day it was. 'I'll do it tonight,' she said.

'What time do you want me there?'

'No!' said Jo, surprising herself with the force of her response. The memory of having put Abbie's niece in danger was still fresh in her mind. There was no way she was going to allow history to repeat itself, least of all with someone she'd grown to love. 'You have to stay away from me until we've caught him. It isn't safe to be around me.'

'What do you mean?' said Aggie. 'Please, Jo, you're scaring me.'

'And promise me, Aggie, that you won't start shadowing my investigation too. The unsub isn't just dangerous, he's now desperate and unpredictable. I wouldn't be able to do my job properly for worrying about you.'

'What about you? Who's going to be watching your back?'

Jo started walking towards the bathroom. 'I'll be fine, Aggie,' she said. 'Now you'll have to excuse me. I've really got to go.'

Chapter 71

'Did you go home like I told you to?' Jo asked.

Nick Carter shrugged, and grinned sheepishly.

'You didn't, did you?' she said.

'Somebody had to brief the early shift,' he replied.

Jo threw her bag down on the desk. 'Now you're playing the guilt card.'

'I managed sixty winks in the conference room,' he told her. 'You'd be surprised how comfy that executive chair is. It tilts right back. You should try it some time.'

'At least I had a shower,' she replied. 'Has anybody mentioned that you stink, Nick? You could do with a shave too.'

He took it well. 'Good honest sweat,' he said. 'And it's a good job I did hang around. Have a look at this.' He handed her a small blue hard-backed notebook in a transparent evidence bag.

'Is this one of the ones from the lock-up?'

'It was dusted for prints before we had a good look at it,' he told her. 'But you don't need to break the seal. I've left it open at the relevant page.'

Jo turned it over. On the second of the two open pages was a list of names handwritten in fine black ink. The first four had been crossed through, but she could still tell that they were those of the victims who had already been attacked: O'Neill, Grimshaw, Dewlay, and Rand. Three dead, one on the mend. And then three more names, clearly added at a later date: ACC Helen Gates, DI Joanne Stuart, and Eric Manson.

'At least he's spelled your name correctly,' said Nick, trying to make light of it.

'Why no mention of Mwamba or Sarah Weston?' she wondered.

'Good question,' he replied.

'Andy Swift was right,' she said, handing back the notebook.

'Your pet profiler?'

'Forensic psychologist. He said that the closer to the unsub I got, the more he'd see me as an obstacle. What we both forgot was that Helen Gates is even more the face of the investigation than I am.'

'You going to give her the good news?' said Nick.

'You haven't?'

He shuffled his feet. 'I thought it'd be better coming from you.'

'While I'm doing that you'd better find out who Eric Manson is. And make sure we've still got eyes on Henry Mwamba. I take it we've still nothing on Clements or his motorbike?'

'Unfortunately not. It's only a matter of time though.'

'Time we haven't got.' Jo sat down. 'I'll get on to ACC Gates, then I'll check on DI Weston. You crack on.'

'Yes, Ma'am!'

He threw a mock salute, spun on his heels, and exited at speed. Jo watched the door close behind him and slumped back in her chair. Though Nick hid it well, she suspected he was still smarting from the fact that she'd made it to DI first, and that she'd basically been parachuted in over his head to lead Operation Alecto. She'd tried so hard not to treat him like a junior. But it was easy to forget when the pressure built up, and especially when she was physically tired and irritable, like now.

She sighed and picked up the phone. 'Ma'am,' she said, as soon as Helen Gates picked up. 'I have an update for you.'

'Finally!'

Jo launched into her report before the ACC had the chance to begin a diatribe. When she'd finished she could tell that Gates was in a much more generous and sombre mood.

'It's a while since I've had a death threat,' she quipped. 'I suppose I should be flattered.'

'It's serious, Ma'am,' said Jo.

'I know that. But has it occurred to you that Clements may have deliberately left that notebook there for you to find, and this is his way of trying to wrong-foot us? Make us take our eye off the ball?'

'I had wondered when I saw that neither Henry Mwamba nor DI Weston were on the list.'

'And what was the other name?'

'Eric Manson.'

'Have you found any connection between that name and Operation Alecto?'

'Not yet, Ma'am.'

'So he could be another distractor. Put there to get us wasting our time chasing shadows while he goes after his real targets?'

You're not just a fourth-floor paper shuffler then, thought Jo. It had been easy to forget that Helen Gates had been a formidable senior investigator before she was dragged kicking and screaming upstairs as part of the Force Diversity programme.

'That's quite possible, Ma'am,' she replied. 'But I can't afford to ignore this Manson as a potential victim. If anything were to happen . . .'

'I know. Duty of care. Rigorous testing of every piece of evidence. They'd have our guts for garters.'

Jo was relieved to note her use of the plural possessive pronoun.

'Speaking of duty of care . . .' Gates continued. 'I'm not being vaccinated with something tested on mice on the off-chance that this lunatic might take a potshot at me. Do you understand?'

'Yes, Ma'am.'

'Are you having one?'

'No, Ma'am.'

'There you go then. What do you plan to do now?'

'Check on DI Weston and Henry Mwamba, and make sure that everything is being done to track down Clements and his motorbike.'

'I can't believe that he hasn't been spotted yet,' said Gates. 'He's had more coverage than David Beckham.'

'Yes, Ma'am. I gather you've done a great job with the newspaper coverage.'

'Don't patronise me, SI Stuart,' said Gates softly. 'And speaking of newspapers, is there any truth in the rumours about you and that Polish reporter?'

Jo had been dreading this. She took a deep breath. 'If you mean, are we friends?' she said. 'Then yes, Ma'am.'

'Just friends?'

'We've had a meal together, two or three times. That's all.'

'Mmm,' said Gates. There was a long pause. 'Be careful, Jo,' she said. 'Mixing business and pleasure is a slippery slope in our world. Try to remember that.'

Chapter 72

'Are you sure this is right?' said Max.

'It's exactly where Mrs Hammond told us,' the uniformed sergeant replied. 'She only lives a quarter of a mile down this lane, and there's nothing else between her and this place.'

'And nobody lives here?'

'Not according to her, nor as far as we're aware. The former occupant went bankrupt. Put a shotgun in his mouth and pulled the trigger.' He shook his head. 'Took me a good six months to forget it and I wasn't the first responder.'

'How long ago was that?'

'Two years this Christmas Eve. He died intestate. They're still trying to track down surviving relatives. A cousin in Canada, they think. Another in Australia. They didn't communicate, so there're no correspondence addresses to go on. Not that there's much to inherit apart from the land, a four-hundred-year-old farmhouse and a couple of falling-down barns, and they've been stripped of anything worth stealing.'

'Could be squatters?' said the firearms team commander.

'With a top-of-the-range SUV?' said the sergeant. 'Unlikely.'

Max stared again at the infrared display on the screen of the drone operator's laptop.

'Anything?' he said.

'Not a dicky bird,' came the reply. 'No vehicles present. No signifi-cant heat sources from any of the buildings.'

'Not a cannabis farm then,' said the sergeant, half-joking.

Max gave him a withering look. 'This is a missing twelve-year-old girl we're talking about,' he said.

'Sorry,' the sergeant mumbled.

'That doesn't mean,' continued the drone operator, 'that there's nobody in any of these buildings. This is the best kit out there, but it can't see through slate roofs and thick stone walls.'

Max opened the car door and got out. He stepped across the nar-row ditch, grasped one of the wayward branches of the hedge with a gloved hand and hauled himself onto the grassy bank.

Across two sloping fields, at the top of a rise, he could see the cluster of stone buildings backlit by the late afternoon sun. The nearest woodland, a small circular copse, was over half a mile away. Anyone fleeing across the fields would be easy to spot even without the drone.

He made his way back to the car and summoned the team leaders to join him by the entrance to the farm track.

'This is how we're going to do it,' he told them. 'I want just five vehicles to start with. I'll be in the first one with Mark Hamblett, who as most of you know is the AKEU negotiator, and Sergeant Watts. Behind us will be the two firearms vehicles, then the dog unit, and finally one of the search team Transit vans with the Enforcer. We'll stop just short of the yard so as not to obscure potential tyre track marks. The drone will stay here with the Forensics unit and the rest of the search team. The drone operator will keep us apprised, by Comms, of any movement. Any questions? No? Right, let's do it.'

Nobody spoke as the procession of vehicles bumped their way up the rutted farm track. They would all, like Max, be running through the range of scenarios ahead. A tense hostage negotiation, a deadly firefight, a nervous pursuit across the fields, a dramatic and successful rescue. Or the possibility that this was all a waste of time. And, worst of all, that they might find Melissa . . . only not alive.

'Stop here!' Max ordered as they approached the gap in the wall that served as the entrance to the farmyard. He turned to look over his shoulder. 'You stay here, Sergeant,' he said. 'I need you to listen in to the Comms channel in case something crops up I should know about.' Then he undid his seat belt, exited the car and waved the firearms commander over.

'I intend to alert potential occupants to our presence by using the loudhailer,' he said. 'If there's a response, we'll follow it wherever it takes us using the normal protocols. If there's no response then I will accompany the officer with the Enforcer and as many of your team as you consider appropriate to check the house is clear.'

'That will be four then,' the firearms commander replied. 'The others will provide cover out here, front and back. If the house is clear, we'll repeat the exercise on the remaining buildings. Permission to deploy?'

'Go ahead,' said Max.

They watched as the officers exited their vehicles. Six of them came forward and hunkered down behind the stone wall, their weapons trained on the windows of the farmhouse. Two further officers began to make their way along the wall towards the rear of the building. While they waited, Max went to the trunk, took out the loudhailer and checked that it was fully charged.

'Good to go,' said the firearms commander.

Max switched the hailer on and held it to his mouth. His words bounced off the stone walls and around the farmyard. He had to speak slowly and pause between each phrase so that the echoes did not obliterate the one that followed.

'Armed Police!' he said. 'This is the National Crime Agency. You are surrounded. I need you to come to the front door, one at a time, with your hands raised where we can see them. Do it now!'

The tension was raw. Almost physical.

'Armed Police!' he repeated. 'Come to the door now. One at a time, with your hands raised where we can see them.'

Max lowered the loudhailer and spoke into his radio mic.

'Foxtrot Alpha Romeo,' he said. 'Is the drone capturing any sign of movement?'

'Negative to that,' came the reply. 'No movement.'

'Right,' said Max, 'we're going in.'

Thirty seconds later the door hung inwards on a single hinge. Max waited as the two pairs of firearms officers worked their way from room to room. His heart thumped in response to every shout.

'Clear!'

'Clear!'

'Clear!'

'Clear!'

'Clear!'

Now the only sounds were footsteps on the stair treads and heavy breathing.

'All clear,' said the last of the officers. He paused, and pointed back the way he had come. 'You might want to start with the bedroom on the left.'

Max climbed the stairs, his mouth dry, his palms slick with sweat. The door was open and the light was now on. He stepped inside.

The first thing that hit him was the acrid smell of methane and rotten eggs. He didn't need to look in the bucket to know what that was. It was the bed beneath the window that drew him.

The duvet lay crumpled on the floor. The wrinkled bottom sheet had a yellow stain running down its centre. A hood lay on one of the pillows. As Max stepped forward, something hard cracked beneath his foot. He stooped, pulled back the duvet and revealed a Ventolin inhaler.

Chapter 73

Jo rang the phone number that Sarah Weston had given her. It went straight to voicemail.

'Sarah, it's Joanne Stuart,' she said. 'We now have definitive proof that Clements is the perpetrator. Please take this seriously and give me a ring back as soon as you get this.'

'Damn!' she said as she speed-dialled the NCA headquarters in Pimlico. 'Please don't go walkabout on me.'

'National Crime Agency, how can I help you?'

'This is Senior Investigator Joanne Stuart calling from Manchester. I urgently need to speak with Sarah Weston. She's part of the Child Exploitation and Online Protection team.'

'I doubt anyone will be in,' he replied. 'It is Sunday. But I'll try her extension.' A nervous forty seconds later, he was back. 'Sorry,' he told her. 'There's nobody answering. I checked with the call handler. She hasn't been in since she signed out on Thursday afternoon. Her diary showed her as having been up in your neck of the woods.'

'I know. She was booked on the 20.17 back to Euston yesterday,' she told him.

'I assume you have clearance, so you can always check the internal list for her work number?'

'I already have it,' said Jo. 'And her personal number.'

'Then I don't know what else to suggest.'

'Put me through to the Duty Officer,' said Jo. 'Tell them it's a State Zero: Emergency Assistance.'

Five minutes later, reassured that everything would be done to track Sarah down and keep her safe, Jo went looking for Nick Carter. Her deputy was talking to two of the passive media search team.

'I haven't been able to reach Sarah,' she told him. 'I'm worried that Clements may have followed her to London, which is why we haven't sighted him or his bike up here.'

'What train was she on?'

'The 20.17.'

'I'll get someone to check the on-board CCTV,' he said. 'Then we'll know for sure.'

'If he knows where she works and lives, he could have got on any of the trains. An earlier one.'

Nick frowned. 'That means checking the concourse CCTV for the past twenty-four hours,' he told her. 'There's only so much we can do at any one time.' His gesture took in the whole of the incident room. 'See for yourself. We don't have the bodies.'

'Then get on to the Transport Police. They've got his photo like everyone else.' People were looking up from their desks and staring at them. Jo lowered her voice and tried to sound conciliatory. 'Sorry,' she said, 'but we've both known Sarah for a long time. She was more than a colleague to me. She was a friend, and . . .'

He held up a hand. 'It's all right,' he said. 'I'll get on to it. And don't worry. She'll be fine.'

'Where are we up to with Henry Mwamba?' she asked.

'I sent DC Hulme to have another word with him.' He glanced at the clock on the wall. 'He should have reported back by now. I'll give him a call. Find out what he's playing at.'

Hulme yawned. He searched in the glove compartment, found a half-empty bag of Fisherman's Friends and popped one in his mouth. He sat back and moved the lozenge slowly around with his tongue, waiting for the hit of menthol and liquorice. If he had been in his own car he could have plugged in his phone and been listening to a trivia quiz. That was the trouble with pool cars. There was beggar all to do when you were just sitting around watching and waiting. Worse when you were on your own. Unless your companion happened to be that motor mouth from K Division CID with the body odour problem.

His radio crackled. It was DS Carter.

'Hulme?'

'Yes, Boss?'

'You were supposed to give me a sitrep?'

'Sorry, Boss. It's just that there was nothing to report.'

'There's always something to report. Even if it's that there's nothing to report.'

'Yes, Boss.'

'Where are you?'

'Hulme.'

'Where in Hulme, Hulme?'

'The Kingdom of Heaven Church of the Mustard Seed.'

'Is this another of your windups, Jimmy?' The barely repressed anger in Nick's voice more than made up for his use of the DC's given name.

'No, Boss. It's on the level,' said Hulme. ' "The kingdom of heaven is like to a grain of mustard seed, which a man took, and sowed in his field: Which indeed is the least of all seeds: but when it is grown, it is the greatest among herbs, and becometh a tree, so that the birds of the air come and lodge in the branches thereof." Matthew 13:31–32.'

'Hulme!' Carter bellowed. 'What the hell are you doing and where is your target? And where is his watcher?'

Hulme swallowed what was left of the lozenge and went into formal mode. 'I ascertained that the target was delivering a homily at the 10.15 a.m. family service at the Kingdom of Heaven Church of the Mustard Seed in Hulme. When I arrived, the designated surveillance officer confirmed that the target had entered the church. I offered to take over while he snatched a breakfast. I then checked for myself that the target was indeed present at the service and then retired to my car to wait for him to leave. I judged it to be unwise and unnecessary to haul him from the service in the middle of his oration.' He paused. 'I trust that was appropriate, DS Carter?'

'What time does this service finish?' said Carter. He sounded mollified, although unrepentant.

'Half eleven, Boss. They're on their way out as we speak.'

'Good. Let me know as soon as you've spoken with him. And then regardless of what he says, you stick to him like a limpet. Got that?'

'Yes, Boss.'

Hulme undid his seat belt and sat up. The congregation was spilling out into the street. He had assumed this would be one of the burgeoning Black Majority Churches, but it was an eclectic mix of race and culture from right across the spectrum. Manchester in a microcosm. There were already more than a hundred men, women, and children blocking the pavement and the narrow street. Concerned that he might miss Mwamba in the crush, he climbed out of the Peugeot 308, alarmed the car, and sauntered over to the opposite side of the street.

Five minutes later, with no sign of his quarry, Hulme politely shouldered his way through the crowd of happy people still congregated outside.

'I'm afraid that the service is ended, Brother,' said one of the ushers standing just inside the entrance.

'I was hoping to have a word with Mr Mwamba,' Hulme said. 'He doesn't seem to have come out yet?'

The usher's eyes lit up.

'Ah, Brother Mwamba!' It rolled off his tongue like a hymn of praise. 'Such a wonderful, uplifting sermon. A shame that you missed it.'

'I'm sure it was. But right now I need to speak with him. Where is he?'

The usher frowned at the brusqueness and impatience of the enquirer. He turned and surveyed the interior of the church. 'He doesn't seem to be here right now. Why don't you ask his son? He'll surely know.'

'His son?'

'Right there. In the blue suit, next to the Sister in the pink dress and hat talking with Pastor Christianson.'

Hulme hurried into the church and down the aisle to where the three of them were standing beside the front pews. 'Excuse me,' he said. 'You're Henry Mwamba's son?'

The man turned and stared at him suspiciously. 'Yes, and this is my wife, his daughter-in-law. And you are?'

He pulled out his warrant card and showed it to them. 'Detective Constable Hulme. I need urgently to speak with your father.'

'Police?' said the pastor. 'What business could the police possibly have with Brother Mwamba?'

'I'm sorry,' said Hulme. 'I don't have time for this. I need to speak with him now. It concerns his safety.'

The two men looked shocked, the daughter-in-law horrified. She gasped and her hand flew to her face.

'His safety,' said the son. 'What do you mean, his safety?'

'He hasn't told you, has he?' Hulme didn't wait for an answer. It would have been superfluous. 'We have reason to believe that someone may be targeting your father,' he said. 'He is supposed to be taking precautions. Now, please, tell me where he is.'

The daughter-in-law looked as though she was about to faint. The pastor reached across and held her steady.

The son grabbed Hulme's arm in a vice-like grip and pointed to a door off to the right. 'He's just left for the Trafford Centre,' he said. 'He's taken our daughter with him.'

His wife began to scream – a high-pitched keen that sent a chill through Hulme's body. He pulled his arm free and raced to the door. On the other side was a parking lot, with an exit out onto the back street. There were a few cars left. None of them contained Mwamba or his granddaughter.

Hulme rushed back inside. 'Ring your father and tell him to return immediately,' he said as he pulled out his own phone. 'Tell me his number while you're at it, and the make of his car.'

'Françoise...' moaned the daughter-in-law, rocking backwards and forwards in the pastor's arms. 'Françoise...'

Her husband, his phone clamped to his ear, moved away the better to hear. Hulme followed him.

'How old is your daughter?' he asked.

'Nine. It's her birthday tomorrow. Dad is going to let her choose a present. We're joining them later – having a meal, going to the pictures.'

'When did they leave?'

'Ten minutes ago? Maybe fifteen?' He put the phone to his other ear and listened intently. His hand trembled.

'Any joy?' said Hulme, instantly regretting his choice of words.

The husband shook his head, his face frozen with fear and helplessness.

'Christ!' DC Hulme exclaimed, as he turned and ran down the aisle.

'Don't blaspheme in God's House,' the pastor called after him.

'Least of your worries,' was his muttered reply. 'Stay here, all of you!' he shouted. 'I'll be back.'

Chapter 74

'Calm down,' said Joanne Stuart.

Hulme wasn't sure if she was talking to him or to DS Carter, whom he could clearly hear cursing him in the background.

'How long ago was this?'

'Within the last fifteen minutes. I'm sorry, Ma'am.' His voice trailed off.

'Not now,' she told him. 'Save it for later. When we've found them both, safe and sound. Now get back in there and put the son on. We need detailed descriptions of them – what they're wearing. And email me any photos of them that he's got on his phone.'

'Yes, Ma'am.'

'And then stay with them. I don't want them charging over to the Trafford Centre and getting in the way. Understood?'

'Yes, Ma'am.'

'Good. Now go.'

She ended the call and turned to face an irate DS Carter.

'I told you he was a bloody liability,' he said.

Jo shrugged her jacket on. 'It's a mistake any one of us could have made, Nick,' she said. 'And, like I told him, this isn't the time for recriminations. We have two people to keep safe. On the flip side, this might just be the opportunity we've been waiting for.'

———————

Jo and Nick burst into the Intu Trafford Centre Security Control Room, closely followed by Carly Whittle. It felt like NASA mission control shortly before lift-off. Serried rows of desks faced a single wall covered with CCTV screens showing live feed of the entrances, food halls and galleries, escalators, cinemas, stores, the parking lots, and the approach roads.

There was an electrifying buzz about the place and a raw intensity about the manner in which operatives studied their monitors. A middle-aged man in a smart suit and with a buzz-cut waved them over.

'DI Stuart?' he said, offering her his hand. 'I'm Les Stanley, the Security Coordinator.'

'SI Stuart,' she replied, 'but it's academic. This is DS Carter and DC Whittle. I understand you have a Comms station ready for us?'

'Over here,' he said, setting off.

'I take it you haven't found them yet?' she asked.

'No. And we certainly haven't spotted anyone who looks as though he could be carrying a rifle. Believe me, he wouldn't have got beyond any of the entrances. But if they are here, I guarantee we'll find them within the next few minutes.'

He led them to a pod containing three desks combined in a horse-shoe shape. Each desk contained a keyboard, three computer monitors, two CCTV monitors, and various headsets. An operative sat before each desk. There were three empty mesh-backed work chairs. Beside each keyboard was a printed list of operational keywords.

'This is Bronze Command Pod One,' he told her. 'I have a duplicate pod just over there. They can both be redesignated as Silver Command if so directed. As I understand it, I'll be continuing to monitor access control, all of our CCTV, and our detection alarm systems. All the information will be available to you here, to Gold Command at GMP

Headquarters, Silver Command at Nexus House, and to all the other relevant stakeholders: GMP specialist units, fire service, emergency medical services, and if it comes to it, special forces. I will also be responsible for the deployment of our own front-line security teams in accordance with your direction.'

'You do know this isn't a full-blown terrorist threat?' said Jo, envisaging the potentially disastrous consequences of an over-the-top response. 'We're talking a known threat: one suspect and one, possibly two, targets.'

'Standard protocol,' said a voice from behind her.

Jo turned. The familiar figure of a senior uniformed officer stood there, holding a clipboard in one hand and a tablet in the other.

'Chief Inspector Sarsfield,' she said. 'What are you doing here?'

'I'm your appointed loggist. As for the scope of the response, I believe that's down to Exercise Winchester Accord. You'll remember that?'

Jo did. The 2016 simulation carried out right here, in and around the Intu Trafford Centre, following the Paris and Brussels terrorist attacks. When the fake suicide bomber had caused outrage by shouting '*Allahu Akbar*'. No one at GMP was likely to forget it.

'We were waiting for you to arrive to implement a controlled evacuation,' Stanley explained.

'We'll see about that,' said Jo, sitting down in one of the chairs and signalling for Nick and Carly to do the same. She put on a pair of headphones and pointed to the communications board in the centre of the pod. 'Are all these channels networked?'

The operative nodded. 'Yes, Ma'am.'

'In which case,' she said, 'please open them all.'

Lights flickered from amber to green.

Jo consulted the list of keywords. 'This is Bravo Charlie One,' she said. 'Golf Charlie One, Sierra Charlie One, please confirm you are receiving.'

'Golf Charlie One receiving.'

'Sierra Charlie One receiving.'

So, Helen Gates was Gold Command, Gordon Holmes Silver Command, and their prime suspect, appropriately, Papa Sierra. Henry Mwamba was Hotel Mike, and his granddaughter Françoise, Foxtrot Mike.

'Papa Sierra, Hotel Mike, and Foxtrot Mike have yet to be located,' she told them.

'Is it correct that Tango One is believed to have arrived on a motorbike?' asked a male voice.

'Who is this?' said Helen Gates. 'Identify yourself using the appropriate keywords.'

'Bravo Charlie Two,' came the reply from the Security Coordinator.

'We don't know for certain,' said Jo. 'Regarding transport, all options should be considered. And we do not, I repeat, do not have a Tango. Golf Charlie One, I have a serious concern. Can you confirm that this operation has not been designated either as an emergency or a terrorist incident?'

'I can confirm that this is not designated as a terrorist incident, although that option remains open. It is designated as an emergency.'

'But . . .' Jo began.

The rules made it clear that for it to constitute an emergency it would have to represent a substantial challenge to GMP's ability to execute its functions. That was not the case. Jo was tempted to argue but knew that would only waste valuable time.

'My concern,' she said, 'is that the implementation of emergency procedures, such as an evacuation, may present a greater threat to public safety than a coordinated stop-and-search protocol. The resultant panic would alert Papa Sierra and make it harder for us to apprehend him. And potentially cause crush injuries to members of the public.'

Jo held her breath. There was a short pause.

'I concur, Bravo Charlie One,' said Gates.

'This is Bravo Charlie Two. We should at least put out a call for Hotel Mike to make himself known to my staff?'

'That would also alert Papa Sierra,' said Jo.

'The safety of Hotel Mike and Foxtrot Mike have to be our prime concern,' Gates responded.

'I concur,' said Gordon Holmes. 'At least it will avoid major panic and make it easier to identify Papa Sierra if he's following them or decides to escape. But it is your decision, Bravo Charlie One.'

Jo stared up at the bank of screens, teeming with men, women, and children blissfully unaware of the unfolding drama. A typical Sunday afternoon. There must be tens of thousands of them. Beside her, DCI Sarsfield had his biro poised, waiting for her decision.

'Make the announcement,' she said. 'But keep it low key. Say his son and daughter-in-law are waiting for him.'

'For information,' said Gordon, while they waited, 'a hazard response unit is on its way. Mobile units are already in place and covering all the major routes into and out of the operational zone. Three intercept teams are en route to you. Paramedics are already on-site and have been briefed.'

No mention of Armed Response.

'What about TFU?' she asked.

'On-call TFU1 have been delayed by an incident,' Gates told her. 'TFU2 are on their way from Manchester Airport, ETA five minutes.'

'I also requested air support,' said Jo.

'NPAS 21 involved in Casevac and unavailable,' Gordon informed them. 'However, the Greater Manchester Fire and Rescue Service AIR Unit drone is en route. ETA four minutes.'

Jo couldn't fault the scale or speed of response. Tactical Firearms officers, dog units, Tactical Aid and Riot Control, all for one man armed with an air rifle, albeit with poisoned pellets. Her acknowledgement was drowned out by the announcement.

'This is a customer service announcement for Mr Henry Mwamba. Would Mr Henry Mwamba please make himself known to the nearest member of staff. Your son and daughter-in-law are waiting for you at the meeting point.'

Excellently done, Jo thought. Not the slightest hint of concern in the tone of the announcer. They watched the bank of screens for an indication that Henry Mwamba had heard and was responding.

The traffic had come to a standstill on all the approach roads. Those exiting the parking lots were having to run the gauntlet of checks by strategically placed motorcycle officers. Still no sign of Mwamba, his granddaughter, or Clements.

'This is Bravo Charlie One,' she said. 'Please ask them to repeat the announcement. And I want repeated text messages sent to his phone.'

A minute passed and still no sign of Mwamba. The Security Coordinator's voice broke in. 'This is Bravo Charlie Two. I have confirmation that TFU2 are on approach and awaiting instructions on channel six.'

The operator beside Jo was pointing to the operational chart.

Jo nodded. 'Bravo Charlie Three, please report your status,' she said.

A male voice responded. 'This is Tango Foxtrot Charlie,' said the Tactical Firearms commander. 'I have six authorised firearms officers. ETA two minutes. A further six on-call officers are on-site and in the process of being briefed and kitted up as we speak.'

Jo assumed that on-call officers referred to some of the traffic cops and Tactical Aid team, emergency-trained in the wake of the Arena Bombing to plug the gap caused by savage central government cuts.

'Be advised that Papa Sierra is not yet located,' she told him. 'Please confirm that you are aware that Papa Sierra is assumed to be armed only with a .177-calibre air rifle? Over.'

'So, advised,' he responded. 'Rules of engagement will apply.'

Jo ran through it in her head. Arrest, contain, neutralise, in that order. Not shoot to kill. Although, in practice, "neutralise" meant a shot to the chest, which would almost certainly be fatal.

A female voice, teetering on the edge of excitement, cut in. 'Vehicle belonging to Hotel Mike has been located. Screen six. Screen six.'

Every head in the room stared up at the bank of screens.

The operator beside Jo pointed it out to her.

'Where is this?' she asked.

'In the Frankie & Benny's parking lot. Right in front of the Great Hall.'

'Can we get a close-up?' she asked.

The camera was already zooming in on a four-year-old red Nissan Qashqai.

'He's still in the car!' she exclaimed. 'Hotel Mike. Is that Foxtrot Mike he's talking to? Can anyone see?'

Mwamba was in the driver's seat, leaning over and talking to someone in the passenger seat. Just the top of the head was visible. A mass of curls. It had to be Françoise.

'Nearest unit, please advise,' said Jo.

A new voice, tight with tension. 'Papa Sierra may be among the trees, on the bank!'

'And there's a motorbike in the bike bay beside the parking lot,' said another voice.

The camera swivelled. Above a sloping grassy bank, on the northwest edge of the parking lot, a figure lurked in the trees. Black jeans, a black hooded top. Was that a backpack?

'Can you confirm, Bravo Charlie One?' Gordon asked.

'Negative,' Jo replied. 'Standby. The build is right . . . but . . .'

The figure moved swiftly through the trees and stopped, half hidden behind the trunk of a tree on the edge of the top of the bank. The camera zoomed in. As the figure began to shrug off the backpack, Jo caught a glimpse of shoulder-length hair and a fledgling beard. Jo's heart began to race.

'Yes! Yes! Yes!' she shouted. 'All units. Papa Sierra sighted in woods above Frankie & Benny's parking lot. Believed armed and dangerous. Approach with caution.'

She switched her attention to the Nissan.

'Stay in the car,' she muttered. 'For God's sake, stay in the car.'

Chapter 75

Henry Mwamba reached into his pocket and turned on his phone. 'Françoise,' he said, 'I'll just let Papa and Mama know we're going to eat first.'

'Can I play on the grass, *Babu*?'

'Of course. But mind the cars and stay nearby.'

He put the phone to his ear.

'What's he doing?' said Jo.

'He's got his phone out,' said Nick Carter. 'He must have switched it on. He's bound to see all the messages we've sent.'

The passenger door opened and they watched the girl jump out.

'No!' Jo exclaimed, unable to stop herself. 'Get back in the car!' She pulled herself together. 'Foxtrot Mike has left the vehicle,' she said. 'She is crossing the parking lot towards the grassed area. She is running up the bank. She is within feet of Papa Sierra. He has moved back out of sight. Now she is running back down again. Where is the firearms commander? Who is the nearest to the parking lot?'

'This is Tango Foxtrot Charlie,' said the TFC. 'ETA one minute. Over.'

'Go directly to the Frankie & Benny's parking lot,' she told him. 'Immediately in front of the main entrance.'

'Roger that,' he replied.

'All other units to the vicinity,' she ordered, 'but hang back. Do not engage. I repeat. Do not engage.'

Jo held her breath as the young girl began to run back up the bank. They saw her grandfather turn to look at her through the window, fear etched on his face. He frantically scrabbled to lower the window. The girl reached the top and turned. Mwamba opened his mouth to shout to her. Clements stepped out from behind his tree and grabbed the girl's arm, pulling her towards him. He clamped her to his chest with his left arm.

'What's that he's holding in his right hand?' someone asked.

Jo instinctively craned forwards. 'Papa Sierra has a gun. It looks like a long-barrelled pistol, possibly a target pistol.'

The girl began to struggle. Below them in the parking lot, the driver's door of the Nissan began to open.

Jo wrenched off her headset and pushed back her chair.

'What are you doing?' Sarsfield asked.

'I'm a trained negotiator and I've met Clements before,' she said. 'I'm going out there. Nick, take over. You've done your Command module. You are now Bronze Command One.'

She made sure her earpiece was secure, switched her Airwave radio on, and jogged towards the door. Carly Whittle paused for a second and then hurried after her.

On the screens behind them the girl was continuing to wriggle in vain. Clements was waving her grandfather towards him with the barrel of his gun.

'SI Stuart, get back in there!' said Gates, as Jo ran down the corridor towards the stairwell.

'You have eyes on,' Jo replied. 'Bravo Charlie One and Sierra Charlie One are perfectly able to manage the situation. Mwamba and his daughter are the responsibility of me and my team. And so is Clements. I don't want to be making life-or-death decisions from a control room.' She was breathing heavily now. 'I need to be where the action is. I need to see it, smell it, feel it. Besides. I'm the only trained negotiator on scene.'

Now she was at the foot of the stairs and racing towards the main exit. Behind her she could hear another set of feet on the stairs. In her earpiece she heard the firearms commander confirm that he was on scene, and Nick Carter describing Henry Mwamba standing beside the Nissan, frozen with fear and uncertainty. Jo burst out onto the esplanade. A member of Intu Trafford Centre security stood by an electric buggy, waiting for her. She leapt into the passenger seat while he switched on the ignition.

As they set off, Carly Whittle jumped onto one of the rear seats. 'You'll need someone to look after the girl,' she said, forestalling Jo's objection.

Off to the right, an unmarked black saloon with flashing blue lights sped towards them, accompanied by a marked Land Rover Defender.

'Tactical Firearms are on scene,' Jo said, her heart pounding in her chest.

'Stop here,' she ordered the driver, less than twenty metres from the Nissan.

Henry Mwamba had left the safety of the Qashqai and had started walking towards the grassed area where his granddaughter was still struggling to free herself.

'Mr Mwamba!' Jo shouted, climbing out of the cart. 'Get back behind your vehicle.'

He turned towards her, exposing his neck. On the bank, Clement raised his pistol.

Before he had a chance to aim and fire, the girl kicked his shin and almost wriggled free. Jo and Carly rushed forward, shouting as they went.

'Bitch!' yelled Clements, lifting the girl up and tightening his grip.

Mwamba had reached the grassed area and was starting up the bank. Without warning, Carly launched herself past Jo, grasped Mwamba around his chest with her left arm, reached between his legs with her right, lifted him clear of the ground and slammed him face first onto the bank. She lay on top of him, depriving Clements of a clear shot.

From behind Jo came a chorus of commands. 'Armed Police! Stay where you are! Drop your weapon! Armed Police!'

Jo glanced over her shoulder. They had fanned out in a semicircle, their weapons trained on Clements. She turned back. Clements had his pistol against the girl's right temple.

'That is an IZH-Baikal MP-46M .177 target air pistol, single-stroke pneumatic,' said a calm male voice. 'Non-lethal except at close range.'

'Potentially laced with a toxin,' Nick Carter reminded them.

'Roger that,' said the TFU commander.

Jo raised both arms out sideways, palms open. 'Darren,' she said, her tone sounding calmer than she felt. 'It's over. Let Françoise go. She's innocent in all of this. You don't want to harm her.'

Her earpiece had gone silent as everyone held their breath. The girl stared wide-eyed at her grandfather sprawled on the grass beneath DC Whittle's body. Clements tightened his grip, causing her to gasp.

'Don't worry, Françoise,' said Jo. 'He isn't going hurt you. Are you, Darren? And nobody is going to hurt you either, Darren. We understand what brought you to this. We can talk about it. Just drop your gun and let her go.'

For a moment it looked as though he might comply. Then he began to inch back towards the cover of the wood.

'Stand still! Armed Police!' they shouted.

Jo knew they were never going to fire. Not so long as that pistol was trained on the girl. Just as she thought they were going to lose sight of him the girl sank her teeth into his hand. He screamed and let go. She ran, stumbled against a trunk, tripped and fell. Jo raced up the bank towards her. She threw herself on the ground and wrapped her arms around the girl.

There was an explosion of voices in her earpiece and from the fire-arms officers yelling at Clements to drop the gun. He was standing six feet away, staring down at her, the weapon hanging by his side. His face was frozen like that of a statue expressing utter disbelief. For a moment she thought he was going to raise the pistol.

'Don't . . .' she began, but the shouts drowned her out.

'Drop your weapon! Do it now! If you do not, we will fire! Drop your weapon! Do it now!'

'Darren, drop the gun!' she shouted. She wondered if he had heard her.

His eyes flickered. He looked up. Made eye contact. Focused.

She nodded her head.

The pistol fell from his hand and bounced against the root of a tree.

'Put your hands behind your head and step away! Do it now!'

Clements looked past her at Henry Mwamba still pinned to the ground beneath Carly Whittle's spread-eagled body. At the semicircle of armed officers, their weapons trained on his chest. At the ring of emergency vehicles fifty yards behind them. There was something about his expression that for a split second caused Jo to fear that he might bend to retrieve the weapon, leaving them no option but to take him down.

'Darren . . .' she began to say.

But he turned his back on them and bolted into the woods.

Chapter 76

'I'm not sending my team in there,' declared the firearms commander. 'He's no longer armed as far as we can tell and they'll be more at risk of shooting each other, or themselves. I need air cover, so that we can track him and be ready for him when he emerges.'

'This is Bravo Charlie One,' said Nick Carter. 'Mobile Units One and Two move to cover the perimeter of the wooded area either side of the Regent Crescent parking lot.'

Jo watched Carly lead Mwamba and his granddaughter over to a paramedic unit.

'Where are the dogs?' she demanded. 'And where is that AIR Unit drone?'

'Right here,' came the reply.

A station wagon had drawn up beside the Land Rover Defender. From behind the raised trunk emerged a man carrying a drone. He moved into an open space and set the drone down on the ground.

'Give me one minute and I'll have this airborne,' he said.

'We don't have a minute,' said Jo. 'Make sure you're patched into the Comms and keep a commentary going. I need to know exactly where he is. And make sure they know he's no longer armed. We need him alive. He may know where that missing girl Melissa is.'

She turned and ran up the slope. The woods were more dense than she'd envisaged. But at least that meant it would slow him down too. She tried to recall the map on the screen in the control room. This patch of trees must be about two hundred and twenty yards long at its narrowest point and no more than a hundred and forty yards wide. They ran behind Frankie & Benny's and encircled the Premier Inn, before petering out along the perimeter road. She decided to head for the longest stretch that curved around the right-hand side of the lodge, guessing that Clements would want to stay in cover for as long as possible.

'AIR Unit One is airborne,' said a new voice.

'Go ahead, AIR Unit One,' said Gordon Holmes.

'I have one person on foot – no, make that two persons on foot – in the wooded area.'

'Please designate furthest of those persons Papa Sierra, and the nearest Juliet Sierra. Proceed.'

'Papa Sierra is one hundred yards ahead of Juliet Sierra, who is closing.'

'Juliet Sierra is also knackered,' muttered Jo as she wove between the trees.

'Papa Sierra is heading towards the western perimeter of the woods where there appear to be ropes strung in the trees adjacent to a parking lot. There are multiple persons in that vicinity.'

'That's the Aerial Extreme ropeway and zipwire,' said the security coordinator anxiously. 'There'll be scores of people on there. Lots of children.'

'Mobile Units One and Two proceed immediately to southern perimeter of Regent Crescent parking lot, Zone Z,' said Nick Carter.

'That does not, I repeat not, include the Tactical Firearms Units,' added Gordon Holmes.

'Roger that,' the TFU commander responded. 'Our involvement would entail an unquantifiable risk to public safety. We have recovered the weapon and are now mobile and on standby, awaiting instruction.'

Jo's breath was laboured. It was hard going over this uneven terrain in a stab vest and boots, with the ground wet and slippery. She could hear the excited chatter of children high in the wooded canopy off to the right. She saw a flash of movement up ahead. Black jeans against the brown tree trunks. Now she caught a glimpse of the black hooded top. He appeared to stumble over some roots, put out a hand and steady himself against a tree, before regaining his balance and hurrying on.

'Papa Sierra has veered left away from the parking lot,' said AIR Unit One. 'Juliet Sierra is closing. Forty yards behind.'

Heartened by the news, Jo raised her pace.

'This is Mobile Unit One. We have blocked the perimeter road opposite the Premier Inn.'

'This is Bronze Command One. Where are you, Mobile Unit Two?'

'Mobile Unit Two. We're opposite the entrance to Aerial Extreme. Two on board. One other, plus dog handler and dog, now on foot.'

'This is AIR Unit One. Papa Sierra has veered right. That is right, right, right. He is now heading west of the Premier Inn towards the perimeter road.' Now there were several voices at once.

'This is Bravo Charlie Two. The perimeter has an electric fence between it and the motorway. Papa Sierra has nowhere to go.'

Jo could see him now, less than twenty yards ahead of her. The trees were beginning to thin out too. 'I have eyes on Papa Sierra,' she said. 'He does not appear to be armed. I repeat he does not appear to be armed.'

'Roger that,' chorused several voices.

'This is Mobile Unit Two. We have Eyes on! Eyes on! Papa Sierra is crossing the perimeter road towards the fence. We are in pursuit.'

Jo burst through the trees and saw Clements directly ahead of her. He had crossed the road and was sprinting towards a marked crossing point. She'd narrowed the distance between them to fifteen yards as he disappeared through a gap in the fence. Behind her she could hear the mobile unit roaring towards them.

'Papa Sierra is on a pedestrian and cycle pathway heading towards the Redclyffe Circle roundabout,' said the drone operator. 'Hold that. He's turning left, left, left, towards the M60 motorway.'

Jo dug deep as she pelted up the ascending slip road after him.

Clements was now abreast of a large yellow sign depicting a tow truck which read Free Recovery, Await Rescue.

If only.

She was five yards behind him as he reached the summit, turned right, and ran straight across the hard shoulder into the slow lane.

Jo stopped and shouted at him. 'Darren – stop! Don't be so stupid.'

Halfway into the second lane, he turned and looked over his shoulder at her.

The first of a line of cars speeding down the slope veered into the fast lane, causing another car to crash into the central barrier. The second car in the line had no time to react, struck Clements head on and threw him onto the windshield, over the roof, and into the path of a diesel tanker.

They saw it all on the screens in the Control Room. They heard the gasp of the drone operator, before he calmly announced: 'Papa Sierra is down. I repeat. Papa Sierra is down.'

Jo closed her eyes and bent over with her hands on her knees, gasping for breath, willing the pounding in her chest to subside. She pressed the button on her Airwave radio to switch it off. 'Shit! Shit! Shit!' she muttered, before leaning on the guard rail and retching onto the bare earth beyond.

Chapter 77

'It's not as though you were in a car,' said Gordon. 'It's not as though it was a pursuit. Not in the technical sense of the word. It wasn't your fault, Jo – not in a month of Sundays. Nobody thinks that, and neither should you.'

All the right words, all in the right order. But it didn't change the facts. A man was dead. An unarmed man. And if she hadn't chased him onto that motorway he'd still be alive.

'He'd already killed three people,' Nick Carter reminded her. 'Wounded one other. And he'd have killed Mwamba if it hadn't been for you.'

'And Carly here,' Jo said.

'And Carly,' he admitted.

Jo turned to her.

'Where did you learn to do a machine-gun takedown, DS Whittle?'

Carly grinned. 'You're not the only mixed martial arts freak in the village, Ma'am.'

'At least DI Weston took your advice,' said Gordon. 'Holed up in a hotel, keeping her head down. Just a shame she didn't let us, or her colleagues know. Would have saved us fretting. I'll give her an earful next time we meet.'

All of this was cold comfort to Jo. She was haunted by the look on Clements's face just before he died. He hadn't been putting himself in harm's way. He was trying to get away. Turning his head, a momentary pause in flight, had been an instinctive response to see where the shouts were coming from. Just enough to slow him down. To set him up. To bring him down. She knew from experience that it would be weeks rather than days before she stopped seeing that look on his face last thing at night, or on waking in the early hours.

It was the first of the debriefing sessions. A man had died during a police operation, so the Independent Police Complaints Commission were already involved. Then there was the internal review to prepare for and, more immediately, a press release to agree.

ACC Gates was calling the room to order.

Jo's phone began to vibrate. She glanced at it surreptitiously. It was Aggie. Well, she would have to wait like everybody else. She switched the phone off and tucked it back in her bag.

Agata swore. '*Gówno!*'

She ended the call on her hands-free and focused on the road ahead. It was an hour since the newspaper had received the call. It had taken another forty minutes for a sub-editor to decide to pass it on.

'This is an important message for Agata Kowalski. Write these numbers down. Fifty-three, fourteen, twenty-five, forty-nine, letter N. Two, forty, thirty-eight, eighty-four, Letter W.'

The caller, a male, had made the person on the front desk repeat the sequence.

'Good,' the caller had said. 'Now make sure she gets it, an' tell 'er time is running out. And the we'ver's not looking good. Not good at all.'

It was only when Agata had played it again and written it down as numbers, instead of words, that she realised what it was. GPS longitude and latitude references. At which point the final sentence chilled her to the bone.

She'd immediately opened Google Earth and entered the coordinates. That took her to a spot in the Delamere Forest, half a mile from a village called Hatchmere. She'd rung Jo from the car, but Jo's phone was off. Agata thanked her lucky stars that she'd entered Max Nailor's number in the contacts of her phone. Max answered on the fourth ring.

'Who is this?' he asked brusquely.

Breathlessly, she told him, and the reason why.

'Read out those numbers,' he said, 'slowly. I'm recording this, but I'm also entering them into my satnav as you give them to me. Right,' he said, 'where are you now?'

She consulted her satnav. 'Bucklow Hill. It says seventeen miles, ETA twenty-seven minutes.'

'Listen, Agata,' he said. 'This could be a windup – it could be a diversion. It could even be a trap of some kind.'

'Or it could be genuine and there's a twelve-year-old girl out there, scared witless and freezing to death!'

'I realise that. But I can't allow a civilian to go charging in there, risking her life and that of the girl. I'm already on my way. I'm also going to get Cheshire Police to send a patrol car and I'm going to call for air support. I need you to promise me that you'll wait at the Hatchmere crossroads. There's a Chinese restaurant there . . .' She heard him clicking away. '. . . the Delamere Fortune Palace. Wait in the parking lot. And please, don't do anything stupid.'

Before she could reply, he was gone.

Chapter 78

To the west, the sun dipped below the mountains of Snowdonia, plunging the lanes into darkness. Agata's headlights automatically switched to full beam, but too late for her to spot the right turn the satnav had been announcing.

'Do a U-turn now.'

No way. The lane was narrow with hedges on either side. She checked the external temperature. It had already dipped to around forty-four degrees Fahrenheit, and it had begun to rain.

Five minutes later the satnav had her back on track and approaching the Hatchmere crossroads. Up ahead on her left was the Chinese restaurant – a single-storey, yellow-rendered building with red roof tiles.

Agata slowed as she reached the entrance to the parking lot. She imagined the young girl, terrified, abandoned, on the verge of hypothermia, took a deep breath and shifted her foot from the brake to the accelerator.

The crossroads was clear. In the distance, off to the right, were twin white beams and a flashing blue light. She drove straight across, past a cluster of cottages on either side, and into the forest. Trees crowded in from either side, their branches meeting overhead, almost leafless after the ravages of the recent storms. Her headlights threw moving shadows deep into the woods.

Now the satnav was telling her that she'd reached her destination. She pulled over into a leaf-strewn lay-by on her left and stopped. Only now did she realise how ill-equipped she was for this situation. Ordinary shoes, no boots, no proper parka. At least there was the light waterproof jacket she kept in the trunk for emergencies. She reached across to the glove box, took out the flashlight that Jo had persuaded her to buy – the one that doubled as an emergency escape hammer – and got out of the car.

The rain was relentless. Despite the cover from the canopy of branches, her hair and clothes were already soaking by the time she managed to pull on the waterproof. She stood there, shining the torch into the woods on either side, realising that she had no idea in which direction to go.

Above the wind whistling in the trees and the patter of the rain on her hood, there came a new sound. The *whup, whup, whup* of an approaching helicopter. Agata looked up. A fierce beam of intense light was slicing through the trees, moving steadily closer. She had to shield her eyes as it hovered overhead, capturing her like a moth in a lamp, before slowly moving away to her left.

Turning her body towards the direction in which the helicopter was moving, Agata trained the beam of her torch on the ground ahead of her. She made out a narrow path, thick with fallen leaves, that led between the trees and disappeared into the bushes ahead. As she plunged into the forest, she was vaguely aware of more white light and blue flashes strobing the road behind her.

The going was hard, the ground uneven. Straggly undergrowth tugged at her jeans and branches slapped her face and body as she shouldered her way through.

The helicopter had stopped and was hovering. There were shouts from behind her that were barely audible above the wind and the sound of the chopping blades.

'Police! Stop! Wait.'

She soldiered on. The trees were thinning out. Suddenly she found herself on the edge of a slight bank above an extensive area of naked wetland, shimmering in the downdraught from the helicopter overhead. Unable to stop, Agata tumbled down the bank. She inhaled deeply and readied herself for the shock of icy water.

She landed with a thump. Her body sank a little and there was a sucking noise. It felt as though she'd landed on a mattress and gently been expelled. She placed her hands on the ground and sat up. She was sitting on a bed of wet peat. And there, forty yards away, in the centre of the searchlight's beam, was a heap of green tarpaulin.

Agata scrambled to her feet. One moment she was bouncing as if on an infant's trampoline, the next pulling her foot from a hole full of stagnant water. Finally, she was there.

The downdraught caught her mid-stride and sent her sprawling on top of the tarpaulin. There was a squeal of protest. A sharp blow to Agata's ribs. She pushed herself to her feet and pulled the tarp away.

Melissa was huddled in a foetal position, swaddled in a dirty parka three times her size. Her lower legs were visible, covered by school uniform trousers. One foot was shoeless, the sock dirty and sodden. Her eyes were closed tight and she was shaking violently. Agata knelt and cradled her in her arms.

'It's alright, Melissa,' she said. 'You're safe now. There's nothing to worry about.'

The helicopter swung away towards the furthest margin of the pit and began, ever so slowly, to descend.

Torches stabbed the darkness. Two police officers appeared.

'That was a bloody stupid thing to do,' said one.

'Leave it, Robbie,' said the other. 'Can't you see the state they're in?'

He knelt down beside them. In his left hand he held an inhaler.

Agata would have thanked him, but her teeth were chattering and the words would no longer come.

Chapter 79

'That was fantastic!'

Jo licked the last of the crème brûlée from the back of her spoon and placed it in the dishwasher. Then she closed the door and switched it on. 'And you shouldn't have gone to all that trouble. Helping me to get my place straight was above and beyond.'

'Don't be daft,' said Aggie. 'I love cooking. And let's face it, neither of us really wanted to go out.'

Jo encircled Aggie's waist with her arms and kissed her. Gently at first, and then with a passionate intensity that was reciprocated, and surprised them both. Jo could feel Aggie's heart beating against her breast like a trapped bird.

'Sorry,' she said, releasing her grip and stepping away.

'Don't be,' said Aggie. 'I needed that and so did you.'

They went through to the lounge.

'There's a drop left in this,' said Jo, raising the bottle of champagne Aggie had bought at Booths to christen the apartment.

'You have it,' said Aggie. 'I have some wine left.'

They sat on the sofa with their glasses, still bathed in the afterglow.

'Max was not best pleased,' said Aggie.

'You did the right thing,' Jo assured her. 'It's what I would have done. Anything could have happened to her.'

Aggie took a sip. 'But she'd been lying out there for over two hours. I don't understand why she didn't just walk back towards the road and flag down a car? That's probably what her captors expected her to do.'

'It's not that simple,' Jo told her, 'when you've been held against your will. Isolated, disoriented, frightened you'll get even more lost. Maybe she reasoned it would be easier for us to find her out there in the open. Maybe she just felt safer.'

'Perhaps they warned her not to move?'

'Maybe.'

'How is she?' Aggie asked.

'Remarkably well under the circumstances. She's had her first session with a specially trained child counsellor. We know that she wasn't physically harmed or sexually abused. It's all about her mental and emotional recovery. Her mother's taking her on a vacation to Disneyworld next week, against professional advice. She'd be better off back at school with her friends.' Jo sipped her champagne. It was slightly flat and very dry after the crème brûlée. She set the glass down on the coffee table. 'It's going to take a long time for her to get over the experience – if she ever does. She's not talking to her father apparently. Blames him for the whole sorry mess. I doubt their relationship will ever be the same again.'

'Are you any nearer to finding out who took her?' Aggie asked.

'No. The most likely scenario is still that O'Neill was behind it. Steve Yates going walkabout was too much of a coincidence. He almost certainly set up the abduction using a series of burner phones. As soon as it became public knowledge that Darren Clements was our prime suspect they had no reason to hold her. That would explain why Yates turned up at Jason O'Neill's place.'

'What did Yates and O'Neill say when you told them that the investigation into the kidnapping was ongoing?'

'Max did that, but he took me along with him. Yates wasn't there; Jason O'Neill was. Max told him he'd been lucky thus far, but his luck was going to run out sometime.'

'What did he say to that?'

Jo made speech marks in the air with her fingers. ' "As my father would have said, 'It isn't a matter of luck. I didn't do it, officer. And neither did Stevie.'" And then as we were leaving he had the cheek to tell me that he owed me one. Presumably for catching the man who'd murdered his father.'

'With friends like that, who needs enemies?'

'That's what Max said. But with any luck, Forensics will come up with some trace evidence from the farm. Then it'll only be a matter of time before it's tracked back to Yates or O'Neill himself. In the meantime, Operation Challenger have Melissa's father under covert surveillance. They're worried he's going to take the law into his own hands, proof or no proof.'

Aggie drained her glass and put it down. 'I can't believe that Darren Clements had been planning it so soon after his sister died.'

'It wasn't immediate. His father leaving was the trigger. We now know he joined a gun club shortly after that, in Jordan Springer's name. He bought the air rifle through them.'

'But I thought he had an air pistol at the Trafford Centre?'

'He did. But it was the rifle he'd used for all the others. We found that in a homemade rack underneath the workbench in the garage he was renting.'

'Where are you up to with the IPCC investigation, Jo?' said Agata.

'That could take months. They may throw a few recommendations around, but I doubt there'll be any serious outcomes for me. I've already been told there's no question of criminal proceedings.'

'I should bloody well hope not.'

'There's always the possibility of a civil prosecution in cases like this. But the father has already made it clear he won't go down that route, and so has Clements' mother. He's had enough pain in his life and more than his fill of the justice system. He just wants to be left in peace and quiet, together with his dog Sandy in that little cottage in the Yorkshire Wolds.'

'Talking of peace and quiet,' said Agata, 'when did you last take a vacation?'

Jo had to think about it. She certainly hadn't taken any beyond the national holidays since joining the NCA. Harry Stone had actually reminded her about it.

'Sometime last year?' she said.

'You must have a mountain of leave entitlement?'

'It doesn't work like that. You can only carry over statutory leave. But I know I've got at least twenty-eight days to take before March 31st. I hadn't really thought about it, what with the change of job, the divorce, moving apartments.'

She tucked her legs up beneath her on the sofa.

'Then it's time you did,' said Aggie. 'Why don't you take a couple of weeks? I could come with you.'

'Together, you mean?'

'Obviously. I'm self-employed. There's no immediate time limit to the job I'm on at the moment. And I could do with a rest myself.'

Jo thought about it. 'I'm on gardening leave. I'm supposed to book some counselling sessions – HR wanting to cover their backs in case I lose the plot. But that's not a problem. I know my boss will back me up.'

'There you go then.'

Agata glanced at her watch. 'Is that television operational?' she asked.

'The guy who delivered it set it up. Why?'

'Do you mind if we have the news on? I have this need to watch it every day. It's almost an addiction. It comes with the territory.'

Jo picked up the remote from the coffee table.

'I think you've missed the National news,' she said. 'But you might just be in time for the Regional . . .'

'And now, for the North West news. Earlier, we brought you the latest update following yesterday's dramatic and fatal climax to the hunt for Darren Clements, the serial killer dubbed by some the Poison Pellet Perpetrator.'

Agata shook her head in disgust. 'The populars love their alliteration. Further confirmation that they lack imagination.'

'Populars?' said Jo.

'You can't call them tabloids any more. Because the heavies like *The Times* and the *Guardian* have all gone down that route.'

'Here we go,' said Jo, pointing to the screen.

Henry Mwamba stood in front of the Kingdom of Heaven Church of the Mustard Seed in the glare of video-camera lights, grinning broadly, a microphone thrust in front of him. It looked as though most of the congregation were assembled on the steps behind him.

'Our Chief Reporter, Derek West, is with Mr Henry Mwamba, who we understand was the next target for Clements, and who is the grandfather of Françoise, the little girl taken hostage by the killer. Go ahead, Derek.'

'Mr Mwamba. We have had hundreds of tweets from members of the public and comments on our website, full of admiration for your bravery in carrying on as normal despite having been warned that the killer had his sights set on you . . .'

'Huh! Brave?' muttered Jo. 'More like arrogant and reckless.'

'Tell us,' the reporter continued, 'how you felt when confronted by Darren Clements in the parking lot at the Intu Trafford Centre?'

Mwamba gave a broad grin. 'Never for a moment,' he said, 'did I doubt that the Lord would keep us safe!'

'Amen!' shouted some of those behind him.

'I prayed to the Lord for salvation and He heard my prayer.'

'Amen! Amen!'

'So, you're saying that God came to your protection?'

Mwamba spread his arms wide. 'Yea, though I walk through the valley of the shadow of death, I will fear no evil.' He turned to the crowd behind him. 'Who else, if not the Lord?'

'How about Greater Manchester Police or the National Crime Agency?' said Jo. 'Or, in your case, Mr Mwamba, Detective Constable Carly Whittle?' She turned off the television and tossed the remote onto the sofa.

'I never got the impression you were in it for public recognition?' said Agata.

'Fat chance, if I was,' said Jo, slumping back into the cushions. 'At times like this, I begin to wonder why I do the job at all.'

'For the Françoises and the Melissas of this world. For that coroner, and for your colleague – what was her name . . .?'

'Sarah. Sarah Weston.'

'. . . who were just doing their jobs. For the innocents in this world who would otherwise have no one to stand up for them. Come on Jo, sit yourself up.'

Agata placed her iPad on the table and switched it on.

'Let's have a look at some vacations? What do you fancy? A fly and flop? Somewhere nice and hot?'

'Where did you have in mind?' said Jo, who despite herself was warming to the idea.

'This time of year, how about the Caribbean?'

Aggie entered it into the TripAdvisor search engine. 'Here you go, this is a brilliant deal. All-inclusive. Montego Bay.'

Jo began to laugh.

'What's the matter?' said Aggie.

'Montego Bay? Are you kidding? And you an investigative reporter?'

'I still don't see . . .'

'Montego Bay. Currently one of the places to avoid in Jamaica – a country with one of the highest murder rates per capita in the entire world? I didn't think you meant a busman's holiday!'

'Alright then,' said Aggie, 'where do you suggest?'

Jo leaned forward, started tapping the screen and then sat back.

'There you go,' she said.

'Iceland?'

'Officially the safest country on earth.'

'It's hardly going to be hot.'

'This is.' Jo tapped again. 'The Blue Lagoon,' she announced. 'Hot thermal springs. In-water massage. Silica mud masks. There's even a bar in the middle so you don't have to get out.'

'When you put it like that,' said Aggie. 'Though it's not the fly and flop I had in mind. More . . . flip-flop.'

That had the two of them howling with laughter. It went on and on, with such intensity that Jo feared she might never catch her breath again. It left her exhausted, but strangely at peace.

Aggie took her hand and drew Jo towards her. As Jo looked into those perfectly imperfect eyes, all the tension she'd been holding in her mind and body leached away, until all that was left was a certainty that this was the beginning of something special.

Afterword

When I handed over the manuscript of *The Blow Out* on February 21st 2018, little did I envisage that eleven days later, on March 4th, two Russian citizens would be subject to a devastating and wicked attack on British soil involving the nerve agent Novichok. Or that Porton Down, the Defence Science and Technology Laboratory, also part of Public Health England, would inevitably become involved. And that attention would consequently be drawn back to the ricin attack on Georgi Markov that formed a part of my research and is referenced in this novel. Then, while working on the copy-edit, it emerged that on May 25th French police had arrested two Egyptian-born brothers in Paris who were plotting an attack using either explosives or the lethal poison ricin!

I am not prescient. It's simply that life, yet again, has proved stranger and far more troubling than fiction.

Bill Rogers
May 2018

Acknowledgments

In addition to all of my longstanding former police and forensics officers, special thanks go to Chris Rainford from the Lancashire Fire and Rescue Service for a special demonstration in drone flying, and for letting my granddaughter come along for the ride. The number of missing persons found, and in some cases rescued, just in time by Chris and those he has trained across the North West is growing apace. Given that Chris is often on call 24/7, finding time to fit us in on a Saturday morning was much appreciated. Also to golf professional David Screeton, who has been trying for over twenty years to tempt me to take up his offer of a free lesson on condition I start playing again – after fifty-three years – for his invaluable advice, and his willingness to become an anonymised character in *The Blow Out*. To Gareth Pardon, my personal trainer, and former Royal Marine Commando, for sharing his experience, and getting my writing arm back to full fitness after injury. And to former colleague and fellow Gooner David How, whose hard-won experience as a Krav Maga exponent and trainer proved invaluable to Jo.

As ever, everyone at Amazon Publishing UK and the Thomas & Mercer imprint has been unfailingly supportive, encouraging, and exceptionally professional. In particular, my editors Jack Butler and

Russel McLean, and copy editor Monica Byles for their usual sensitive, empathetic, and insightful suggestions, as well as Hatty Stiles, Nora Dunne, Victoire Chevalier, Emily Meade, and Nicole Wagner, who effortlessly completed the package.

About the Author

Bill Rogers is the author of ten earlier crime fiction novels featuring DCI Tom Caton and his team, set in and around Manchester. The first of these, *The Cleansing*, was short-listed for the Long Barn Books Debut Novel Award and was awarded the e-Publishing Consortium Writers Award 2011. *The Pick, The Spade and The Crow* was the first in a new series featuring Senior Investigator Joanne Stuart, on secondment to the Behavioural Sciences Unit at the National Crime Agency, located on Salford Quays, Manchester. SI Jo Stuart first appeared as a promising junior member of Tom Caton's team. Formerly a teacher and schools inspector, Bill has four generations of Metropolitan Police officers behind him. He is married with two adult children, four grandchildren and three great-grandchildren. He lives near Manchester.